Samuel Smiles, George Reid

Life of a Scotch Naturalist

Thomas Edward

Samuel Smiles, George Reid

Life of a Scotch Naturalist
Thomas Edward

ISBN/EAN: 9783337404475

Printed in Europe, USA, Canada, Australia, Japan

Cover: Foto ©Raphael Reischuk / pixelio.de

More available books at **www.hansebooks.com**

LIFE OF A SCOTCH NATURALIST.

Thomas Edward

LIFE

OF

A SCOTCH NATURALIST:

THOMAS EDWARD,

ASSOCIATE OF THE LINNÆAN SOCIETY.

By SAMUEL SMILES,

AUTHOR OF "LIVES OF THE ENGINEERS," "SELF-HELP," "CHARACTER,"
"THRIFT," ETC.

PORTRAIT AND ILLUSTRATIONS BY GEORGE REID, A.R.S.A.

PREFACE.

The history of the humblest human life is a tale of marvels. Dr. Johnson said that there was not a man in the street whose biography might not be made interesting, provided he could narrate something of his experiences of life, his trials, his difficulties, his successes, and his failures.

I use these words as an introduction to the following biography of my "man in the street." Yet Thomas Edward is not an ordinary man. Eighteen years since, I mentioned him, in "Self-Help," as one of the most extraordinary instances of perseverance in the cause of science that had ever come under my notice.

Nor was he a man of any exalted position in society. He was a shoe-maker then; he is a shoe-maker still. For nearly thirty years he has fought the battle of scientific poverty. He is one of those men who live *for* science, not *by* science. His shyness prevented him pushing himself forward; and when he had done his work, he was almost forgotten.

How he pursued his love of nature; how he satisfied his thirst for knowledge, in the midst of trials, difficulties, and troubles—not the least of which was that of domestic poverty—will be found related in the following book. Indeed, it may be said of him that he has endured as much hardship for the cause of science as soldiers do in a prolonged campaign. He spent most of his nights out-of-doors, amidst damp, and wet, and cold. Men thought him mad for enduring such risks. He himself says, "I have been a fool to nature all my life."

He always lamented his want of books. He had to send his "findings" to other naturalists to be named, and he often lost them. But books could not be had without money; and money was as scarce with him as books. He was thus prevented from taking rank among higher-class naturalists. He could only work in detail; he could not generalize. He had to be satisfied with the consolation that Mr. J. Gwyn Jeffreys once gave him. "Working naturalists like yourself," said he, "do quite as much good service in the cause of science as those who study books." Edward, however, doubted this; for he considered works on natural science to be a great help to the working naturalist. They informed him of what others had done, and also of what remained to be done.

Those who would know something of what Edward has accomplished in only *one* department of his favorite subject should consult Messrs. Bate and Westwood's "History of the British Sessile-eyed Crustacea," where his services to the cause of science are fully and generously acknowledged. Of the numerous Crustacea mentioned in that work, Edward collected a hundred and seventy-seven in the Moray Firth, of which twenty were New Species.

In 1866, Edward was elected an Associate of the Linnæan Society—one of the highest honors that science could confer upon him. Since then, however, he has been able to do comparatively little for the advancement of his favorite study. He had been so battered about by falling from rocks in search of birds, and so rheumatized by the damp, wet, and cold to which he was exposed at night—for he was obliged to carry on his investigations after his day's work was over—that he was unable to continue his investigations in natural history.

In the Appendix will be found a Selection of the Fauna of Banffshire, prepared by Edward. I have been able to find room for only the Mammals, Birds, Fishes, and Crustacea. I wish it had been possible to give the Star-fishes (*Rayed Echinodermata*), Mollusks, Zoophytes, and other objects; but this would have filled up the book, and left no room for the Biography.

It was not my intention to have published the book in the ornate form in which it now appears. But my friend Mr. Reid, being greatly interested in the man and his story, and having volunteered to illustrate the work "for love," I could not withstand his generous offer. Hence the very fine portrait of Edward, so exquisitely etched by Rajon; and the excellent wood-engravings of Whymper and Cooper, which illustrate the volume.

It is scarcely necessary to say that the materials

of the book have been obtained from Edward himself, either by written communication or by "word
of mouth." Much of it is autobiography. Edward
was alarmed at the idea of what he had communicated being "put into a book." He thought it
might do me an injury. "Not a copy," he said,
"would be bought in Banff."

However this may be, the writing of the Biography has given me much pleasure. It has led me to
seek health amidst the invigorating breezes of the
North; and to travel round the rugged shores of
Aberdeen and Banff, in search of the views of bays
and headlands with which Mr. Reid has so beautifully embellished the book.

It may be objected—"Why write the life of a
man who is still living?" To this it may be answered, that Edward has lived his life and done his work.
With most of us, "*Hic jacet*" is all that remains to
be added. If the book had not been written now, it
is probable that it never would have been written.
But it may be asked, "Is the life really worth writing?" To this question the public alone can give
the answer.

LONDON, *November*, 1876.

CONTENTS.

CHAPTER I.

EARLY YEARS.

CHAPTER II.

SCHOOLS AND SCHOOL-MASTERS.

CHAPTER III.

APPRENTICESHIP.

CHAPTER IV.

RUNS AWAY FROM HOME.

Sets out for the Kettle.—His Provisions.—His Money.—Tries to sell his Knife.—Ruins of Dunnottar Castle.—Bervie.—Encounter with Tramps.—Montrose.—Sells his Knife.—Sleeps in a Hay-cock.—Arbroath.—Sailors' Wives.—Dundee.—Long-tailed Titmouse.—Cupar. —Reaches the Kettle.—His Reception.—Sets out for Home.—Uncivility of a Gamekeeper. — Adventure with a Bull.—Rests near Stonehaven.—Reaches Aberdeen.—Reception at Home.....Page 74

CHAPTER V.

RESUMES WORK.

Offers himself as a Sailor.—Resumes Shoe-making.—Wild Botanical Garden.—Tanners' Pits for Puddocks.—The Picture - shops.—The *Penny Magazine.*—Castlegate on Fridays.—Gun-makers' Windows. —Tries to emigrate to America as a Stowaway.—He fails.—Joins the Aberdeenshire Militia.—Chase of a Butterfly.—Is apprehended. —Is reprimanded and liberated.—Enlists in the 60th Rifles.—Assists as a Pew-opener.—Leaves Aberdeen for Banff........... 85

CHAPTER VI.

SETTLES AT BANFF.

His Employment.—Finds Time to follow his Bent.—His Caterpillars among the Workmen.—His Landlady.—Marries a Huntly Lass.— Settled for Life.—Self-education in Natural History.—Stuffs Birds. —His Want of Education.—Want of Books.—Shy and Friendless. —Avoids the Public-house.—His Love of Nature.—The Ocean.— The Heavens.—Makes a Collection.—His Gun and Paraphernalia. —His Equipment.—Sleeps Out - of - doors at Night.—Exaggerated Rumors about him. — Frequents Boyndie Church - yard.—Lies in Holes during Rain.—Disagreeable Visitors.—Awful Night in Boyndie Church-yard.—Moth-hunting at Night.—Terrible Encounter with Badgers.. 94

CHAPTER VII.

NIGHT WANDERERS.

Animals wandering at Night. — Their Noises and Cries. — The Roe-deer and Hare.—The Rabbit.—A Rabbit Fight.—The Fox.—The

CHAPTER VIII.

FORMS A NATURAL-HISTORY COLLECTION.

CHAPTER IX.

EXHIBITS HIS COLLECTION AT ABERDEEN.

CHAPTER X.

RESUMES HIS FORMER LIFE AND HABITS.

CHAPTER XI.

BEGINS TO PUBLISH HIS OBSERVATIONS.

CHAPTER XII.

RAMBLES AMONG BIRDS.

CHAPTER XIII.

LITERATURE AND CORRESPONDENCE.

CHAPTER XIV.

BY THE SEA-SHORE.

CHAPTER XV.

DISCOVERIES AMONG THE CRUSTACEA.

CHAPTER XVI.

DISCOVERIES AMONG ZOOPHYTES, MOLLUSKS, AND FISHES.

CHAPTER XVII.

ANTIQUITIES—KITCHEN-MIDDENS.

CHAPTER XVIII.

CONCLUSION.

FAUNA OF BANFFSHIRE.

ILLUSTRATIONS.

By GEORGE REID, A.R.S.A.

OTHER ILLUSTRATIONS.

BANKS AND BRAES O' DON.

LIFE OF A NATURALIST.

CHAPTER I.

EARLY YEARS.

THOMAS EDWARD was born at Gosport, Portsmouth, on Christmas-day, 1814. His father, John Edward, was a private in the Fifeshire militia. Shortly after his enlistment at Cupar, he went to Aberdeen to join his regiment. While stationed there, he became acquainted with, and afterward married, Margaret Mitchell, a native of the place.

Not long after John Edward's marriage, his regiment was ordered to Portsmouth. Toward the close of the Continental war, militia regiments were marched hither and thither, from one end of the country to another. The regular troops had mostly left England, to meet the armies of Napoleon in the Peninsula and the Low Countries. The militia were assembled in camps along the coast, or were stationed in garrisons to hold watch and ward over the French prisoners confined there. Hence the appearance. of the Fifeshire militia at Gosport, where the subject of our story was born.

When the Battle of Waterloo had been fought, and peace fell upon Europe, the English army returned from abroad. The militia were no longer needed for garrison duty, and the greater number of them were sent home. The Fifeshire militia were ordered to Fife, and took up their quarters at Cupar. During that time, John Edward's wife and family resided at the village of Kettle, about six miles south-west of the county town. They lived there because John was a native of the place, and had many relatives in the village.

At length the militia were disembodied. Edward returned to Kettle, and resumed his trade of a hand-loom linen-weaver. After remaining there for some time, he resolved to leave for Aberdeen. His wife liked neither the place nor the people. Kettle was a long, straggling, sleepy village. The people were poor, and employment was difficult to be had. Hence Edward did not require much persuasion to induce him to leave Kettle and settle in Aberdeen, where his wife would be among her own people, and where he would be much more likely to find work and wages to enable him to maintain his increasing family.

Arrived at Aberdeen, John Edward and his wife "took up house" in the Green, one of the oldest quarters of the city. Their house was situated at the foot of Rennie's Wynd, near Hadden's "Woo mill." There was really a Green in those days, lower down the hill. The Denburn ran at the foot of the Green. There were also the Inches, near the mouth of the Dee, over which the tide flowed daily.

Since then the appearance of that part of Aberdeen has become entirely changed. Railways have blotted out many of the remnants of old cities.* The Green is now covered

---

* Some antiquarian writers are of opinion that the Green was the site of ancient Aberdeen. For instance, Sir Samuel Forbes, of Foveran, in his "Description of Aberdeenshire" (1715), says, "From the end of the last-mentioned straight street [the Upper Kirkgate], there runs another southward and obliquely [the Nether Kirkgate], leading also to the town churches, and terminates in a pretty broad street, lying flat, and called the Green, the seat of the ancient city; where the river Dee receives a small rivulet, called the Denburn, covered with a bridge of three arches."—Turreffs's *Antiquarian Gleanings*, p. 290.

with houses, factories, and the Aberdeen Railway-station—
its warehouses, sidings, and station rooms. A very fine
bridge has been erected over the Green, now forming part
of Union Street; the Palace Hotel overlooking the railway-
station and the surrounding buildings.

Thomas Edward was brought up in his parents' house in
the Green, such as it was sixty years ago. It is difficult to
describe how he became a naturalist. He himself says he
could never tell. Various influences determine the direction of a boy's likings and dislikings. Boys who live in
the country are usually fond of birds and birdnesting; just
as girls who live at home are fond of dolls and doll-keep-
ing. But this boy had more than the ordinary tendency
to like living things; he wished to live among them. He
made pets of them; and desired to have them constantly
about him.

From his birth he was difficult to manage. His mother
said of him that he was the worst child she had ever nursed.
He was never a moment at rest. His feet and legs seemed
to be set on springs. When only about four months old,
he leaped from his mother's arms, in the vain endeavor to
catch some flies buzzing in the window. She clutched him
by his long clothes, and saved him from falling to the
ground. He began to walk when he was scarce ten months
old, and screamed when any one ventured to touch him.
And thus he went on, observing and examining—as full of
liking for living things as he was when he tried to grasp
the flies in the window at Gosport.

When afterward asked about the origin of his love for
natural history, he said, "I suppose it must have originated in the same internal impulse which prompted me to
catch those flies in the window. This unseen something—
this double being, or call it what you will—inherent in us
all, whether used for good or evil, which stimulated the
unconscious babe to get at, no doubt, the first living animals he had ever seen, at length grew in the man into an

irresistible and unconquerable passion, and engendered in him an insatiable longing for, and earnest desire to be always among, such things. This is the only reason I can give for becoming a lover of nature. I know of none other."

While living at Kettle, the child began to walk. He made friends with the cats and dogs about the house. He was soon able to toddle out-of-doors. At first he wished to cultivate the acquaintance of the cocks and hens and ducks, of which the village was full; but they always ran away before he could get up to them and caress them.

There was, however, another and a much more dangerous creature whose acquaintance he sought to make. This was a sow called Bet, with a litter of pigs. Whenever he was missing, he was found looking in at the pigs. He could not climb over the paling, but could merely look through the splits.

The sow was known to be ferocious, and she was most so when she had a litter of pigs. Edward's mother was afraid lest the sow should injure him by biting his hands or face through the bars of the cruive.* Therefore she warned him not to go near the beast; but her warnings were disregarded. When she asked, "Where's Tam?" the answer invariably was, "Oh, he's awa wi' the pigs."

One day the boy disappeared. Every hen-house, every stable, every pig-sty, and every likely corner of the village, was searched; but in vain. Tom was lost! He was then little over a year old. He could not have gone very far. Somebody raised the cry that he had been "stolen by the gypsies!" It was remembered that some tinkers had been selling their brooms and pans in the village that afternoon; and it was immediately concluded that they had kidnaped the child. It was not so very unreasonable, after all. Adam Smith, the author of "The Wealth of Nations," had

---

* *Cruive*, a pig-sty.

been kidnaped by a gypsy woman when a child at Kirk-caldy, many years before; and such things live long in popular recollection.

A hue and cry was accordingly got up in Kettle about the bairn that had been stolen by the gypsies. Their camp was known to be in the neighborhood, about three miles off. Tom's uncle and three other men volunteered to go early next morning. The neighbors went to their homes, except two, who remained with the mother. She sat by the fire all night — a long, wretched, dreary night. Early in the morning the four men started. They found the gypsy camp, and stated their grievance. They "wanted the child that had been kidnaped yesterday." "What?" said the chief gypsy; "we never kidnap children: such a dishonest deed has never been laid to our charge. But, now that you are here, you had better look for yourselves."

As the searchers were passing through among the carts and tents, they were set upon by a number of women and girls, and belabored with every kind of weapon and missile. Those who had neither sticks nor ropes used their claws. The men were unmercifully pummeled and scratched before they could make their escape. They reached Kettle in a deplorable state—without the child!

All hopes of his recovery in that quarter being ended, another body of men prepared to set out in another direction. But at this moment they were amazed by a scream outside the house. All eyes were turned to the door, when in rushed the pig-wife, and, without the least ceremony, threw the child into his mother's lap. "There, woman, there's yer bairn! but for God's sake keep him awa frae yon place, or he may fare war next time." "But whar was he?" they exclaimed in a breath. "Whar wud he be but below Bet and her pigs a' nicht!"*

---

* The question occurred, How did the child get among the pigs? He could not have climbed over the paling; he must have been lifted

When the family removed to Aberdeen, young Edward was in his glory. The foot of Rennie's Wynd was close to the outside of the town. He was enabled to roam into the country by way of Deeside and Ferryhill. Close at hand were the Inches — not the Inches of to-day, but the beautiful green Inches of sixty years ago, covered with waving algæ. There, too, grew the scurvy-grass, and the beautiful sea-daisy. Between the Inches were channels through which the tide flowed, with numerous pots or hollows. These were the places for bandies, eels, crabs, and worms.

Above the Inches, the town's manure was laid down, at a part now covered by the railway-station. The heaps were remarkably prolific in beetles, rats, sparrows, and numerous kinds of flies. Then the Denburn, at the foot of the Green, yielded no end of horse-leeches, powets (tadpoles), frogs, and other creatures that abound in fresh or muddy water. The boy used daily to play at these places, and brought home with him his "venomous beasts," as the neighbors called them. At first they consisted, for the most part, of tadpoles, beetles, snails, frogs, sticklebacks, and small green crabs (the young of the *Carcinus mœnas*); but as he grew older, he brought home horse-leeches, asks (newts), young rats—a nest of young rats was a glorious prize—field-mice and house-mice, hedgehogs, moles, birds, and bird'snests of various kinds.

The fishes and birds were easily kept; but as there was no secure place for the puddocks, horse-leeches, rats, and such-like, they usually made their escape into the adjoining houses, where they were by no means welcome guests. The neighbors complained of the venomous creatures which the young naturalist was continually bringing home. The horse-leeches crawled up their legs and stuck to them, fetch-

---

over. There was an old sweetheart of the quondam militia-man, whom he had deserted in favor of Margaret Mitchell. It was believed that she had maliciously lifted the child over the palings, and put him among the pigs, most probably from spite against her old lover.

ing blood; the puddocks and asks roamed about the floors; and the beetles, moles, and rats sought for holes wherever they could find them.

The boy was expostulated with. His mother threw out all his horse-leeches, crabs, birds, and bird'snests; and he was strictly forbidden to bring such things into the house again. But it was of no use. The next time that he went out to play he brought home as many of his "beasts" as before. He was then threatened with corporal punishment; but that very night he brought in a nest of young rats. He was then flogged; but it did him no good. The disease, if it might be so called, was so firmly rooted in him as to be entirely beyond the power of outward appliances. And so it was found in the end.

Words and blows having failed to produce any visible effect, it was determined to keep him in the house as much as possible. His father, who was a hand-loom weaver, went to his work early in the morning, and returned late at night. His meals were sent to him during the day. The mother, who had her husband's pirns to fill, besides attending to her household work, was frequently out of the way; and as soon as she disappeared, Tom was off to the Inches. When any one made a remark about her negligence in not keeping a tighter hold of the boy, her answer was, " Weel, I canna be aye at his heels." Sometimes he was set to rock the cradle; but on his mother's arrival at home, she found the rocker had disappeared. He was also left to play with the younger children; but he soon left them to play by themselves.

He was occasionally sent a message, though he rarely fulfilled it. He went to his old haunts, regardless of the urgency of the message. One morning he was sent to his father's workshop with his breakfast; but instead of going there, he set off for the Stocket, several miles from town, with two other loons.* Tom induced them to accompany

---

* In the North, *loons* and *queans* are boys and girls.

him. The Stocket was a fine place for birds and bird's-nests. They searched all day, and returned home at night. The father never received his breakfast: it was eaten by Edward and the loons.

As a punishment for his various misdoings, he was told one morning that he was to be confined to the house all day. It was a terrible punishment, at least to him. Only a portion of his clothes was given him, that he might not go out; and as a further precaution, his mother tied him firmly to the table-leg with a thick wisp of thrums. She also tied his wrists together with a piece of cord. When she went out on family affairs, Tom's little sister was set to watch him. But he disengaged himself from his bonds almost as quickly as the Davenport brothers. With a mixture of promises and threats, he made his little sister come to his help; and the two together pushed the table close to the grate, when, putting the rope which confined his legs between the ribs, it soon burned asunder, and he was free. He next tried to find his clothes, but his mother had hidden them too securely. He found a coat of his elder brother's, much too big for himself: nevertheless he put it on.

His mother's feet were now heard on the stair. Tom hid himself at the back of the door, so that he might rush out as soon as she entered. The door was opened; his mother rushed in, screaming, and Tom ran away. The table to which the rope had been attached was on fire, and the house would soon have been in a blaze. In quenching the flames of the rope attached to the boy's leg, he had forgotten, in his hurry, to quench the burning of the rope still attached to the table. Hence the fire. But Tom was now at liberty. He soon got rid of his shackles, and spent a glorious day out-of-doors. He had a warm home-coming at night; but the less said of that, the better.

In fact, the boy was found to be thoroughly incorrigible. He was self-willed, determined, and stubborn. As he could not be kept at home, and would not go a message, but was

always running after his " beasts," his father at last determined to take his clothes from him altogether; so, one
morning when he went to work, he carried them with him.
When the boy got up, and found that he had nothing to
wear, he was in a state of great dismay. His mother, having pinned a bit of an old petticoat round his neck, said to
him, " I am sure you'll be a prisoner this day." But no !
His mother went down-stairs for milk, leaving him in the
house. He had tied a string round his middle, to render
himself a little more fit for moving about. He followed
his mother down-stairs, and hid himself at the back of the
entry door; and as soon as she had passed in, Tom bolted
out, ran down the street, and immediately was at his old
employment of hunting for crabs, horse-leeches, puddocks,
and sticklebacks.

His father, on coming home at night with Tom's clothes
in his hand, looked round the room, and asked, " Is he in
bed ?" " Na !" " Far* is he ?" " Weel, I left him here
when I gaed to the door for milk, and when I came back
he was awa; but whether he gaed out o' the window or
up the lum,† I canna tell." " Did ye gie him ony claes ?"
"No !" " Most extraordinary !" exclaimed the father, sitting down in his chair. He was perfectly thunderstruck.
His supper was waiting for him, but he could not partake
of it. A neighboring woman shortly after entered, say-

---

* The pronunciation of the Aberdeenshire dialect is peculiar. For
instance, *far* is where; *fat,* what; *tee,* to ; *dee,* do ; *feel,* fool ; *peer,* poor ;
byeuk, book ; *been,* bone, etc. It is said that Jane Maxwell, the hand-
some and beautiful Duchess of Gordon, was in the habit of amusing
George III. by repeating phrases in Aberdonian doric ; and that his
majesty plumed himself on his ability to interpret them. The duchess one day tried his mettle with the following : " A gangrel bodie oot
o' the toon o' Stanhive was i' the way o' wan'erin the kwintra wi' a
bit basket owre 'er gardie, crying, ' Fa'll buy my black doctors fulpit in
a peel ?' " The gangrel bodie was a leech-seller of Stonehaven, and of
course the " doctors " were " whelped " in a pool.

† *Lum,* chimney.

ing, " Meggy, he's come !"   " Oh, the nickem !"* said Tom's mother, " surely he's dead wi' cauld by this time.   Fat *can* we do wi' him ?   Oh, Mrs. Kelmar, he'll break my very heart !   Think o' him being oot for haill days without ony meat !   Often he's oot afore he gets his breakfast, and we winna see him again till night.   Only think that he's been out a' the day 'maist naked !   We canna get him keepit in frae thae beasts o' his !"

" He'll soon get tired o' that," said Mrs. Kelmar, " if ye dinna lick him."   " Never !" roared old Edward ; " I'll chain him in the house, and see if that will cool him."   " But," rejoined Mrs. Kelmar, " ye maunna touch him the night, John."   " I'll chain him to the grate !   But where is he ? Bring him here."   " He's at my fireside."   By this time, Tom, having followed at her heels, and heard most of what was said about him, was ready to enter as she came out. "Far hae ye been, you scamp ?" asked his mother.   " At the Tide !"   His father, on looking up, and seeing the boy with the old petticoat about him, bedabbled by the mud in which he had been playing, burst into a fit of laughter.   He leaned back on his chair, and laughed till he could laugh no more.

" Oh, laddie," said the mother, " ye needna look at me in that way.   It's you that he's laughin' at, you're sic a comical sicht.   Ye'll gang to that stinkin' place, man, till ye droun yoursel, and sine ye winna come back again." Tom was then taken in hand, cleaned, and scrubbed and put to bed.   Next morning his father, before he went out, appeared at the boy's bedside, and said, " If ye go out this day, sir, I'll have you chained."   " But," replied Tom, " ye hinna a cooch ;"† for he had no notion of any thing being chained but dogs.   " Never mind," said his father, " I'll chain you !"

---

* *Nickem*, a person given to mischievous tricks.   The word is also used as an endearing phrase : my *bonnie nickem* is equivalent to my *little dear.*

† *Cooch*, a dog-kennel.

The boy had no inclination to rise that day. He was hot and cold alternately. When he got up in the afternoon, he was in a "gruize."* Then he went to bed again. By the evening he was in a hot fever. Next day he was worse. He raved, and became delirious. He rambled about his beasts and his birds. Then he ceased to speak. His mouth became clammy and his tongue black. He hung between life and death for several weeks. At length the fever spent itself, leaving him utterly helpless.

One afternoon, as he was gradually getting better, he observed his mother sitting by his bedside. "Mother," said he, "where are my crabs and bandies that I brocht hame last nicht?" "Crabs and bandies!" said she; "ye're surely gaun gyte;† it's three months sin ye were oot!" This passed the boy's comprehension. His next question was, "Has my father gotten the chains yet?" "Na, laddie, nor winna; but ye maunna gang back to yer auld places for beasts again." "But where's a' my things, mother?" "They're awa! The twa bottoms o' broken bottles we found in the entry, the day you fell ill, were both thrown out." "And the shrew-mouse ye had in the boxie?" "Calton [the cat] took it." This set the boy a-crying, and in that state he fell asleep, and did not waken till late next morning, when he felt considerably better. He still, however, continued to make inquiries after his beasts.

His father, being indoors, and seeing the boy rising and leaning upon his elbow, said to him, "Come awa, laddie. It's long since ye were oot. The whins, and birds, and water-dogs‡ at Daiddie Brown's burnie will be a' langin to see ye again." The boy looked at his mother and smiled, but said nothing. In a few days he was able to rise, but the spring was well advanced before he was able to go out-of-doors.

* *Gruize*, a rigor, generally preceding a cold or fever.
† *Gaun gyte*, becoming insane, or acting foolishly.
‡ Water-rats.

He then improved rapidly. He was able to go farther and farther every day. At first he wandered along the beach. Then he roamed about over the country. He got to know the best nesting places—the woods, plantations, and hedges—the streams, burns, locks, and mill-dams—all round Aberdeen. When the other boys missed a nest, it was always "that loon Edward" that took it. For this he was thrashed, though he was only about four years old.

One of his favorite spots was the Den* and quarries of Rubislaw. There were five excellent places in the den for bird'snests and wild flowers. But he went to the quarries chiefly to find the big bits of sheep's silver, or mica, in the face of the rocks. Edward was much astonished at the size of the rocks. He knew how birds made their nests; he knew how flowers and whins grew out of the ground; but he did not know how rocks grew. He asked his parents for the reason. They told him that these rocks had existed from the beginning. This did not satisfy him, and he determined to ask one of the men at the quarry, who certainly ought to know how the rocks grew. "How do the rocks grow?" asked he of a quarry-man one day. "Fat say ye?" Tom repeated the question. "To the deil wi' ye, ye impudent brat, or I'll toss ye owre the head o' the quarry!" Tom took to his heels and fled, never looking back.

Another favorite haunt was Daiddie Brown's burnie. There were plantations and hedges near it, and fields close at hand on either side. Its banks were thickly clothed with wild raspberries and whins—the habitats of numerous birds. The burn itself had plenty of water-dogs, or water-rats, along its banks. That neighborhood has now been entirely overbuilt. The trees, the hedges, the whins, and even the burn itself, have all been swept away.

Tom's knowingness about bird'snests attracted many of

---

* *Den*, dean, a dingle or small valley.

his boy-fellows to accompany him in his expeditions. He used to go wandering on, forgetful of time, until it became very late. On such occasions the parents of the boys became very anxious about them; and knowing that Tam Edward was the cause of their being kept so long away from home, they forbade them accompanying him again on any account. When he asked them to go with him a bird-nesting, their answer usually was, " Wha wad gang wi' you? Ye never come hame!" Even when Tom did get any boys to follow him, he usually returned alone.

On one occasion he got some boys to accompany him to a wood at Polmuir, about two miles from town, on a bird-nesting expedition. While they were going through the wood, a little separated, one of them called out, "A byke, a byke,* stickin' on a tree, and made o' paper!" A byke was regarded as a glorious capture, not only for the sake of the honey, but because of the fun the boys had in skelpin' out the bees. Before they had quite reached the spot, one of the youngest boys yelled out, "Oh! I'm stung, I'm stung!" He took to his feet, and they all followed. After they had run some distance, and there being no appearance of a foe, a halt was made, and they stood still to consider the state of affairs. But all that could be ascertained was, that the byke was on a tree, that it was made of paper, and that it had lots of yellow bees about it.

This so excited Tom's curiosity that he at once proposed to go back and take down the paper byke. His proposal was met with a decided refusal; and on his insisting upon going back, all the other boys ran away home. Nothing daunted, however, he went back to that part of the wood where the byke had been seen. He found it, and was taking it from the under side of the branch to which it was attached, when a bee lighted upon one of his fingers and stung it severely. The pain was greater than from any

---

* *Byke*, a bees' nest.

sting that he had ever had before. He drew back, and sucked and blew the wound alternately, in order to relieve the pain.

Then he thought, "What can I do next?" There the byke hung before him. It was still in his power to remove it—if he could. To leave it was impossible. Although he had nothing to defend himself from the attacks of the bees, nor any thing to put the byke into when he had taken it down, still he would not go without it. His bonnet could scarcely do. It was too little and too holey. His stockings would not do, because he wished to take the byke home whole. A thought struck him. There was his shirt! That would do. So he took off his jacket, and disrobed himself of his shirt. Approaching the tree very gently, though getting numerous stings by the way, he contrived to remove the byke from the branch to which it was hanging, and tucked it into his shirt. He tied the whole up into a sort of round knot, so as to keep all in that was in.

It was now getting quite dark, and he hurried away with his prize. He got home in safety. He crept up the stair, and peeped in at the key-hole to see that the coast was clear. But no! he saw his father sitting in his chair. There was an old iron pot in a recess on one side of the stair, in which Tom used to keep his numerous "things," and there he deposited his prize until he could unpack it in the morning. He now entered the house as if nothing had happened. "Late as usual, Tam," said his father. No further notice was taken. Tom got his supper shortly after, and went to bed.

Before getting into bed, he went a little out of the way to get undressed, and then, as much unseen as possible, he crept down beneath the blankets. His brother, having caught sight of his nudity, suddenly called out, "Eh, mother, mother, look at Tam! he hasna gotten his sark!" Straightway his mother appeared at the bedside, and found that the statement was correct. Then the father made his

appearance.   "Where's your shirt, sir?"   "I dinna ken."
"What! dinna ken?" addressing his wife—"Where's my
strap?"   Tom knew the power of the strap, and found that
there was no hope of escaping it.

The strap was brought.   "Now, sir, tell me this instant,
where is your shirt?"   "It's in the bole on the stair."   "Go
and get it, and bring it here immediately."   Tom went and
brought it, sorrowfully enough, for he dreaded the issue.
"And what have you got in it?"   "A yellow bumbees'
byke."   "A what?" exclaimed his father and mother in a
breath.   "A yellow bumbees' byke."   "Did I not tell you,
sir," said his father, "only the other day, and made you
promise me, not to bring any more of these things into the
house, endangering and molesting us as well as the whole
of our neighbors?   Besides, only think of your stripping
yourself in a wood, to get off your shirt to hold a bees'
byke!"

"But this is a new ane," said Tom; "it's made o' paper."   "Made o' fiddlesticks!"   "Na, I'll let ye see it."
"Let it alone; I don't want to see it.   Go to bed at once,
sir, or I shall give you something [shaking his strap] that
will do you more good than bees' bykes!"

Before the old couple went to bed, they put Tom's shirt
into a big bowl, poured a quantity of boiling water over it,
and, after it was cold, they opened the shirt, and found—a
wasps' nest!

CHAPTER II.

SCHOOLS AND SCHOOL-MASTERS.

Edward was between four and five years old when he went to school. He was sent there principally that he might be kept out of harm's way. He did not go willingly; for he was of a roving, wandering disposition, and did not like to be shut up anywhere. He hated going to school. He was confined there about four hours a day. It might seem very little to some, but it was too much for him. He wanted to be free to roam about the Inches, up the Denburn, and along the path to Rubislaw, birdnesting.

The first school to which he was sent was a dame's school. It was kept by an old woman called Bell Hill. It was for the most part a girls' school, but Bell consented to take the boy, because she knew his mother and wished to oblige her. The school-room was situated at the top of a long stair. In fact, it was the garret of an ordinary dwelling-house.

We have said that Tom did not like school. He could not be reconciled to spend his time there. Thus he often played the truant. He was sometimes arrested on his way to school by the fish-market. It was then held in the Shiprow, where the post-office now stands. There were long rows of benches on which the fish were spread out. The benches were covered in, and afforded an excellent shelter on a rainy day.

Tom was well known to the fish-wives. "Here comes the queer laddie," they would say as they saw him approaching. And when he came up, they would ask him, "Weel, man, fat are ye gaun to speer* the day?" Tom's

---

* *Speer*, to ask a question.

inquiries were usually about fish—where they came from, what their names were, what was the difference between the different fishes, and so on. The fish-market was also a grand place for big blue flies, great beetles with red and yellow backs (burying beetles), and daylight rottens. They were the tamest rats he had ever seen, excepting two that he used to carry about in his pockets. His rats knew him as well as a dog knows his master.

But Tom's playing the truant and lingering about the fish-market soon became known to his mother; and then she sent for *her* mother, Tom's grannie, to take him to school. She was either to see him "in at the door," or accompany him into the school itself. But Tom did not like the supervision of his grannie. He rebelled against it. He played the truant under her very eyes. When grannie put him in at the door, calling out "Bell!" to the school-mistress up-stairs, Tom would wait until he thought the old woman was sufficiently distant, and then steal out, and run away, by cross streets, to the Denburn or the Inches.

But that kind of truant-playing also got to be known; and then grannie had to drag him to school. When she seized him by the "scruff o' the neck," she had him quite tight. It was of no use attempting to lie down or sit down. Her hand was like a vise, and she kept him straight upon his feet. He tried to wriggle, twist, turn himself round as on a pivot, and then make a bolt. She nevertheless held on, and dragged him to school, into the presence of Bell Hill, and said, "Here's your truant!" Tom's only chance was to go along very quietly, making no attempt to escape grannie's clutches, and then, watching for an opportunity, he would make a sudden dart and slip through her fingers. He ran, and she ran; but in running, Tom far outstripped her; for though grannie's legs were very much longer than his, they were also very much stiffer.

The boy was sent one morning to buy three rolls for breakfast; but after he had bought the rolls, instead of going home, he forgathered with three loons, and accompanied them to the Denburn. He got a lot of horse-leeches, and was in the act of getting another, when, looking in the water, he saw the reflection of grannie approaching. When he felt her fingers touching his neck, he let go the stone under which the horse-leech was, and made a sudden bound to the other side of the burn. He heard a heavy splash in the water. His comrades called out, "Tam, Tam, ye're grannie's droonin'!" But Tam neither stopped nor looked back. He flew as fast as he could to the Inches, where he stopped to take breath. The tide coming in, drove him away, and then he took refuge on the logs, near the Middens; after which he slunk home in the evening.

His mother received him thus: "Ye're here again, ye ne'er-do-well! creepin' in like a thief. Ye've been wi' yer ragamuffins: yer weet duds tell that. That's wi' yer Inches, an' tearin' an' ridin' on the logs, an' yer whin bushes. But ye may think muckle black shame o' yersel, man, for gaun and droonin' yer peer auld grannie." "I didna droon her," said Tom. "But she may hae been drooned for you; ye didna stay to tak her oot." "She fell in hersell." "Haud yer tongue, or I'll take the poker t'ye! Think shame, man, to send her hame in sic a filthy state. But where's the bread I sent ye for?" "It's a' eaten." "We wad hae had a late breakfast if we had waited till now, and sine ye've no gottin it after a'. But ye'll see what yer faither 'ill say to ye when he gets hame!"

Tom was in bed by that time. He remained awake until his father returned in the evening. He was told the whole story by his wife, in its most dreadful details. When he heard of grannie's plash into the burn, and coming home covered with "glaur," he burst out into a long and hearty laugh. Tom heard it with joy. The father then remarked that grannie should "beware of going so near the edge of such a dirty place." Then Tom felt himself reprieved, and shortly after fell asleep.

The scape-grace returned to school. He did not learn a
great deal. He had been taught by his mother his A B C,
and to read words of three letters. He did not learn much
more at Bell Hill's school. Bell's qualifications as a teacher
were not great. Nevertheless, the education that she gave
was a religious education. She prayed, or, as Edward called
it, "groaned," with the children twice a day. And it was
during one of her devotional exercises that the circumstance
occurred which compelled Bell Hill to expel Tom Edward
from her school.

Edward had been accustomed to bring many of his
"beasts" with him to school. The scholars were delighted
with his butterflies, but few of them cared to be bitten or
stung by his other animals, and to have horse-leeches crawling about them was unendurable. Thus Edward became a
source of dread and annoyance to the whole school. He
was declared to be a "perfect mischief." When Bell Hill
was informed of the beasts he brought with him, she used
to say to the boy, "Now, do not bring any more of these
nasty and dangerous things here again." Perhaps he promised, but generally he forgot.

At last he brought with him an animal of a much larger
sort than usual. It was a kae, or jackdaw. He used to
keep it at home, but it made such a noise that he was sent
out with it one morning, with strict injunctions not to
bring it back again. He must let it go, or give it to somebody else. But he was fond of his kae, and his kae was
fond of him. It would follow him about like a dog. He
could not part with the kae; so he took it to school with
him. But how could he hide it? Little boys' trousers
were in those days buttoned over their vest; and as Tom's
trousers were pretty wide, he thought he could get the kae
in there. He got it safely into his breeks before he entered the school.

So far so good. But when the school-mistress gave the
word "Pray," all the little boys and girls knelt down, turn-

ing their backs to Bell. At this movement the kae became fractious. He could not accommodate himself to the altered position. But seeing a little light overhead, he made for it. He projected his beak through the opening between the trousers and the vest. He pushed his way upward; Tom squeezed him downward to where he was before. But this only made the kae furious. He struggled, forced his way upward, got his bill through the opening, and then his head.

The kae immediately began to *cre-waw! cre-waw!* "The Lord preserv's a'! Fat's this, noo?" cried Bell, starting to her feet. "It's Tam Edward again," shouted the scholars, "wi a craw stickin' oot o' his breeks!" Bell went up to him, pulled him up by his collar, dragged him to the door, thrust him out, and locked the door after him. Edward never saw Bell Hill again.

The next school to which he was sent was at the Denburn side, near by the venerable Bow brig, the oldest bridge in Aberdeen,* but now swept away to make room for modern improvements. This school consisted wholly of boys. The master was well stricken in years. He was one of the old school, who had great faith in "the taws,"† as an instrument of instruction. Edward would have learned much more at this school than at Bell Hill's, had he not been

---

* The Rev. James Gordon, in his "Description of both Towns of Aberdeen" (1661), says: "The bruike called the Den Burne runs beneath the west side of the citie; upon the brink quhairoff a little stone bridge, at that pairt wher the brooke entereth the river Dee, the Carmelites of old had a convent, whoes church and quholl precinct of building wer leveled with the ground that very day that the rest of the churches and convents of New Aberdeen wer destroyed. There remayneth now onlie ane kilne, which standeth in the outmost south corner of the citie, known this day by the name of the Freer Kilne."

† The "taws" consist of a leather strap about three feet long, cut into tails at the end. Sometimes the ends are burned, to make them hit hard. They are applied to the back, or the "palmies"—that is, the palm of the hand.

so near his favorite haunt, the Denburn. He was making rapid progress with his reading, and was going on well with his arithmetic, when his usual misfortune occurred.

One day he had gone to school earlier than usual. The door was not open, and to while away his time he went down to the Denburn. He found plenty of horse-leeches, and a number of the grubs of water-flies. He had put them into the bottom of a broken bottle, when one of the scholars came running up, crying, "Tam, Tam, the school's in!" Knowing the penalty of being behind time, Tom flew after the boy, without thinking of the bottle he had in his hand. He contrived, however, to get it into the school, and deposited it in a corner beside him, without being observed.

All passed on smoothly for about half an hour, when one of the scholars gave a loud scream, and started from his seat. The master's attention was instantly attracted, and he came down from the desk, taws in hand. "What's this?" he cried. "It's a horse-leech crawlin' up my leg!" "A horse-leech?" "Yes, sir, and see," pointing to the corner in which Tom kept his treasure, "there's a bottle fu' o' them!" "Give me the bottle!" said the master; and, looking at the culprit, he said, "You come this way, Master Edward!" Edward followed him, quaking. On reaching the desk, he stopped, and, holding out the bottle, said, "That's yours, is it not?" "Yes." "Take it, then; that is the way out," pointing to the door; "go as fast as you can, and never come back; and take that too," bringing the taws down heavily upon his back. Tom thought that his back was broken, and that he would never get his breath again.

A few days after, Tom was preparing to go out, after breakfast, when his mother asked him, "Where are ye gaun the day, laddie?" "Till my school," said he. "To your school, are ye? Where is't? at the Inches, or the Middens, or Daiddie Brown's burnie? where is't?" "At the fit o' the Green." "At the fit o' the Green! But hoo lang is it since ye was putten awa frae that school?" Tom was silent. He saw that his mother had been informed of his expulsion.

In a little while she was ready to go out. She took hold of her son by the cuff of the neck, and took him down to the Green. When she reached the school, for the purpose of imploring the master to take her son back, she knocked at the door, and the master at once appeared. Before she could open her mouth, the master abruptly began, "Don't bring that boy here! I'll not take him back—not though you were to give me twenty pounds! Neither I, nor my scholars, have had a day's peace since he came here." And with that he shut the door in her face before she could utter a single word. She turned and came away, very much vexed. She kept her grip on the boy, but, standing still to speak to a neighbor, and her hold getting a little slacker, he made a sudden bolt and escaped.

As usual, he crept in late in the evening. His father was at home, reading. On entering, Tom observed that he stopped, fixing his eyes upon him over the top of his book, and looked at him steadily for some time. Then, laying down his book, he said, "And where have you been, sir?" The boy said nothing. "It's no wonder that you're dumb. You've been putten out of your school a second time. You'll be a disgrace to all connected wi' you. You'll become an idler, a ne'er-do-well. You'll get into bad company. You'll become a thief! Then you'll get into jail, and end your days in misery and shame. Such is the case with all that neglect their schooling, and disregard what their parents bid them."

Tom was at last ashamed of himself. He said nothing until supper-time; and then he asked for his supper, as he was hungry. "Perhaps you are," said his father; "and you shall get no supper this night, nor any other night, until you learn to behave yourself better. Go to bed, sir, this moment!" Tom slunk away, and got to bed as soon as possible. When the lights were out, and all were thought to be abed, a light hand removed the clothes from over Tom's head, and put something into his hand. He found it to be "a big dad o' bread-and-butter." It was so like the kind motherly heart and hand to do this. So Tom had his supper, after all.

He was next sent to the Lancaster School in Harriet Street. There were two masters in this school. The upper classes were in the highest story, the other classes in the lowest. The master of the lower class, to which Tom belonged, knowing his weakness, ordered him, on entering, not to bring any of his beasts to that school. He was to pay more attention to his lessons than he had yet done, or he would be punished severely. He did not bring any thing but his school-books for a long time, but at last his usual temptation befell him. It happened in this way:

On his way to and from school, along School Hill, he observed a sparrow's nest built in the corner part of a spout. He greatly envied the sparrow's nest; but he could only feast his longing eyes at a distance. He tried to climb the spout once or twice, but it was too high, and bulged out at the top. The clamps which held the spout to the wall were higher at the top than at the bottom. He had almost given up the adventure in despair, when one day, on going to school, he observed two men standing together, and looking up in the direction of the nest. Boy-like, and probably thinking that he was a party concerned in the affair, he joined them, and listened to what they were talking about. He found that the nest interfered with the flow of water along the spout, and that it must be removed; and that the whole water-way along the spout must also be cleaned out.

Tom was now on the alert, and watched the spout closely. That day passed, and nothing was done. The next day passed, and still the men had not made their appearance. But on the third day, on his way to school, he observed a man and a boy placing a long ladder against the house. Tom stopped, and, guessing what was about to be done, he intended to ask the man for the nest and its contents. The man was about to ascend the ladder, when, after feeling his pockets and finding that something had been forgotten, he sent the boy back to the shed for something or other—most probably a trowel. Then, having struck a light and set fire to his pipe, the man betook himself to the church-yard, which was near at hand.

A thought now struck Tom. Might he not take the nest himself without waiting for it, and perhaps without getting it, after all? He looked about. He looked into the church-yard gate, nearly opposite. He saw nobody. The coast was clear. Tom darted across the street and went rapidly up the ladder. Somebody shrieked to him from a window on the other side. It staggered him at first. But he climbed upward; got to the nest, and, after some wriggling and twisting, he pulled it away, and got down before either the man or the boy had returned.

It was eggs that he wanted, but, lo and behold! here was a nest of five well-fledged birds. Instead of taking the birds home, Tom was foolish enough to take them with him to school. He contrived to get the nest into the school unobserved, and put it below the form on which he was seated, never thinking that the little things would get hungry, or try to make their escape. All went on well for about an hour. Then there was a slight commotion. A chirrup was heard. And presently the throats of all were opened— "*Chirrup! chirrup!*" Before the master could get the words "What's that?" out of his mouth, the birds themselves answered him by leaving their nest and fluttering round the school-room, the boys running after them! "Silence! Back to your seats!" cried the master. There was now stillness in the school, except the fluttering of the birds.

The culprit was called to the front. "This is more of your work, Edward, is it not?" "Yes, sir." "And did I not tell you to bring no more of these things here?" "Yes, sir; but I only got them on my way up, or I wouldn't have brought them here." "I don't believe it," said the master. "Yes, it's true, it's true," shouted some of the scholars. "Silence! How do you know?" "We saw him harryin' the nest as we came up School Hill." "How?" "He was on the top of a long ladder takin' the nest oot o' a spoot." "Well, sir," he said to Edward, "you are one of the most daring and determined little fellows that I have ever heard of. It seems you will follow nobody's advice. If you do not give up your tricks, you will some day fall and break your neck. But as you have told me the truth, I will forgive you this once. But remember! it's the last time. Now go, collect your birds, and take them away."

Edward groped about to collect the birds, but few of them were left. The windows having been let down, they had all escaped except one. He got that one, and descended to the street. There he recovered two other "gorbals." He went home with his three birds; but, his sister being ill, his mother told him to take them away, because they made such a noise. In the course of the day he gave them to another boy, in exchange for a little picture-book containing "The Death and Burial of Cock-robin."

Next morning he went back to school, and from that time forward he continued to obey the master's orders. He never brought any more "beasts" there. He was at the Lancaster school about eighteen months, though he was occasionally absent. He did not learn very much. The Bible was used as the reading-book, and when he left school he could read it fairly. He could also repeat the Shorter Catechism. But he knew very little of arithmetic, and nothing of grammar. He had only got the length of the rule of two—that is, he could add up two lines of figures. He could not manage the multiplication-table. He could only multiply by means of his fingers. He knew nothing of writing.

We must mention the cause of his leaving his third and his last school. He had entirely given up bringing "beasts" with him; but he had got a bad name. It was well known that he had been turned out of all the schools which he had formerly attended on account of bringing his "beasts" with him. Better kill a dog, it is said, than give him a bad name. In Edward's case, his bad name was attended with very serious results.

One morning, when the boys were at their lessons and the master was at his desk, a sudden commotion occurred. The master gave a loud scream, and, jumping to his feet, he shook something from his arm, and suddenly put his foot upon it. Then, turning in Edward's direction, he exclaimed, "This is some more of your work, Master Edward." Not hearing what he said, Edward made no reply. Another boy was called forward, and both stooping down, they took up something and laid it on a sheet of paper. On rising, the boy was asked what it was. "It's a Maggy Monny Feet," he said. "Is its bite dangerous? Is it poisonous?" The boy could not tell.

Edward was then called to the floor. "You've been at your old trade, Edward, I see; but I'll now take it out of you. I have warned you not to bring any of your infernal beasts here, and now I have just found one creeping up my arm and biting me. Hold up!" Edward here ventured to say that he had not brought the beast, that he had not brought any thing for a long while past. "What! a lie too?" said the master: "A lie added to the crime makes it doubly criminal. Hold up, sir!" Tom held up his hand, and the master came down upon it very heavily with the taws. "The other!" The other hand was then held up, and when Tom had got his two hot hands, the master exclaimed, "That's for the lie, and this for the offense!" and then he proceeded to bring the taws heavily down upon his back. The boy, however, did not cry.

"Now, sir," said the master, when almost out of breath,

"will you say now that you did not bring it?"   "I did not;
indeed, sir, I did not!"   "Well, then, take that," giving him
a number of tremendous lashes along his back.   "Well,
now?"   "I did not!"   The master went on again: "It's
your own fault," he said, "for not confessing your crime."
"But I did not bring it," replied Edward.   "I'll flog you
until you confess."   And then he repeated his lashes, upon
his hands, his shoulders, and his back.   Edward was a mere
mite of a boy, so that the taws reached down to his legs,
and smote him there.   "Well, now," said the master, after
he was reduced to his last effort, "did you bring it?"   "No,
sir, I did not!"

The master sat down exhausted.   "Well," said he, "you
are certainly a most provoking and incorrigible devil."   The
master had a reddish nose, and a number of pimples on
his face, which were of the same hue.   When he got into a
rage, it was observed that the protuberances became much
brighter.   On this occasion his organ became ten times red-
der than before.   It was like Bardolph's lantern in the poop.
Some of the boys likened his pimples to large driblets of
blood.

After resting for a while in his chair, Edward standing
before him, he called to the boy whom he had first brought
to his assistance, "William, bring forward that thing!"   The
boy brought forward the paper, on which lay a bruised cen-
tipede.   "Now, then," said the master, "did you not bring
that venomous beast here?"   "I did not, sir!"   The whole
school was now appealed to.   "Did any of you see Edward
.with that beast, or any other beast, to-day or yesterday?"
No answer.   "Did any of you see Edward with any thing
last week or the week before?"   Still no answer.   Then,
after a considerable pause, turning to Edward, he said, "Get
your slate.   Go home, and tell your father to get you put
on board a man-of-war, as that is the best school for all
irreclaimables such as you."   So saying, he pointed to the
door.   Tom got his slate and his books, and hurried down-

stairs.   And thus Edward was expelled from his third and last school.

On reaching home, he told his parents the circumstances connected with his expulsion.   He also added that he wouldn't go to school any more; at all events, he wouldn't go back to "yon school."   He would rather go to work. He was told that he was too young to work; for he was scarcely six years old.   His father proposed to take him to the Lancaster school on the following day, for the purpose of inducing the master to take back the boy.

The next day arrived.   His father came home from his work for the purpose of taking the boy to school; but Tom had disappeared.   He would not go back.   He went first to the fish-market, where he spent the greater part of the day.   Then he went down to the Inches.   From thence he went toward the logs, and while there with a few more boys preparing sparrow-traps, one of them called out, "Tam, there's yer faither!"   Tom immediately got up and ran away.   His father, following him, called out "Stop, sir! stop, sir! come back, come back, will you!"   Tom's father was a long, slender man, and could not stand much running. He soon dropped behind, while Tom went out Dee-side way like a lamp-lighter.   He never stopped until he reached the Clayholes.   Not seeing his father following him, he loiter-ed about there until it was nearly dark; he then returned, keeping a close lookout, and ready to run off again.   At length, about dark, he got back to the logs.

It must be mentioned that on the spare ground above the Inches large piles of logs were laid, some of them of great size.   The logs were floated down the Dee, and were laid there until the timber merchants found it convenient to take them away.   Little care being exercised in putting up the piles, there were often large openings left at the ends.   Instead of going home, the boy got into one of these openings, and crept in as far as he could get.   But though he was in a measure out of sight, he soon found that he could obtain very little shelter for the night. He was barefooted, and his clothes were thin and raggy. The wind blew through the logs, and he soon became very cold. He shivered till his teeth chattered. The squeaking and jumping of the rats, of whom there seemed to be myriads, kept him awake. It was so different from being snug in his warm bed, that he once thought of getting out of his hole and running home. But he was terrified to do that, and thus encounter his father's strap—his back being still so sore from the effects of his flogging at school. The cold continued to increase, especially toward the small hours of the morning. Indeed, he never experienced so bitterly cold a night in the whole course of his life.

At length morning began to dawn. The first streaks of light were tinging the eastern sky, when Tom prepared to get out of his hole and have a run in the open ground to warm himself. He was creeping out of the logs for the purpose, when in the dim morning light he thought he saw the figure of a man. Yes! it was his father. He saw him moving about among the saw-pits, the logs, and the piles of wood. Tom crept farther into his hole among the logs; and, on looking out again, he found his father had disappeared. Half an hour later he appeared again; and after going over the former ground, he proceeded in the direction of the Inches. In a few minutes he descended to the channel, doubtless with the intention of crossing, as the tide was out at the time.

Now, thought Tom, is my opportunity. He crept out of his hole, went round the farther end of the logs, up Lower Dee Street, past the carpet-weaver's, up Carmelite Street, and then home. Just as he reached the top of the stair, Mrs. Kelmar, the kindly "neibour," who had been kept up all night by the troubles of the Edward family, took him by the collar, and said, "Eh, laddie, ye hae gien yer folk a sair nicht o't! But bide a wee, I'll gang in wi' ye!" As she entered the door, she exclaimed, "Here he's again,

Maggie, a' safe!"   "Oh, ye vagaboon!" said the mother, "where hae ye been a' nicht?   Yer faither's oot seekin' ye. I wonder how I can keep my hands aff ye."   "No, no, Maggie," said Mrs. Kelmar, "ye winna do that.   But I'll tell ye what ye'll do.   Gie him some meat, and let him get to his bed as fast as he can."   "His bed?" said his mother; "he shanna bed here till his faither comes in."   "Just gie him something, Maggie, and get him oot o' the road." After some parleying, Tom got something to eat, and was in bed, with the blankets over him, before his father returned.

"Weel, John," said Mrs. Kelmar, "ye hinna gotten him?" "No."   "Ye hinna gaun to the right place!"   "The right place!" said John, "who on earth could tell the right place for such a wandering Jew as he is?"   "Well, I've got him." "Where?"   "At the head o' the stair!"   "And where is he now?"   "Where he should be."   "That's in Bridewell!"   "No, no, John, dinna say that."   "Where, then?" "In his bed."   "What! here?   And before I have paid him for his night's work?"   "Now, John, just sit doun and have a cup o' tea wi' Maggie and me before you go to your wark; and if ye hae ony thing to say to the laddie, ye can say it when he gets up."   "You always take his part, Mrs. Kelmar, always!"

Tom lay quaking in bed.   He heard all that was said. He peeped out of the blankets; but when he saw his father sit down he knew that all was safe.   And when he had had his friendly cup o' tea, and had gone to his work, Tom fell fast asleep.   He did not awake until midday, when his father returned to dinner.   Being observed to move in his bed, his father ordered him to get up.   This set him a-crying, and he exclaimed that "he wudna gang back to yon school."   His mother now asked the reason why he was so bitter against going to "yon school."   He then told them how he had been treated by the master, and how his back was sore yet.

His back was then looked at, and it was found that his shirt was hard with clotted blood, and still sticking to his skin. The wales extended right down to his legs. Means were adopted to soften the shirt and remove it from the skin. But while that was being done, the boy fell back and fainted away. On coming to himself, he found his mother bathing his brow with cold water, and Mrs. Kelmar holding a smelling-bottle to his nose, which made his eyes run with water. A large piece of linen, covered with ointment, was then put upon his back. His father went away, ordering him to keep the house, and not to go out that day.

Whatever may have passed between his parents he did not know. He was in bed and asleep when his father returned at night. But he was never asked to return to the Lancaster school.

He had now plenty of time for excursions into the country. He wandered up the Dee and along the banks of the Don on both sides. He took long walks along shore— across the Aulten Links to the Auld Brig, and even up to the mountains, which at Aberdeen approach pretty near to the coast.

During one of his excursions on the hills of Torrie, near the commencement of the Grampians, while looking for blackberries and cranberries, Edward saw something like the flash of an eel gliding through among the heather. He rushed after it, and pounced down upon it with both hands, but the animal had escaped. He began to tear up the heather, in order to get at it. His face streamed with perspiration. He rested for a time, and then began again. Still there was no animal, nor a shadow of one.

At this time another boy came up, and asked, "What are ye doing there?" "Naething." "D'ye call that naething?" pointing to about a cart-load of heather torn up. "Have ye lost ony thing?" "No." "What are ye looking for, then?" "For something like an eel." "An eel!"

AULTEN LINKS, ABERDEEN.

quoth the lad; "do ye think ye'll find an eel amang heather?   It's been an *adder*, and it's well ye have na' gotten it.
The beast might have bitten ye to death."   "No fear o'
that," said Edward.   "How long is it sin' ye saw it?"
"Some minutes."   "If that's the case, it may be some
miles up the hills by this time.   Which way was it gaun?"
"That way."   "Well," said the lad, "you see that heap o'
stones up there? try them, and if you do not find it there,
you may gang hame and come back again, and then ye'll
just be as near finding it as ye are now."   "Will ye help
me?" asked Edward.   "Na, faith, I dinna want to be bitten
to death."   And so saying, he went away.

Edward then proceeded to the pile of stones which had
been pointed out, to make a search for the animal.   He
took stone after stone off the heap, and still there was no
eel.   There were plenty of worms and insects, but these he
did not want.   A little beyond the stones lay a large piece
of turf.   He turned it over, and there the creature was!

He was down upon it in an instant, and had it in his hand! He looked at the beast. It was not an eel. It was very like an ask, but it was six or seven times longer.

Having tightened his grip of the beast, for it was trying to wriggle out of his hand, he set out for home. He struck the Dee a little below where the Chain Bridge now stands, reaching the ford opposite Dee village, and prepared to cross it. But the water being rather deep at the time, he had to strip and wade across, carrying his clothes in one hand and the "eel" in the other. He had only one available hand, so that getting off and on his clothes, and wading the river breast-high, occupied some time.

On reaching the top of Carmelite Street, he observed his mother, Mrs. Kelmar, and some other women, standing together at the street door. He rushed in among them with great glee, and, holding up his hand, exclaimed, "See, mother, sic a bonnie beastie I've gotten!" On looking at the object he held in his hand, the conclave of women speedily scattered. They flew in all directions. Edward's mother screamed, "The Lord preserv's! what the sorrow's that ye hae noo?" "Oh, Meggy, Meggy," said Mrs. Kelmar, "it's a snake! Dinna let him in! For ony sake dinna let him in, or we'll a' be bitten!" . The entry door was then shut and bolted, and Tom was left out with the beast in his hand.

Mrs. Kelmar's husband then made his appearance. "What's this, Tam, that has caused such a flutter among the wives?" "Only this bit beastie." Kelmar started back. "What, has it not bitten you?" "No!" "Well," he added, "the best thing you can do with it is to take it to Dr. Ferguson as fast as you can, for you can't be allowed to bring it in here."

Dr. Ferguson kept a druggist's shop at the corner of Correction Wynd, near the head of the Green. He had a number of creatures suspended in glass jars in his window. Boys looked in at these wonderful things. They were the admiration of the neighbors. Some said that these extraordinary things had come from people's "insides." Tom had often been there before with big grubs, piebald snails, dragon-flies, and yellow puddocks. So he went to Dr. Ferguson with his last new prize.

He was by this time surrounded by a number of boys like himself. They kept, however, at a respectable distance. When he moved in their direction they made a general stampede. At length he arrived at the doctor's door. When the doctor saw the wriggling thing that he was holding in his hand, he ordered him out of the shop, and told him to wait in the middle of the street until he had got a bottle ready for the reception of the animal. Tom waited until the bottle was ready, when he was told that when he had got the snake in he must cork the bottle as firmly as possible. The adder was safely got in and handed to the doctor, who gave Tom fourpence for the treasure. Next day it appeared in the window, to the general admiration of the inhabitants.

Tom hastened home with his fourpence. On entering the house, he encountered his father, who seized him by the neck, and asked, "Where's that venomous beast that you had?" "I left it with Dr. Ferguson." "But have you no more?" "No." "That's very strange! You seldom come home with so few things about you. But we shall see." The boy was then taken into the back yard, where he was ordered to strip. Every bit of clothing was shaken, examined, and searched; the father standing by with a stick. Nothing was found, and Tom was allowed to put on his clothes and go up-stairs to bed.

CHAPTER III.

APPRENTICESHIP.

THE boy was learning idle habits. He refused to go back to the Lancaster school. Indeed, from the cruel treatment he had received there, his parents did not ask him to return. He had now been expelled from three schools. If he went to a fourth, it is probable that he might also have been expelled from that. It would not do for him to go scouring the hills in search of adders, or to bring them home, to the " terrification " of his neighbors. He himself wished to go to work. His parents at last gave their consent, though he was then only about six years old. But poor people can always find something for their children to do out-of-doors. The little that they earn is always found very useful at home.

Edward's brother, who was about two years older than himself, was working at Craig and Johnston's tobacco works. On inquiry, it was found that the firm was willing to take young Edward at the wage of fourteen-pence a week. The tobacco-spinners worked in an old house situated at the end of the flour-mill in St. Nicholas Street. Each spinner had three boys under him—the wheeler, the pointer, and the stripper. Edward went through all these grades. As a stripper he could earn about eighteen-pence a week.

The master was a bird-fancier, so that Edward got on very well with him. The boy brought him lots of nests and young birds in summer, and old birds which he trapped during winter. The master allowed him to keep rabbits in the back yard ; so that, what between working and playing, attending to his rabbits and catering for their food, his time passed much more happily than it had done at school.

After being in the tobacco works for about two years, Edward heard that boys were getting great wages at a factory at Grandholm, situated on the river Don, about two miles from Aberdeen. The high wages were a great attraction. Tom and his brother took the advantage of a fast-day to go to the mill and ask for employment. The manager told the boys that he wanted no additional hands at that time, but that he would put their names down, and let them know when he required their services.

They returned, and told their parents what they had done. Both father and mother were against the change, partly because of Tom's youth, and partly because of the distance Grandholm was from Aberdeen. Tom, however, insisted that he could both work and walk; and at last his parents gave their consent.

There was another reason besides the high wages which induced Tom to wish to be employed at Grandholm. He kept this to himself. He had often seen the place before, though only at a distance. But who that has seen the banks and braes of the Don, from the Auld Brig* to the Haughs of Grandholm, can ever forget it? Looking down from the heights above the Brig of Balgownie, you see the high broad arch thrown across the deep and dark winding Don. Beneath you, the fishermen are observed hauling to

---

* The Auld Brig is also called the Brig o' Balgownie. Byron, who lived for some years at Aberdeen in his boyhood, says: "The Brig of Don, near the 'auld toun' of Aberdeen, with its one arch and its black deep salmon-stream, is in my memory as yesterday. I still remember the awful proverb which made me pause to cross it, and yet lean over it with a childish delight—being an only son, at least by the mother's side:

"'Brig o' Balgownie, wight [strong] is thy wa';
Wi' a wife's ae son on a mear's ae foal
Down thou shalt fa'.'"

BRIG O' BALGOWNIE.

THE SPIRES OF ST. MACHAR.

the shore their salmon-nets. Westward of the Auld Brig
the river meanders among the bold, bluff banks, clothed to
the summit with thick embowered wood. Two or three
miles above are the Haughs, from which a fine view of the
Don is obtained, with the high wood-covered bank beyond
it; and, over all, the summits of the spires of St. Machar,
the cathedral church of old Aberdeen.

It was to roam through these woods and amidst this
beautiful scenery that young Edward so much desired to
be employed at the Grandholm factory. Nor was he disappointed in his expectations. Scarcely three days had
elapsed ere a letter arrived at the Edwards' house, informing both the boys that they would be employed at the mill
at the usual wages. The hours were to be from six o'clock
in the morning till eight o'clock in the evening.

The boys had accordingly to be up by about four in the
morning, after which they had to get their breakfast, and to
walk two miles to their work. They were seldom home at

night before nine. It was delightful in summer, but dreary in winter, when they went and came in the cold dark nights and mornings. The wages of the boys were at first from three to four shillings a week each, and before they left the mill their wages were from five to six shillings a week.

The boys were first put into the heckling shop. They were next transferred to a small mill at the end of the larger one. Young Edward worked there. His business was to attend at the back of a breaker—to take away the cases when they were full, and put empty ones in their places. He was next set to attend two carding-machines; and from these to the roving or spinning side, three of which he frequently kept before he left. This was the highest work done in that room.

"People may say of factories what they please," says Edward, "but I liked this factory. It was a happy time for me while I remained there. It was situated in the centre of a beautiful valley, almost embowered among tall and luxuriant hedges of hawthorn, with water-courses and shadowy trees between, and large woods and plantations beyond. It teemed with nature and natural objects. The woods were easy of access during our meal-hours. What lots of nests! What insects, wild flowers, and plants, the like of which I had never seen before! Prominent among the birds was the sedge warbler,* which lay concealed in the reedy copses, or by the margin of the mill-lades. Oh! how I wondered at the little thing! how it contrived to imitate almost all the other birds I had ever heard! and none to greater perfection than the chirrup of my old and special favorite, the sparrow."

One day he saw a kingfisher—a great event in his life! What a beautiful bird! What a sparkling gem of nature! Resplendent in plumage and gorgeous in color—from the

---

* Called also the English mocking-bird, and the Scottish nightingale.

bright turquois blue to the deepest green, and the darker
shades of copper and gold.   Edward was on a nesting excursion, with some little fellows like himself, along the
braes of the Don, and at some distance above the Auld
Brig, when he first saw this lustrous bird.   "I was greatly
taken," he says, " with its extraordinary beauty, and much
excited by seeing it dive into the stream.   I thought it
would drown itself, and that its feathers would eventually
become so clogged with water that it would not be able to
fly.   Had this happened—which, of course, it did not—my
intention was to have plunged in to the rescue, when, as
a matter of course, I would have claimed the prize as my
reward.   Thus buoyed up, I wandered up and down the
river after the bird until the shades of even came down and
forced me to give up the pursuit; and I then discovered,
having continued the chase so long, that I was companion-
less, and had to return home alone.

"It so happened that for a month or two during summer-time, owing to the scarcity of water, one part of the
factory worked during the night-time and the other during
the day-time, week and week about.   This was a glorious
time for me.   I rejoiced particularly in the night work.
We got out at six in the morning, and, instead of going ·
directly home, I used to go up to the woods of Scotston
and Scotston Moor, scour the country round them, and
then return home by the Auld Brig.   Another day I
would go up to Buxburn, range the woods and places about
them, and then home by Hilton or Woodside.   Or, again,
after having crossed Grandholm Bridge, instead of going
up by Laurie Hillock, I went away down Don side, by
Tillydrone, the Aulten (old Aberdeen), through the fields
to the Aulten Links, whipped the whins there, then over
the Broad Hill, and home by Constitution Street.   I would
reach it, perhaps, about dinner-time, instead of at seven in
the morning, although I had to be back at the mill again
by eight o'clock at night.

"Once, on a Saturday, after having visited Buxburn, I went round by the back of the Dancing Cairns to the Stocket and the woods of Hazelhead, then down the Rubis-law road, and home in the evening. Ah! these were happy days. There were no taws to fear, and no tyrannical dominie to lay them on. True, the farm people did halloo at me at times, but I generally showed them a clean pair of heels. The gamekeepers, also, sometimes gave me chase, but I managed to outstrip them; and although no nests were to be got, there was always something to be found or seen. In winter-time, also, when the canal was frozen, a mile of it lay in our way home, and it was capital fun to slide along, going to and coming from our work. This was life, genuine life, for the young. But, alas! a sad change was about to come; and it came very soon."

The boys remained at Grandholm factory for about two years. Their father thought that they ought both to be apprenticed to some settled trade. The eldest boy left first, and was apprenticed to a baker; then Tom, the youngest, left, very much to his regret, and was bound apprentice to a shoe-maker. He was eleven years old at that time. His apprenticeship was to last for six years. His wages began at eighteen-pence a week, with sixpence to be added weekly in each succeeding year. He was to be provided by his master with shoes and aprons. The hours were to be from six in the morning to nine at night, two hours being allowed for meals.

The name of Edward's master was Charles Begg. His shop was situated at the highest part of Gallowgate. He usually employed from two to three workmen. His trade consisted chiefly in manufacturing work of the lightest description, such as ladies' and children's boots and shoes. He himself worked principally at pump-making, and that was the branch of the trade which young Edward was taught.

Begg was a low-class Cockney. He was born in London, where he learned the trade of shoe-making. He had gradually wandered northward, until he reached Inverness, where he lived for some time. Then he went eastward to Elgin, then to Banff, until at last he arrived at Aberdeen, where he married and settled. Begg was a good workman; though, apart from shoe-making, he knew next to nothing. It is well, however, to be a good workman, if one does his work thoroughly and faithfully. The only things that Begg could do, besides shoe-making, were drinking and fighting. He was a great friend of pugilism; though his principal difficulty, when he got drunk, was to find any body to fight with in that pacific neighborhood.

It was a great misfortune for the boy to have been placed under the charge

CHARLES BEGG'S SHOP, GALLOWGATE.

of so dissolute a vagabond. He had, however, to do his best. He learned to make upper-leathers, and was proceeding to make shoe-bottoms. He would, doubtless, have learned his trade very well, but for the drunkenness of his master, who was evidently going headlong to ruin. He was very often absent from the shop, and when customers called, Edward was sent out by his mistress to search the public-houses frequented by Begg; but, when found,

he was usually intoxicated.   The customers would not return, and the business consequently fell off.   When drunk,
Begg raved and swore ; and after beating the boy in the
shop, he would go up-stairs and beat his wife.

Shoe-makers are usually very fond of pets, and especially
of pet birds.   Many of the craft have singing-birds about
them, and some are known to be highly skilled and excellent bird-fanciers.   But Begg had no notion of pets of any
kind.   He had no love whatever for the works of nature,
and detested those who had.   Edward had been born with
the love of birds and living creatures, and Begg hated him
accordingly.   Begg used to rifle his pockets on entering
the shop, to see that Edward had nothing of the kind about
him.   If he found any thing, he threw it into the street—
his little boxes with butterflies, eggs, and such-like.   Many
a blow did he give Edward on such occasions.   He used
to say that he would "stamp the fool out of him ;" but he
tried in vain.

One afternoon, when Edward had finished his work, and
was waiting for the return of his master in order to go to
dinner, he was sitting with a sparrow on his knee.   It was
a young sparrow which he had trained and taught to do a
number of little tricks.   It was his pet, and he loved it
dearly.   While he was putting the sparrow through its
movements, the master entered.   He was three parts drunk.
On looking at the bird on Edward's knee, he advanced, and
struck Edward such a blow that it laid him flat on the floor.
The bird had fluttered to the ground, and was trampled on.

When Edward was about to rise, he saw that Begg was
going to kick him.   Raising up his arm to ward off the
blow, Begg's foot came in contact with it, and, losing his
balance, he reeled, staggered against the wall, and fell backward.   He gathered himself together and got up.   If an·
gry before, he was furious now.   Edward, seeing that he was
again about to resume his brutality, called out that he would
shout for help, and that he wouldn't be struck again with-

out a cause. " Without a cause, you idle blackguard! sitting playing with some of your devils instead of doing my work!" " I had no work; it was done three hours ago, and I was waiting to go to my dinner." " It's not near dinner-time yet." " It's four o'clock!" " I didn't know it was so late: well, you may go."

Tom seized the opportunity of picking up his poor and innocent bird from the floor. He found it was still breathing. He put it tenderly in his bosom, and hastened homeward. His mother was not surprised at his lateness, which was very usual, in consequence of the irregularity of his master's hours. " But what's the matter wi ye?" she said; " your face is bleedin', and ye hae been greetin'." " Look," said he, taking the harmless and now lifeless bird from his breast and holding it up, " that would gar ony body greet;" and his tears fell on the mangled body of his little pet. " I wouldn't have cared so much for myself," he said, " if he had only spared my bird." Then he told his mother all that had happened, and he added that if Begg struck him again without a cause he would certainly run away. She strongly remonstrated against this; because, being bound apprentice for six years, he must serve out his time, come what would.

On returning to the shoe-maker's shop in the afternoon, Edward was met at the door by his master, who first shook him, and then searched him ; but, finding there was nothing about him, he was allowed to go to his seat. And thus three years passed. The boy learned something of his trade. The man went on from bad to worse. In his drunken fits he often abused and thrashed his apprentice. At last the climax came. One day Edward brought three young moles to the shop. The moles were safely ensconced in his bonnet. When Begg found the moles, he killed them at once, knocked down Edward with a last, seized him by the neck and breast, dragged him to the door, and with a horrible imprecation threw him into the street. Edward was a good deal hurt; but he went home, determined from that day he would never again serve under such a brute.

Begg called at his mother's next day, and ordered the boy to return to his work. Edward refused. Begg then invoked the terrors of the law. "He would compel Edward to fulfill his apprenticeship. He would prosecute his father, and his two sureties, and make them pay the penalty for breaking the boy's indenture." This threat gave Edward's mother a terrible fright, especially when her boy insisted that he would not go back. The family were left in fear and commotion for some time. But at last, as nothing further was heard of the threatened prosecution, they dismissed it from their minds.

What was Edward to do next? He was thoroughly sick of his trade, and wished to engage in some other occupation that would leave him freer to move about. He would be a sailor! He had a great longing to see foreign countries, and he thought that the best way of accomplishing this object was to become a sailor. On mentioning the matter to his parents, he was met with a determined and decided refusal. They tried to dissuade him by various methods. "Man," said his father to him, "do you know that sailors have only a thin plank between them and death? Na, na! If you're no gaun back to Begg, you must find some other master, and serve out your time. Bide ye at the shoemaker trade; and if ye can make siller at it, ye can then gang and see as mony countries as ye like."

Such was his father's advice, but it did not suit young Edward's views. He wanted to be a sailor. He went down to the harbor, and visited every ship there, in order to offer himself as a cabin-boy. He asked the captains to employ him, but in vain. At last he found one captain willing to take him, provided he had the consent of his father. But this he could not obtain, and therefore he gave up the idea for a time.

Then he thought of running away from home. He could

not get away by sea; he would now try what he could do by land. He had often heard his parents talking about the Kettle, and of his uncle who had gone in search of him to the gypsy camp. Edward thought he would like to see this uncle. He might perhaps be able to help him to get some other and better employment than that of shoe-making. His thoughts were very undefined about the matter. But he certainly would not go back to work again with Charlie Begg, the drunken shoe-maker.

GRANDHOLM MILLS.

4

CHAPTER IV.

RUNS AWAY FROM HOME.

At last Edward determined to run away from home, and from Charlie Begg's cruelty, and to visit his wonderful uncle at the Kettle. The village is situated nearly in the centre of the county of Fife, about a hundred miles from Aberdeen. Edward did not know a step of the road, but he would try and do his best to reach the far-off place.

The first thing that he wanted was money. All his earnings had gone into the family purse, and were used for family expenses. One day, when his mother had gone out, leaving Edward to rock the cradle, he went to look at the money-box, and found only a solitary sixpence in it. He wanted sevenpence in all—that is, a penny to get across Montrose Bridge, and sixpence to cross the Tay at Dundee. He took the sixpence from the box, and fancied that he might be able to raise another penny by selling his knife. He took two quartern loaves of bread, put some oatmeal into a parcel, and, bundling his things together, and giving the cradle a final and heavy rock, he left the house, and got away unseen.

He ran up Deeside until he came to a high bank, near where the Allanvale cemetery now stands. He went in among the bushes, took off his working duds, and put his Sunday clothes on; then, tying the former in a bundle, he dug a hole among the sand and shingle, and thrust them in, stamping upon them to press them down. He covered up the whole with grass, leaves, and shingle. Putting his stockings and shoes together, and swinging them over his shoul-

der, he set out barefoot for Kettle.   He thought he might
be able to accomplish the journey in about two days.

Away he sped. Time was precious. The way was long,
and his provender was small.   He had only sixpence.   He
soon tried to raise the other penny.   He met with two
herd-boys and a girl.   He said to the boys, " Will ye buy
a knife? I'll give it you cheap."   "No."   He passed
through Stonehaven, about sixteen miles from Aberdeen,
and up a steep brae on to Bervie.

Edward was not much influenced by the scenery through

RUINS OF DUNNOTTAR CASTLE.

which he passed.   He was anxious to push on without loss
of time.   But one thing he could not help seeing, and that
was the ruins of Dunnottar Castle.   They lay on his left
hand, on a lofty, rock-bound cliff, betwixt him and the sea.
They seemed to be of great extent, but he could not turn
aside to visit the ruins.   They reminded him, however, of
the numerous stories he had heard about them at home—
of the Covenanters who had been thrust into the Whigs'
Vault at Dunnottar, where many of them died; of others
who had tried to escape, and been battered to pieces against

the rocks, while attempting to descend to the sea-shore ; and of the Regalia of Scotland, which had been concealed there during the wars of the Commonwealth. Thoughts of these things helped him on his way; but the constant thought that recurred to him was, how he could sell his knife and raise the other penny.

As he was approaching Bervie, he met some lads on the road, and asked them, " Will you buy a knife ?" " Where did you steal it ?" said the lads. Off went Edward, followed by a volley of stones. He walked on for a long time, until he got hot and tired. By that time he had walked about twenty-five miles. Then he sat down by the side of a spring to eat his oatmeal, and swallow it down with water.

After resting himself for a time, he started up, and set off at full speed for Montrose. On his way he saw numerous things that he would have liked to take with him, and numerous woods that he would have gone into and searched with right good will; but the thought of the journey before him put all other things aside. Kettle was still a long way off; and, besides, he still wanted the additional pontage penny, in order to cross Montrose bridge. He went on and overtook a girl. He asked her if she would buy a knife. " No !"

He next overtook a man and woman with a lot of bairns. They looked rather suspicious. He tried to avoid them, and walked faster, but the man addressed him : " Stop a minute, laddie; ye're in an awfy hurry !" " Yes," said Edward, " I am in a hurry." " But have ye ony baccy ?" " No, I have no baccy." " Try if he has ony clink," said the woman. " Have ye ony brass ?" " No." " Take him, ye sheep," said the woman to her husband, " and squeeze him." Tom, on hearing this, immediately betook himself to his heels, and, being a good runner, soon left them far behind.

At length he reached Montrose. Seeing some boys gaz-

ing in at a shop-window, he went up to them and asked
if they would buy a knife. "No!" Edward thought he
would never get rid of his knife. He must raise a penny
to get over Montrose bridge, and yet he had nothing but
his knife to sell. He could not break into his sixpence.
Then he bethought him of offering the knife to the bridge-
keeper; and if he refused to buy it, he would try and run
the blockade. He went up to the bridge, looked at the entrance, and felt that he could not run across with success.

DISTANT VIEW OF MONTROSE.

He went away from the bridge, and determined again to
sell his knife. Walking up the river, he came to some men
working at a large building. He asked if any of them
wanted a knife. After a little bargaining, one of the men
said he would give a penny for it. Edward was delighted.
He rushed back to the bridge, gave the bridge-keeper the
penny, and crossed in double-quick time on his way to Arbroath.

It was now getting dark. He had walked all day, and

was now very tired. He was desirous of putting up somewhere for the night. But first he must have his supper. He sat down by a little rill, and, with the help of the water, eat some more of his meal and a piece of his quartern loaf. After he had refreshed himself, he thought he could walk a few more miles. He had now walked forty miles. The twilight being long in the North, and the month being July, he went on until he came to what he thought would be a good beild* for the night. This was a field in which there were a number of hay-cocks. He crossed the wall, went up to a hay-cock, pulled a lot of hay out, then ensconced himself inside, and soon fell fast asleep.

Toward morning he was wakened up by something scratching at his brow. On putting his hand up, he found it was a big black beetle, trying to work its way in between his skin and his bonnet. He wished he had had his box with him to preserve the beetle, but he could only throw it away. As he lay awake he heard the mice squeaking about him. It was still dark, though there was a glimmering of light in the east. Day was about to break. So he got out of his hole, shook the hay from him, crossed the wall, and resumed his journey.

Though he felt stiff at first, he soon recovered his walking powers, and reached Arbroath by daylight. Every body was in bed excepting one woman, whom he saw standing at the end of a close-mouth. He went up to her and asked which was the road to Dundee. When she began to speak, he saw that she was either drunk, or daft, or something worse. He went away, walked through several other streets, but found no one astir. The town was asleep. Then he sat down on a door-step and eat some of his loaf. He was just beginning to fall asleep, when some men who passed woke him up. They told him the road to Dundee, and he instantly set off in that direction.

---

* *Beild*, shelter.

As he went on his way, he came up to a man who was tramping along like himself. He belonged to Dundee, was a weaver by trade, and had been traveling through the country in search of work. The man asked Edward where he had come from, whither he was going, where he had slept, and what money he had to carry him to the end of his journey. On hearing that he had only enough to carry him across the ferry at Dundee, the weaver gave him a penny, saying that he would have given him more but that the penny was all the change he had.

Shortly after, they overtook two women, who turned out to be two sailors' wives. They had come from Aberdeen. The ship in which their husbands sailed had been chartered · to Dundee, and would not enter the port of Aberdeen for some time; hence the journey of the wives to Dundee. The weaver, on hearing where they came from, pointed to his little companion, and said, " Here's a laddie that comes frae the same place, and as his wallet's no very weel filled, perhaps ye might gie him a copper or two." One of the women looked hard at Edward, and said, " I've surely seen ye before, laddie. Did ye ever frequent the fish-market i' the Shipraw ?" " Yes." " And ye had sometimes tame rottens wi' ye ?" " Yes." " Ah ! I thocht sae. I used to help my mother wi' her fish, and was sure that I had seen ye i' the market."

Then they asked him where he was going ? " Till the Kettle," he said. " Till the what did ye say, laddie ?" " The Kettle !" How they laughed ! They had never heard of such a place before. But when their laughter had settled down, they gave the boy twopence ; and as they parted, one of the women said, " Tak' care o' yer feet, laddie, when ye step intil the Kettle."

On reaching Dundee, Edward crossed the Firth of Tay by the ferry-boat, and reached Newport, in the county of Fife. From thence he walked on to Cupar. He was very much bewildered by the manner in which the people told him the direction of the roads. They told him to go south or north, or east or west. He had no idea of these geographical descriptions. One man told him to "gang east a bit, then turn south, syne haud wast."

He went in the direction indicated, but he could proceed no farther. He sat down on a stone at the side of the road, and fell fast asleep. A gentleman passing in a gig, called out to him, "Boy! boy! get up! Don't lie sleeping in the sun there; it's very dangerous." On wakening up he was much dazed, and he did not at first remember where he was. When he finally got up, he asked the gentleman the road to Cupar. On being properly directed, he set off again.

The road along which he passed lay for some time through a wood. Among the various birds which he saw and heard, he observed a group of little round birds not much bigger than a hazel-nut, with very long tails. They squeaked like mice, and hung to and went round about the slenderest twigs. He had never seen such little birds before. He did not know their names, but he afterward found that they were the long-tailed titmouse. The little things were the young brood of the parent bird, which was, no doubt, hanging or flying somewhere near them.

Edward went into the wood to see them and follow them. As he passed along he was called to from behind, and a man came up and seized him by the collar. The man, doubtless a keeper, roughly asked him where he was going. "Naewhere." "What are you doing here, then?" "Naething." "What's that in your bundle?" "My stockings and shoes." "Let me see." His bundle was then overhauled, and nothing being found in it but his stockings and shoes, he was allowed to depart, with the injunction "never to return there again, unless he wished to be sent to jail."

After walking a few miles, he reached Cupar, and, passing through it, went on toward Kettle. Coming to a small burn, he washed and dried his feet, and put on his stockings and shoes, rubbing the dust from off his clothes preparatory to arriving at his destination. He reached Kettle in the evening, and soon found his uncle. But the reception he met with did not at all meet his expectations: it was any thing but cordial. After some inquiries, the uncle came to the conclusion that the boy had done some mischief, and had run away from his parents to hide himself in the Kettle. He could not believe that the boy had come so far merely to see him. The old man's relations were all dead, or had removed from the place. He was merely lodging with a friend. The house in which he lodged was full, and there was no spare bed for Edward. At length the woman of the house said that she would make up a bed for him in the place where she kept her fire-wood.

When the boy had got his supper, he was asked if he could read. "A little." The Bible was got, and he was asked to read two chapters. He was next asked if he could sing. "No." He was then told that he might go to bed. The bed was soft and sweet to the tired boy. As he went to sleep he heard the people of the house reading the Bible and singing a psalm.

He slept very sound, and would have slept much longer but for his being wakened up next morning for breakfast. The rain fell very heavily that day. The boy began to feel very weary and lonesome, and wished again to be at home. He had taken no thought, until now, of the results of his leaving so suddenly. He thought of what his father and mother might think of his disappearance. He wondered whether he might now get away to sea.

But how was he to get home? He had now only a poor half-penny left. However, he had still a gully; perhaps he might be able to sell that. After considering the matter, he resolved to set out for Aberdeen, rather than be a burden to the people at the Kettle. He told his uncle that he would leave next day. The uncle said nothing. The boy

was up early next morning, got his breakfast, and also a
big piece of bread, which he put into his bundle. His uncle
accompanied him a little way along the road, and at parting gave him eighteen-pence. Edward was overjoyed. He
would now be able to get home with money in his pocket.

As he approached Newport, he came up to three men
standing on the road. Two of them were gentlemen, and
the third seemed to be a gamekeeper. He was showing
them something which he had shot in the adjoining wood.
Edward went forward, and saw that it was a bird with blue
wings and a large variegated head. "What do you want?"
said the gamekeeper to Edward. "To have a sight of the
bird, if you please." "There, then!" said the gamekeeper, and he swung the bird in his face, nearly blinding him.
When the water was out of his eyes, and he could see, he
found that they had gone along the road. He followed
them, still expecting to see the bird, and to have it in his
hand; but the gamekeeper was relentless.

At length he reached the pier, just as the ferry-boat was
reaching the landing-place. He had another pleasant voyage across the ferry to Dundee. His object now was to
push on to the field where he had slept among the hay.
He arrived at the place, but there were no hay-cocks. The
field was cleared. He found some whins in the neighborhood, and went in among them, and slept there until the
sun was well up the sky. He started up, and went rejoi-
cing on his way. He passed through Arbroath, and was
speeding on briskly to Montrose, when he came up to a
man standing in the middle of the road, holding a bull by
a rope. He asked the boy if he would hold the bull for a
few minutes until he went to a house, which he pointed to,
near at hand. "I will give you something if you do," said
the man. "Yes, I will," said Edward, "if you'll not be
long." "No," said the man, "I'll not be long."

On getting hold of the rope, Edward found that he was
likely to have a difficult job. Scarcely had the man disap-

peared ere the bull began to snort, and kick, and jump. The brute threw up its head, and bounded backward with such force that the boy was nearly upset. Instead of holding the rope short, as he had been told, he let it go, though he still held by it at the far end. Away went the bull along the road, dragging the boy after him. So long as the full stretch of rope lay between them, Edward did not care so much; but when the animal rushed into a field of corn, he let go altogether, and resumed his journey.

He had not gone far before he found, on looking back, that he was hotly pursued by the animal. Observing his danger, Edward rushed into a clump of trees standing by the roadside, and, throwing down his bundle, he proceeded to climb one of them. He had only ascended a few yards when the brute came up. The bull snorted and smelled at his bundle, threw it into the ditch with his horns, bellowed at the boy up the tree, gave a tremendous roar, then dashed out of the wood, and set off at full speed down the nearest by-way. Edward was flurried and out of breath : he rested in the tree for a short time, then descended, and ran along the road for some miles, until he thought that he was out of reach of further danger.

This was the only adventure that he met .with on his homeward journey. He passed through Bervie without molestation. But instead of reaching Aberdeen that night, as he had intended, he rested near Stonehaven. He went through the town, and got into a corner of the toll-bar dike, where he sat or lay until day-break. He then got up, and commenced the last stage of his journey.

On reaching the neighborhood of Aberdeen, he went to the hole in the bank by Deeside where he had left his week-day clothes, and found them all right. But before going home he went down Deeside and turned up Scraphards to look at a laverock's nest, which was still there. Then he went past Ferryhill House, through Dee village, and struck the water-side by the path now known as Affleck Street, and got home at breakfast-time, after an absence of a week.

His mother was in. "Where hae ye been now, ye vagaboon?" "At my uncle's." "Where?" "At the Kettle." "And hae ye been a' the way to Fife, you vagrant?" Tom then told his story; his mother following it up with a long and serious lecture. She reproached him for the dishonesty which he had committed, in taking the sixpence out of the box when he went away. "Weel, mother," said he, "here's the sixpence for the one I took." He had saved the sixpence out of the eighteen-pence his uncle had given him when he left Kettle. "No," she replied, "the crime is the same, after all, and you are sure to be punished for it yet."

Then she urged him to go back to his trade, for he was far better at work than stravaigin* about the country like an evil-doer. Edward asked if his father would not consent now to his going to sea. She did not think he would; she thought that to go back to his work was the best thing of all. She herself would not hear a word more about his going to sea.

---

* *Stravaigin*, idle, wandering, or strolling.

CHAPTER V.

RESUMES WORK.

Instead of going directly back to his work, Edward went down to the harbor to ascertain whether any of the captains would accept of his services as a sailor. He went from ship to ship for three days. Some captains were willing to take him with an indenture, which would have to be signed by his father. Others were willing to take him without his father's consent; but in that case they required two sureties to sign the indenture. These were serious obstacles—too serious to be got over—and on the third afternoon he left the harbor with a sorrowful heart. There were several skippers of coasting vessels, and of lime and coal hulks, who would have taken him for four years; but these were not the kind of ships that he wished to sail in.

Being thus forced, though very reluctantly, to give up all thoughts of going to sea, he now considered whether it might not be possible to learn some other trade less hateful to him than that of a shoe-maker. But his parents would not hear of any change. They told him that his former master was willing to take him back, and to give him a shilling a week more during the ensuing year, and two shillings more during his last, or fifth, year. But Edward strongly objected to return to the master who had so cruelly used him.

Not wishing, however, to withstand his parents' advice any longer, he at last consented to go on with his trade. But, instead of serving out his time with his former master, he found a pupil-master in Shoe Lane, who was willing to employ him, and to improve him in his business. Edward agreed to give the master, for his trouble, a percentage of his earnings, besides his pupil-money, and a share of the fire and light.

Edward's work at this place was mostly of the lighter and smaller sort. His employer was of a much kindlier nature than the last, and he got on very well with him. Edward was also, in a measure, his own master. He could still look after his birdnesting. That was his strongest attraction out-of-doors. He did not rob the birds of their eggs. His principal pleasure was to search for their nests, and to visit them from time to time. When the eggs were hatched, and the little birds were grown and ready to fly, he would take one or two, if they were singing-birds, and rear them for himself, or for other bird-fanciers.

It was about this time that Edward began what he called his Wild Botanical Garden. His parents had left the Green, and removed to another quarter of the town. Behind the house, and behind the adjoining houses, was a piece of waste ground about ten feet wide. It was covered with stones, bits of bricks, and broken tiles. Edward removed these from the ground, and put them in a corner by themselves, covering them with earth. He dug over the ground, manured it, and turned it over again. Then he divided the space into compartments for the reception of plants and flowers. These were brought from the fields, the woods, and the banks adjoining the Dee and the Don. He watered and tended them daily; but, alas! they would not flourish as they had done on their native soil. He renewed them again and again. The rasp, the wild strawberry, the fox-glove—or dead men's bells, as it is there called—the hemlock, some of the ferns, and many of the grasses, grew pretty well; but the prettiest and most delicate field flowers died away one by one.

His mother, who delighted in flowers, advised him to turn the ground into an ordinary garden. Now, although

Edward loved garden flowers, he very much preferred those which he found in the woods or growing by the way-side, and which he had known from his infancy. Nevertheless, he took his mother's advice; and knowing many of the places near the town where the gardeners threw out their rubbish, he went and gathered from thence a number of roots, flowers, and plants, which he brought home and planted in his garden. The greater number of them grew very well, and in course of time he had a pleasant little garden. He never planted more than one specimen of each flower, so that his garden was various in its beauty. The neighbors, who had at first sneered at him as a fool, on seeing his pretty garden, began to whisper that the "loon" was surely a genius, and that it was a pity that his father had not made him a gardener, instead of a shoe-maker. Edward himself often wished that his parents had been of the same mind as the neighbors.

Near the back of the house in which Edward lived was an old tannery, with a number of disused tanning-pits, full of water. These, he thought, would be a nice place for storing his powets and puddocks.* He got a large pail, went to a place where these creatures abounded, and brought back a large cargo, heaving them into the pit. But they did not thrive. They nearly all died. He next put about thirty newts there, but he never saw them again, dead or alive. At last he gave up this undertaking.

About the same time he used to make a tour among the book-sellers of the town, to inspect the pictures which they had in their windows. These visits proved a source of great profit and pleasure to him. He learned something from the pictures, and especially from the pictures of animals. He found that there was more to be gained from a visit to the picture-shops than from a visit to the public-house. When he saw a book that he could buy, he bought it, though his means were still very small.

---

* Tadpoles and frogs.

It was in this way that he became acquainted with the *Penny Magazine*. He bought the first number,* and liked it so well that he continued to take it. He especially liked those parts of it which related to natural history. Among the other publications which he bought was one called the *Weekly Visitor*. It cost only a half-penny. It had good pictures, and gave excellent stories, which were usually of a religious tendency. He read this little publication over and over again. Nor did he ever lose the opportunity of going

CASTLEGATE ON FRIDAYS.

to the Castlegate on Fridays, to see the pictures and picture-books, which were usually exposed for sale on market-days.

The gun-makers' windows were also a source of attraction, for they often had stuffed birds exhibited in them. There was also a window devoted entirely to stuffed birds

---

* The *Penny Magazine* was published in 1832, when Edward would be about eighteen years old.

near the entrance to the police-office in Watch Lane, and another in Meal Market Lane, both of which attracted a large share of his attention. The sight of these things first gave Edward the idea of preserving animals. The first beast he stuffed was a mole, and he was very proud of it.

The shoe-making trade having become very flat, Edward left Shoe Lane, after having been there for about twenty months. He then went to work at a shop on the Lime Quay, near the harbor. He had steady work there for some time, at set wages. Though he had less time to attend to his natural-history pursuits, he still managed to attend to his garden and his "family," as his mother termed his maingie* of beasts. Trade again recovering, he went back to work at the old place. But this did not continue long. The men had to be paid off; and then Edward did not know what to do.

At that time, emigration to America was the rage. Trade was very depressed throughout the country. There were bread riots in many of the manufacturing towns. Numbers of laborers were without work, and without the means of living. Aberdeen shared in the general depression; and many persons emigrated to the United States, where there was a better demand for labor. Edward wished to emigrate too, but he had no money. He had only a few shillings to spare. But might he not contrive to emigrate as a stowaway?

This course is frequently adopted at the ports from which ships sail for America. A boy gets on board, conceals himself in the hold, and after the ship has got out of sight of land he makes his appearance on deck, usually half starved. Edward determined to try this method of escaping from Aberdeen, and more especially from his shoe-making trade. He knew one of the sailors on board the ship which he had selected; and although the sailor was strongly opposed to

---

* *Maingie*, many—"a great lot." From the German word *Menge*.

the project, Edward prevailed upon him to make an opening in the cargo, so as to admit him into a hole near the
bow of the ship. Here, amidst some boxes and coils of
rope, Edward deposited three dozen biscuits and two bottles of water.

He waited outside, hovering about the quay, until the
day of sailing arrived. But the ship did not sail until five
days after the advertised time. When the emigrants went
on board, Edward went with them. For three days and
nights he lay among the coils of rope, feeding upon his biscuits and water. On the forenoon of the fifth day he was
in his berth ; and just as the vessel was about to be loosed
from her moorings, Edward's friend came along the hold in
breathless haste, and inquired (for he was in the dark) " if
he was there." " Surely," replied Edward. " For the love
of God," said the sailor, " come out at once, and get on
shore. You have time yet. Simon Grant [the town's offi-
cer] and a lot of his sharks have come, and they are about
to rummage the ship from stem to stern for runaways. So
make haste and come out; you have no chance now."

Edward still delayed. He did not like to leave his hole.
But hearing an unusual commotion going on, amidst a great
deal of angry speaking, and fearing the worst, he at last
very unwillingly crept from his berth, went on deck, and
leaped on shore just as the ship was leaving the quay. He
afterward learned that the town's officer was in search of
another class of stowaways, who, it seems, had been carried
on board in boxes or barrels. Edward found that he could
not see the world after this method ; and he returned home,
defeated and mortified.

The Aberdeenshire militia having been called out in 1831,
Edward enlisted in the regiment. He was only about eighteen years old at the time. When the men assembled, they
were found to be a very bad lot—mere riffraff—the dregs
of the neighborhood. They were regardless both of law
and order. Seldom a night passed without the patrol bring-

ing in numbers to the guard-house for being drunk and disorderly. Even during parade many of the men were put under arrest for insubordination, chiefly because of the insulting language they used toward their officers.

The militia were only embodied for four weeks. During the first fortnight, the awkward squads were drilled without arms of any sort. It was only during the last fortnight that they were provided with muskets and bayonets. The company to which Edward belonged was drilling one day on the links. It was a bright, sunny afternoon. The company was marching along near the lower part of the links, when a large brown butterfly flitted past. Edward saw it in an instant. He had never seen the like of that butterfly before!* Without thinking for a moment of what he was doing, he flew after it—among the bents and sand hillocks, grasping after it with his hand.

> "A very hunter did he rush
>   Upon the prey : with leaps and springs
>   He followed on from brake to bush."

The butterfly eluded him; it flew away before him. Again he rushed after it, losing his bonnet in the hunt. He was nearing the spot where it had alighted. He would catch it now, when suddenly he was gripped by the neck! He looked round, and saw it was the corporal of his company, with four militia-men behind him.

Looking Edward sternly in the face, the corporal said, "What's up, Edward?" "Nothing." "The deuce!" "No, it wasn't that—it was a splendid butterfly." "A butterdevil!" "No! it was a butter-*fly!*" "Stuff!" said the corporal; "are you mad?" "No; I don't think I am." "You look like a madman; and I'll tell you what it is, you'll have to pay for this." "For what?" "For breaking away from the ranks during drill. I am sent to arrest you and take you to the guard-house: so come along!"

---

* It proved to be a *brown fritillery.*

And away they marched—two militia-men before, two behind, and Edward and the corporal in the centre. By this time a number of persons had collected, the younger people calling out to their companions to come and see the mad militia-man.

On crossing the links, the prisoner and his escort encountered one of the officers of the regiment, accompanied by a group of ladies. "Where are you going with that boy?" said the officer, addressing the corporal. "To the guardhouse!" "What! more insubordination?" "Yes." "This is most dreadful; what has he done?" "He broke the ranks during drill, and although Sergeant Forbes called him back, he ran away after what he calls a butterfly." There was a short silence, after which the ladies were observed tittering and laughing. "What did you say, corporal?" "He ran out of the ranks after a butterfly." "What! ran away from his exercise for the sake of an insect! Most extraordinary. Is he mad, corporal?" "Well, the sergeant thinks so; and that's the reason why I have got four men to help me to take him; but I don't think that he's mad." "He must be drunk, then?" "No, I don't think he's drunk either." "He must be either mad or drunk: did he ever behave so before?" "No, not to my knowledge."

The officer and the ladies retired, and talked together. After about five minutes had elapsed, the officer returned, and said to the corporal, "Are you quite sure that the prisoner behaved himself properly before his ridiculous chase after the butterfly?" "I know of nothing whatever against him, sir." "Call him forward." Edward advanced toward the officer. "Well, sir, what have you to say about breaking the ranks during drill, and running after the butterfly? Are you subject to fits of insanity?" Edward did not reply. "Can't you speak, sir?" cried the officer, angrily. "Yes, sir," replied Edward; "but you have asked questions that I can not answer." "What induced you to leave the ranks, and run after a harmless insect?" "I really do not know, unless it was from a desire to possess the butterfly."

Looks were exchanged between the officer and corporal, when the former, calling Edward aside, said to him, " I dare say, young man, you are not aware that the crime which you have committed against military discipline is a very severe one. This constant disobedience to orders must be put a stop to. But as this is your first offense, and as these ladies have interceded for you, I shall endeavor to obtain your acquittal, in the hope that you will closely attend to your duty in future." Addressing the corporal, he added, " Take him back to the ranks, and tell Sergeant Forbes that I will speak to him about this affair." This was Edward's first and last military offense, and he served out the rest of his time with attention and diligence.

Edward disliked returning to his trade. His aversion to it was greater even than before. He disliked the wages, which were low ; but he still more disliked the manner in which the masters treated their men. They sometimes kept them idle for days, and toward the end of the week they would force them to work night and day in order to finish their jobs. Edward liked his militia life much better ; and, in order to get rid of the shoe-making, and continue his soldier's life, he enlisted in the 60th Rifles. When his mother heard of the decision he had come to, she expressed herself as strongly opposed to it ; and, working upon the young man's feelings, which were none of the hardest, he at last promised not to go, and arrangements were made to get him off. Thus ended Edward's military career.

Before he left Aberdeen, he assisted his father as beadle (or pew-opener) in the North Church, King Street. He continued in this office for about two years. He liked the occupation very well, and was sorry to leave it, when he finally left Aberdeen to settle at Banff.

CHAPTER VI.

SETTLES AT BANFF.

Edward was about twenty years old when he left Aberdeen and went to Banff to work at his trade. He found a master there willing to employ him. Shoe-making had not improved. Men worked long hours for little wages. The hardest worker could only earn a scanty livelihood. Though paid by the piece, the journeymen worked in the employers' shops. Their hours were from six in the morning till nine at night. They had scarcely an interval of time that they could call their own.

Edward found the confinement more miserable than the wages. And yet he contrived to find some time to follow his bent. He went after birds, and insects, and butterflies. He annoyed his shopmates almost as much as he had annoyed his school-fellows. In summer-time, he collected a number of caterpillars, and put them in a box beside him in the workshop, for the purpose of watching them, and observing their development into the chrysalis state.

In spite of his care, some of the caterpillars got out and wandered about the floor, sometimes creeping up the men's legs. Some of the workmen did not care, but one of them was almost thrown into convulsions when he knew that a "worm was out." The other men played tricks upon him. When any of them wanted a scene, they merely said, "Geordie, there's a lad oot!" Then Geordie would jump to his feet, and would not sit down again until he was assured that all the worms were fast in their boxes.

Edward was forced to keep his caterpillars in the workshop, as the landlady with whom he lodged would not allow any of his "vermin," as she called them, to enter her house. He had one day taken in about a dozen caterpillars of the puss moth, and asked her for a box to hold them in. The landlady told him at once to get out of the house with his "beasts." She never could understand her lodger. She could not fathom "fat kin o' a chiel he was. A'body tried to keep awa frae vermin but himsel'!"

The idea again recurred to Edward of saving money enough to enable him to emigrate to the United States; but this was prevented by his falling in love! Man proposes: God disposes. He met with a Huntly lass at the farm of Boyndie. He liked her, loved her, courted her, married her, and brought her home to the house which he had provided for her in Banff.

Edward was only twenty-three years old when he brought his wife home. Many may think that he was very imprudent in marrying so early. But he knew nothing about "Malthus on Population." He merely followed his natural instincts. What kept him would keep another also. It turned out, however, that he had married wisely. His marriage settled him for life. He no longer thought of emigrating to America. Then, his marriage gave him a happy home. His wife was bright and cheerful, and was always ready to welcome him from his wanderings. They were very poor, it is true; but mutual affection makes up for much. Perhaps they occasionally felt the bitterness of poverty; for Edward's earnings did not yet amount to more than about nine shillings and sixpence a week.

Another result of Edward's marriage was, that it enabled him to carry on his self-education in natural history. While he lived in lodgings, he had few opportunities for collecting objects. It is true, he explored the country in the neighborhood of Banff. He wandered along the sands toward Whitehills, and explored the rocky cliffs between Macduff and Gamrie. He learned the geography of the inland country and of the sea-coast. He knew the habitats of various birds and animals. Some of the former he procured and stuffed; for by this time he had acquired the art of preserving birds as well as insects. But while he lived in lodgings he had no room for stuffed birds or preserved moths and butterflies. It was only when he got a home of his own that he began to make a collection of these objects.

It was a great disadvantage to him that his education should have been so much neglected in his boyhood. He had, it is true, been at three schools before he was six years old; but, as we have already seen, he was turned away from them all because of his love of "beasts." He had learned comparatively little from his school-masters, who knew little themselves, and perhaps taught less. He was able to read, though with difficulty. Arithmetic was to him a thing unknown. He had not even learned to write. It was scarcely possible that he could have learned much in his boyhood, for he went to work when he was only six years old.

An attempt was made to teach him writing while he was apprenticed to Begg, the drunken shoe-maker. He asked leave to attend a writing-school held in the evening. His master could not, or would not, understand the meaning of his request. "What!" said he, "learn to write! I suppose you will be asking to learn dancing next! What business have you with writing? Am I to be robbed of my time to enable you to learn to write?" Edward's parents supported the application, and at last the master gave his consent. But there was always some work to do, or something to finish and carry home to the master's customers, so that Edward rarely attended the writing-school; and at the end of the quarter he knew very little more of penmanship than he did at the beginning.

Edward had to begin at the beginning with every thing. As we have already said, he knew next to nothing of books. He did not possess a single work on natural history. He did not know the names of the birds and animals that he caught. For many years after he had begun his researches his knowledge of natural objects was obtained. by chance. He knew little of the nature and habits of the creatures that he went to seek; he scarcely knew where or how to find them. Yet his very absence of knowledge proved a source of inexhaustible pleasure to him. All that he learned of the form, habits, and characteristics of birds and animals was obtained by his own personal observation. His knowledge had been gathered and accumulated by himself. It was his own.

It was a misfortune to Edward that, after he had attained manhood, he was so shy and friendless. He was as solitary as Wordsworth's Wanderer. He had no friend of any sort to direct him in his studies; none even to lend him books, from which he might have obtained some assistance. He associated very little with his fellow-workers. Shoe-makers were a very drunken lot. Edward, on the contrary, was sober and thoughtful. His fellow-shoe-makers could not understand him. They thought him an odd, wandering, unsettled creature. Why should he not, as they did, enjoy himself at the public-house? Instead of doing this, Edward plodded homeward so soon as his day's work was over.

There was, however, one advantage which Edward possessed, and it compensated him for many difficulties. He was an intense lover of nature. Every thing that lived and breathed had charms for him. He loved the fields, the woods, the moors. The living presence of the earth was always about him, and he eagerly drank in its spirit. The bubbling brooks, the whispering trees, the aspects of the clouds, the driving wind, were all sources of delight. He felt himself free amidst the liberty of nature.

The ocean in its devious humors—sometimes peacefully slumbering, or laving the sands with murmuring kisses at his feet; then, full of life and motion, carrying in and out the fishermen's boats along the shores of the Firth ; or, roaring with seeming agony, dashing itself in spray against the rock-bound coast—these sights and scenes were always a source of wonderment. As his wanderings were almost invariably conducted at night, he had abundant opportunities of seeing, not only the ocean, but the heavens, in their various aspects. What were these stars so far off in the sky? Were they worlds? Were they but the outposts of the earth, from which other worlds were to be seen, far beyond the ken of the most powerful telescope?

To use Edward's own words, " I can never succeed in describing my unbounded admiration of the works of the Almighty; not only the wonderful works which we ourselves see upon earth, but those wondrous and countless millions of orbs which roll, both near and far, in the endless immensity of space—the home of eternity.

" Every living thing that moves or lives, every thing that grows, every thing created or formed by the hand or the will of the Omnipotent, has such a fascinating charm for me, and sends such a thrill of pleasure through my whole frame, that to describe my feelings is utterly impossible."

Another advantage which Edward possessed, besides his intense love of nature, was his invincible determination. Whatever object in natural history he desired to possess, if it were possible to obtain it, he never rested until he had succeeded. He sometimes lost for a time the object of which he was in search, because he wished to observe its traits and habits. For this purpose, he would observe long and carefully before obtaining possession of it. By this means he was enabled to secure an amount of information in natural history such as no book, except the book of nature, could have supplied him with.

Edward proceeded to make a collection of natural objects early in the spring of 1838. He was then twenty-four years old, and had been married about a year. He had, a short time before, bought an old gun for four and sixpence ; but

it was so rickety that he had to tie the barrel to the stock
with a piece of thick twine. He carried his powder in a
horn, and measured out his charges with the bowl of a
tobacco - pipe. His shot was contained in a brown - paper
bag. A few insect bottles of middling size, some boxes for
containing moths and butterflies, and a botanical book for
putting his plants in, constituted his equipment.

As he did not cease shoe - making until nine at night,
nearly all his researches were made after that hour. He
had to be back to his work in the morning at six. His
wages were so small that he could not venture to abridge
his working hours. It was indispensably necessary for him
to husband carefully both his time and his money, so as to
make the most of the one and the best of the other. And,
in order the better to accomplish this, he resolved never to
spend a moment idly, nor a penny uselessly.

On returning home from his work at night, his usual
course was to equip himself with his insect boxes and bottles, his botanical book, and his gun ; and to set out with
his supper in his hand or stowed away in his pocket. The
nearest spring furnished him with sufficient drink. So long
as it was light, he scoured the country, looking for moths,
or beetles, or plants, or birds, or any living thing that came
in his way.

When it became so dark that he could no longer observe, he dropped down by the side of a bank, or a bush,
or a tree, whichever came handiest, and there he dozed or
slept until the light returned. Then he got up, and again
began his observations, which he continued until the time
arrived when he had to return to his daily labor. It was no
unusual circumstance for him—when he had wandered too
far, and come upon some more than usually attractive spot
—to strip himself of his gear, gun and all, which he would
hide in some hole ; and, thus lightened of every thing except his specimens, take to his heels, and run at the top of
his speed, in order to be at his work at the proper time.

On Saturdays he could only make his observations late at night. He must be home by twelve o'clock. Sabbath-breaking is an intolerable sin in Scotland, and Edward was never a Sabbath-breaker. It was a good thing for his mental and physical health that there was a seventh day during which he could not and would not work. But for his seventh day's rest, he would have worked night and day. On Sundays he went to church with his wife and family. After evening service he took off his best clothes, and donned his working dress. Then he took a few hours' sleep in his chair or lying across his bed, before setting out. He thus contrived to secure a few hours' observation on Monday mornings before six o'clock.

His neighbors used to say of him, "It is a stormy night that keeps that man Edward in the house." In fact, his neighbors were completely bewildered about his doings. They gave vent to all sorts of surmises about his wanderings by night. Exaggerated rumors spread about among the towns-people. He went with a gun! Surely he couldn't be a poacher or a burglar? That was impossible. It was well known that he lived soberly and honestly, denying himself many things, and never repining at his lot, though living a life of hardship. But what could he mean by wandering about at night among wild, lonely, and ghost-haunted places? They wouldn't have slept in Boyndie church-yard for worlds! And yet that was one of Edward's favorite spots!

He went out in fine starlit nights, in moonlight nights, and in cold and drizzling nights. Weather never daunted him. When it rained, he would look out for a hole in a bank, and thrust himself into it, feet foremost. He kept his head and his gun out, watching and waiting for any casualties that might happen. He knew of two such holes, both in sand-banks and both in woods, which he occasionally frequented. They were foxes' or badgers' dens. If any of these gentry were inside when he took up his position, they did not venture to disturb him. If they were out, they did the same, except on one occasion, when a badger endeavored to dislodge him, showing his teeth. He was obliged to shoot it. He could often have shot deers and hares, which came close up to where he was; but they were forbidden animals, and he resisted the temptation. He shot owls and polecats from his ambuscades. Numbers of moths came dancing about him, and many of these he secured and boxed, sending them to their long sleep with a little drop of chloroform. When it rained heavily, he drew in his head and his gun, and slept until the first streaks of light appeared on the horizon; and then he came out of his hole and proceeded with his operations.

At other times he would take up his quarters for the night in some disused buildings—in a barn, a ruined castle, or a church-yard. He usually obtained better shelter in such places than if he were seated by the side of a stone, a bush, or a wall. His principal objection to them was, that he had a greater number of visitors there than elsewhere—such as polecats, weasels, bats, rats, and mice, not to speak of hosts of night-wandering insects, mollusks, beetles, slaters, centipedes, and snails. Think of having a polecat or a weasel sniff-sniffing at your face while asleep! or two or three big rats tug-tugging at your pockets, and attempting to steal away your larder! These visitors, however, did not always prove an annoyance. On the contrary, they sometimes proved a windfall; for, when they came within reach, they were suddenly seized, examined, and, if found necessary, killed, stuffed, and added to the collection.

The coldest places in which Edward slept at night were among the rocks by the sea-side, on the shingle, or on the sea-braes along the coast. When exposed to the east wind, these sleeping-places were perishingly cold. When he went inland, he could obtain better shelter. In summer-time, especially, he would lie down on the grass and sleep soundly, with the lock of his gun for his pillow and the canopy of

heaven for his blanket. His ear was always open for the
sounds of nature, and when the lark was caroling his early
hymn of praise, long before the sun had risen, Edward would
rise and watch for day-break—

> "When from the naked top   •
> Of some bold headland he beheld the sun
> Rise up, and bathe the world in light."

In the course of his wanderings inland he was frequently
overtaken by storms in the hills. He carried no cloak, nor
plaid, nor umbrella, so that he often got completely soaked
before he could find shelter.

One of the most remarkable nights Edward ever spent
was under a grave-stone in the church-yard of Boyndie.
The church of this parish was at one time situated in the
midst of the church-yard; but as it was found inconven-
ient, and at a considerable distance from the bulk of the
parishioners, it was removed inland, leaving but a gable-end
of the old church standing. The church-yard, however, is
still used as a burying-place. It stands on a high piece of
ground overlooking the sea, about two miles west of Banff.
In clear days, the bold, rugged, precipitous coast is to be
seen, extending eastward as far as Crovie Head. But the
night of which we speak was very dark; the sky was overhung with rolling clouds; the sea was moaning along the
shore. Edward expected a wild night, as he had seen the
storm brewing before he left home. Nevertheless, he went
out as usual.

He had always regarded a thunder-storm as one of the
grandest sights. He rejoiced in the warring of the elements by day, and also by night when the inhabitants of
the earth were wrapped in sleep. As he approached old
Boyndie, the storm burst. The clouds were ripped open,
and the zigzag lightning threw a sudden flood of light over
land and sea. Torrents of rain followed, in the midst of
which Edward ran into the church-yard, and took shel-

BOYNDIE CHURCH-YARD.

ter under a flat tombstone supported by four low pillars. There was just room enough for him to lie down at full length. The storm was not yet at its height. The thunder pealed and crashed and rolled along the heavens, as if the universe were about to be torn asunder and the mighty fragments hurled out into infinity. It became louder and louder—nearer and nearer. The lightning flashed in red and yellowish. fiery streams; each flash leaving behind it a suffocating, sulphurous odor. Then followed torrents of rain and hail and lumps of ice.

After the thunder-storm the wind began—lightly at first, but, increasing rapidly, it soon blew a hurricane. The sea rose, and lashed its waves furiously along the coast. Although Edward had entertained no fear of the thunder, he now began to fear lest the tremendous fury of the wind would blow down the rickety gable-end of the old church of Boyndie; in which case it would have fallen upon the tombstone, under which he lay.

The hurricane lasted for about an hour, after which the wind fell. Midnight was long past, and morning was approaching. Before leaving the tombstone, Edward endeavored to obtain a few minutes' sleep. He had just begun to doze, when he was awakened by a weird and unearthly moaning. He listened. The moaning became a stifled scream. The noise grew louder and louder, until it rose into the highest pitch of howling. What could it be? He was in the home of the dead! Was it a ghost? Never! His mind revolted from the wretched superstition. He looked out to see what it could be, when something light in color dashed past like a flash, closely followed by another and a darker object. After the screaming had ceased, Edward again composed himself to sleep, when he was wakened up by a sudden rush over his legs. He looked up. The mystery was solved! Two cats—a light and a dark one—had been merely caterwauling in the grave - yard, and making night hideous, according to their usual custom.

By this time the day was beginning to break, and Edward prepared to leave his resting-place and resume his labors. He felt very stiff as he crept from under the tombstone, where he had been lying in a cramped position. He was both cold and wet; but his stiffness soon wore off; and after some smart running in the open air his joints became a little more flexible, and, shortly after, he returned home.

Edward had frequent mishaps when he went out on these nocturnal expeditions. One summer evening he went out moth-hunting. The weather was mild and fair, and it gave promise of an abundant "take" of moths. He had with him his collecting-box under his arm, and a phial of chloroform in his pocket. His beat lay in a woody dale, close by the river's side. He paced the narrow footpath backward and forward, snapping at his prey as he walked along the path.

The sun went down. The mellow thrush, which had been pouring forth its requiem to the parting day, was now silent. The lark flew to its mossy bed, the swallow to its nest. The wood-pigeon had uttered its last coo before settling down for the night. The hum of the bee was no longer heard. The grasshopper had sounded its last chirp; and all seemed to have sunk to sleep. Yet nature is never at rest. The owl began to utter its doleful and melancholy wail; the night-jar (*Caprimulgus Europæus*) was still out with its spinning-wheel-like *birr, birr;* and the lightsome roe, the pride of the lowland woods, was emitting his favorite night bark.

The moths continued to appear long after the butterflies had gone to rest. They crowded out from their sylvan homes into the moth - catcher's beat. These he continued to secure. A little drop of the drowsy liquid, and the insect dropped into his box, as perfect as if still in nature's hands. Thus he managed to secure a number of first-rate specimens — among others, the oak egger moth, the uni-

corn hawk - moth, the cream - spot tiger - moth, the angle-
shades, the beautiful China-mark, the green silver-line, and
various other specimens. He hoped to secure more; but
in the midst of his operations he was interrupted by the
approach of an extraordinary-looking creature.

He was stepping slowly and watchfully along his beat,
crooning to himself, "There's nae luck aboot the house,"
when, looking along the narrow footpath, he observed something very large, and tremendously long, coming toward
him. He suddenly stopped his crooning, and came to a
standstill. What could the hideous - looking monster be?
He could not see it clearly, for it had become dark, and the
moon was not yet up. Yet there it was, drawing slowly
toward him. He was totally unarmed. He had neither
his gun nor even his gully knife with him. Fear whisper-
ed, "Fly! fly for your life!" but courage shouted, "No!
no! stand like a man and a true naturalist, and see the
worst and the best of it!" So he stood his ground.

At length the animal gradually approached him. He
now observed that it consisted of three large and full-
grown badgers, each a short distance behind the other, the
foremost being only about sixteen yards from where he
stood. He had for some time been on the lookout for a
badger to add to his collection, and now he hoped to be
able to secure one. He rushed forward; the badgers suddenly turned and made for the river along-side of which his
beat had extended. He wrapped a handkerchief round his
hand to prevent the animals biting him, threw off his hat,
and bolted after the badgers. He was gaining on them
rapidly, and as he came up with the last, which was bolting
down into the river, he gave it a tremendous kick; but, in
doing so, he fell suddenly flat on his back in the midst of
the path. When he came to himself, he began to feel if
his legs were broken, or if his head were still on. Yes, all
was right; but, on searching, he found a tremendous bump
upon the back of his head as big as a turkey's egg.

Such was the end of his night's moth-hunting. But his head was so full of badgers, and he was so confused with his fall, that when he reached home and went to sleep, he got up shortly afterward, loaded his gun for the purpose of shooting a badger, and as he was in the act of putting a cap on the nipple, he suddenly awoke!

CHAPTER VII.

NIGHT WANDERERS.

ALTHOUGH it is comparatively easy to observe the habits of animals by day, it is much more difficult to do so at night. Edward, as we have already said, was compelled by circumstances to work at shoe-making by day, and to work at natural history by night.

"It would have been much easier work for me," said Edward, in answer to an inquiry made as to his nocturnal observations, "had it been my good fortune to possess but a single trustworthy book on the subject, or even a single friend who could have told me any thing about such matters. But I had neither book nor friend. I was in a far worse predicament than the young and intending communicants at the parish church of Boyndie were, who, when asked a question by the good and pious minister, and returning no answer, were told that they were shockingly in the dark —all in the dark together. Now, they had a light beside them, for they had their teacher in their midst; but I had no light whatever, and no instructor. It was doubly dark with me. It was decidedly the very blackness of darkness in my case. The only spark or glimmer I had was from within. It proceeded from the never-ceasing craving I had for more knowledge of the works of nature. This was the only faintest twinkle I 'had to lighten up my path, even in the darkest night. And that little twinkle, together with my own never-flagging perseverance, like a good and earnest pilot, steered me steadily and unflinchingly onward."

Although Edward was frequently out in winter-time, especially in moonlight, his principal night-work occurred between spring and autumn. The stillest, and quietest, and usually the darkest, part of the night — unless when the moon was up—was from about an hour after sunset until about an hour before sunrise. Yet, during that sombre time, when not asleep, he seldom failed to hear the sounds or voices, near or at a distance, of midnight wanderers prowling about. In the course of a few years he learned to know all the beasts and birds of the district frequented by him. He knew the former by their noises and gruntings, and the latter by the sound of their wings when flying. When a feathered wanderer flew by, he could tell its call-note at once, and often the family as well as the species to which it belonged. But although he contrived to make himself acquainted with the objects of many of these midnight cries and noises, others cost him a great deal of time and labor, as well as some dexterous manœuvring.

The sounds of the midnight roamers, as well as the appearance of the birds and animals, were invariably more numerous during the earlier part of the year. In the spring and early part of summer they were always the most lively. Toward the end of summer the sounds became fewer and less animated; and the animals themselves did not appear so frequently. Woods were the principal lodging-places of birds and animals. There were fewer in the fields; still fewer among the rocks or shingle by the sea-shore, except in winter; and in the hills, the fewest of all.

When he made his first night expeditions to the inland country, the hoarse-like *bark* of the roe-deer, and the timid-like *bleak-bleak* of the hare puzzled him very much. He attributed these noises to other animals, before he was able, by careful observation, to attribute them to their true sources. Although the deer wanders about at all hours of the night, occasionally grunting or barking, it does not usually feed at that time. The hare, on the other hand, feeds even during the darkest nights, and in spring and the early part of summer it utters its low cry of *bleak-bleak*. This cry is very different from that which it utters when snared or half shot. Its cry for help is then most soul-pitying: it is like the tremulous voice of an infant, even to the quivering of its little innocent lips.

While Edward found that the deer and the hare were among the animals that wandered about a good deal in the dark, he did not find that the rabbit was a night-roamer, although he occasionally saw it moving about by moonlight. He often watched the rabbits going into their burrows at sunset; and he also observed them emerging from them a little before sunrise. But there was one thing about the rabbit that perplexed and puzzled him. It did not emit any cry, such as the hare does; but he often heard the rabbit *tap-tap* in a particular manner. How was this noise caused? He endeavored to ascertain the cause by close observation.

Early one morning when he was lying under a whin-bush, about twenty yards from the foot of a sandy knoll, where there were plenty of rabbits' holes, he was startled by hearing a loud tap-tapping almost close to where he lay. The streaks of day were just beginning to appear. Parting the bush gently aside and looking through it, he observed a rabbit thud-thudding its hind feet upon the ground close to the mouth of another rabbit's hole.

Edward continued to watch the rabbit. After he had finished his tapping at the first hole, he went along the hillock and began tap-tapping at another. He went on again. He would smell the ground about the hole first, and would sometimes pass without tapping. At last he got to a hole where his progress was stopped. After he had given only two or three thuds, out rushed a full-grown rabbit, and flew at the disturber of the peace. He rushed at him with such fury that they both rolled headlong down hill, until they reached the bottom.

There they had a rare set-to — a regular rabbit-fight. Rabbits are fools at fighting. Their object seems to be to leap over each other, and to kick the back of their enemy's

head as they fly over; each trying to jump the highest and
to kick the hardest. It is a matter of jumping and kick-
ing. Yet rabbits have an immense power in their hinder
feet. They often knock each other down by this method
of fighting. They also occasionally fight like rams—knocking their heads hard together. Then they reel and tumble,
until they recover, and are at it again, until one or the other
succumbs.

Edward is of opinion that the method pursued by the
male rabbits, of tapping in front of their neighbors' holes,
is to attract the attention of the females. When the male
comes out instead of the female, a fight occurs, such as that
above described. At other times, the rabbit that taps is
joined by other rabbits from the holes, and a friendly con-
ference takes place. But, besides this loud beating with
their heels, the rabbits possess another method of communicating with their fellows. They produce a sound like
tap-pat! which is the sign of danger. Edward often saw
numbers of them frisking and gamboling merrily about the
mouths of their burrows; but when the sound of *tap-pat*
was heard, the whole of the rabbits, young and old, rushed
immediately to their holes.

Among the true night-roamers are the fox, the otter, the
badger, the polecat, the stoat, the weasel, the hedgehog, the
rat, and almost the whole family of mice. These are, for
the most part, nocturnal in their habits. No matter how
dark or tempestuous the night, they are constantly prowling about. Even at the sea-shore, the otter, the weasel, and
the mice often paid Edward a visit. When on the hills or
moors, he often saw the weasel, and sometimes the fox;
but the fields and the sides of woods were the places where
they were most frequently met with. All these animals,
like the deer and hare, have their peculiar and individual
calls, which they utter at night.

Thus the fox may be known by his *bark*, which resembles that of a poodle-dog, with a little of the yelp in it;

and he repeats this at intervals varying from about six to eighteen minutes between each. When suddenly surprised, the fox gives vent to a sharp, harsh-like growl, and shows and snaps his teeth. "I once," says Edward, "put my walking-staff into the mouth of a fox just roused from his lair—for foxes do not always live in holes—to see how the fellow would act. He worried the stick, and took it away with him. I have, on three different occasions, come upon two foxes occupying the same lair at the same time—twice on the cliffs by the sea, and once among the bushes in an old and disused quarry. In one instance, I came upon them in midwinter, and in the other two cases during summer."

The badger utters a kind of snarling *grunt*. This is done in quick succession. Then he is silent for a short time, and again he begins in the same strain. The otter, and most of the other night-roamers, have a sort of *squeak*, which they utter occasionally. But though there is a difference between them, which Edward could distinguish, it is very difficult to describe it in words. Their screams, however, differ widely from their ordinary call. The scream is the result of alarm or pain, perhaps of a sudden wound; the call is their nightly greeting when they hold friendly converse with each other; but the difference in the screams can only be learned by the ear, and can scarcely be described by words.

The field-mice—the "wee timorous beasties" of Burns—besides their squeaking, lilt a low and not unmusical ditty for hours together. Edward often heard them about him, sometimes quite near him, sometimes beneath his head. He occasionally tried to clutch them, but on opening his hand he found it filled with grass, moss, or leaves. The result of his observations was, that several, if not the whole, of the mouse race are possessed, more or less, of the gift of singing.

The otter, polecat, stoat, and weasel have a knack of *blowing* or *hizzing* when suddenly come upon, or when placed at bay. The three latter stand up on their hind feet in a menacing attitude. Sometimes they suddenly dart forward and give battle when they see no other way of escape. This is especially the case with the females when they have their young about them. Edward once saw a weasel, after hiding her family among a cairn of stones, ascend to the top, and, muttering something all the while, by her threatening attitude and fierce showing of her teeth dared any one to approach her under penalty of immediate attack.

A bite of a weasel, or polecat, or badger, or otter is any thing but agreeable. The bites of the weasel and the polecat are the worst. There seems to be some poison in their bites, for the part bitten soon becomes inflamed, and the bite is long in healing. The whole of this group of animals are of the same bold, fearless, and impetuous disposition. They are also remarkably impertinent and aggressive, not hesitating to attack man himself, especially when they see him showing the slightest symptoms of cowardice. Take the following illustrations, communicated by Edward himself :

" Returning one morning from an excursion in the Buchan district, when between Fraserburgh and Pennan, I felt so completely exhausted by fatigue, want of sleep, and want of food (for my haversack had become exhausted), that I went into a field near the road, lay down by a dike-side, and fell fast asleep. I had not slept long, however, when I was awakened by something cold pressing in betwixt my forehead and the edge of my hat. There were some small birds in my hat which I had shot, and they were wrapped in wadding. On putting up my hand to ascertain the meaning, I got hold of a weasel, which had been trying to force its way in to the birds. I threw him away to some distance among the grass, and went to sleep again. The fellow came back in a few minutes, and began the same trick. I gripped him hard this time, and tossed him across the dike* into another field, but not before he had bitten my hands. I began to close my eyes once more, when again the prowler approached. At last, despairing of peace, I left the spot where I had been seated, and went into a small plantation about a hundred yards off, and now I thought I would surely get a nap in comfort. But the weasel would not be refused. He had followed in my track. I had scarcely closed my eyes before he was at me again. He was trying to get into my hat. I awoke and shoved him off. Again he tried it, and again he escaped. By this time I was thoroughly awake. I was a good deal nettled at the pertinacity of the brute, and yet could not help admiring his perseverance. But thinking it was now high time to put an end to the game, instead of falling asleep, I kept watch. Back he came, nothing daunted by his previous repulses. I suffered him to go on with his operations until I found my hat about to roll off. I then throttled, and eventually strangled, the audacious little creature, though my hand was again bitten severely. After getting a few winks of sleep, I was again able to resume my journey."

Edward was once attacked by two pertinacious rats in a similar manner. He was making an excursion between Banff and Aberdeen, and had got to a place near Slains Castle, beyond Peterhead. It had been raining all day. It was now growing dark, and he looked about for a place to sleep in. He observed a dilapidated building, which looked like the ruins of a threshing-mill, as it stood near a farm-steading. He entered the place, and found only a small part of the roof still standing. It was, however, sufficient to protect him from the rain, which was still falling. There was a pile of stones and rubbish immediately under the roof, and having gathered together as much dry grass

---

* *Dike* or *dyke*, in the north, means a stone or earth wall, not a ditch, as it means in the south.

as he could find, and spread it on the stones, he lay down in a reclining position. In this position he soon fell fast asleep.

How long he had slept he did not know, but he was awakened by a quivering sort of motion about his head. He at first thought it was caused by the sinking of the stones, and that his head was going down with them. He sat bolt-upright, clutched his gun and wallet to save them, and felt the stones with his hands to ascertain whether they had sunk or not. They were quite undisturbed. He again lay down, thinking that he had only been dreaming. But before he could fall asleep, the movement under his head again commenced. Thinking it might be a weasel, and not wishing for his company, he moved to one side, adjusted his bedding, moved the grass, and prepared to lie down again.

His sleep this time was of very short duration, for the tug-tugging again commenced. He now raised his hand, at the same time that he opened his eyes, and seized hold, not of a weasel, but of a rat. He threw him away, thinking that that would be enough. Being assured that there were no weasels there—for rats and weasels never associate—he now thought he should be able to get a little sleep. He had no idea that the rat would return.

But in this he was disappointed. He was just beginning to sleep, when he heard the rat again. He looked up, and found that two rats were approaching him. So long as there were only two, he knew he could manage them. He allowed them to climb up the stones and smell all about him. One of them mounted his face and sat upon it. They next proceeded to his wallet, and endeavored to pull it from under his head. They had almost succeeded in doing so, when he laid hold of his wallet and drove them off.

Being now in a sort of fossilized state, from wet and cold, Edward did not attempt to sleep again, but rose up from his bed of stones, secured all his things, and marched away to recover his animal heat and resume his explorations.

Speaking of the otter as a night-roamer, Edward observes: "I am not aware who first burlesqued the otter as an amphibious animal. He must have known very little of the animal's true habits, and nothing at all of its anatomical structure. The error thus promulgated seems to have taken deep root. That the otter is aquatic in habits, is well known. He goes into the water to fish, but he is forced to come up again to breathe. In fact, a very small portion of the otter's life is spent in the water. There are many birds that are far more aquatic than the otter. There are some, indeed, that never leave the water night nor day; yet no one calls them amphibious birds. I have seen the otter, in his free, unfettered, and unmolested condition, both in the sea and the river, go into the water, and disappear many a time, and I have often watched for his re-appearance. The longest time that he remained under water was from three to four minutes; the usual time was from two to three minutes. I have also watched numbers of water birds, who have also to descend for their food, and I must say that the greater number of them exceed the otter in the time that they remain below water. Some of them remain double the time. I once saw a great northern diver remain below water more than nine minutes. A porpoise that I once watched remained down about ten minutes; and so on with other sea-birds and animals."

Many of these night-roaming animals—such as the weasel, rat, badger, otter, and polecat—are seen during the day; but these may only be regarded as stray individuals, their principal feeding-time being at night. The rat may forage in the day-time, and the weasel is sometimes to be seen hunting when the sun is high. But there was one circumstance in connection with the manners and habits of these creatures which surprised Edward not a little, which was, that although he very seldom saw any of them in the evening, or until after it was dark, he never missed seeing them in the morning, and sometimes after it had become daylight. The same remark is, in a measure, applicable to many of the night insects, to land crustaceans, beetles, many of the larger moths, sand-hoppers, and slaters.

One of the most severe encounters that Edward ever had with a nocturnal roamer was with a polecat or fumart* in the ruined castle of the Boyne. The polecat is of the same family as the weasel, but it is longer, bigger, and stronger. It is called fumart because of the fetid odor which it emits when irritated or attacked. It is an extremely destructive brute, especially in the poultry-yard, where it kills far more than it eats. Its principal luxury seems to be to drink the blood and suck the brains of the animals it kills. It destroys every thing that the gamekeeper wishes to preserve. Hence the destructive war that is so constantly waged against the polecat.

The ruined castle of the Boyne, about five miles west of Banff, was one of Edward's favorite night haunts. The ruins occupy the level summit of a precipitous bank forming the eastern side of a ravine, through which the little river Boyne flows. One of the vaults, level with the ground, is used as a sheltering place for cattle. Here Edward often took refuge during rain, or while the night was too dark to observe. The cattle soon got used to him. When the weather was dry, and the animals fed or slept outside, Edward had the vault to himself. On such occasions he was visited by rats, rabbits, owls, weasels, polecats, and other animals.

One night, as he was lying upon a stone, dozing or sleeping, he was awakened by something pat-patting against his legs. He thought it must be a rabbit or a rat, as he knew that they were about the place. He only moved his legs a little, so as to drive the creature away. But the animal

---

* *Fumart* from *ful merde*, old French.

THE CASTLE OF THE BOYNE.

would not go. Then he raised himself up, and away it
went; but the night was so dark that he did not see what
the animal was. Down he went again to try and get a
sleep; but before a few minutes had elapsed, he felt the
same pat-patting: on this occasion it was higher up his
body. He now swept his hand across his breast and thrust
the intruder off. The animal shrieked as it fell to the
ground. Edward knew the shriek at once. It was a polecat.

He shifted his position a little, so as to be opposite the
door-way, where he could see his antagonist betwixt him
and the sky. He also turned upon his side in order to have
more freedom to act. He had in one of his breast-pockets
a water-hen which he had shot that evening; and he had
no doubt that this was the bait which attracted the polecat. He buttoned up his coat to his chin, so as to prevent
the bird from being carried away by force. He was now
ready for whatever might happen. Edward must tell the
rest of the story in his own words:

" Well, just as I hoped and expected, in about twenty
minutes I observed the fellow entering the vault, looking
straight in my direction. He was very cautious at first.
He halted, and looked behind him. He turned a little, and
looked out. I could easily have shot him now, but that
would have spoiled the sport; besides, I never wasted my
powder and shot upon any thing that I could take with
my hands. Having stood for a few seconds, he slowly advanced, keeping his nose on the ground. On he came. He
put his fore-feet on my legs, and stared me full in the face
for about a minute. I wondered what he would do next—
whether he would come nearer or go away. When satisfied
with his look at my face, he dropped his feet and ran out
of the vault. I was a good deal disappointed, and I feared
that my look had frightened him. By no means. I was
soon re-assured by hearing the well-known and ominous
squeak-squeak of the tribe. It occurred to me that I was

about to be assaulted by a legion of polecats, and that it might be best to beat a retreat.

"I was just in the act of rising, when I saw my adversary once more make his appearance at the entrance. He seemed to be alone. I slipped quietly down again to my former position, and waited his attack. After a rather slow and protracted march, in the course of which he several times turned his head toward the door—a manœuvre which I did not at all like—he at last approached me. He at once leaped upon me, and looked back toward the entrance. I lifted my head, and he looked full in my face. Then he leaped down, and ran to the entrance once more, and gave a *squeak.* No answer. He returned, and leaped upon me again. He was now in a better position than before, but not sufficiently far up for my purpose. Down went his nose, and up, up he crawled over my body toward the bird in my breast-pocket. His head was low down, so that I couldn't seize him.

"I lay as still as death; but, being forced to breathe, the movement of my chest made the brute raise his head, and at that moment I gripped him by the throat. I sprung instantly to my feet, and held on. But I actually thought that he would have torn my hands to pieces with his claws. I endeavored to get him turned round, so as to get my hand to the back of his neck. Even then, I had enough to do to hold him fast. How he screamed and yelled! What an unearthly noise in the dead of night! The vault rung with his howlings. And, then, what an awful stench he emitted during his struggles! The very jackdaws in the upper stories of the castle began to *caw.* Still I kept my hold. But I could not prevent his yelling at the top of his voice. Although I gripped and squeezed with all my might and main, I could not choke him.

"Then I bethought me of another way of dealing with the brute. I had in my pocket about an ounce of chloroform, which I used for capturing insects. I took the bottle out, undid the cork, and thrust the ounce of chloroform down the fumart's throat. It acted as a sleeping draught: he gradually lessened his struggles. Then I laid him down upon a stone, and, pressing the iron heel of my boot upon his neck, I dislocated his spine, and he struggled no more. I was quite exhausted when the struggle was over. The fight must have lasted nearly two hours. It was the most terrible encounter that I ever had with an animal of his class. My hands were very much bitten and scratched, and they long continued inflamed and sore. But the prey I had captured was well worth the struggle. He was a large and powerful animal—a male; and I desired to have him as a match for a female which I had captured some time before. He was all the more valuable, as I succeeded in taking him without the slightest injury to his skin."*

The birds that roam at night are more easily described. Although the bat comes out pretty early in the evenings, it is not on night insects that he chiefly feeds: it is rather on the day insects which have not yet gone home to their rest. The bat flies mostly at twilight, and inhabits ruins and buildings as well as hollow trees in the woods.

---

* An encounter between an eagle and a polecat in the forest of Glen Avon, Banffshire, is thus described in the "New Statistical Account of Scotland:" "The eagle builds its aerie in some inaccessible rock, and continues from year to year to hatch its young in the same spot. One of these noble birds was killed some years ago which measured upward of six feet from tip to tip of the wings. One of the keepers of the forest being one day reclining on the side of a hill, observed an eagle hovering about for his prey, and, darting suddenly down, it caught hold of a polecat, with which it rose up, and flew away in the direct of an immense cliff on the opposite hill. It had not proceed ed far when he observed it abating its course, and descending in a spiral direction until it reached the ground. He was led by curiosity to proceed toward the spot, which was about a mile distant from him, and there he found the eagle quite dead, with his talons transfixed in the polecat. The polecat was also dead, with its teeth fixed in the ea- gle's gullet."

The owl is a nocturnal bird of prey. It flits by, as the twilight deepens into night, and hoots or howls in hollow and lugubrious tones. Though Edward was by no means given to fear, he was once scared at midnight by the screech of a long-eared owl (*Strix otus*). It was only about the third or fourth night that he had gone out in search of specimens. When he began his night-work he was sometimes a little squeamish; but as he became accustomed to it, he slept quite as soundly out-of-doors as in bed. He was as fearless by night as by day. No thought of ghosts, hobgoblins, water-kelpies, brownies, fairies, or the other supposed spirits of darkness, ever daunted him. But on this particular night he had one of the most alarming and fearful awakenings that he had ever experienced.

There had been a fearful thunder-storm, during which he had taken shelter in a hole in the woods of Mountcoffer. He had fallen asleep with his head upon the lock of his gun. Before he entered the burrow, he had caught a field-mouse, which he wished to take home alive. He therefore tied a string round its tail, attaching the other end of the string (which was about six feet long) to his waistcoat. The little fellow had thus the liberty of the length of his tether.

While Edward was sleeping soundly, he was awakened by something tug-tugging at his waistcoat; and then by hearing a terrific series of yells, mingled with screeches, close at his head. He was confused and bewildered at first, and did not know where he was, or what the dreadful noises meant. Recovering his recollection, and opening his eyes, he looked about him. He remembered the mouse, and pulled back the string to which it had been attached. The mouse was gone: nothing but the skin of its tail remained. He looked up, and saw an owl sitting on a tree a few yards off. He had doubtless begun to scream when he found that his capture of the mouse was resisted by the string attached to its tail. Edward emerged a little from his burrow, and drew out his gun for the purpose of shooting the owl; but before he could do this, the owl had taken to his wings and fled away with his booty.

Besides the long-eared owl, Edward also met with the brown owl—the only two species that he met with in his district, or of which he can speak from personal observation. Both of these owls uttered a *too-hoo* when sinking down upon their prey; and after they had secured it, they would fly away without any further noise; but if obstructed, they would both set up a loud screech. Edward had many opportunities of witnessing this trait in their characters. The best instance occurred in the wood of Backlaw.

"Near the centre of this wood," he observes, "and not far from the farm of the same name, there is a small piece of stagnant water. I was reclining against a tree one night, listening to a reptilian choir—a concert of frogs. It was delicious to hear the musicians endeavoring to excel each other in their strains, and to exhibit their wonderful vocal powers. The defect of the concert was the want of time. Each individual performer endeavored to get as much above the concert-pitch as possible. It was a most beautiful night—for there are beautiful nights as well as days in the North—and I am certain that these creatures were enjoying its beauty as much as myself. Presently, when the whole of the vocalists had reached their highest notes, they became hushed in an instant. I was amazed at this, and began to wonder at the sudden termination of the concert. But, looking about, I observed a brown owl drop down, with the silence of death, on to the top of a low dike close by the orchestra.

"He sat there for nearly half an hour, during which there was perfect silence. The owl himself remained quite motionless, for I watched him all the time. Then I saw the owl give a hitch, and move his head a little to one side. He instantly darted down among the grass and rushes, after which he rose with something dangling from his claws. It was a frog : I saw it quite distinctly. He flew up to a tree behind the one against which I was leaning. I turned round a little, and looked up to see how the owl would proceed with his quarry — whether he would tear him in pieces, or gobble him up whole. In this, however, I was disappointed. Although I moved very quietly, the quick eye or ear of the owl detected me, and I was at once greeted with his *hoolie-gool-oo-oo* as loud as he could scream. I might have shot him ; but my stock of powder and lead was very low, and I refrained. Besides, he soon put it out of my power by taking wing and flying off with his prey."

There were two other birds which Edward often observed prowling about in the twilight in search of food—namely, the kestrel and merlin. On one occasion he shot a specimen of the latter, when it was so dark that he could scarcely see it. He did not know that it was a hawk. He thought it was a goat - sucker by its flight. Many of the birds of prey roamed about by night as well as by day. The harsh *scream* of the heron, the *quack* of the wild duck, the *piping* of the kittyneedy (common sandpiper), the *birnbeck* of the moor-fowl, the *wail* of the plover, the *curlee* of the curlew, and the *boom* of the snipe, were often heard at night, in the regions frequented by these birds. Then again, by the sea-side, he would hear by night the shrill *piping* of the redshank and ring-dotterel, and the *pleck-pleck* of the oyster-catcher, as they came down from their breeding-grounds to the shore, to feed or to hold their conclaves.

The coot and water-hen sometimes get very noisy after sunset. The land-rail *craiks* the whole night through, until some time after the sun rises. The partridge, too, either moves about or is on the alert during spring and summer, as may be known by its often-repeated *twirr-twirr*. " The only bird we have here," says Edward, " that attempts to give music at the dead hours of night is the sedge-warbler. It appears to be possessed of the gift of song during the night as well as the day, and it is by no means niggardly in exercising its vocal powers.

"Well do I remember," he continues, "how the little mill-worker, of scarcely ten years of age, was struck with admiration and almost bewildered with delight at the first of this species he had ever heard exhibiting its mimicking powers; whereas now I considered this to be neither more nor less than the bird's own natural melody. And if there be any change in the delight with which I hear the sedge-warbler, although I have now turned the corner of ten times six, and have become an old cobbler instead of a juvenile factory operative, yet when I hear the little songster, I drink in the pleasure with even greater delight than I did in those long-past years."

The rook, too, is in a measure nocturnal in his habits during a certain term of the year, especially when building his nest or when bringing up his progeny. From the time when the foundation of the nest has been laid to the end of the matrimonial proceedings for the year, and until the last chick has left the nest, the rookery is in a state of continual *caw-cawing* from morning till night. As the young brood of rooks grow up, their appetites increase, and hence the incessant labor of their parents in scouring the country for worms and grubs to furnish them with their late supper or their early morning breakfast.

"I once," says Edward, "during one of my country excursions, slept beside a very large rookery in the woods of Froglen. Slept? no, I could not sleep! I never was in the midst of such a hideous bedlam of cawings. I positively do not believe that a single member of that black fraternity slept during the whole of that night. At least I didn't. If the hubbub slackened for a moment, it was only renewed with redoubled vehemence and energy. I found the rookery in the evening in the wildest uproar, and I left it in the morning in the same uproarious condition. I took good care never to make my bed so near a rookery again. Still,

in all justice, I must give the rook the very first and highest
character for attention to its young. It is first out in the
morning to search for food, and the last to provide for its
family at night. The starling is very dutiful in that way;
but the rook beats him hollow."

"As a rule," says Edward, "so far as I have been able to
observe, the sky-lark is the first songster in the morning,
and the corn-bunting the last at night. It was no uncommon thing to hear the lark caroling his early hymn of praise
high up in the heavens before there was any appearance
of light, or before I thought of rising to recommence my
labors. Nor was it unusual to hear the bunting stringing

FRASERBURGH.

together his few and humble notes into an evening song
long after sunset, and after I had been compelled to suc-
cumb from want of light to pursue my researches. So far
as I can remember, I do not think that I have heard the
sky-lark sing after sundown.

"Among the sylvan choristers, the blackbird is the foremost in wakening the grove to melody, and he is also among
the latest to retire at night. As soon as the first streaks
of gray begin to tinge the sky, and break in through the
branches amidst which he nestles, the blackbird is up, and
from the topmost bough of the tree he salutes the new-born
day. And when all the rest of the birds have ended their

daily service of song and retired to rest, he still continues to tune his mellow throat, until darkness has fairly settled down upon the earth.

"After the sky-lark and blackbird have heralded the coming day, the thrush rises from her couch, and pours out her melodious notes. The chaffinch, the willow-wren, and all the lesser songsters then join the choir, and swell the chorus of universal praise."

6*

CHAPTER VIII.

FORMS A NATURAL-HISTORY COLLECTION.

BANFF was the central point of Edward's operations. Banff is a pleasant country town, situated on the southern shore of the Moray Firth. It lies on a gentle slope inclining toward the sea. In front of it is the harbor. Although improved by Telford, it is rather difficult of access, and not much frequented except during the fishing season. Westward of Banff, a low range of hills lies along the coast. The burns of the Boyne, Portsoy, and Cullen cross the range, and run into the sea.

The fishing town of Macduff, which may be considered the port of Banff, lies about a mile to the eastward. To reach it, the river Deveron is crossed by one of Smeaton's finest bridges. The harbor of Macduff is more capacious and more easy of entrance than that of Banff. Many foreign vessels are to be seen there in the fishing season, for the purpose of transporting the myriads of herrings which are daily brought in by the fishermen.

Eastward of Macduff the coast becomes exceedingly rocky. The ridges of the hills, running down toward the sea, seem to have been broken off by the tremendous lashings of the waves at their feet, and thus the precipitous rocks descend in several places about six hundred feet to the shore. The coast scenery at Gamrie is unrivaled on the eastern shores of Scotland. The cliffs are the haunts of myriads of sea-fowl. "On a fine day," says Edward, "and under the mild influence of a vernal and unclouded sun, the scene is particularly beautiful. The ocean lies tranquil, and

stretched out before the spectator like an immense sheet of
glass, smiling in its soft and azure beauty, while over its surface the kittiwake, the guillemot, the razor-bill, and the puffin, conspicuous by the brilliant orange and scarlet of its bill
and legs, are beheld wheeling with rapid wing in endless
and varying directions. On firing a gun, the effect is start-
ling. The air is immediately darkened with the multitudes
of birds which are roused by the report. The ear is stunned by the varied and discordant sounds which arise. The
wailing note of the kittiwake, the shrill cry of the tammy-
norie, and the hoarse voice of the guillemot, resembling, as
it were, the laugh of some demon in mockery of the intrusion of man amidst these majestic scenes of nature—all these
combined, and mingled occasionally with the harsh scream
of the cormorant, are heard above the roar of the ocean,
which breaks at the foot of these tremendous and gigantic
precipices."

The view from the heights of Gamrie on a summer evening is exceedingly fine. The sea ripples beneath you. Far
away it is as smooth as glass. During the herring season,
the fishing-boats shoot out from the rocky clefts in which
the harbors are formed. Underneath are the fishing-boats
of Gardenstown ; to the right those of Crovie. Eastward
you observe the immense fleet of Fraserburgh vessels, about
a thousand in number, creeping out to sea. Westward are
the fishing-boats of Macduff, of Banff, Whitehills, Portsoy,
Cullen, Sandend, Findochtie, and the Buckies, all making
their appearance by degrees. The whole horizon becomes
covered with fleets of fishing-boats. Across the Moray
Firth, in the far distance, the Caithness Mountains are relieved against the evening sky. The hills of Morven and
the Maiden's Pap are distinctly visible. The sun, as it descends, throws a gleam of molten gold across the bosom of
the firth. A few minutes more, and the sun goes down,
leaving the toilers of the sea to pursue their labors amidst
the darkness of the night.

Gamrie Head is locally called Mohr Head.* The bay of Gamrie is a picturesque indentation of the coast, effected by the long operation of water upon rocks of unequal solidity. The hills, which descend to the coast, are composed of hard graywacke, in which is deeply inlaid a detached strip of moldering old red sandstone. The waves of the German Ocean, by perpetual lashing against the coast, have washed out the sandstone, and left the little bay of Gamrie —the solid graywacke standing out in bold promontories — Mohr Head on the one side, and Crovie Head on the other.

The fishing village of Gardenstown lies at the foot of the Gamrie cliffs. It is reached by a steep winding path down the face of the brae. The road descends from terrace to terrace. The houses look like aeries, built on ledges in the recesses of the cliff. As you proceed toward the shore, you seem to look down the chimneys of the houses beneath. The lower and older part of the village is close to the sea. The harbor seems as if made in a cleft of the rocks. The fishers of this village are a fine race of men, with a grand appearance. They are thorough Northmen; and but for their ancestors having settled at Gamrie, they might have settled in Normandy, and "come in with the Conqueror" at the other end of the island.

A little eastward of Gardenstown is the little fishing village of Crovie, containing another colony of Northmen. Farther out to sea is the majestic headland of Troup. It is the home of multitudes of sea-birds. Its precipices are penetrated with caves and passages, of which the most remarkable are Hell's Lum and the Needle's Eye. Hell's Lum† consists of a ghastly opening on the slope of the hill near Troup Head. From this opening to the sea there is a subterranean passage about a hundred yards long, up which, on the occasion of a storm, the waves are forced

---

* The Celtic name for *Big Head.*   † *Lum,* or chimney.

with great fury, until they find their escape by the " Lum "
in the shape of dense spray.   The other opening, the Needle's Eye, runs quite through the peninsular rocky height.
It is about a hundred and fifty yards long, and is so narrow that only one person at a time can with difficulty make
his way through it.

Eastward of Troup Head, the scenery continues of the
same character.   The fishing village of Pennan, like Gardenstown, lies at the foot of a ledge of precipitous rocks,
and is inclosed by a little creek or bay.   From the summit
of the Red Head of Pennan, the indentations of the coast

BAY OF ABERDOUR.

are seen to Kinnaird's Head in the east, and to the Bin Hill
of Cullen in the west.

The scenery of this neighborhood, besides its ruggedness
and wildness, is rendered beautiful by the glens or dens
which break through the ridges of rock and form deep ravines, each having its little streamlet at the bottom, winding its way to the sea.   The water is overhung by trees or
brush-wood, sometimes by bowlders or gray rocks like but-
tresses, which seem to support the walls of the den.   These
winding hollows are rich to luxuriance with plants and
flowers—a very garden of delight to the botanist.   Heaths,

furze, primroses, wild rasps, wild strawberries, whortleber-
ries, as well as many rare plants, are to be found there;
while the songsters of the grove—thrushes, blackbirds, and
linnets—haunt the brush-wood in varying numbers.

The most picturesque and interesting of these dens are
those of Troup, Auchmedden, and Aberdour. The dens,
when followed inland, are found to branch out into various
lesser dens, until they become lost in the moors and mosses
of the interior. The Den of Aberdour is particularly beautiful. At its northern extremity, near where it opens upon
the sea, the rift in the glen is almost overhung by the ruins of the ancient church of Aberdour,* said to have been
founded by St. Columbanus, who landed on this part of the
coast to convert the pagan population to Christianity. The
Bay of Aberdour, with its bold headland, forms the sea entrance to this picturesque valley.

The coast-line of Banffshire, without regarding the indentations of the bays, extends for about thirty miles along the
southern shores of the Moray Firth. This was the principal scene of Edward's explorations. His rounds usually extended coastwise, for about seven miles in one direction,
and about six in another. He also went inland for six

---

* The modern church is at New Aberdour, nearer the centre of the
population; but the church-yard at Old Aberdour is still used as the
parish burying-ground. Nothing can be more disgraceful than the
state of some of the country burying-places in Scotland. The graves
at Aberdour are covered with hemlocks and nettles! And yet some
money seems to have been spent in "ornamenting" the place. The
ruins of the ancient church have actually been "harled"—that is, be-
spattered with a mixture of lime and gravel! Think of "harling"
Melrose Abbey! The money spent in whitewashing the ruins would
certainly have been better expended in removing the bits of old cof-
fins, cutting down the hemlocks and nettles, and putting the burying-
ground into better order. The queen has shown a good example in
ordering the church-yard of Crathie to be improved. But that of
Braemar is still in a wretched state, being covered with hemlocks
and nettles.

miles. But he very often exceeded these limits, as we shall afterward find.

Having referred to the coast-line, we may also briefly refer to the inland portion of the county. Banffshire is of an irregular shape, and extends from the southern shores of the Moray Firth in a south-westerly direction toward Cairngorm and Ben Macdhui—the highest mountain knot of the Grampians. The middle portion of the county is moderately hilly. Glen Fiddick, Glen Isla, and Strath Deveron follow the line of hills which descend in a north-westerly direction from the Grampians toward the sea.

The county generally is under cultivation of the highest order. The valleys are intersected with rich meadows and pasture-lands, which are stocked with cattle of the choicest breeds. There are numerous woods and plantations, both luxuriant and verdant, though there is a great want of hedges. Agriculture is gradually extending upward toward the mountains. Moors and morasses are fast disappearing. In places where the wail of the plover, the birr of the moorcock, and the scream of the merlin were the only sounds, the mellow voice of the lark, the mavis, and the blackbird are now to be heard in the fields and the woods throughout the country.

In the extreme south-western district lies the great mountain knot to which we have already referred. The scenery of this neighborhood can scarcely be equaled, even in Switzerland, though it is at present almost entirely unknown. Cairngorm, Benbuinach, Benaven, and Ben Macdhui surround Loch Avon and the forest of Glen Avon. The Banffshire side of Ben Macdhui forms a magnificent precipice of fifteen hundred feet, which descends sheer down into the loch. This lonely and solemn lake is fed by the streams flowing from the snows that lie all the year round in the corries of the mountains above. These streams leap down from the bare and jagged cliffs in the form of broken cataracts. One of these falls has a descent of nine hundred fect.   The parish of Kirkmichael, in which this scenery occurs, is almost unpeopled.   It has only one village—Tomintoul—the highest in Scotland.   The people who inhabit it and the other hamlets of the parish are of a different race and religion, and speak a different language, from those who inhabit the middle and lower parts of the county.[*]

To return to the labors of our naturalist.   For about fif-

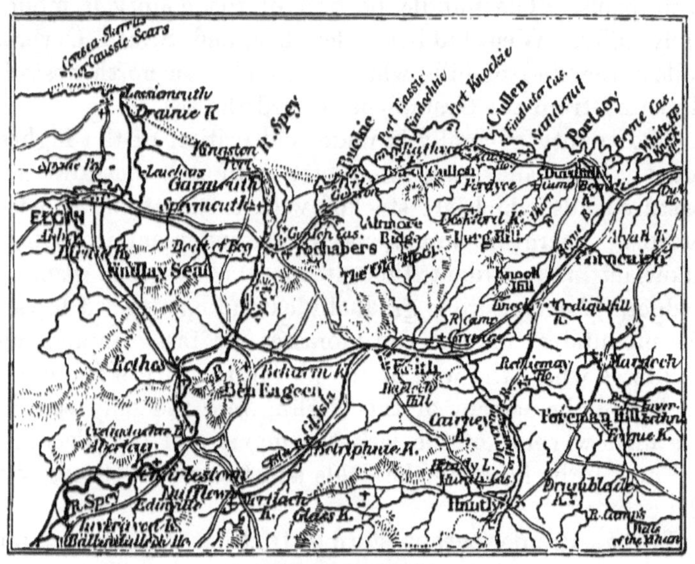

MAP OF BANFFSHIRE.

teen years Edward made the greater part of his researches at night.   He made them in the late evening and in the early morning, snatching his sleep at intervals between the departing night and the returning day.

---

[*] Their race is Celtic, whereas the inhabitants of the sea-shore are for the most part Scandinavian.   Their language is Gaelic, whereas that of the rest of the county is Scoto-English.   Their religion is Roman Catholic, whereas that of the lower part of the county is Protestant.   There are many districts in Scotland where, in consequence of the inaccessibility of the roads, the Reformation never reached

His rounds, we have said, extended coastwise along the
shore of the Moray Firth, for about seven miles in one direction and about six in another.   His excursions also extended inland for about five or six miles.   He had thus
three distinct circuits.   Although he only took one of them
at a time, he usually managed to visit each district twice a
week.

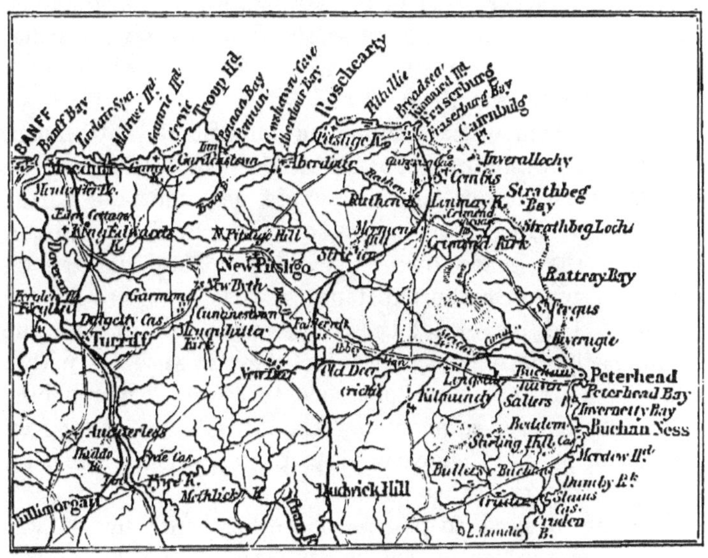

AND NORTH ABERDEENSHIRE.

Having sometimes wandered too far, as he frequently
did, he divested himself of his hunting paraphernalia, rolled
them up together, hid them in a hole or some convenient
place, and then ran home as fast as he could, in order to be
at his work at the proper time.   He once ran three miles
in twenty minutes.   He measured the time by his watch—
for he had a watch then, though, like himself, it is worn out
now.

Occasionally, when kept late at work, he was prevented
from enjoying his evening ramble.   After going to bed,

and taking a short sleep, he would set out in the dark, in order to be at the place where he had appointed, from whence he worked his way homeward in the morning toward Banff.

But though he made it a general practice during his nightly excursions to return home in time for the morning's work, he occasionally found it necessary to deviate a little from this rule. When he was in search of some particular bird, he was never satisfied or at rest until he had obtained it. On one occasion two geese, the first of their kind that he had ever seen, caused him to lose nearly a whole week before he could run them down.

He saw them while walking out one Sunday afternoon. They were swimming about on a piece of water near the town. He went out before daylight next morning to the same place. But he saw no geese. He waited for an hour, and then they made their appearance. They alighted on the water within a short distance of the bar where he was sitting. Had his object been to secure them at once, he could easily have shot them, for they were both within reach of his gun. But he wished to observe their habits, and he waited for some time. Having satisfied himself on this head, he next endeavored to possess them. He shot one of them; the other flew away.

He now desired to possess the other bird; but it was with extreme difficulty that he could accomplish his object. Though the goose returned, it was so extremely shy that it could scarcely be approached. It was only by making use of many precautions, and resorting to some very curious stratagems, that Edward was able to capture the bird. A week elapsed before he could secure it. He shot it on Saturday, but he did not recover it until the following morning.

On another occasion a little stint (the least of the sandpipers) cost him two days and a night. It was the first bird of the kind he had ever seen — and it was the last. Though he was occasionally within a mile or two of Banff during the pursuit of the bird, and though he had not tasted food during the whole of his absence, lying during part of the night among the shingle on the sea-shore, yet he never once thought of leaving the chase until final success crowned his efforts. We must allow him to tell the story in his own words:

"I once had a desperate hunt after a little stint (*Tringa minuta*). Returning home one evening along the links,* I heard a strange cry coming, as it seemed, from the shore. I listened for some time, as I knew it was the season (September) for many of our migratory species to visit us. Never having heard the cry before, I was speedily on the beach. But it was growing dark, and I had not cat's eyes. The sound, too, ceased so soon as I had gained the beach. After groping about for some time, I thought I espied a rather large flock of birds at some distance along the shore. I approached cautiously, and found that I was correct; the flock consisting chiefly of ringed plovers, dunlins, and sanderlings. From the latter circumstance, and from the fact that the cry was that of a sandpiper, I was pretty sure that a stranger was among them. Although I could see well enough that the birds were on the wet sand between me and the water, I could not make them out distinctly. Once or twice I thought I could distinguish one considerably smaller than the others, but I soon felt that I had been mistaken. I was now in a state of great excitement. Every limb shook like an aspen-leaf, or a cock's tail on a windy day. What was I to do? True, I might have fired at them, but the odds were greatly against my being successful.

"It was now fairly dark, and the birds had retired to rest on a ridge of rocks which intervenes between the sands and the links. Instead of returning home, as any one else

---

* *Links*, sandy, flat ground, sometimes covered with grass, lying along the sea-shore.

would have done, I laid myself down in a hollow till morning, to wait their first appearance, in the hope of attaining my object. It proved a wet and windy night ; but daylight brought with it a fine morning. With it also came two gunners from Banff, striding along the beach on a shooting excursion. This vexed me to the very heart. The birds were not yet astir, but I knew they would rise at the approach of the men, who would doubtless attempt to shoot them. Just as I anticipated, up went the birds; crack! crack! went the shots; and down fell several birds. Rising from my stony couch, I rushed at once to the spot to see the victims, and found them all to consist of sanderlings, dunlins, and one ringed plover. The gunners were strangers to me, but I ventured to ask them to abstain from firing until I had satisfied myself about the bird I sought; but they seemed unable to understand why one bird could be of more interest than another, and they told me that, as there were plenty of them, I could fire away and take my chance. I declined to shoot with them, but eagerly watched each time they fired; and if a bird fell, I went and examined it; but I did not meet with the one I sought. The men at last got tired and went away.

"It was now my turn; but, unhappily, the birds, from being so often fired at, had become extremely shy, so that to get near them for my purpose was all but impossible. By perseverance, however, I at length made out one, as I thought, a good deal smaller than the others. I succeeded in creeping a little nearer. They rose; I fired, and down fell four. I rushed, breathless, hoping to pick up the bird in which I took such interest. But, alas! no. It was not there. Away went the remaining birds to the sea; then, turning, they rounded a point or headland called Blackpots, and disappeared from view. From this, and from their not returning, I knew that they had gone to the sands at Whitehills, about three miles distant, to which place I proceeded. But no sooner had I reached there, than back they flew in the direction from which they had come.   Back I went also, and found them at the old place.

Just as I reached them, away they flew once more, and, of course, away I went likewise.   In this way we continued nearly the whole day—they flying to and fro, I following them.   Toward evening my strength beginning to fail, and feeling quite exhausted, I gave up the chase, and once more took up my abode among the shingle, in the hope that they might again return there for the night.   Just as I wished and expected, and while it was yet light, they came and alighted about thirty yards from where I lay.   Away went fatigue, hunger, and thoughts of home!   In fact, the sight of this object of my day and night's solicitude made me a new creature.   Off went the messengers of death.   Two of the birds fell; the rest fled once more to the sea.   I followed, but had not proceeded far when I observed one falter.   Leaving its companions, it bent its course toward where I stood, and suddenly dropped almost at my feet. As I picked up the little thing, I could not but feel thankful that my patience and perseverance had at last been crowned with success.   It was the first little stint I had ever shot, and the only one I have ever seen in this neighborhood."

In thus pursuing his researches, Edward lost much of his time, and, in proportion to his time, he also lost much of his wages.   But his master used to assist him in making up his lost time.   It was a common remark of his, "Give Tam the stuff for a pair of shoes at night, and if he has any of his cantrips in view, we are sure to have them in the morning ready for the customer."   Edward took the stuff home with him, and, instead of going to bed, worked at the shoes all night, until they were finished and ready for delivery.   He had another advantage in making up for lost time.   His part of the trade was of the lightest sort.   He made light shoes and pumps.   He was one of those who, among the craft, are denominated *ready*.   He was thus able to accomplish much more than those who were engaged at heavier work. This, together with his practice of spending not a moment idly, was much in his favor.

He also contrived to preserve his specimens during his meal hours, or in his idle times "betwixt pairs" — while, as shoe-makers would say, they were " on the hing." During the long winter nights he arranged the objects preserved, and put them in their proper cases. In order the better to accomplish this work, he did not go to bed until a very late hour. As he was not able to afford both fire and light, he put out the lamp when engaged upon any thing that could be done without it, and continued his labors by the light of the fire.

When forced to go to bed, he went at once, and, having slept at railway speed for an hour or an hour and a half, he was up again and at work upon his specimens. He felt as much refreshed, he said, by his sound sleep, as if he had slept the whole night. And yet during his sleep he must have had his mind fixed upon his work, otherwise he could not have wakened up at the precise time that he had previously appointed. Besides stuffing his own birds, he also stuffed the birds which other people had sent him, for which he was paid.

One of the objects which he had in view in making his "rounds" so frequently was to examine the traps he had set, in order to catch the beetles, grubs, and insects which he desired to collect. His traps were set with every imaginable organic material — dead birds, rats, rabbits, or hedgehogs; dead fish, crabs, or sea-weed. He placed them everywhere but on the public roads—in fields and woods, both on the ground and hung on trees; in holes, in old dikes; in water, both fresh and stagnant. Some of these traps were visited daily, others once a week, while those set in water, marshy places, and in woods, were only visited once a month. He never passed any dead animal without first searching it carefully, and then removing it to some

sheltered spot.   He afterward visited it from time to time.
Fish stomachs, and the refuse of fishermen's lines, proved a
rich mine for marine objects.   By these means he obtained
many things which could not otherwise have been obtained;
and he thus added many rare objects to his gradually growing collection.

He was, however, doomed to many disappointments.
One of these may be mentioned.   Among his different
collections was a large variety of insects.   He had these
pinned down in boxes in the usual manner.   He numbered
them separately.   When he had obtained the proper names
of the insects, his intention was to prepare a catalogue.   He
knew that there were sheets of figures sold for that and
similar purposes, but he could not afford to buy them.   He
accordingly got a lot of old almanacs and multiplication-ta-
bles, and cut out the numbers.   It was a long and tedious
process, but at length he completed it.

When the insects were fixed and numbered, Edward removed the cases into his garret preparatory to glazing them.
He piled them one upon the other, with their faces downward, in order to keep out the dust.   There were twenty
boxes, containing in all nine hundred and sixteen insects.
After obtaining the necessary glass, he went into the garret
to fetch out the cases.   On lifting up the first case, he found
that it had been entirely stripped of its contents.   He was
perfectly horrified.   He tried the others.   They were all
empty!   They contained nothing but the pins which had
held the insects, with here and there a head, a leg, or a
wing.   A more complete work of destruction had never
been witnessed.   It had probably been perpetrated by rats
or mice.

His wife, on seeing the empty cases, asked him what he
was to do next.   "Weal," said he, "it's an awfu' disappointment; but I think the best thing will be to set to
work and fill them up again."   To accumulate these nine
hundred and sixteen insects had cost him four years' labor!

And they had all been destroyed in a few days, perhaps in a single night!

It will be remembered that Audubon had once a similar disappointment. On leaving Henderson, in Kentucky, where he then lived, he left his drawings, representing nearly a thousand inhabitants of the air, in the custody of a friend. On returning a few months later, and opening his box, he found that a pair of Norway rats had taken possession of the whole, and gnawed up the drawings into little bits of paper. Audubon did what Edward now determined to do. He went out into the woods with his gun, his note-book, and pencils, and in the course of about three years he again filled his port-folio.

Edward duly carried out his purpose. He went moth-hunting as before; he hunted the moors and the woods, the old buildings and the grave-yards, until, in about four more years, he had made another collection of insects; although there were several specimens contained in the former collection that he could never again meet with.

Edward had now been observing and collecting for about eight years. His accumulations of natural objects had therefore become considerable. By the year 1845, he had preserved nearly two thousand specimens of living creatures found in the neighborhood of Banff. About half the number consisted of quadrupeds, birds, reptiles, fishes, crustacea, star-fish, zoophytes, corals, sponges, and other objects. He had also collected an immense number of plants. Some of the specimens were in bottles, but the greater number were in cases with glass fronts. He could not afford to have the cases made by a joiner; so he made the whole of them himself, with the aid of his shoe-maker's knife, a saw, and a hammer.

In order to make the smaller cases, he bought boxes from the merchants; and in breaking them up, he usually got as many nails as would serve to nail the new cases together. To make the larger cases, he bought wood from the carpenters. He papered the insides, painted the outsides, and glazed the whole of the cases himself. The thirty cases containing his shells were partitioned off, each species having a compartment for itself. This was a difficult piece of work, but he got through it successfully. There were about three hundred cases in all.

His house was now filled with stuffed birds, quadrupeds, insects, and such-like objects. Every room was packed with the cases containing them, his shoe-making apartment included. What was he to do with them? He had, indeed, long had a project in his mind. In the first place, he wished to abandon the shoe-making trade. He was desirous of raising money for the purpose of commencing some other business. He also wished to have some funds in hand, in order to prosecute his investigations in natural history. How could he raise the requisite money? He thought that he might raise a part of it by exhibiting his collection. Hence his large accumulation of specimens, and his large collection of cases.

There was a feeing fair held twice a year at Banff, on market-days, called Brandon Fair. Young lads and lasses came in from the country to be feed, and farmers and their wives came in to fee them. It was a great day for Banff. All the shows and wild beasts, the dwarfs and giants, the spotted ladies and pig-faced women, accompanied by drums and trumpets, converged upon Banff on that day. The town, ordinarily so quiet, became filled with people—partly to hire and be hired, and partly to see what was to be seen. The principal streets were kept in a continual row until the fair was over.

Edward gave an exhibition of his collection at the Brandon Fair in May, 1845. He took a room in the Trades' Hall, and invited the public to inspect his " Collection of Preserved Animals, comprising Quadrupeds, Birds, Fishes, Insects, Shells, Eggs, and other Curiosities."

The local paper called the public attention to the rare

and beautiful objects contained in Edward's Collection —"the results of his own untiring efforts and ingenuity, without aid, and under discouraging circumstances which few would have successfully encountered..... Our young friends especially should visit the collection: it will both amuse and instruct them. They will learn more from seeing them in half an hour than from reading about them in half a year."

Edward took the inhabitants by surprise. They had never been able to understand him. His wanderings by night had been matter of great wonderment to them. The exhibition fully explained the reason of his frequent disappearances. When his public announcement was advertised, some of the better classes called at his house in Wright's Close, to ascertain if it was true. True, indeed! He pointed to the cases of stuffed birds and animals which nearly filled his house. Then the question came, "What made you a naturalist?"

"When I was first asked this question," says he, "I was completely dumfoundered! I had no notion that a naturalist could be *made*. What! make a naturalist, as you would make a tradesman! I could not believe that people became naturalists for pecuniary motives. My answer to those who put the question invariably was, and still is, *I can not tell*. I never knew of any external circumstance that had any thing to do with engendering in my mind the never-ceasing love which I entertained for the universal works of the Almighty; so that the real cause must be looked for elsewhere."

In preparing for the exhibition of his collection, Edward brushed up his specimens and cleaned his cases, before removing them to the Trades' Hall. But in looking over his collection, he found that he had sustained another serious loss. He regarded it at the time as a heart-rending catastrophe. Some time before, he had put nearly two thousand dried and preserved plants into a box, which he had placed at the top of the stair, in order to be out of harm's way. The plants were all dried and preserved. They were the result of eight years' labor employed in collecting them. But when he went to overhaul the box, he found that the lid had been shoved to one side, and that numerous cats had entered it and made it their lair. The plants were completely soaked, and rendered utterly worthless. The box smelled so abominably that he was under the necessity of making a bonfire of it in the back-yard.

All this was exceedingly disheartening. Nevertheless, he removed his remaining collection to the place appointed for exhibiting it. He had no allurements, no music, no drums nor trumpets, as the other show-people had. His exhibition was held in an upper room, so that the sight-seers had to mount a long stair before they could see the collection. Nevertheless, many persons went to see it; and the result was, that Edward not only paid his expenses, but had something laid by for future purposes.

He went on collecting for another exhibition, and increased his specimens. He replaced, to a certain extent, the plants which had been destroyed by the recklessness of the cats. He obtained some wonderful fishes and sea-birds. His collection of eggs was greatly increased. He now prepared for a second exhibition at the Brandon Fair, 1846. On that occasion he was able to exhibit many old coins and ancient relics.

This exhibition was more attractive and more successful than the first. It yielded a better remuneration; but, what was more satisfactory, Edward was much complimented by those who had inspected his collection. It excited general applause. In short, it was considered by Edward himself to be so successful as to induce him to remove the collection to Aberdeen, for exhibition in that important city.

CHAPTER IX.

EXHIBITS HIS COLLECTION IN ABERDEEN.

BANFF was a comparatively small and remote town, whereas Aberdeen was the centre of Northern intellect and business. At Banff, comparatively few persons knew much about natural history or science; while Aberdeen had two universities, provided with professors, students, and all the accompaniments of learning. It also contained a large and intelligent population of educated business men, tradesmen, and artisans.

Edward was sanguine of success at Aberdeen. It was his City of Expectations. He was now doubly desirous of giving up shoe-making, and devoting himself to natural history. For this purpose he wanted means and a settled income. He intended to devote the proceeds of his exhibition in several ways. He had, indeed, almost settled them in his own mind. He would, in the first place, make arrangements for opening a coffee-house or provision-shop for the employment and support of his family. He would next purchase some works on natural history by the best authors. He would probably also buy a microscope and some other necessary scientific instruments. Alnaschar, in "The Arabian Nights," with the basket of glass at his feet, did not dream more of what he would do with his forthcoming income than Edward did of what he would do with the successful results of his exhibition at Aberdeen.

But Edward must now be up and doing. The cases had to be put in order; new objects had to be added to the collection; new birds had to be stuffed; some of the groups had to be arranged in dramatic form.   One of these consisted of the Death of Cock Robin.   There was the sparrow perched upon a twig, warrior-like, with his bow in one of his feet, and his arrow-case slung across his back.   There was the redbreasted robin lying on a green and mossy knoll, with the arrow shot by the sparrow sticking in his little heart; and in a burn meandering close by, there was a silvery fish with its little dish, catching Robin's life-blood. There was also a great black beetle, with a thread and needle, ready to sew his shroud.

In another case, the Babes in the Wood were represented—two robin-redbreasts covering their tender bodies with leaves.   There was a case of mice, entitled " Pussy from Home:" the mice, large and small, were going into and coming out of a meal-bag, which they were rifling.   There was another large case, containing a number of small birds in a state of great excitement, darting and pecking at an object in the middle of the case, which proved to be a weasel, attempting to rob a yellow bunting's nest, containing six eggs, one of which the weasel had rolled out.   Perhaps the best case was the one containing a pheasant, with six young birds, all beautifully stuffed.   For this Edward was offered three guineas before he left Banff.

At length all was ready, and Edward, with a light heart, left Banff for Aberdeen.   The collection was taken in six carriers' carts — the largest that could be found.   Edward could not take it by railway, for there were no railways then in Banff.   The whole family accompanied the collection.   It consisted of Edward, his wife, and five children. They set out early in the morning of Friday, the 31st of July, 1846—a memorable day in Edward's history.   The six cart-loads arrived safe at Aberdeen on the evening of the following day.

Edward had previously taken the shop No. 132 Union Street, for the purposes of his exhibition.   This street is the finest in Aberdeen—perhaps the finest in Scotland.   It is wide and broad, and about a mile long. The houses are of hewn granite, some of them of massive and noble architecture. Union Street is the representative street of the Gray City.

Handbills were issued, and advertisements published in the local journals, announcing the opening of the exhibition. In the handbill it was stated that "the objects comprising this collection have been collected in the counties of Banff and Aberdeen, and preserved by a single individual, and that individual a journeyman shoe-maker. They have been exhibited by him in Banff, to the delight and admiration of every visitor—all being surprised at the beauty, order, and multitude of the various objects—some going so far as to doubt the fact of the proprietor being a shoemaker, saying that it was impossible for a person of that trade being able to do any thing like what they saw before them.

"Thomas Edward takes the liberty of stating that the collection is allowed by eminent naturalists to be one of the greatest curiosities ever offered for public inspection in this quarter, amounting, as it does, to above two thousand objects; and being the work of one individual, who had to labor under every disadvantage, having none to tell how or where to find the different objects; none to teach him how to preserve these objects when found; no sound of promised reward ringing in his ears to urge him on in his singular course; no friend to accompany him in his nightly wanderings; help from none; but solely dependent on his own humble abilities and limited resources.

"Were it possible for words to describe, in adequate terms, the unexampled assiduity and unwearied perseverance with which Thomas Edward has labored in the formation of his collection, it would surprise every individual capable of reflection. Such not being the case, a visit to the exhibition can alone enable the public to form any idea of the extent of his labors. The ocean, the rocky shore,

the shingly and sandy beach ; the meadows, the cultivated
fields, the whinny knowes, the woods ; the running brooks,
the stagnant pools, the muddy and unsavory ditches, the
marshy flats ; old walls, ruined towers, and heath-clad hills
—have all been visited and anxiously searched in order to
procure the objects which compose the collection."

Such was Edward's appeal to the people of Aberdeen to
come and see his collection. The terms were very mod-
erate — "Ladies and Gentlemen, 6d.; Tradespeople, 3d.;
Children, half-price." The *Aberdeen Journal* thus noticed
the collection : "We have been particularly struck with
the very natural attitudes in which the beasts and birds of
prey are placed ; some being represented as tearing their
victims, others feeding their young, and some looking side-
ward or backward, with an expression of the eye which indicates the fear of interruption. The birds are very beautiful, and the entomological specimens will be found exceedingly interesting."

On the Thursday following his arrival in Aberdeen, Edward opened his collection. He was in hopes that there
would be a rush to see the objects which he had collected
with so much difficulty during the last eight years. He
believed in himself, though others did not yet believe in
him. But there was no rush—no eager multitude crowd-
ing the door of No. 132. Indeed, very few persons called
to see the collection. These might, however, tell their
friends of its interest, and the rush might still come. But
he waited in vain. The rush never came.

The principal people who called upon him during the
first ten days were stuffed-bird sellers, and persons who
pestered him to buy nearly every thing of a bestial kind,
alive or dead. Some of the articles offered were monstrosities or delusions, such as double chickens, double mice, a
kitten with a rat's head, a double-headed dog, a rat with
two tails, both curled up like a pig's, and such-like objects.
These people were all bowed to the door.

Several ladies called upon Edward to consult him about their favorite pets. One had a lap-dog that was sick; another a bird that was lame; others had crippled or diseased cats. He was asked to come and see a pig that had broken one of its legs. A gentleman called upon him one day about an old and favorite rabbit whose front teeth had grown so forward that it could not eat—"Would he come and cut them off?" "No! he had not time. He must attend to his exhibition."

Very few people came. Those who did come knew very little about natural history. Their ignorance of the works of nature seemed to Edward surprising. Only a few knew any thing, excepting about the commoner sorts of animals. As to the number, and nature, and habits of living creatures, they appeared to know next to nothing. The transformation of insects was a mystery to them. They could not see how it was possible for an ugly caterpillar to become transformed into a beautiful butterfly. Edward felt very much for the ignorance of men of his own class: it was simply deplorable.

Dr. Macgillivray, Professor of Natural History in Marischal College, Aberdeen, called upon Edward, and was much pleased with his collection of Banffshire fauna. The professor told him that the inhabitants of Aberdeen were not yet prepared for an exhibition of this kind. There was not even a public museum in the city; no collection of natural objects; no free library; nothing for the enlightenment of the higher and nobler faculties of man. To this cause Edward, in a great measure, attributed the failure of his exhibition. Some of the professors who afterward called to see the collection told Edward that "the people of Aberdeen were not yet prepared for such an exhibition, especially as it had been the work of a poor man. He had come several centuries too soon."

Several of the persons who examined the exhibition did not believe that it had been the work of Edward at all.

Among his better-class visitors was a gentleman who frequently came in as he passed, and carefully examined the specimens. He sometimes gave Edward half a crown, and would not take any change back. The gentleman was an inveterate and persistent interrogator. His questions were usually of a personal character. But Edward had by this time prepared a *bag of forgetfulness,* into which he put all the disagreeable things that were said to him ; and, once there, he remembered them no more. Edward believed that his visitor belonged to the medical profession, and that he was connected with a neighboring dispensary.*

One day the visitor arrived, and, without looking at the specimens, he went directly up to Edward, and asked, " Well, how are you getting on ?" " Very poorly," was the answer. "And no wonder !" said the visitor. " How ?" " How !" he almost shouted, " because the people here don't believe in such a thing. I am sure of it, from what I know and have heard myself."

" But if they would only come !"

" Come ? that's the very thing. It seems they'll not come. And although they did, what satisfactory evidence is there that what they see is the result of your own unaided and individual labor? You are quite a stranger here. You should have had some persons of high standing in the city to take you under their patronage—say the professors of both colleges, or the provost and town-council. Oh ! you needn't shake your head and look at the floor. It would have been much better."

" I never considered myself in a position," said Edward, " to ask such a favor."

" Then you'll not succeed here unless you do something of the sort."

" In that case, then," said Edward, " I'll be plain enough to tell you that I never will succeed."

---

* It was afterward found that the visitor was Dr. Cadenhead, one of the principal physicians and oculists of the city.

7*

"You are too stiff — too unbending," said the doctor. "Then, you know very well that you have nobody in Aberdeen to confirm your extraordinary statement. You say that the whole of this collection is entirely the work of your own hands, and that it is your own exclusive property !"

"Yes. I bought the game birds; and as· regards the others, I procured the whole of them myself — preserved them and cased them, just as you see them."

"And had you to work for your living all that time ?"

"Yes; and for the living of my family too."

"Then you have a wife and a family ?"

"Yes, I have five children."

"The devil !"

"No, sir; I said children."

"Ah yes, I know; I beg your pardon. But do you mean to say that you have maintained your wife and family by working at your trade all the while that you have been making this collection ?"

"Yes."

"Oh, nonsense ! How is it possible that you could have done that ?"

"By never losing a single minute, nor any part of a minute, that I could by any means improve."

"Did you ever hear of any one else who had ever done the like before ?"

"No. But thousands might have done it, and much more too."

"Well, I don't believe it. I have never heard of such a thing, and I have never read of such a thing !"

"But I never thought," said Edward, "that I was doing any thing that any one else might not have done. I was quite unaware of the fact that I was doing any thing in the least way meritorious. But if I have, as a journeyman shoe-maker, done any thing worthy of praise, then I must say that there is not a working-man on the face of the earth that could not have done much more than I have done; for of all the occupations that are known, that of shoe-making is surely the very worst."

"Had you been an outside worker, I would not have thought so much about it; but even then it would have been surprising.   But having to work from morning to night in a shoe-maker's shop—where these things can neither be seen nor found—the thing is perfectly inconceivable.   I'll give my oath that, so far as Aberdeen is concerned — or, I believe, any other place — there is not a single working-man who could, by himself, have done any thing of the sort.   I tell you that there is no person who knows the laboring people and their circumstances better than I do; and I tell you again, that, situated as they are, the thing is quite impossible.   They have neither the learning nor the opportunities necessary for scientific pursuits; nor yet the time nor the money to spare for the purpose.   No, poor devils! they need all their time and all their money to eke out their bare and half-starved existence."

"I quite agree with you," replied Edward, "in some of your remarks; but I am sorry to say that the wretchedness you allude to is in too many cases attributable to themselves, and also to their slatternly and improvident wives.   They do not go into the fields to drink in the sweets of nature, but rush unthinkingly into the portals of hell, and drown their sorrows in whisky.   In this way they beggar themselves and pauperize their families."

"There is doubtless something in that," said the doctor, "but I spoke in general.   Of course, there are exceptions. It would appear that you are one, and a most extraordinary one too.   And here it is that I am most puzzled.   I can't understand how you have done all this single-handed.   Besides, you must have read a great deal.   You must have had access to the best scientific works; and you must also have possessed sufficient means to enable you to collect and arrange these things as they now are."

"Permit me to say, sir," said Edward, "that I am not

a book - learner, nor have I ever read any scientific works. I never had any access to them.   Nor do I possess any means besides those that I have earned by hard and constant work."

"What! have you no education? no access to scientific works?"

"No, sir."

"Then how the deuce did you manage?"

"Well, I think I have told you that several times before. But I'll tell you again — this time in a few words. My chief school was the earth, and my principal teacher was nature.   What I have been able to do, has been done by economizing every farthing of money, and every moment of time."

"Do you mean to say that you got no education, and had no money, but what you worked for?"

"I do; and—"

"Confounded nonsense!"

"Allow me to proceed.   It is not always those who have the most money and the best education that do the most work, either in natural history or any thing else."

"Oh yes!   That's all very well; but it's not to the point. But [looking at his watch] I find I must go.   I'll call again; for I am determined to be at the bottom of this affair."

The next time he called, Edward was standing at the door. "Well," said he, "I can't wait to-day, for I have to go into the country, and I can't be home for a week.   But here's your fare."   "No, no," said Edward; "you haven't been in."   "Very well, here goes!" and he pitched the fare in among the birds.   When Edward went to look at the fare, instead of a penny, he found a crown-piece.   The gentleman never called again.   By the time he returned from the country the exhibition was at an end.

As Edward had announced in his handbill that he had been an inhabitant of Aberdeen, and worked at the Grandholm Mills in his boyhood, some of his old companions called upon him at the exhibition. The paragraph in the handbill was as follows: "The idea of having a collection of the works of nature was first formed by him (the exhibitor) in very early life, and while traversing the country in the vicinity of Aberdeen, but more particularly when wandering among the delightful haughs of Grandholm, where he went to work when little more than nine years of age. Should this come under the notice of any of those who were mill-mates with Thomas Edward, they perchance may remember the boy they all wondered at so much because he would not join in their youthful sports, but rather chose to wander alone through the woods or by the banks of the Don, in quest of those objects, the pursuit of which in after-years cost him so much labor, time, and expense."

As nearly twenty years had passed since Edward had worked at the spinning-mills, he failed to recognize his early companions when they called, until they mentioned some circumstance or conversation which brought them to his recollection. Some walked round the collection before they made themselves known to him, while others did so as they entered. But one and all agreed that though they might have imagined that Edward had done something toward making the collection, they could not believe that he had done it all by himself while working at his trade. They were working-men themselves, and knew what they had to contend with, in the form of want of time, want of means, and difficulties of all sorts. These considerations only tended to heighten their sense of astonishment the more.

Some of Edward's other acquaintances also called, and they, like the others, declared that it was perfectly impossible for any working-man to have made such a collection by himself without any extraneous aid. One of his old shop-mates called frequently, and Edward endeavored to convince him that the thing was quite feasible; but he insisted that he must have got assistance or help in some way or another.

"Well," said Edward, "you remember how I worked beside you in the old garret in Shoe Lane ; how I was never idle, and was always busy at something, whether I had shoemaking to do or not. Very well. I continued the same practice after I left you ; and when I got a wife, instead of growing lazier, I became more ardent than ever. I squeezed the pith and substance out of every moment to make the most of it; and raxed and drew every farthing out like a piece of india-rubber, until I could neither rax nor draw it any more. I have thus endeavored to make the most and the best of every thing."

A new idea seemed to strike the man. "But did ye no get some bawbees wi' yer wife ?"

"No," said Edward, "not a bawbee. But, though poor in cash, she brought me a dowry worth more than all the money ever coined !"

"Trash, man ! trash ! Fat could be better than siller till a puir man ?"

"Well, I'll tell you. She brought me a remarkably sound and healthy body, strong bones, and a casket well filled with genuine common sense, or, rather, a mind far superior to that usually possessed by the majority of her sex. Now that's what I call better than money. And I can tell you, also, that if young men were to look out for such wives, they would be able to lead their lives to much better purpose than they now do. Your tap-rooms, and dram-shops, and public-houses would then have fewer and far less eager customers. And, if I am not much mistaken, there would be many more happy homes and happy families, especially among the poor ; instead of the miserable, heart-sickening, disease-engendering hovels, which are a curse and a stain upon our so-called civilization."

"Ye'll be a temperance-man, then, are ye ?"

"Yes ; I'm temperate enough. And if wives would look more to their husbands' comfort, as well as to the interests of their own families, there would be far more temperance-men, as you call them, than there are now. I'm not a member of the Temperance Society; nevertheless, I am in favor of every thing that would make people more sober and diligent, and tend to man's good, both here and hereafter."

"But," continued the man, "are ye satisfied that ye got nae help in the way I hinted?"

"None whatever."

"But far did ye learn the wrightin' [carpentering], the paintin', and the glazin'?"

"At my ain fireside, where every thing good should be learned. My teachers were — first, 'Necessity;' and, secondly, another teacher, of whom you may not have heard, called WILL."

"Ye're a mystery," said the man.

"Perhaps I may be," answered Edward; "but I'll just tell you three things, whether you may understand the 'mystery' or not. My neighbors in Banff say of me that 'that man surely means to tak' the world by speed o' fit.' My shopmates say that 'Tam is just the lad for taking time by the forelock;' and many of the inhabitants say, 'Whoever may be seen lounging about at the lazy corners, you'll never see Edward among them.' Now, these are three little nuts which I hope you will crack among your shopmates; and I hope they will do them good."

One day two ladies came to see the exhibition. They looked over the collection, and one of them came up to Edward and looked him straight in the face. She asked him if he belonged to Aberdeen.

"Well," he replied, "although I was not born in Aberdeen, still I may say I belong to it. My mother was an Aberdeen woman, and I was brought up here until I went to Banff." "Ah," said the lady, "I thought so. Your countenance and appearance are very much the same as they were when I last saw you." "Indeed!"

"Were you not at one time a private in the Aberdeenshire militia?" "I was; but what of that?" "Allow me to explain: do you remember running out of the ranks one day while at drill, and flying after a butterfly?" "I do," said Edward.

"And of being pursued and taken prisoner by a corporal and four men of your company, when you were brought up before the officer, who gave you your liberty?"

"Yes," said Edward, "all that is true." "And perhaps you remember that there was a group of ladies with the officer?" "Oh yes, I remember that." "Well, then, I was one of those ladies; and I first proposed to the others that we should intercede with the captain to let you off."

The lady then proceeded to explain that she herself was an entomologist, and had been greatly pleased with the collection. Edward, on his part, thanked her most cordially for the good service she had been able to do for him on the links that day, now so long past. "But, now," she added, "as one good turn deserves another, will you come and take your tea and supper with us some evening?" Edward was thunderstruck at this proposal, for he was an exceedingly shy and bashful man, though he had been such a "hempy" in his youth. "Oh no!" said he, "I can not venture on taking such a liberty." "I'll have no denial," said the lady; "there will be only a few friends who wish to make your acquaintance."

The idea of being exhibited as a lion was perfectly revolting to Edward; so he again protested that he could not accept the invitation, however kindly it was meant. "No, no; you *must* come. There's my card and address, and when I have fixed the day, I'll send you an invitation. Good-day. Now remember! one good turn deserves another!" And away she went, leaving Edward looking rather sheepish, and fumbling in his hand a piece of elegantly got-up and highly aromatic pasteboard.

When the servant came with the invitation two days later, Edward returned a message that it was impossible for him to accept the invitation, because he could not leave his collection. The servant again returned, and invited him to attend the party after the exhibition had been closed for the night. He again politely refused.

The lady never returned to the exhibition ; and Edward felt that he had grievously offended her by refusing her invitation. Yet, had she known of his position at the time, her heart would have melted with pity at his sufferings. But this was of too touching and too delicate a nature to be explained to her. By that time, although Edward's doom was not altogether sealed, still he knew, humanly speaking, that his fate was inevitably fixed, and that he had no visible means of escape from his lamentable position.

We have said that when Edward opened his exhibition in Aberdeen, he expected that there would be a large influx of visitors to see the collection of objects in natural history, which he had made with so much labor and difficulty. But there was no rush whatever. The attendance was always very small. The exhibition-room was for the most part empty. Edward at first thought that he had fixed the price too high ; but he could remedy that defect. The better classes had failed him ; now he would try the working-people. He would call " the millions " to his aid. Accordingly he reduced the entrance-price to a penny.

But " the millions " never came. So far as Edward's collection was concerned, their minds seemed as hard and impenetrable as the adamantine houses in which they lived. Their hearts, he thought, were made of their native granite. Still he would make another effort. He now advertised more widely than before, thinking that extended publicity might prove successful. He had bills printed by the thousand ; he employed sandwichmen to carry them about, to distribute them in the market, in the principal thoroughfares, at the gates of the factories and principal working-places, and in every place resorted to by working-people. To accommodate them, he opened the exhibition at eight instead of ten in the morning; and kept it open until ten o'clock at night.

It was of no avail. The millions did not come. The attendance even fell off. Some days only a few pence were taken; on other days nothing. Days, weary days, went on, and still there was no success. Yet Edward had plenty of advisers. Some thought that the collection should have been exhibited near the centre of the town, where the working-classes lived. Edward was fain to think that there might be something in this. He found a large room which he thought would answer the purpose; but he was required to pay the rent beforehand, and to give security for ten pounds. This was entirely out of the question, for he could not give security for "ten bawbees." One person, who had been a showman, advised him to have immense placards outside, and to have a band of music to attract the people. He must have show and hubbub. "That was the thing that attracted folk; whereas his exhibition was all in the inside." But Edward would not have any of such attractions.

In short, the exhibition was fast approaching its end. The rent of the shop had to be paid, and he had no money to pay it. His wife and family had to be maintained, and he had no means of maintaining them. All that he took at the door was required to pay the cost of the bills and advertisements. By the end of the third week he was deep in debt. Though he had been earning small wages, he had never before been in debt. To think of being in debt was in itself an agony. What was he to do? He was sinking deeper and deeper, with no prospect of deliverance.

By the Friday of the fourth week he had altogether lost hope. He had taken nothing in the shape of money that day. His exhibition was entirely deserted. He sunk into the lowest state of despondency. About three o'clock he received a letter from his master at Banff, telling him that if he did not return immediately to his work, he would be under the necessity of giving his employment to another. "Return immediately!" That was impossible. What was he to do with his collection? How was he to defray his debt?

It is scarcely to be wondered at, if, under these deplorable circumstances, despair—despair of the worst description—should have got the better, at least for a time, of his over-taxed and oversensitive brain. He was in a strange place—a place which had once known him, but knew him no more. His wife and his five children were altogether dependent upon him, though they were at present living with his aged and infirm parents. He was deep in debt, for which, if not liquidated, his collection would be seized—a collection, rather than part with which he would have sacrificed his life. At the same time, the loss of work, starvation, and ruin stared him in the face. Is it surprising that, thus situated, despair should for a time have got the mastery over his better and sounder judgment?

The afternoon was far advanced. His dinner, which had been brought to him an hour before, still lay untasted. He was pacing up and down the apartment, pondering over his miserable position, when his father entered. Edward was looking so agitated that the old man inquired what ailed him? He said he was going out, and went toward the door, fearing lest his wife or any of his children might appear. His father stepped between him and the door, remonstrating with him, and saying that he was not fit to go out in such a state. But a woman entering attracted his father's attention, and Edward was thus allowed to slip away unobserved.

Edward rushed down Union Street, on his way to the sands. At first he thought of going to the Dee at the Craiglug; but he bethought him that it would be better to go to the sea-shore, where it might be thought his death was accidental. From the time of his leaving the shop in Union Street until about four hours after, when he recovered his senses, his memory remained almost a complete blank. He had a vague idea of crossing the links, and seeing some soldiers at the foot of the Broadhill. But beyond that he remembered next to nothing. Unlike a dream, of which one remembers some confused ideas, this blank in his mental life was never filled up, and the purpose for which he wandered along the sands left little further impression upon his memory. He remembered, however, the following circumstances:

He had thrown off his hat, coat, and waistcoat before rushing into the sea, when a flock of sanderlings lighted upon the sands near him. They attracted his attention. They were running to and fro, some piping their low, shrill whistle, while others were probing the wet sand with their bills as the waves receded. But among them was another bird, larger and darker, and apparently of different habits from the others. Desirous of knowing something of the nature of this bird, he approached the sanderlings. They rose and flew away. He followed them. They lighted again, and again he observed the birds as before. Away they went, and he after them. At length he was stopped at Don mouth. When he recovered his consciousness, he was watching the flock of birds flying away to the farther side of the river. He had forgotten all his miseries in his intense love of nature. His ruling passion saved him.

How long the chase lasted he never could tell. It must have occupied him more than an hour. He found himself divested of his hat, coat, and vest; and he went back to look for them. He had no further desire to carry out the purpose for which he had descended to the sea. His only thought was about the strange bird among the sanderlings: " What could it be?" Perhaps the bird had been his Providence. He tried to think so.

In the mean time he was very cold. He found his coat, vest, and hat a long way down the beach. On his return, he found that he had been followed by some people, who

MOUTH OF THE DON.

were watching him. When he returned, they followed him until he reached his clothes; and when they saw him dressed and ready to depart, they disappeared. Not wishing to cross the links again that night, he turned and went up Don side to the new bridge, and took the road from thence into the town.

It was late before he got home. Being still very much depressed, and feeling very unwell, he went almost immediately to bed, thinking that he might be able to hide his grief yet a little longer from those who were near and dear to him—dearer to him now than ever. But, alas! the ordeal he had passed through during the day had been most dreadful, and he was racked by conflicting and torturing thoughts during the whole of his sleepless night.

Morning, anxiously wished-for morning, came at last. Although still feverish from excitement, and very unsettled in his mind, he got up, dressed, and went down to the sea-shore a little after daylight, eagerly searching for the strange bird of the preceding evening. But, although he walked several times along the sands, from the bathing-machines to the mouth of the Don, he never saw it. He saw its companions, the sanderlings; but the providential bird had gone. So far as Edward knew, he never saw the like of that bird again.

Although chagrined at his disappointment, he felt himself, on the whole, more refreshed and settled in his mind than when he left home. After breakfast—the first food he had taken since the previous morning—he went to Union Street to open his exhibition. As he was not disturbed by visitors, he had plenty of time for reflection. He had now to consider how he could honorably extricate himself from the trap into which he had so unwittingly and so unfortunately fallen.

The only way which presented itself was by making a terrible sacrifice—namely, by selling the whole of his collection. It took him many long and bitter heart-pangs before he could arrive at this conclusion. But force, stern force, prevailed over all other considerations. He must, so far as he could, get honorably out of debt, although not a farthing of balance might remain. Yes: his eight years' collection of birds and natural objects must go, so that he might stand upright before the world. Accordingly, an advertisement appeared in the newspapers offering the collection for sale.

After the announcement appeared, several gentlemen called and told him that he was quite wrong in offering his collection for sale. He had several letters from Banff to the same effect. Some of his correspondents there offered their suggestions and advice. They said that as the collection had been made in Banffshire, it properly belonged to Banffshire; and that it would be an everlasting slur upon the county if it were allowed to go elsewhere. One gentleman of influence requested Edward to delay the sale for a few days, in order that he might be enabled to obtain subscriptions, so as to secure the collection for Banff. Twenty pounds could easily be collected in Banff for such a purpose. If the subscribers did not themselves buy it, there was a scientific society in Banff that would certainly buy it, to form the nucleus of a collection of Banffshire fauna.

Edward accordingly postponed the sale for some days. He had great faith in his correspondent, who was himself a member of the society in question. The gentleman had considerable influence in the district, and would doubtless do what he could to raise the requisite money to purchase the collection. But, alas, how futile are promises! Words! mere words! Days passed, and no further communications arrived. Edward was now pressed for his debts, and he could no longer postpone the sale of the collection. The spark of hope that had been kindled in his breast died out. All hope of salvation from any quarter had fled. He must meet his difficulties as he best could. It was now the middle of the sixth week, and his expenses were increasing daily.   Accordingly, he accepted the offer of twenty pounds and ten shillings for the whole of his collection!

It was a bitter pang to part with it; but the thing must be done. Howling was of no use. Edward was even glad to get that paltry sum, in order to be at last set free. The gentleman (Mr. Grant) who bought the collection wished it for his boy, who had a taste for natural history. The specimens were removed to his house at Ferryhill. They were afterward packed up and sent to his place in St. Nicholas Street, where they were stored up in some damp

THE SHORE AT ABERDEEN.

and unsuitable room; and, being otherwise neglected, it is believed that the whole collection eventually went to ruin.

Perhaps Edward might have got more money for his collection if he had broken it up and offered it in lots. Professor Dickie was willing to buy a number of his specimens, and to pay a good price for them; but this would have involved a considerable loss of time, and also a considerable increase of expense. He was therefore under the necessity of disposing of the whole at once.

"Whatever," says Edward, "may have been the real cause of my ruin and want of success, I must say that, although I was not supported and encouraged, I had no real claim upon the inhabitants of Aberdeen. I certainly do owe many of them — particularly those of the upper and middle classes of society—a deep debt of gratitude for their courteous attention and their offered hospitality. Although circumstances did not allow me to avail myself of their kindness, I have never forgotten the unfeigned favors which they proffered me. I know that some of them were deeply offended at my refusing their invitations ; but had they known of my deplorable position at the time, I feel certain that their feeling of offense would have given place to the deeper and softer feeling of pity for the unfortunate."

CHAPTER X.

EDWARD had left Banff on the 31st of July, 1846, full of hope; after six weeks, he returned to it full of despair. He had gone to Aberdeen with his collection, accompanied by his wife and family; he returned from it alone and on foot, without a single specimen of his collection, and without a penny in his pocket that he could call his own. He felt ruined, disappointed, beggared—his aims and hopes in life blasted. He was under the necessity of leaving his wife and children at Aberdeen; for they could not travel fifty miles to Banff on foot.

Edward felt terribly crushed on re-entering his desolate home. A strange-like heaviness of mind came over him. The place was drear and lonesome. It was so different from what it had once been. It was no longer enlivened by the prattle of his children, or the pleasant looks of his wife. There was neither fire, nor food, nor money. The walls, which only a few weeks before had been covered with his treasures—the results of the hard labor of years— were bare and destitute. The house was desolation itself.

After remaining there for a short time, a neighbor came in and asked Edward to come to his house and get some food. He most gladly assented to the proposal. He afterward went to see his master, and arranged with him as to the re-commencement of his work. This was easily accomplished, as Edward was considered a Don at his trade.*

---

* Master shoe-makers, in those days, employed Men's men (that is, men who made men's shoes), Women's men, Boot men, and Pump

After this had been settled, he went to pay a short visit to a friend at Gardenstown, until his wife and family had returned from Aberdeen. Edward could not bear to remain in his house until they had come back: nor could he yet pay for their journey. But the carrier, who had taken the collection and the family to Aberdeen, cheerfully consented to bring the latter back free.

It was during this interval that Edward lived for a few days with his friend, Mr. Gordon, of Gardenstown. The place had long been one of Edward's favorite haunts. He was able, in a sort of way, to enjoy the coast scenery, to see the busy fishermen going out to sea in the evenings, and to listen to the noisy clamor of the sea-fowl at Gamrie Mohr.

When Edward knew that his wife and family had reached Banff, he returned home, and was joyfully met by his wife and bairns. Home had already begun to look more homely. There was a fire to sit down beside, and a family circle to converse with. Care, despondency, and despair had already, to a certain extent, been cast aside. There would yet be peace and plenty about the fireside. Edward threw off the showman's garb, and donned that of the hard-working sutor.* Next morning he was busy at his trade, sewing, hammering, and "skelping away at the leather."

During the ensuing autumn and winter he passed his time at his ordinary daily work. He refrained from going out at night. He had parted with all his objects in natural history, and he did nothing, as yet, to replace them. But his mind had been at work all the while. As spring advanced, he found it impossible to check his ruling pas-

---

men, according to the branch they worked at. Those who excelled in proficiency were called Dons. Edward was a Don Pump man. Few excelled him at that part of the business. It was for this reason that his master objected to his leaving the shop so often on his natural-history excursions, as he could find no one else to do this part of the work so well.

* *Sutor*, shoe-maker.

sion. His day's work done, he again started with his gun
on his shoulder, his insect-boxes and appendages slung
round his back, his plant-case by his side, and a host of pill-
boxes, small bottles, and such-like, packed in his pockets.
Away he went, with heart as light as a feather, to search,
as long as light remained, for tenants of the woods, the
fields, and the sea-shore.

When daylight faded into darkness, he would sit down,
as usual, for a nap—it did not matter where—by the side
of a rock, on a sand-bank, in a hole in the ground, in a dry
ditch, under the cover of a bush, behind a dike, in a ruined
castle, or by the side of a tree : it was all the same to him.
There he lay until the first peep of morning appeared,
when he started up and was at work again. He continued,
until he thought he had just sufficient time left to get to
his workshop by the appointed hour.

His zeal was more than renewed. It was redoubled.
He proceeded with even greater perseverance than before.
His few friends warned him in vain. They thought he
might spend his energies to some better purpose. If their
advice staggered him, it was only for an instant. "One
look," he says, "at my cobbler's stool dispelled every consideration. My wish was, at some time or other, to wrench
myself free from my trade."

He adopted the self-same plan that he had formerly employed. As soon as his day's work was over, he started on
his nightly expedition. During five months of the year he
slept out—excepting on Saturday and Sunday nights, or
when the weather was stormy. To his former equipment
he added a small trowel for digging up plants and grubs,
and a hammer for splitting fossils or chipping off parts of
any rock that he might wish to preserve.

At first he used chip-boxes, to carry the insects which he
collected during his tours ; but he found them such a worry
that he was obliged to use something else. He once
bought so many chip-boxes from a druggist, that he refused

to sell him any more until his stock had been replenished. Edward carried in them slugs, caterpillars, snails, worms, spiders, shells, various sorts of insects, eggs of small birds, and every other little knickknack that he wished to preserve. Here is his description of his hunting paraphernalia :

"My coat had eight pockets, four outside and four inside. The two lower inside ones were 'meal - pocks' for size. My waistcoat, too, had four rather big receptacles : the term 'waistcoat-pockets' could scarcely describe them. Besides these, I had a number of bags or wallets hung over my shoulders, or tied round my middle, or under my coat, according to their intended uses. I had also several queer-looking things which I carried in my hands, and called 'accessories;' for there is no other specific name for the articles. Nevertheless, all had their quota of chip - boxes, except my butterfly and moth case, and my plant - book. These were generally kept sacred for their respective purposes."

On one occasion Edward went out for a three days' ramble among the Balloch hills, between Keith and Huntly, about twenty miles south-west of Banff. The purport of his journey was to collect butterflies, moths, and various objects. He had not his gun with him, but he had many more chip - boxes than usual. A friend of his had often urged him to bring him a lot of ants for some birds, and Edward determined to satisfy him. He had been very successful in his search, and had also filled many boxes for his friend.

On the afternoon of the third day, while he was busily engaged on a wild, wide, and desolate moor, he was startled by a sudden flash of lightning. Had he been attending to the weather instead of to his own pursuits, he might have seen the brooding clouds wending their way toward him from the south. He might then have found some convenient shelter from the impending storm. But after the first flash of lightning, it broke upon him almost at once. He

had scarcely got his things put in order, and the ant-boxes
deposited in his coat-pocket, when down came the deluge.
None but those who have been under the influence of hill-
rains can have any idea of their tremendous force. It is
like the downpour of a cataract. The rain falls in sheets,
in waves, almost solid. Nothing but the stiffest weather-
proof can keep the water out.

Edward's first thought was shelter! But where could he
find it? Not a house was to be seen; not a wall, not a tree,
not a bush. He could not find even a hole in a sand-bank.
There was nothing that he could see around him but a
dreary, bleak, wide-spread moor. Nevertheless, he set off,
running as fast as he could, in the hope of at length reaching some friendly haven. After having run a long time
amidst thunder and lightning, through water, moss, and
heather, he stopped for a moment to consider where he
was running. There was still no sign of a house, or hut,
or shealing. The place where he stood was crossed by numerous paths, but he knew just as much of the one path as
he did about the other. The country round him was one
wide expanse of moor-land. There was nothing before him
but moor, moor, moor! He saw no object that could serve
to guide him. He merely saw the outlines of the nearest
hills faintly visible through the watery haze; but he did
not recognize them. He began to feel himself lost on a
lonesome moor.

He was now at his wits' end. Having been for some
time without food, he was becoming faint. And yet he
could not remain where he was. He again began to run.
The sky was now almost as black as night, and the sheets
of rain were falling as heavily as before. Only the vivid
flashes of lightning enabled him to trace the direction in
which he was going. He plunged into bog after bog, ex-
tricated himself, and then ran for life. Sometimes he came
to a likely track and followed it; but it led to nothing—
only to a succession of tracks which led off in various di-

rections across the moor.   At last he ran straight forward, without paying any regard to tracks.   By continuing in this course he eventually came to a road—a gladsome sight, because it must lead to some dwelling or other.   But which way should he go?   He knew nothing of the direction of the road, for he had altogether lost his reckoning, and every landmark was invisible.

After a few moments' consideration, he bethought him of the direction in which Huntly might possibly lie; and as that town was his intended destination, he faced about, as he thought, in that direction, and commenced running again at full speed.   After having run for about a mile, he came in sight of his destined haven—a house.   It stood on a slight elevation, with its back to the road, and was surrounded by a turf-and-stone wall.   Collecting his remaining strength, he ran up the slope, cleared the dike at a bound, and rushed into the house without further ceremony.

He found two little maidens inside, who looked rather frightened at his sudden appearance.   And no wonder! He must have looked more like a lunatic than a naturalist. Being completely exhausted, he threw himself right down on a seat without speaking a single word.   When he recovered his breath, he asked pardon of the little damsels for running in so unceremoniously; "he had been overtaken by the storm."   He asked them if he might be allowed to rest there until the storm ceased?

"I dinna ken," said one of the girls; "oor mither's nae in.   She's oot breakin' sticks; but," she added, "I dare say ye may."

There was a good fire of sods and peats on the floor. Edward went toward it, with his dripping clothes, to dry himself.   He now began to look at his belongings.   He first took off his hat, which was the hiding-place for many of his treasures.   He found that the bundles of rare moss which he had picked up on the moor, and also the flies which he had pinned into the crown of his hat, were all right. His hat was usually two-storied; we wish we could have given a section of it. The lower part contained his head, and the other, above it, separated by a thin piece of board, contained mosses, birds' eggs, butterflies, insects, and such-like.

He next proceeded to take off some of his wallets; but, just as he had begun to remove them, he heard the girls behind him twittering and giggling. Turning round, he saw one of them pointing to his back, and trying to suppress her mirth. He could not imagine the reason. Another and yet another stifled laugh! On his looking round again, they rushed out of the room; and then he heard them exploding with laughter. The cause of their merriment was this: the storm of rain had soaked Edward to the skin. Every pocket and wallet was full of chip-boxes and water. The glue of the boxes had melted; the ants, worms, slugs, spiders, caterpillars, and such-like, had all escaped, and were mixed up in a confused mass. They shortly began to creep out of the innumerable pockets in which they had been contained. It was because the girls had seen the mixture of half-drowned spiders, beetles, ants, and caterpillars creeping up the strange man's back, that they rushed from the place, and laughed their full out-of-doors.

Edward was now left to himself. The girls had doubtless gone to fetch their mother. He began to think of beating a retreat, as he seemed to have been the cause, in some way, of the girls leaving the house. But at that moment a woman of prodigious size and attitude appeared at the threshold. She stood stock-still, and looked at the stranger furiously. He addressed her, but she gave no reply. He addressed her again, louder; but she was still silent. He looked at her again. In one hand she grasped a most formidable-looking axe, while in the other she held what looked like the half of a young tree. She was tall,

8*

stout, and remarkably muscular; her hair was of a carroty-red color, and thickly matted together; her dress was scanty; she was bare-legged, but wore a pair of old unlaced boots, such as are usually worn by plow-men. With her axe in one hand and her pole in the other — with her clenched teeth and fierce aspect—Edward could entertain no other idea of her than that she was mad, and that her intention was to brain him with her axe! He could not rush past her — her space filled the door-way. He could not over-power her, for she was much more powerful than he was. His suspense was dreadful.

At last she moved one step forward; then another, until Edward thought he might plunge past her and escape. But no; she opened her lips and spoke, or rather yelled, "Man, fat the sorra brocht ye in here, an' you in siccan a mess? Gang oot o' my hoose, I tell ye, this varra minit! Gang oot!" This appeal brought Edward to himself again. He apologized to her for entering her house, and begged her to let him remain until the rain had ceased. "Not a minit!" was the sharp rejoinder; "ye'll pit my hoose afloat. Be-sides yer vermin, ye'll pit's a' in a hobble if ye dinna gang oot!"

He protested that he had nothing to do with vermin; but as he spoke he lifted up his hand to wipe something off his cheek. It was a hairy oobit! He was in a moment alive to the woman's expostulations. On looking to his clothes, he found that he was a moving mass of insect life. He cleared the room in a bound, regardless of the woman's axe and cudgel. He went into an old shed, threw off his coat and waistcoat, and found them a mass of creeping things. On searching his pockets, he found that all the chip-boxes had given way, and that the whole of the collec-tion which he had made during the last three days was lost. He might have collected the insects from his clothing, but he had nothing to put them in. He now found that he was the lunatic, and not the woman. Before he departed, he apologized to her for the trouble he had caused her, and then he departed homeward—a sadder if not a wiser man.

After this adventure he never again resorted to *chip*-boxes. He used little bottles for holding beetles and various insects. He had also a light, flat box, about nine inches square, for containing the more fragile portion of the insect tribe, such as butterflies and moths. Before he pinned them down, he gave them a drop of chloroform to put them to sleep, and prevent them destroying their beautiful plumage. When he met these tender creatures reposing on a flower, he would always, if possible, drop a little chloroform upon them, and thus end their struggles. Then he boxed them. By this means he secured many splendid specimens,

His hat was also an excellent insect-box, and a convenient receptacle for many things. He had a false crown put in the upper part of it, well stored with pins. And even when he went out to walk with his wife and children, he would occupy part of his time in looking for and storing up moths and butterflies, so that not an opportunity nor a moment's time was lost.

He carried his caterpillars in a tin box, with several compartments; and his snails in a similar box of smaller dimensions. His eggs, after being emptied, were put into a sort of canister; and being well packed with cotton wool, they very seldom broke, although he carried them about with him for days together.

Whenever he shot a bird or animal, his first business was to fill up the mouth and nostrils with cotton wadding, and then to search for the wounds and fill them up. By this means he always got his specimens home clean. This he found to be indispensably necessary with sea-birds, if he wished to bring them home unsoiled.

Being unable to purchase presses for his plants, he used heavy flat stones, and boxes filled with gravel and dry sand.

These answered very well, and were all the presses he ever had.

After his first exhibition at Banff, Edward became a general referee as to all natural and unnatural objects found in the district. People of all sorts brought " things " to him, to ascertain what they were. Sometimes they were rare objects, sometimes they were monstrosities. His decision did not always satisfy the inquirers; and then they sent the objects to some other person, who, they thought, knew better. They always found, however, that Edward had been right in his decisions. When he knew with certainty, he gave his opinion. When he did not know the object, he said he could not give an opinion. And this was, doubtless, the best course to adopt.

Several of his friends told him that he ought to extend his investigations into Aberdeen, and even into Elgin. They did not offer to help him, but they advised him to go. He had now eight of a family, and his wages, allowing for extra work, only amounted to about fifteen or sixteen shillings a week. To range the counties of Aberdeen, Banff, and Elgin, in search of objects in natural history, while he was maintaining his family on such slender wages, was therefore an altogether impossible task.

His wife was his best helper. She bound all his upper leathers, and also the upper leathers of several of the other workmen. The wages paid to her were distinct from the wages paid to Edward. Very often, instead of spending her earnings on clothes or bringing the money home, she would buy for her husband bottles for his insects, wood for his bird-cases, or powder and shot for his gun. None of his advising friends ever helped him in this way.

And yet Edward did extend his investigations farther into Banffshire, and even into Aberdeenshire. With that view he obtained a certificate, drawn up by the clerk of the peace, and signed by sixteen justices of the peace, enabling him to go over the country with his gun, in search of birds and other things. He always carried this certificate with him; and when he presented it to a gamekeeper, he was allowed to go wherever he pleased. The certificate was as follows:

"These are to certify that the bearer, Thomas Edward, shoe-maker, who is in height about five feet six inches, has dark eyes and hair, much pock-pitted, round-shouldered, and about thirty-five years of age—is, in addition to his other calling, engaged in collecting and preserving various objects of Natural History, particularly those objects which relate to Ornithology (Birds), Oalogy (Eggs), Entomology (Insects), Helminthology (Worms, etc.), and Conchology (Shells);—That, for the purpose of procuring Ornithological Specimens, he is under the necessity of using a Gun, but in doing so, We, the undersigned, have never heard of a single case of poaching being brought against him; and, as far as we know, he is not in the habit of killing Game of any sort, nor of destroying property of any description, which, were he in the practice of so doing, being so frequently out with his Gun, he could not, we think, have escaped public notice so long—having resided in this town for a period of sixteen years, during which time he has borne an unimpeachable character.

["James Duff, J.P., etc, etc.]

"Banff, *March*, 1850."

Edward was now in the prime of life, yet he was drawing very heavily upon his constitutional powers. Sleeping out-of-doors nightly, whether the weather was fair or foul, subjected him to many attacks of cold and rheumatism. Yet he had no sooner recovered than he was out again at his nightly work. He was still as wild a birdnester as he had ever been in his youth. He would go to any distance or to any place to find a bird or a bird's-nest that was new to him. He would run up a tree like a squirrel, and come down again with the birds or the nest.

He would also walk or climb up a precipice when a nest was to be had. Of course, he had many falls. But what of that, if the object was gained? The most dangerous fall that he ever had was at Tarlair. The circumstance may be described, as a specimen of the dangers which Edward ran in his pursuit of natural history. The author went to see the place, and was afraid to look down into the chasm among the rocks into which the naturalist had fallen.

The little valley of Tarlair is about three miles east of Banff: it is not far from Macduff. The road to Tarlair is along the bare bluff coast; and when you reach the top of a lofty point, you see beneath you a green grassy valley indenting the rocks. At the inner end of the valley is a little well - house, where inland people come during summertime, to drink the mineral waters.*　Eastward of Tarlair the rocky cliffs ascend higher and higher—rising to their loftiest height in the almost perpendicular cliff of Gamrie Mohr.

The place at which Edward met with his accident is at the projecting point of the valley above mentioned, where the rocks begin to ascend. Not far from the mouth of the valley there is, in the face of the rock, a very large, high, and wide-mouthed cave or chasm, fronting the sea. The back wall of the cave, as well as the sides, contain a number of strange-like openings, and fantastical projections, one of which is called "the pulpit." Edward often sat in the cave, and also slept in it; but he never preached in it, though he several times brought down sea-gulls and hoodie-crows with his gun. The bottom of the cave is thickly covered with stones and bowlders thrown in by the sea, which, in storms, dashes with great fury into its innermost recesses.

In the roof, and near the front of the cave, a few martins build their nests every season. As Edward was coming home one morning from his night's work, and while he was walking under the cliff, intending to come out at Tar-

---

* This is the place so well described in "Johnny Gibb of Gushetneuk." "There was a little house, too, at the foot of the north bank, where a drop of whisky could be got somehow in cases of emergency, as when the patient got 'hoven' with the liberal libations of salt-water previously swallowed, or when the taste lay strongly in that direction; but this was no part of the recognized regimen."

TARLAIR—VIEW OF NORTH COAST OF BANFFSHIRE.

lair, he observed one of the martins flying out of the cave, and shot it. Instead of dropping at his feet, it fell on the top of the cliff. How was he to get at the bird? He might have gone round a considerable way, and thus reached the top of the rock; but this would have involved the loss of considerable time, and he was anxious to get home to his work.

There was another way of getting at the bird, and that was by scrambling directly up the face of the cliff. He determined on adopting the latter course. Usually, when ascending rocks, he used to tie his gun to his back, as both hands were required to grip and clutch the edges of the rock above him. But on this occasion, not wishing to lose further time by buckling on his gun, he determined, dangerous though it was, to ascend the precipice gun in hand. By grasping the stones above him with his hands and nails, and putting the tips of his shoes into the crevices of the rocks, or sometimes only on to a little tuft of grass, he contrived to haul himself up. He managed very well until he reached about the middle of the ascent, where a bend occurs in the rocks. There he became fixed. To come down, unless headlong, was impossible; and to go up seemed equally impracticable. In that case he would have had to drop his gun, and smash it to bits on the rocks below. This he could not afford to do. Still, he could not stay there. With bated breath and steady eye, he clutched a little projection of rock standing out far above him. He caught it, clambered a little way up, then secured a firmer footing, and at last reached the summit in safety.

His troubles were not over. They were only beginning. He looked about for the bird. It lay only a few yards from him. It was on the edge of the cliff, and seemed apparently dead. On stooping to pick it up, it fluttered, raised one of its wings, and went over the precipice. In his eagerness to catch it, or perhaps from the excited state in which he was from mounting the cliff, Edward grasped at the bird, missed it, lost his footing on the smooth rock, and fell over the precipice. His gun fell out of his hand and lodged across two rocks jutting out from the beach below. Edward fell upon his gun and smashed it to pieces; but it broke the force of the blow, and probably saved his life. A fall of at least forty feet on rocks and stones would certainly have killed most men, or at least broken many of their bones. When afterward endeavoring to recall his feelings on the occasion, Edward said, "I remember that on losing my balance my gun slipped from my hand, and I uttered the exclamation, 'Oh God!' Then my breath seemed to be cut by a strong wind which made me compress my lips. I shut my eyes, and felt a strange-like sensation of a rushing sound in my ears; and then of coming, suddenly and violently, with a tremendous thud, upon the stony rock."

His breath was gone, and it was long before he could recover it. He was for a time utterly senseless. On slightly recovering consciousness, he thought he was under the influence of a nightmare. He seemed to be in bed, and saw before him hideous faces, grinning and grimacing, like so many demons. He tried to shake them off, to shut them out. But no! the monsters were still there in all their hideousness, and still he was utterly helpless.

At length two plow-men, who had been working in the adjoining field, and seen Edward fall over the cliff, came forward to its edge, and looked down upon him wedged among the rocks. "Ye're no dead yet, are ye?" said one of the men. Edward was unable to make any answer. "Fa is't?" said the other man. "Ou! it's that feel chiel* that's aye gaun aboot wi' his gun and his wallets!" The men looked down again in consternation, with eyes that seemed about to leap from their sockets. Edward at length began to feel about him. He felt himself wedged in as in a vise, between

---

* *Feel chiel,* foolish fellow.

two long and oval pieces of rock, and quite unable to set himself free. The two countrymen went round by the Tarlair pathway, in order to get Edward out of his fixture. It seemed to him an age before they arrived.

They at first took him by the shoulder and tried to lift him out; but this was so painful to him that at last they desisted. They then tried to remove one of the rocks between which he lay clasped : this also proved fruitless. Edward then observed that the other rock, which they had not yet tried to remove, consisted of a loose shale. It had either dropped from the cliff, or been tossed inshore by the sea. Edward desired them to try and move it a little; but their joint efforts proved unavailing. Many attempts were made to no purpose. A stout fisherman then appeared on the scene. He put his shoulder to the rock, and the block was at last moved sufficiently far so as to enable Edward to be dragged out of the vise.

He sat down and felt himself all over. His left shoulder and left side were extremely sore. The back of his head was also very painful. But he was thankful to find that neither his arms nor his legs were broken. He was not so sure about his left ribs. He was very much bruised and cut on that side. One of the splinters of the gun-stock was found sticking through his coat. An old copper powder-flask, which he had in his left pocket, was as flat as a flounder : all its contents were dashed out.

Edward entreated the men to help him to get to the cave. He thought that, if left there for a time, he would soon recover. He got upon his feet with difficulty, and found that his spine had been hurt. With the help of two of the men, he was at last able to walk very slowly to the cave. They urged him to allow them to carry him to the cottage near the mineral well. But he preferred to rest in the cave. They prepared a bed of sea-weed for him, on which he lay down. His protectors then left him, and, spite of his pain, he fell asleep. He must have slept some time, for he was awakened by the murmuring of the sea, which was fast approaching the cave.

Finding that his sickly feeling had left him, and that he was on the whole much better, although his left side and shoulder were still very painful, he gathered himself together and rose to his feet. He staggered about a little at first; but he was at last able to return in search of his gun. He found it in a woful plight. The stock was broken to bits, and the barrel and lock were laid in the hollow. He gathered up the fragments of the companion of his travels for so many years; and, divesting himself of the heaviest of his wallets, he left them in a corner of the cave. Then, keeping hold of the rocks, he contrived to reach the inner side of the Tarlair valley. From thence he had a weary walk to Banff. He took many rests by the way, and at length reached home in the afternoon, sore, sick, and weary, and went to bed. His wounds were then looked to. It was found that none of his ribs were broken, and that he had only sustained some severe contusions. It was, however, nearly a fortnight before he could do any work. A month elapsed before he could walk to Tarlair for the wallets and remains of his gun, which he had left in the hollow of the cave.

To support his family during his illness, he was forced to sell a considerable portion of the collection which he had made during the last few years. Although it was not so large as that which he had exhibited at Aberdeen, it contained many rarer birds, insects, crustacea, zoophytes, and plants; and it was, on the whole, much better got up. He sold about one hundred cases at this time, consisting chiefly of preserved birds, insects, and eggs. He also sold about three hundred plants, and more than two hundred zoophytes, besides about one hundred minerals or fossils. Among the plants were a great number unnamed. He had as yet no botanical books, and the friends to whom he applied could not supply the names. They considered them very rare, if not new and unnamed.

It was a great blow to him to sell a portion of his second collection. But he had no help for it. It was his only savings-bank. When other means failed him, he could only rely upon it. He had no friends in his neighborhood to help him. His specimens went to many places, far and near. A considerable portion of them went to Haslar, near Southampton, where one of the hospital surgeons was making a collection of objects in natural history.

CHAPTER XI.

BEGINS TO PUBLISH HIS OBSERVATIONS.

SHORTLY after Edward's return from Aberdeen, he made the acquaintance of the Rev. James Smith, of the manse of Monquhitter, about eight miles south-east of Banff. Mr. Smith had some works on natural history, which he lent to Edward; and they enabled him to ascertain the names of some of the birds which he discovered in the neighborhood.

One day, while walking along the sea-coast, Edward shot a bridled guillemot (*Uria lachrymans*), a bird not before known to frequent the district. When he informed Mr. Smith of the circumstance, the reverend gentleman thus wrote to him: "The discovery of the bridled guillemot at Gamrie is very interesting, and affords another confirmation of the remark that there are many things yet to be found out, almost at our doors, by those who have a relish for the works of nature, and who will make a good use of the faculties which the Almighty has bestowed upon them. In my own case, I have now almost *no* opportunity in my power for prosecuting researches in natural history out-of-doors; and, even if I had, there is so little sympathy for any proceedings of this nature, that I should to a certainty be regarded by almost all my parishioners as half-mad, or at least as childish, and neglecting my more serious duties. Still, I always feel a strong interest in the subject, and in any discovery which is made in regard to it."

As Edward had no narrow-minded parishioners to encounter, he went on with his researches. Mr. Smith strongly encouraged him to persevere. He also advised him to note down the facts which came under his notice, and to publish the results of his observations. This surprised Edward. "Why," said he, "I can not write for the publishers." "You must learn to write," said Mr. Smith; "and in order to write correctly you must study grammar."

He importuned Edward so much, that at last he said he "had no use for grammar." "You can not write without it," said Mr. Smith. "But," returned Edward, "I have no intention of writing." "You *must* write," said Mr. Smith. "You must write down all that you learn respecting the objects you are collecting. It is a duty that you owe to society, and it will be very selfish on your part if you do not publish the results of your observations."

After about half an hour's arguing, Edward asked, "How long do you think it would take me to learn grammar?" "Well," said Mr. Smith, "I do not think you would take very long to learn it. But," he added, "you will require to relinquish your outdoor pursuits during that time." "If that be the case, Mr. Smith, I am afraid that I can not become a pupil. But if I have any time left after I have done with nature, then perhaps I may begin to study grammar; but not till then."

Mr. Smith's advice, however, was not without its good results. Edward *did* begin to note down his observations about natural objects, and he published them from time to time in the local paper, the *Banffshire Journal.* When the present author asked for a sight of the articles, Edward replied, "I think I could supply you with scraps of a good number, although, on looking over my stock, I find that a great many have disappeared. My family and friends have dealt very freely with them. In fact, they were found good for 'kinlin'.'* The most of what I wrote in the local papers is lost, forever lost."

---

* Kindling fires.

Among the articles which he was able to collect, we find descriptions of rare moths, rare birds, and rare fishes. Perhaps one of the first articles which he published was a description of a " death's-head moth " found in the parish of Ruthven — one of the most wonderful, as it is one of the most extraordinary, of insects.

" In its caterpillar state," says Edward, " it has the power of making a pretty loud snapping-like noise, which has been compared by some to a series of electric sparks. The chrysalis squeaks, but more particularly when about to change; and as to the perfect insect itself, it is gifted with a voice which it has the power of modulating at pleasure, being sometimes of a plaintive nature, then mournful, then like the moaning of a child, then again like the squeaking of a mouse. This, together with the fact that it carries on a portion of its back—that part called the thorax—an impression of the front view of a human skull (hence its name of death's-head), has made it an object of the greatest terror and dislike among the ignorant and superstitious. It is looked upon, not as the handiwork of the Almighty, but as the agent of evil spirits. The very shining of its large bright eyes, which sparkle like diamonds, is believed to represent the fiery element from which it is supposed to have sprung. On one occasion these insects appeared in great abundance in various districts of Bretagne, and produced great trepidation among the inhabitants, who considered them to be the forerunners, and even the causes, of epidemic diseases and other calamities. In the Isle of France it is believed that any down or dust from their wings falling on the eyes causes immediate blindness. All this is, of course, merely the result of superstitious prejudice.

" The death's-head is said to be the largest moth we have, and is, in fact, the largest found inhabiting Europe, save the peacock moth. Be this as it may, it is a very large insect, measuring from five to six inches across the wings, and having a body proportionately long and thick. The caterpillar, which is smooth, and of a greenish yellow, with minute black dots all over, and with seven or eight bluish stripes on the sides, having a horn above the tail, is likewise very large, being, when full grown, about six inches long. It feeds on the potato, the deadly-nightshade, the jasmine, and the *Lycium barbarum*, and other plants of as dissimilar a nature."

In another article he mentioned the herald moth (*Scaliopteryx libatrix*), a specimen of which was presented to him by Mrs. G. Bannerman. He describes this beautiful insect as occurring in great profusion in some of the Southern parts of England, but as very rare in the North. It is called the "herald" moth, because it is said to indicate the approach of winter.

The peacock butterfly (*Papilio Io*) was caught in Duff House garden, close to Banff. Although common in England, this butterfly is very rare in Scotland. Morris makes no mention of its ever having been seen in the North. A great flock of these butterflies passed over a part of Switzerland in 1828, when they were described as a swarm of locusts. This circumstance led Edward to insert some observations regarding that destructive insect, the *Locusta migratoria*, which passed over this country in the year 1846, the ever-memorable potato-famine year.

"Great numbers," he says, "were found in the counties of Aberdeen, Banff, and Moray. Several were also got in the sea at Aberdeen, as well as near Banff. Some of those found were very large, being two and a half inches long, and nearly as thick as one's little finger; their wings expanding to about four inches in breadth. Nine of this size were found by one individual in a turnip-field at the Stocket, near Aberdeen. They were brought to me while I was there with my first unfortunate collection. But, large though this may seem, it is nothing to others. We are told that in India there are locusts of a yard in length. I do not vouch for the fact; it is no story of mine. Pliny tells it; and from him we have it. Some found in the sea at Aberdeen were offered there for sale as 'fleein'-fish,' and no less a sum than ten shillings was sought for them. Strange sort of flying-fish this! Truly it may have been said that the entomological and ichthyological school-masters were both abroad in those days. It may, however, be remarked that something of a similar kind took place among ourselves not very long ago, so that we have little room to laugh at the Aberdonians. A person having picked up a *galerite* (a species of fossilized sea-urchin of the cretaceous system), near by our harbor, was showing it to some individuals, when one of them, no doubt puzzled, said, 'Oh! it's just something that *somebody has made.*' But to return to the locusts. Those of which we have been speaking arrived in the month of August and the beginning of September. Now, this year it would appear that something of the same kind had taken place, as numbers have been picked up in various parts of the country. Three have, at least, been found with us, viz., two near the Moss of Banff, and one at Cornhill; another at Mintlaw, Aberdeenshire. I have also one from Lerwick, where it is said they have been rather plentiful in the corn-fields; as also in the Zetland Islands, in Unst, and the rest of the bare and isolated Skerries. In some of the Western isles, I believe, they have actually proved a complete pest.

"As may be expected, there are many species of this creature, as there are of every thing else; but those here alluded to are perhaps the most redoubtable of them all, as being the most destructive, the best known from their migratorial flights, and being, as already hinted, the species that constituted one of the awful plagues of Egypt in the days of Moses. They were doubtless the same that wasted the land of Canaan, and caused such a terrible famine, of which we read in the book of Joel. A wind drove them into the sea; their dead bodies were again cast on shore in such heaps that the Hebrews were obliged to dig large pits in which to bury them. In this country, we have about twenty-five different kinds belonging to the same family, of which the foregoing is one; but, of course, they are all of small size, and therefore may be said to be comparatively harmless."

In another article Edward mentions another insect almost equally destructive. A friend of Edward at Turriff found four *saw-flies* in a piece of a fir-tree that was being cut up for fire-wood. They are called *saw-flies* "from the fact that the female possesses, posteriorly, an instrument by which she perforates, or rather saws, holes in trees, into which she drops her eggs. From this it will be seen that the larvæ are wood-feeders. In this country they are by no means numerous, and it is well that they are not, or our forests would shortly disappear; for in places where they abound, such as in Norway, they destroy hundreds of thousands of trees in a season. It is only the growing, and not the dead, wood that they attack. The young grubs, as soon as they emerge from the egg, cut their way right into the very heart of the solid timber, and there they gnaw and bore in every possible direction. By this means, the tree is either killed, or so injured, that ultimately it pines and dies. The fly itself has no English name, but is known to entomologists by the term of *Sirex juvencus.*"

In another article, Edward mentions the fact of a spider (*Aranea domestica*) having lived in one of his sealed-up cases for twelve months without food. He had before written to his reverend friend on the subject, but Mr. Smith informed him that he had no books on entomology, and could give him no information. Edward says of his spider, that, after the case had been sealed up, he saw him walking over the birds contained there, until at last he became stationary in one of the corners. "Toward noon of the second day of his incarceration he commenced operations, and by breakfast-time of the day following his web was completed. The little artisan was then observed to walk slowly and very sedately all over the newly formed fabric, seemingly with the view of ascertaining if all was secure. This done, the aperture was next examined, and with more apparent care than was bestowed upon the rest of the structure. This wonderful mechanical contrivance— which serves at least the fourfold purpose of store-house, banqueting-hall, watch-tower, and asylum in times of danger—being found all right, the artificer then took up his station within it, no doubt to await the success of the net which he had spread, and from whence, had fortune proved kind, he would boldly have rushed out to secure his struggling prey. There was, however, no fly to be caught within the case. He was the only living thing in it; and there the patient creature remained without food for the space of more than twelve months."*

The notices on natural history, which appeared from time to time in the local journal, had the effect of directing general attention to the observation of natural objects; and numerous birds, fishes, insects, caterpillars, shells, and plants were sent to Edward for examination.

In one of his notes he mentions a cinereous shearwater (*Puffinus cinereus*) found on the beach near Portsoy. This led him to give a very vivid account of the stormy petrel. Another of the specimens sent to him was a *Dy-*

---

* "The superstitious notion that a spider shut up without food for a year is transformed into a diamond has probably cost many of these insects their lives; and if the eradication of ancient prejudices be as serviceable to science as the discovery of new truths, the poor spiders may console themselves with the honor of martyrdom as justly as the innumerable frogs, who betrayed, amidst their tortures, the mystery of galvanism. In this, as in other things, people have obtained a very different and perhaps more important result than they had expected. It appears that though spiders do not turn to diamonds, they can live a long time without food. An insect of this species, inclosed in a box for this rational purpose, was found alive after the poor sufferer had been forgotten for five years."—*Ackermann's Repository*, Jan., 1815.

phalcanthus longispinus, from the fossil diggings of Gamrie. "How strange!" he says. "Here we have an animal, or perhaps I should rather say a stone, part of which had once been a creature enjoying life, but now how changed! How long is it since it lived, died, and became thus transformed? Years ago, nay ages, many ages, long anterior to the creation of man. How wonderful, and yet how true!"

Of another specimen he says:

"Here, again, is a black, pink, yellow, and brown creature, with crests and ornaments like a duchess—just, in fact, like a lady of the olden time dressed up and decorated for a ball, with her head stuck full of feathers, her ribbons flying, and fan in hand; in other words, a caterpillar of the vaporer moth, found in a garden at Buckie.

"And, lastly, though not least, a specimen of the mountain bladder fern (*Cystopteris montana*), found on Benrinnes by a gentleman from England, and sent to me as a rarity. It was only in 1836 that this fern was made known as British, having then been for the first time met with by a party of naturalists on Ben Lawers. Since that time, however, it has been found in a ravine between Glen Dochart and Glen Lochy, Perthshire. It is also found on the mountains of North Wales, on the Alps, and on the Rocky Mountains of North America."

Many rare birds were sent to him for examination, notices of which he recorded in the local paper. Thus, he obtained the little crake (*Crex pusilla*), a bird that had not before been found in the neighborhood, from a land-surveyor at Whitehills. The mountain finch (*Fringilla montifringilla*) was sent to him from Macduff, where it had been driven ashore during a recent storm. A greater shrike or butcher bird (*Lanius excubitor*)—a bird that had not before been found in Scotland—was found dead at Drummuir Castle, and sent to him for preservation. The spoonbill (*Platalia lucordia*) and bee-eater (*Merops apiaster*)—very rare birds— were also found at Boyndie.

Of the latter bird, Edward says, " This is a splendid bird, as rare as the last, if not more so.   If we except the breast, which is of a bright yellow, encircled by a black ring, and some other orange and brown scattered here and there, it may be said to be of a beautiful verdigris green.   The two middle tail feathers are about an inch longer than the others.   The bill is longish and pointed.   Though termed bee-eaters, they also feed on beetles, gnats, grasshoppers, flies, etc.   The most of these they capture on the wing, somewhat after the fashion of the goat-sucker and swallow. Although a scarce bird with us, they are common in their native countries.   In Asia Minor and the adjacent lands to the north, and in Northern Africa, they are said to be so abundant as to be seen flying about in thousands."

Among the rarer birds found in the district were the Bohemian wax-wing, or chatterer (*Bombycilla garrula*), whose native home is Bohemia — the black redstart (*Phœnicurus tithys*), a bird that had never before been met with in Scotland.   Edward, in describing this bird, says, " It is quite possible that it may have visited the country before; but, from the neglect, or rather contempt, with which natural science is regarded in this part of the country, it may have visited us, and even bred among us, unknown and unrecorded.   There is plenty of work among us for naturalists.   A great deal has yet to be learned regarding the various branches of natural science.   There is nothing better calculated for the purpose than *attentive and accurate local observers.*"

On one occasion, when out shooting on the sands west of Banff, Edward brought down a very rare bird.   It was a brown snipe (*Macroramphus griseus*), a bird well known in North America, but not in Britain.   Here is Edward's story :

" Taking a stroll the other day to the west of the town, with my gun in hand, to get the air, I crossed the sands at the links, and, looking along them, I observed a pretty

large group of my old and long‑loved favorites — birds.
Wishing, instinctively as it were, to know what they were,
I went cautiously forward to take a nearer view.   I found
that they consisted for the most part of ring‑dotterels and
dunlins, with a few golden plovers.   I was somewhat as‑
tonished at seeing the plovers, for they are by no means a
shore bird with us at this season of the year—nor, in fact,
at any time, except when driven by snow.   But there they
were, and no mistake.   Not yet satisfied, however — for I
thought I could distinguish one that did not exactly belong
to any of those already mentioned—I wished to go a little
nearer, and on doing so was glad to find my conjectures
fully confirmed; but what the stranger was I could not tell.
I saw enough, however, to convince me that it was a rare
bird.   There is no getting an easy shot at a stranger.   The
dotterels are constantly on the lookout for squalls; and
when any thing suspicious appears, they immediately rise
and fly away.   A shot, however, after a good deal of wind‑
ing and twisting, was fired, and, although at rather long
range, broke one of the stranger's legs.   This had the effect
of parting him from his companions—they flying seaward,
and he to the shingle which intervenes betwixt the sands
and the links.   Here he dropped, seemingly to rise no
more.

"Having reloaded, in case of need, I then ran, as well as
I was able, to pick him up.   I gained the place, and after
some difficulty, having passed and repassed him several
times, I at last found my bird lying stretched out at full
length among the pebbles, and to all appearance a corpse.
It was now that I ascertained with satisfaction and pride
that the great rarity I had met with was neither more nor
less than a specimen of the brown snipe, and a splendid
one it was too, being evidently an old bird.   Being almost
intoxicated with delight, I sat down, and, having taken
some cotton wadding from my pocket to wrap round the
injured leg, and stop up any other wound that he might

have received, I took him up for that purpose.   But, alas! there is many a slip between the cup and the lip.

"Away flew the bird just as I was about to lay him on my knee; he actually slipped out from among my very fingers.   I fired both barrels as soon as I could get hold of my gun, sitting though I was.   But on the bird went, whistling as he flew, despite the dangling of his shattered limb, but whether in derision at my stupidity, or exulting in his own miraculous and fortunate escape, I can not tell. Reaching the burn mouth of Boyndie, he again alighted among the tumbling waves there.   It was now gloaming, and what between one thing or other, I was rather like an aspen-leaf than any thing else.   Follow, however, I did; I searched the place, and was just on the eve of giving up the pursuit as hopeless — having, as I thought, beat the ground over and over again to no purpose—when up rose the bird from among my very feet.   Both barrels were again emptied, but with little apparent effect.   The last one made him scream somewhat harshly, and falter a little in his flight, but that was all.   On he sped.   Darkness now put an end to any further operations for that day.   Next day, however, and for many days after, I was out; but, although I searched the coast as far as the sands of White-hills on the one side, and the burn of Melrose on the other, I could find no traces of the bird.   And thus I lost perhaps one of the greatest ornithological rarities that have ever visited the district."

One of the most vivid descriptions which Edward insert-ed in the *Banffshire Journal* was a narrative of a day's adventures on Gamrie Head.   The editor, in introducing it to his readers, said that it reads not unlike a chapter of Audubon or Wilson.   The reader will judge for himself:

"Having promised to visit some friends in Gardenstown, to partake of their hospitality during the festive season of the new year, I left home with that object on the morning of the 31st of December, 1850.   I passed through Mac-

GAMRIE HEAD.

9*

duff, and took the path which leads along the cliffs, hoping thereby to meet with something rare or strange in the ornithological world, and worthy of my shot. In this way I had nearly reached the highest point of Gamrie Head without meeting with any thing but the common tenants of these rocky braes, when my attention was attracted by the screaming of a number of birds at the bottom of the cliff. On looking over, I observed that they consisted of several hooded and carrion crows, together with two ravens, two Iceland gulls (*Laurus Icelandicus*), and a number of other dark-colored gulls, apparently immature specimens of the great black-backed species, one of which, in perfect plumage, was standing and picking at an object floating in the water close to the rock, and about which all the other birds were screaming. It appeared to me, and it afterward proved to be the case, that they were making food of the object about which they were fighting; but the black-backed bird kept them all at bay, allowing none to approach, not even the ravens themselves.

"Having feasted my eyes for a while on the Icelanders, the thought struck me that I would descend the cliff in order to procure one of them, if possible, and also to get a nearer view of the object which had drawn the various birds together. Accordingly, observing a narrow track near me, I commenced my descent, but I had only proceeded a short distance when I found myself on the brink of a precipice. I was about to return, when, accidentally looking over, I observed a portion of the rock jutting out a little beyond the one on which I stood, and about four feet and a half below it. I now concluded that, if I could gain this rock, I would still find the path to enable me to continue downward. With these hopes, and having laid down my gun, I swung myself down upon the rock. I had no sooner done so than I heard a low growl, as if proceeding from a rabid dog; and on looking along the rock, I was a good deal surprised at seeing two foxes standing in a rather slouching attitude at the other end of the shelf, apparently very much discomfited at my unwarrantable intrusion.

"Another look at the place and its surly occupants was enough to convince me of the unmistakable truth that, instead of having met with a path leading to the bottom of the cliffs, I had only found one to a fox's lair. My first impulse was to ascend the rocks, but in this I was completely baffled. The brow of the cliff to which I wished to ascend was fully as high as my breast, and overhung the rock on which I stood. I had nothing of the nature of a step to put my foot on to aid myself up, and nothing to lay hold of with my hands but small tufts of withered grass and some small stones, all of which gave way as soon as any stress was put upon them. The last and the only remaining object within my reach was a stone about twice as large as my head, and partially imbedded among the grass. I took hold of the big stone with both hands, and succeeded in drawing myself about half - way up, when it suddenly gave way. The stone came into collision with my right shoulder, and would in all likelihood have borne me along with it to the bottom of the cliff, had it not been that at that instant I got hold of a short tuft of heath with my mouth, by the aid of which, and by using my fingers as a beast would its claws, I was enabled to regain my former position.

"It was now quite evident that I would require to descend the cliff by some means or other; but how? That was a matter for deep consideration. I was standing on the brink of a precipice—had two cunning fellows to deal with—had to hold on, at least with one hand, to the rock above in order to maintain my equilibrium—and had to keep a steady eye on my companions, for fear lest they should rush at me and throw me over the cliff.

"Such being the case, ·was I not in a pretty fix? If there were any means of escape, it was from the point near

which the foxes were. But how could I dislodge them to
get at that point? The space on which we stood was only
from about two feet and a half to one foot broad, and
about nine feet long, projecting to some distance over the
cliff beneath. To have shot them, and rid myself of their
presence in that fashion, was, from my position, utterly impossible.

"At length a thought struck me, and, with the view of
putting it in execution, I laid down my gun close to the
back of the shelving, out of harm's way; then crouching
down with my feet toward my shaggy friends, who kept
up a constant chattering of their teeth during the whole
time, and pushing myself backward until I reached the
nearest, I gave him a kick with my foot on the hind-quar-
ters, which produced the desired effect; for I had no sooner done so than I felt first the feet of one, and then of the
other, passing lightly along my back, and, before I had
time to lift up my head, they had bolted up the precipice,
and disappeared.

"I was now master of the place, though not of the situation. On looking over the cliff, I found that there was no
way of getting down but by leaping into a crevice of the
rocks, more than eight feet beneath me, and in a slanting
direction from where I was. This was a doleful discovery,
but there was no help now; so, taking off my coat, shot-
belt, and powder-flask, that I might be so much the lighter,
and have the free use of my arms, I threw them down to
the bottom of the rock. I next bound the gun to my back,
having previously emptied it of its contents. I then crawled
over the edge of the rock, and hung dangling in the air for
a little, like the pendulum of a clock. I would have given
all that I ever possessed in the world to have been again in
the foxes' den, stinking though it was. For then, and not
till then, did I discover, to my sorrow, that a rugged portion of a rock projected over the entrance to the aperture
to which I wished to descend, and that, in leaping, I would

require to go beyond it in order to reach the landing underneath. To accomplish such a feat seemed to me impossible.

"I hung thus, being afraid to make the leap, though up I could not get, until my hands began to give way; when, mustering all my remaining strength, and having taken the last swing with some force, I let go my hold to abide by the dreadful alternative, for I had little hope of gaining the desired haven. Most fortunately, however, I did gain it; but, in doing so, I received a severe blow on the left temple from the rock I had so much dreaded. I also lost my cap, which fell off when my head struck the rock. From this cavity or chink, which was the worst that I ever had to deal with, I managed—by leaping and swinging from one rocky shelf and cavity to another, and by crawling from crag to crag, alternately, as circumstances required it — to reach a huge stone, which evidently had once formed a part of the higher portion of the cliff, but had, at a by-gone period, by some means or other, become detached from it, and on rolling down had found a temporary resting-place there.

"Beyond this stone I found my leaping was at an end, for I had now arrived at the top of a rather rough and almost perpendicular declivity, fully fifty feet from the bottom, and bounded on both sides by steep and overhanging cliffs. Before me was the sea; behind and above me was an insurmountable barrier of three hundred feet of cliff. Although I had descended thus far, there was no human possibility of my being able to re-ascend by the same path. In such a place — alone, and almost powerless — bruised and nearly worn out with exertion—what could I do? Throw myself down, and meet my fate at once, or wait till help should arrive? But where was help to come from? Two boats had already passed from Gardenstown, both of which I hailed, but they sailed along on their way. Perhaps they were too far out at sea to hear my cries, or to notice my signals of distress.

"Despairing of success, I sat down to consider what was next to be done. While thus resting, I observed a falcon (*Falco peregrinus*) sailing slowly and steadily along, bearing something large in his talons. On he came, seemingly unconscious of my presence, and alighted on a ledge only a few yards from where I sat. I now saw that the object he carried was a partridge. Having fairly settled down with his quarry on the rock, I could not help wondering at and admiring the collected ease and cool composure with which he held his struggling captive (for it was still alive) until death put an end to its sufferings. There was no lacerating with his beak at the body of the poor and unfortunate prisoner, in order, as it were, to hasten its termination; no expanding of the wing to maintain his equilibrium; although the last and dying struggle of the bird caused him to quiver a little.

"All being now over, with one foot resting upon his game and the other on the rock, silent and motionless as a statue, the noble captor stood, with an inquiring eye gazing at the now lifeless form of his reeking prey, seeming to doubt the fact that it was already dead. But there was no mistake. The blood, oozing from its mouth and wounds—its body doubtless pierced by the talons of the conqueror—already began to trickle down the sides of the dark cliffs, dyeing the rocks in its course. Satisfied at last that life was fairly extinct, an incision was then made in the neck or shoulder of the victim, and into this the falcon thrust his bill several times, and each time that it was withdrawn it was covered with blood. This being done, and having wrenched off the head, which he dropped, he then began not only to pluck, but to skin his food, from the neck downward; and, having bared the breast, commenced a hearty meal by separating the flesh from the sternum into portions, with as much apparent ease as if he had been operating with the sharpest surgical instrument. I should have liked well to have seen the end of the work thus begun; but, unfortunately, a slight movement on my part was detected by the quick eye of the falcon, and my nearness was discovered. Having gazed at me for a few, and only for a few, seconds with an angry and piercing scowl, mingled with surprise, he then rose, uttering a scream so wild and so loud as to awaken the echoes of the surrounding rocks; while he himself, with the remains of his feast, which he bore along with him, rounded a point of the cliff and disappeared; and there is no doubt that he ended his repast in unmolested security.

"I was glad — nay, proud — of this unlooked-for occurrence, as I had never before, on any occasion, had the pleasure of witnessing any of those noble birds in a state of nature, or while engaged in devouring their prey, and that, too, among the rugged fastnesses of their natural retreat. In consequence of having paid particular attention to the movements of the falcon, I was enabled to bring to maturity an opinion, the seeds of which were sown many years ago — viz., that if painters, engravers, and preservers of animals would endeavor to get lessons from nature, and work accordingly, the public would not be so often duped as they are, by having to pay for false representations and caricatured figures, instead of the genuine forms of these noble birds.

"The falcon had no sooner fled than the reality of my own situation again burst upon my mind. I had as little prospect of relief from passers-by as ever; and, becoming a prey to evil forebodings, I felt cold and sick at heart. It was now afternoon, and daylight would soon be on the wane. I had no time to lose, for it was necessary that something should be done to extricate myself, if possible, before dark. The only way of doing so was by sliding down the declivity, be the consequences what they might. Accordingly, I unloosed the gun from its place on my back, and having taken my garters, which were very long, from my legs, I tied them together, then attached one end of them to the gun, and holding the other end in my hand, I

dropped it as far as the string would allow, and then, let-
ting go, I heard the gun clash to the bottom.   I next took
the two napkins which had bound the gun to my back, and
wound them round my head, in order to save it as much as
possible from the edges of the rocks.   I then stretched myself upon the rocky slope, with my feet downward, and was
ready for the descent, when, repenting, I would again have
drawn myself up.   But the scanty herbage which I held by
gave way, and I was hurled down, whether I would or no,
and with such violence that, on landing among the rocks, I
became quite unconscious.

"On recovering, I found myself lying at the foot of the
cliff, sick and very sore.   I found that I had bled profuse-
ly from the nose and one of my ears.   My first impulse, on
recovering, was to move my limbs to ascertain if any of
them were broken, when, to my inexpressible joy and thankfulness, I found them whole, though somewhat benumbed.
Becoming thirsty, and observing a pool of water at a short
distance, I attempted to rise, but my spine pained me so
much that I was obliged to lie down again without being
able to reach the desired spot.   The thirst increasing, I
dragged myself to the water.   I thrust my mouth into it,
and had partaken of a draught before I discovered that, instead of fresh, I had swallowed *salt*, water!

"If I was ill before, I was worse now.   Having sickened
and vomited again, I revived a little; and after I had washed
the blood from my face and head, I was enabled to sit up
with my back against a rock.   While thus seated, I observed all the articles which had been dropped, except my
cap, which, however, I afterward found.   After sitting for
about half an hour, I made another attempt to rise, and
succeeded, though I reeled about like a drunken fellow,
and could scarcely stand steady without the aid of my gun,
which I found was not so much bruised as I had expected.
Having again assumed my coat and other appendages, I
then endeavored to load my gun, with the view of procur-

ing one of the Icelanders which I had seen from the top of
the cliff. This, however, proved a very difficult matter;
and when I had loaded the gun, I found, to my disappointment, that I could not bring it to bear upon the object. I
made the attempt several times, but was at last obliged to
abandon the hope I had entertained of obtaining either of
the birds.

"I was vexed at this, for both came several times within
easy shot. All my hopes of procuring the birds being at an
end, I then proceeded to view the object in the water round
which the birds were hovering, and I was surprised to find
it to be the carcass of an animal of a very singular appearance. It was not until I had looked at it for some time
that I could bring my memory to bear upon it. I then
thought, and I have since been fully confirmed in the opinion, that I discovered in it a specimen, or rather the putrid
remains, of the spinous shark. It wanted the head, which
had been broken off by the fish having been dashed against
the rocks by the waves. The tail was also broken off, but
still hung by a filament to the body. In shape it somewhat resembled the tail of the common dog-fish; but there
evidently had been two fins on the back, nearer to the pos-
terior than the anterior portion of the animal, though these
had been broken or rubbed off. The skin, which was of a
dark-blue color, and had a leathery appearance, was thickly
beset with curved thorns or spines (whence the animal's
name), nearly all of which were more or less damaged. I
know of nothing that I could liken these thorns or spikes
to but the thorns or spikes which may be seen on the stem
of an old rose-bush—with this exception, that the spikes of
the fish are larger. From its position in the water, though
close to the rocks, I could not make out its girth in any
part whatever; but from where the head had joined the
body to the tip of the tail it was about two yards in length.
Having fully satisfied myself that the present specimen,
from its decomposed state and the holes perforated in it by

the gulls, was beyond the state for preservation, I again left it, that the impatient birds might once more descend and recommence their banquet.

"I now wished to get to a sandy beach at some distance to my left, known as Greenside, from which I knew that a path led to the top of the cliff. On my way thither I met with a very serious obstacle in the form of a huge rock, whose base extended into the sea; and, as a matter of course, as I could not get round it, I required to get over it. I was then far from being in a condition to climb a rock. However, I had no alternative. The tide, then about to come in, would have shown me no mercy. Accordingly, my gun was once more on my back, and on hands and knees, for feet here were of no use, and with the aid of my mouth, I succeeded in crawling over, and, with some further difficulty, I contrived to reach Greenside. Instead of holding on to Gardenstown, I turned my face toward home, where I arrived betwixt five and six in the evening, with the impression of the last day of 1850 so deeply stamped upon my body and mind, that it will not easily, if ever, be obliterated from either."

CHAPTER XII.

RAMBLES AMONG BIRDS.

THE Rev. Mr. Smith must have felt surprised at the graphic manner in which Edward described the birds of the district. The truth is, that Edward, though he had acquired his principal knowledge from observation, had also learned something from books. Mr. Smith had lent him such books as he had in his library, and also referred him to the articles on natural history in the *Penny Cyclopedia.* Although Edward did not accept his friend's advice as to the study of grammar, yet he learned enough for his purpose. It is not so much by recollecting the rules of grammar that one learns to write, as by the careful reading of well-written books. After that, grammar comes, as it were, by nature. Besides, if a man feels keenly, he will be sure to write vividly. This was precisely Edward's position.

Mr. Smith thought it unfortunate that Edward's contributions to natural history should be confined to the local newspaper. He asked permission to send an account of his observations to a scientific journal. Edward expressed his fears lest his contributions might not be found worthy of notice. He was always shy and modest: perhaps he was too modest. There are cases in which shyness is almost a misfortune. A man may know much; but, because of his shyness, he declines to communicate his information to others. He hides his secret, and nobody is the wiser for his knowledge. He is too bashful. He avoids those who might be friendly to him, and who might help him. Edward often stood in his own light in this way.

Mr. Smith, however, persevered. He obtained from Edward some notes of his observations, and, after correcting them, he offered to send them to the *Zoologist*, and publish them under his own name. "I have no doubt," he said, "that the articles would be acceptable to the editor; but, if you do not approve of this plan, I hope you will not for a moment allow me to interfere with you. At all events, I trust that you will have no objection to let the information be known to a much wider circle of readers, and especially of zoologists, than are likely to consult the pages of the *Banffshire Journal*."

Edward at last gave his consent; and in the *Zoologist* for 1850* Mr. Smith inserted a notice of the sanderlings which had been shot by Edward on the sands of Boyndie. In the following year Mr. Smith inserted in the same magazine a notice of the spinous shark which Edward had seen under Gamrie Head.† "In order," says Mr. Smith, "to determine whether it was the spinous shark or not, I sent Mr. Edward the 39th volume of the 'Naturalist's Library,' which contains an account, by Dr. Hamilton, of Edinburgh, of the Squalida, or family of sharks, and in which there is a colored engraving of this particular shark. In reply, Mr. Edward observes, 'I have now no doubt whatever that the animal discovered and examined by me was the spinous shark.' "

In another article Mr. Smith described Edward in the following terms: "I have oftener than once made mention in the *Zoologist* of Mr. Thomas Edward, shoe-maker in Banff, who is a zealous admirer of nature and an excellent preserver of animals. Occasionally he tears himself, as it were, from the employment to which necessity compels him, and slakes his thirst for the contemplation of zoological scenes and objects by a solitary ramble amidst the mountains and hills which so greatly abound in the upper portion

---

* *Zoologist*, 1850: 2915.   † *Zoologist*, 1851: 3057.

of the shires of Aberdeen and Banff. Of some of his adventures during a ramble of this description he has sent me an account. This I consider so interesting that I have rewritten it, and now submit it for insertion in the *Zoologist.* The facts, the ideas, and the reflections are all his own, and in many parts I have retained his own impressions. Upon the accuracy and the minuteness of his observations, and upon his veracity of character, the utmost reliance may at all times be placed."

The paper that follows consists of the description of a ramble, extending over several days, in the hill districts near Noth and Kirnie. It is not necessary to transcribe the whole paper; but we may select the following passages as showing the keen observation as well as the character of the man. Edward had entered a narrow glen, at the bottom of which runs the burn called Ness Bogie. He was listening to the voice of the cuckoo, and the *clap-clap* of the ring-pigeons, which rose in great numbers, when an abrupt turn of the road brought him, suddenly and unexpectedly, within a few yards of a beautiful heron.

" I immediately stood still," he says. " The upright and motionless attitude of the bird indicated plainly that he had been taken by surprise; and for the moment he seemed, as it were, stunned and incapable of flight. There he remained, as if fastened to the spot, his bright yellow eye staring me full in the face, and with an expression that seemed to inquire what right I had to intrude into solitudes where the human form is so rarely seen. As we were thus gazing at each other, in mutual surprise at having met in such a place, I observed his long slender neck quietly and gradually doubling down upon his breast. His dark and lengthened plumes were at the same time slightly shaken. I knew by this that he was about to rise; another moment, and he was up. Stretching his long legs behind him, he uttered a scream so dismal, wild, and loud that the very glen and hills re-echoed the sound, and the whole scene was instantly filled with clamor. The sandpiper screamed its *kittie-needie ;* the pigeon *cooed ;* the pipit, with lively emotion, came flying round me, uttering all the while its *peeping* note ; the moor-cock sprung with whirring wing from his heath lair, and gave forth his well-known and indignant *birr birr-bick ;* the curlew came sailing down the glen with steady flight, and added to the noise with his shrill and peculiar notes of *poo-elie poo-elie coorlie coorlie wha-up ;* and, from the loftier parts of the hills, the plovers ceased not their mournful wail, which accorded so well with the scene of which I alone appeared to be a silent spectator. But I moved not a foot until the alarmed inmates of the glen and the mountain had disappeared, and solemn stillness had again resumed its sway."

On the following day, while crossing the Clashmauch, on his way to Huntly, Edward observed a curlew rise from a marshy part of the hill, to which he bent his steps in hopes of finding her nest. In this, however, he was disappointed ; but, in searching about, and within a few feet of the remains of a wreath of snow, he came upon a wild duck lying beside a tuft of rushes. It may be mentioned that there had been a heavy snow-storm, which had forced the plovers and wild ducks to abandon their nests, though then full of eggs, and greatly interrupted the breeding season in the Northern counties. Edward proceeds :

"As I imagined she was skulking with a view to avoid observation, I touched her with my stick, in order that she might rise ; but she rose not. I was surprised, and on a nearer inspection I found that she was dead. She lay raised a little on one side, her neck stretched out, her mouth open and full of snow, her wings somewhat extended, and with one of her legs appearing a little behind her. Near to it there were two eggs. On my discovering this, I lifted up the bird, and underneath her was a nest containing eleven eggs ; these, with the other two, made thirteen in all : a few of them were broken. I examined the whole of them, and found them, without exception, to contain young birds.

This was an undoubted proof that the poor mother had sat upon them from two to three weeks. With her dead body in my hand, I sat down to investigate the matter, and to ascertain, if I could, the cause of her death. I examined her minutely all over, and could find neither wound nor any mark whatever of violence. She had every appearance of having died of suffocation. Although I had only circumstantial evidence, I had no hesitation in arriving at the conclusion that she had come by her death in a desperate but faithful struggle to protect her eggs from the fatal effects of the recent snow-storm.

"I could not help thinking, as I looked at her, how deep and striking an example she afforded of maternal affection. The ruthless blast had swept with all its fury along the lonesome and unsheltered hill. The snow had risen higher, and the smothering drift came fiercer, as night drew on; yet still that poor bird, in defiance of the warring elements, continued to protect her home, and the treasure which it contained, until she could do so no longer, and yielded up her life. That life she could easily have saved, had she been willing to abandon the offspring which nature had taught her so fervently to cherish, and in endeavoring to preserve which she voluntarily remained and died. Occupied with such feelings and reflections as these, I know not how long I might have sat, had I not been roused from my reverie by the barking of a shepherd's dog. The sun had already set, the gray twilight had begun to hide the distant mountains from my sight, and, not caring to be benighted on such a spot, I wrapped a piece of paper, as a winding-sheet, round the faithful and devoted bird, and, forming a hole sufficiently large for the purpose, I laid into it the mother and the eggs. I covered them with earth and moss, and over all placed a solid piece of turf; and having done so, and being more affected than I should perhaps be willing to acknowledge, I left them to molder into their original dust, and went on my way."

Having thus related an instance of maternal affection on the part of the wild duck, let us cite a still more remarkable instance of brotherly sympathy and help on the part of the common tern (*Sterna hirundo*), called pickietars in the neighborhood of Banff.

"Being on the sands of Boyndie one afternoon at the end of August, I observed several parties of pickietars busily employed in fishing in the firth. As I was in want of a specimen of this bird, I loitered about on the beach, narrowly watching their motions, and hoping that some of them would come within range of my gun. The scene around was of no common beauty. In the azure heaven not a cloud was to be seen, as far as the eye could reach; not a breath of wind was stirring the placid bosom of the firth. The atmosphere seemed a sea, as it were, of living things; so numerous were the insects that hummed and fluttered to and fro in all directions. The sun, approaching the verge of the horizon, shot long and glimmering bands of green and gold across the broad mirror of the deep. Here and there several vessels were lying becalmed, their whitened sails showing brightly in the goldened light. An additional interest was imparted by the herring-boats which were congregating in the bay; their loose and flagging sails, the noise of the oars, and the efforts of the rowers, told plainly enough that a hard pull would have to be undergone before they could reach their particular quarters for fishing, in the north-eastern part of the firth.

"While I stood surveying with delight the extended and glorious prospect, and witnessing with admiration the indefatigable evolutions of the terns in their search for food, I observed one of them break off from a party of five, and direct his course toward the shore, fishing all the way as he came. It was an interesting sight to behold him as he approached in his flight—at one moment rising, at another descending—now poised in mid-air, his wings expanded but motionless, his piercing eye directed to the waters be-

neath, and watching with eager gaze the movements of their
scaly inhabitants—and now, as one of them would ever and
anon come sufficiently near the surface, making his attack
upon the fish in the manner so thoroughly taught him by
nature. Quick as thought, he closed to his side his out-
spread pinions; turned off his equilibrium with a movement almost imperceptible; and, with a seeming careless-
ness, threw himself headlong into the deep so rapidly that
the eye could with difficulty keep pace with his descent.
In the least space of time he would be seen sitting on the
water, swallowing his prey. This being accomplished, he
again mounted into the air. He halts in his progress.
Something has caught his eye. He lets himself down; but
it is only for a little, for his expected prey has vanished
from his sight.

"Once more he soars aloft on lively wing; and, having
attained a certain elevation, and hovering, kestrel-like, for a
little, with quick-repeated strokes of his pinions he rapidly
descends. Again, however, his hoped-for victim has made
its escape; and he bounds away in an oblique direction,
describing a beautiful curve as he rises without having
touched the water. Shortly after, he wings his way nearer
and nearer to the beach; onward he advances with zigzag
flight, when suddenly, as if struck down by an unseen hand,
he drops into the water within about thirty yards of the
place where I am standing. As he righted and sat on the
bosom of the deep, I was enabled distinctly to perceive
that he held in his bill a little scaly captive, which he
had snatched from its home, and which struggled violently to regain its liberty. Its struggles were in vain; a few
squeezes from the mandibles of the bird put an end to its
existence.

"Being now within my reach, I stood prepared for the
moment when he should again arise. This he did so soon
as the fish was dispatched. I fired, and he came down with
a broken wing, screaming as he fell into the water. The

report of the gun, together with his cries, brought together
the party he had left, in order that they might ascertain
the cause of the alarm. After surveying their wounded
brother round and round, as he was drifting unwittingly toward the shore with the flowing tide, they came flying in a
body to the spot where I stood, and rent the air with their
screams. These they continued to utter, regardless of their
own individual safety, until I began to make preparations
for receiving the approaching bird. I could already see
that it was a beautiful adult specimen; and I expected in
a few moments to have it in my possession, being not very
far from the water's edge.

"While matters were in this position, I beheld, to my
utter astonishment and surprise, two of the unwounded
terns take hold of their disabled comrade, one at each wing,
lift him out of the water, and bear him out seaward. They
were followed by two other birds. After being carried
about six or seven yards, he was let gently down again,
when he was taken up in a similar manner by the two who
had been hitherto inactive. In this way they continued
to carry him alternately, until they had conveyed him to
a rock at a considerable distance, upon which they landed him in safety. Having recovered my self-possession, I
made toward the rock, wishing to obtain the prize which
had been so unceremoniously snatched from my grasp. I
was observed, however, by the terns; and instead of four,
I had in a short time a whole swarm about me. On my
near approach to the rock, I once more beheld two of them
take hold of the wounded bird as they had done already,
and bear him out to sea in triumph, far beyond my reach.
This, had I been so inclined, I could no doubt have prevented. Under the circumstances, however, my feelings
would not permit me; and I willingly allowed them to perform without molestation an act of mercy, and to exhibit
an instance of affection, which man himself need not be
ashamed to imitate. I was, indeed, rejoiced at the disap-

pointment which they had occasioned, for they had thereby rendered me the witness of a scene which I could scarcely have believed, and which no length of time will efface from my recollection."

On another occasion Edward exhibited the same closeness, minuteness, and patience of observation with regard to the turn-stone (*Strepsilas interpers*), a bird which is an inhabitant of the sea-shore, and has a wide geographical range, though it has rarely been seen on the shores of the Moray Firth. In Edward's ornithological excursions, it was not so much his object to kill birds as to observe their manners and habits. He very often made his excursions without a gun at all. In a letter to the author, he observes: "In looking over my printed articles, you will find a great number of notices of the habits and workings of various species. I spent so much time in observation, that I had little time to spare to write out the results; and what I did write did not seem to be much appreciated. Perhaps this is not to be wondered at. It appears that the compilers of works on natural history in this country do not care for details of the habits of the animals they treat of. They rather glory in the abundance of technical descriptions they can supply. These may seem scientific, but they are at the same time very dry. In fact, natural history is rendered detestable to general readers. We want some writers of the Audubon and Wilson class to render natural history accessible to the public at large."

If Edward himself could have been rescued from his shoe-maker's seat, we might probably have had the book which he indicates. He was full of love for his subject; he was patient and persevering in his observations; and, notwithstanding his great disadvantages, it will be observed that his style of writing was vivid and graphic. With respect to the turn-stone, which Edward described in 1850,*

* First in the *Banffshire Journal*, December 31st, 1850; and afterward copied by Mr. Smith in the *Zoologist*, April, 1851.

it does not appear that any ornithological writer, excepting Audubon, had particularly described it, although Edward had never read Audubon's work. The Rev. Mr. Smith observed: "It is consistent with my knowledge that Mr. Edward has never read the account given by Audubon of the habits of the turn-stone. I mention this as a proof, among others, of the accuracy and minuteness with which he makes his observations. He is the only European, so far as I have the means of ascertaining, who has described the efforts which are put forth by the bird in question in cases of difficulty, not only with its bill, but with its breast also." The following is Edward's description of the bird:

"The turn-stone is a very interesting bird, from its peculiar form and singular habits. It is a strong, thick bird, with rather short, thick legs; long expanded toes; and full, broad breast. Its bill is in the form of an elongated cone, strong at the base, on the culmen rather flattened, and with a curve inclining upward toward the tip. The habits of the bird are singular, more particularly with respect to the method which it adopts to procure food—which is, as its name denotes, by turning over small stones in search of the insects beneath them, on which it feeds. When the object which it wishes to turn over is too large for the bill to do so, the breast is applied; and it would seem that the birds are willing to assist each other, just as masons or porters will do in turning over a stone or a bale of goods. I may here take the liberty of mentioning an incident concerning the turn-stone which came under my own observation.

"Passing along the sea-shore to the west of Banff, I observed on the sands, at a considerable distance before me, two birds beside a large-looking object. Knowing by their appearance that they did not belong to the species which are usually met with in this quarter, I left the beach and proceeded along the adjoining links, an eminence of shingle intervening, until I concluded that I was almost opposite to the spot where the objects of my search were employed.

Stooping down, and with my gun upon my back prepared for action, I managed to crawl through the bents and across the shingle for a considerable way. At length I came in sight of the two little workers, who were busily endeavoring to turn over a dead fish which was fully six times their size. I immediately recognized them as turn-stones. Not wishing to disturb them, and anxious at the same time to witness their operations, I observed that a few paces nearer them there was a deep hollow among the shingle, which I contrived to creep into unobserved.

"I was now distant from them about ten yards, and had a distinct and unobstructed view of all their movements. In these there was evinced that extraordinary degree of sagacity and perseverance which comes under the notice only of those who watch the habits of the lower creation with patience and assiduity, and which, when fully and accurately related, is not unfrequently discredited by individuals who, although fond of natural history, seem inclined to believe that every thing in regard to animals must necessarily be false, or at least the result of ignorance, unless it has been recorded in books which are considered authorities on the subject.

"But to return. Having got fairly settled down in my pebbly observatory, I turned my undivided attention to the birds before me. They were boldly pushing at the fish with their bills, and then with their breasts. Their endeavors, however, were in vain: the object remained immovable. On this they both went round to the opposite side, and began to scrape away the sand from beneath the fish. After removing a considerable quantity, they again came back to the spot which they had left, and went once more to work with their bills and breasts, but with as little apparent success as formerly. Nothing daunted, however, they ran round a second time to the other side, and recommenced their trenching operations with a seeming determination not to be baffled in their object, which evidently was to undermine the dead animal before them, in order that it might be the more easily overturned.

"While 'they were thus employed, and after they had labored in this manner at both sides alternately for nearly half an hour, they were joined by another of their own species, which came flying with rapidity from the neighboring rocks. Its timely arrival was hailed with evident signs of joy. I was led to this conclusion from the gestures which they exhibited, and from a low but pleasant murmuring noise to which they gave utterance so soon as the new-comer made his appearance. Of their feelings he seemed to be perfectly aware, and he made his reply to them in a similar strain. Their mutual congratulations being over, they all three set to work; and after laboring vigorously for a few minutes in removing the sand, they came round to the other side, and, putting their breasts simultaneously to the fish, they succeeded in raising it some inches from the sand, but were unable to turn it over. It went down again into its sandy bed, to the manifest disappointment of the three. Resting, however, for a space, and without leaving their respective positions, which were a little apart the one from the other, they resolved, it appears, to give the work another trial. Lowering themselves, with their breasts close to the sand, they managed to push their bills underneath the fish, which they made to rise to about the same height as before. Afterward, withdrawing their bills, but without losing the advantage which they had gained, they applied their breasts to the object. This they did with such force and to such purpose that at length it went over and rolled several yards down a slight declivity. It was followed to some distance by the birds themselves, before they could recover their bearing.

"They returned eagerly to the spot from whence they had dislodged the obstacle which had so long opposed them; and they gave unmistakable proof, by their rapid and continued movements, that they were enjoying an ample repast as the reward of their industrious and praiseworthy labor. I was so pleased, and even delighted, with the sagacity and perseverance which they had shown, that I should have considered myself as guilty of a crime had I endeavored to take away the lives of these interesting beings at the very moment when they were exercising, in a manner so happily for themselves, the wonderful instincts implanted in them by their Creator. When they appeared to have done and to be satisfied, I arose from my place of concealment. On examining the fish, I found it to be a specimen of the common cod. It was nearly three feet and a half long, and it had been imbedded in the sand to the depth of about two inches."

One of Edward's greatest pleasures was in rambling along the sea-shore, to observe the habits of the sea-birds. The multitude of birds which frequent the shores of the Moray Firth are occasioned by the shoals of herrings, which afford food not only for thousands of fishermen, but for millions of sea-birds. To show the number of birds that frequent the coast, it may be mentioned that during the storm that occurred in December, 1846, Edward counted between the Burn of Boyne and Greenside of Gamrie, a distance of about nine miles, nearly sixty of the little auk, which had been driven ashore dead, besides a large number of guillemots and razor-bills. Numbers of these birds were also found lying dead in the fields throughout the county.

And yet the little auk has a wonderful power of resisting the fury of the waves. "It is a grand sight," says Edward, "to see one of these diminutive but intrepid creatures manœuvring with the impetuous billows of a stormy sea. Wave follows wave in rapid succession, bearing destruction to every thing within reach; but the little auk, taught by nature, avoids the threatened danger, either by mounting above the waves or by going beneath them, re-appearing unhurt as they spend their fury on the shore. The eye for a time wanders in vain among the turbulent surge to catch an-

VILLAGE OF PENNAN.

other sight of the little sailor bird.   One unaccustomed to
such a scene would be apt to exclaim, 'Poor little thing!   It
is buried amidst the foam!'   Have a little patience.   See!
there it is, once more, as lively as ever, and ready to master
the approaching billow.   Its descent among the waves may
have been merely in search of food, for it is only betwixt
the waves, while inshore during a storm, that the bird can
descend for that purpose.   The bird is known in our locality
by the curious term of the 'nor-a-wa-wific,' from the sup-
position that it comes from Norway."

The rocky coasts along the east shore were the most
attractive scenes for our naturalist.   Not only the wildest
scenery, but the wildest birds, were to be found in that
quarter.   Gamrie Mohr and Troup Head were especially
favorite places.   We have already described Edward's adventures near the former headland.   Here is his description
of his visit to Troup Head:

"Sailing in a little bark, with a gentle breeze blowing, I
had ample opportunities of viewing the various birds as
they approached, and as they flew past.   Passing in front
of the several sea-fowl nurseries of Troup, I beheld scenes
truly magnificent—scenes which could not have failed to
create feelings of the deepest interest in a mind capable of
appreciating the sublime and beautiful workings of nature.
Having landed at the most famed of these nurseries, in order to view the scene with advantage—here, I thought, as
I gazed at the white towering cliffs which had laughed to
scorn the angriest scowl of the most mighty wave that ever
spent its fury at their base, and defied the stormiest blast
from the icy north; where the largest gull in its midway
flight appears no larger than the smallest of its kind; where
the falcon breeds beside and in perfect harmony with the
other inhabitants of the rocky cliffs; where multitudes of
birds, of various forms and hues, from the snowy whiteness
of the kittiwake to the sable dye of the croaking raven,
have found a resting-place whereon to build their nests and

deposit their young—here, I thought, as I was about to leave the busy throng — even here, man, the noblest creature, though too often degrading himself beneath the lowest of animals, might learn lessons of industry and affection from these humble monitors of nature."

During breeding-time the clamor of the sea-birds is tumultuous, though the lashing of the sea at the foot of the cliffs tends to a great extent to lull their noise; but toward evening all becomes still again.   Edward frequently ascer-

THE RED HEAD OF PENNAN.

tained this by personal experience.   Being in the neighborhood of Pennan one day, he went along the Head, in order, if possible, to get a sight of the far-famed eagles of the promontory.   He was unsuccessful on the occasion.   He had loitered by the way, and the declining day at length warned him to leave the place without seeing the coveted sight. His road westward lay along the coast.   With disappointed hopes, he trudged along, scarcely thinking how the hours were flying.   At length it became dark as he approached the broom braes of Troup.   He found himself fairly benighted.   At the same time, he was tired and weary.   He had endured many outs and ins, ups and downs, that day. His intention was to have gone to the house of his old shop-mate at Gardenstown and spend the night; but now he felt, from his worn-out condition, that it would have taken him nearly two hours' walking to reach the place.   He therefore determined to stay where he was, or rather, to go down to a sleeping-place near Troup Head, to ascertain how his feathered friends conducted themselves during the night-time.

His sleeping-place was a very wild one.   It was no other than Hell's Lum.   He knew the place well.   He had entered it both from the sea-side and from the land-side.   He had been in it in storm and calm, in clouds and sunshine. And now he was about to spend the night in it.   The weather was, however, calm; the sea was like a sheet of glass; so that he had little fear of getting a wetting during his few hours' stay.   While in the "Lum," he was at the back of the cliffs, and in close proximity with the breeding-places of the myriads of sea-fowl.   It was now the busiest part of the season.   The birds had been very clamorous during the day, but as night came on their clamor ceased. With the exception of a few screams—while, perhaps, the birds were being displaced in their nests—the night was silent, though Edward kept awake and listened for nearly the whole time.

But with the first glimmerings of daylight, and just as he was beginning to move and to creep out of the pit, Edward thought that he heard some of the birds beginning to whimper and yawn, as if ready for another day's work; and by the time he had rounded Crovie Head, he beheld the cliffs alive, and the multitude of sea-birds again in full operation.

CHAPTER XIII.

LITERATURE AND CORRESPONDENCE.

A GREAT misfortune befell Edward in 1854: his friend, the Rev. Mr. Smith, died. He was a man whose richly cultivated mind and warm heart endeared him to all with whom he came in contact. He was almost the only man of culture in the neighborhood who appreciated the character of Edward. He not only made himself his friend, but became his helper. Edward was under the impression that people looked down upon him and his work because he was a poor shoe-maker. There were other persons who knew of Edward's perseverance, self-denial, and uncomplainingness, and also of his efforts to rise into a higher life; but they did not help him as Mr. Smith did. The true Christian gentleman treated the poor man as his friend. He treated him as one intelligent man treats another. The shoe-maker from Banff was always made welcome at the minister's fireside at Monquhitter.

Mr. Smith helped Edward with books. He lent him such books as he had from his own library; and he borrowed books from others, in order to satisfy Edward's inquiries about objects in natural history. He wandered about the fields with him, admiring his close observation; and he urged him to note down the facts which he observed, in order that they might be published to the world.

In one of the last letters addressed by Mr. Smith to Edward he observed: "It is, I conceive, the great defect in the natural sciences that we know so little of the real habits and instincts of the animal creation. In helping to fill up this gap, your personal minute and accurate observations will be of no little service; although individuals, solemn and wise in their own conceit, may look upon some of them as so strange as to be altogether fabulous; and *that* for no better reason than because during all their lives—having exercised their faculties only in eating, drinking, and sleeping—the things related have never come under the notice either of their eyes or their ears."

We find, from a letter of Professor Dickie, that Mr. Smith endeavored to obtain employment for Edward as a preserver of British birds for the natural history collection in King's College, Aberdeen. Many kindly letters passed between Edward and the minister of Monquhitter, sometimes about newly discovered birds, at other times about the troubles and sicknesses of their respective families. Mr. Smith's suggestion that Edward should note down his observations for publication was not, as we have seen, without effect, as the latter afterward became a contributor to the *Naturalist*, the *Zoologist*, the *Ibis*, the *Linnæan Journal*, and other natural history publications.

In one of Edward's articles in the *Zoologist*, he thus refers to a circumstance which happened during one of the last excursions he took with his reverend friend. He is referring to the partridge (*Perdrix cinerea*). "A very cunning and faithful mother is the female; for when she has eggs, she never leaves her nest without hiding them so carefully that it is almost impossible to detect their whereabouts; and if you take her by surprise, away she hobbles on one leg, and a wing trailing on the ground, as if wounded!.... Wandering about the Waggle Hill one day with my friend, the Rev. Mr. Smith, I chanced to observe a moorfowl squatted on the ground among the heather, close to my feet; in fact, I stood above her before I noticed her. Being summer-time, I at once guessed the nature of the case. On my friend coming up, I drew his attention to the bird over which I stood. 'Oh,' he said, 'she's surely dead, Mr. Edward.'   'Oh, no,' said I; 'there are eggs or young beneath her.'   'Well,' he answered, 'if so, it is certainly a very wonderful circumstance; but we shall see.' Then, stooping down, he touched the bird, but she did not move.   'She must be alive,' he said, 'because she is warm; but she must be wounded, and not able to rise or fly.' 'Oh no,' I once more said; 'she has something beneath her which she is unwilling to leave.'   The bird allowed him to stroke her without moving, except turning her head to look at him.   On my friend's dog Sancho coming up and putting his nose close to her, she crept away through the bushes for some distance, and then took to flight, leaving a nest and fifteen eggs exposed to our gaze.   Before leaving, we carefully closed up the heather again, so as to conceal as much as possible the nest and its beauteous treasure; and I need not say that we were both delighted with what we had seen.   Mr. Smith was particularly struck with the incident, as he had never seen any thing of the kind before; and he remarked, 'I verily believe that I could not have credited the fact if I had not seen it myself,' and he afterward spoke of it with the greatest admiration."

Edward also numbered among his friends the Rev. Alexander Boyd, of Crimond.   It was through the Rev. Mr. Smith that Edward was first introduced to him.   Mr. Smith was anxious that Edward should examine and observe the birds of Strathbeg, near which the village of Crimond is situated.   Crimond is about thirty-five miles from Banff, ten miles from Peterhead, and about seven from Fraserburgh.

The loch of Strathbeg was at one time of limited extent. It was connected with the sea at its eastern extremity; but a hill of sand having, about the beginning of last century, been blown across the opening during a furious east wind, the connection between the loch and the sea was closed, and it became a fresh-water loch, as it remains to this day.   The scenery in the neighborhood is by no means picturesque; but the loch is very attractive to sportsmen, in consequence of the number of wild fowl that frequent it, or that breed among the islands and marshes at its western extremity.

The Rev. Mr. Boyd was the parish minister of Crimond. His hospitable manse was always open to Edward when he visited the neighborhood. In one of Mr. Boyd's letters to Edward, he said: "We have exactly the sort of room that will suit you, and you will be left at liberty to pursue your researches at your convenience; the room being so situated that you can go out or come in at any hour of the day or night, without any one being the wiser. There will always be something in the cupboard to refresh you before starting at day-break, or when you come home at night, though every one in the house may be asleep. And you may continue with us the whole week, if you be so disposed. My coble will always be at your service, and I hope to be able to accompany you on some of your rambles, though I am not nearly so agile now as I have been. . . . . Mrs. Boyd is now quite well, though she had a long illness after you were here; and we have a young specimen of zoology to show you which is worth all the rare birds of Strathbeg put together!"

The number of water-fowl that Edward found about the loch was very great. During winter-time it was the haunt of birds from far and near, in prodigious numbers. In summer-time it was the breeding-place of numerous birds of a different kind. The people of the neighborhood say that "all the birds of the world come here in winter." In angry weather, when the ocean is tempest-tossed, the sea-birds fly in, and, mingling with the natives, constitute a very motley group. The number of birds is so great that when a gun is fired they rise *en masse*, and literally darken the air, while their noise is perfectly deafening.

The swans are among the largest birds that frequent the loch. Edward found the beautiful white hooper (*Cygnus ferus*), and the no less fair and elegant Polish swan (*Cygnus immutabilis*). The geese were innumerable: the bean goose (*Anser segetum*), the pink-footed goose (*A. brachy-rynchus*), the white-pointed goose (*A. erythropus*), the barnacle goose (*A. leucopsis*), the brent goose (*A. brenta*), the Canadian goose (*A. Canadensis*), and even the Egyptian goose (*A. Egyptiacus*). The last mentioned was first detected by Mr. Boyd himself. In a letter to Edward, dated the 24th of November, 1853, he said: "One morning lately I was informed that there was a strange bird of the goose tribe in my mill-dam. I sallied forth with a telescope in one hand and a double-barrel, loaded with No. 1, in the other. I first took a leisurely look at him with the former at less than one hundred yards distance, when I made the following observations: Size and appearance those of a small wild goose; head, brown and gray mixed; back, rich brown, lightish; breast and neck, gray; tail, dark or black; tips of wings, ditto, and glossy; legs and bill, reddish; a dark ring round the neck, and a dark spot right on the centre of the breast. He was nibbling the tender grass on the dam banks. I then approached nearer. Instead of flying, he merely swam away to the other side of the pond, and seemed either very tired or else accustomed to the presence of man. I was quite within shot of him, but, from his tameness, I conjectured that he was some fancy animal escaped from a gentleman's demesne. I then went for some corn, and scattered it on the banks, and as soon as I moved away he came to eat it. When startled, he generally makes a circuit of a quarter of a mile and returns again; but latterly he goes to the loch of Strathbeg all night, and returns in the morning for his corn. I am afraid he will not be spared long, although I have sent word in several directions that he is not to be shot. I should be glad if he would become domesticated. I wish you would look over some of your books and tell me what he is. I have not seen a bird of the same kind before."

From Mr. Boyd's minute description of the bird, Edward was enabled to inform him that it could be nothing else than a specimen of that rare species, the Egyptian goose. After about two months' sojourn in Mr. Boyd's mill-pond, the bird flew away on the day preceding the great snow-storm of January, 1854, and never returned. Mr. Boyd was afterward enabled to ascertain the correctness of Edward's information. He was in Liverpool, and while visiting a poulterer's yard, he observed a bird exactly like the one that had taken shelter in his mill-pond. On inquiring its name, he was informed that it was an Egyptian goose.

The mallard, the widgeon, the teal, the gargancy, the pintail, the ferruginous, the harlequin, the shoveler, the shieldrake, and the eider-duck, visited the loch in vast numbers. The ducks were ten times more numerous than the geese. There were the scaup (*Fuligula marila*), the tufted (*F. cristata*), the red-headed pochard or dun-bird (*F. ferina*), and the golden-eyed garrot (*Clangula garrotta*). The red-necked grebe and the black-chinned grebe also bred in the loch. Herons, bitterns, spoonbills, glossy ibises, snipes, woodcocks, green sandpipers, ruffs, dotterels, gray phalaropes, were also to be seen. These were the birds that mostly frequented the loch in winter. There were numerous flocks of gulls of various species, and other shore-birds, which only made visits to the loch for shelter during storms.

When spring approached, the birds became restless. The flocks began to break up, and flights of birds disappeared daily. At length the greater part of the winter birds left, except a few stragglers. An entirely different set of birds now began to make their appearance. You could now hear the shrill whistle of the redshank, the bright carol of the lark, the wire-like call of the dunlin, the melancholy note of the wagtail, the boom of the snipe, and the pleasant peewit of the lapwing. There were also the black-headed bunting, the ring-dotterel, the wheat-ear, the meadow pipit, the reed warbler, the rose linnet, the twite, the redshank, the black-headed gull, and the arctic tern, which bred in suitable localities round the loch. Among the remaining birds were several specimens of the skua, coots, water-hens, swifts, and several kinds of swallows. The whimbrel, green-shank, water-rail, pied wagtail, roseate tern, and water-ouzel also frequented the neighborhood of the loch, but did not breed there.

In an account of "The Birds of Strathbeg," which Edward afterward published in the *Naturalist*, he mentioned the curious manner in which the ring-dotterel contrives to divert attention from her nest.

While strolling along the sands in the month of July, a friend who was with him fired at a tern. Without knowing what he had fired at, Edward saw a ring-dotterel before him, which, he thought, must be the bird. It was lame, and dragging its wing behind it as if it had been sorely wounded. It lay down, as if dead. Edward came up, and put his hand down to secure it. The bird rose and flew away. Then it dropped again, hobbled and tottered about, as if inviting him to pursue it. "I stood a few seconds," says Edward, "considering whether I would follow or not; then off I started, determined to have it. Away went the bird, twiddling and straddling, and away I followed in hot pursuit. Round and round the sand-hillocks we scrambled until I was perfectly wearied. Nothing but the novelty of the affair could have kept me in pursuit of the wounded bird.

"In this way we continued, until I saw that I could make nothing of it by fair means; so I doubled round and met it fair in front. I was about to take hold of it, when, to my amazement, it rose and flew. Its flight, however, was of short duration, as it again suddenly dropped down, and lay on the sand as if dead. 'You are mine now at last,' said I, as I observed it fall. I accordingly proceeded to take it up, in order to put it in my pocket. But, lo! it rose again and flew away; when once more it suddenly dropped behind one of the larger hillocks. It was a beautifully marked specimen, and, fearing lest I should lose it altogether, I determined to put a stop to the wild-goose chase. Having put my gun in readiness, I proceeded in the direction in which the bird fell. But it did not rise. I searched all round, but there was no bird! I met my friend, and inquired if he had fired at a ring-dotterel. No; he had only shot at a tern. 'But, by-the-bye,' he added, 'I found a nest and the young of that bird as I came along.'

"In a few minutes we stood beside the young ones. The spot I found to be only about three yards in advance of where my attention was first attracted to the apparently wounded bird. Having collected the little downy things, and placed them in a hollow among the sand, we again took our departure. In doing so, what should we meet but my old friend the dotterel, which again commenced its former pranks! But, no! It was too late; the truth had oozed out. The bird had completely deceived me, and my friend laughed heartily at my mistake."

During one of Edward's visits to Crimond Manse, to which some gentlemen of the neighborhood had been invited to meet him, Mr. Boyd, after dinner, when the ladies had left the room, expressed his surprise that something had not been done to enable Edward to obtain more time to pursue his researches in natural history. The gentlemen present cordially agreed with him. Mr. Boyd then proposed to insert a notice in the *Fraserburgh Advertiser*, and to circulate it extensively in the neighborhood. The following forms part of the article:

" During the past month our district has been visited by Mr. Edward, from Banff, a naturalist of no mean attainments, and one who, we doubt not, will soon bring himself into public notice, both by his indefatigable researches into natural science, and his valuable contributions to various scientific periodicals..... While there are few branches of natural history in which he does not take an interest, it is in ornithology that he shines most conspicuously, and in this he was much encouraged by the late Rev. Mr. Smith, of Monquhitter..... We cordially wish Mr. Edward every success in the various fields of research upon which he has entered. It is but justice to a most deserving person to draw attention to his praiseworthy endeavors, in the midst of many difficulties, to perfect his knowledge of natural history, and to recommend it to all around him, especially the young. Happy would it be if our tradesmen were to take a leaf out of Mr. Edward's book, and, instead of wasting their time, squandering their means, and imbittering their existence in the haunts of dissipation, they would sally forth in these calm summer evenings to rural scenes and sylvan solitudes, to woo Nature in her mildest aspect; to learn a lesson from the moth or the spider; to listen to the hum of the bee or the song of birds; to mark the various habits and instincts of animals, and thus to enrich their minds with useful and entertaining knowledge."

Mr. Boyd's object in publishing this notice was to attract the attention of the working-classes to the study of natural history; and. with this object he was of opinion that Edward should endeavor to disseminate among them the information which he had acquired during his long experience. He proposed that Edward should get up a series of rudimentary lectures on natural history, illustrated by specimens of birds and other objects. The lectures were first to be delivered in Banff, and, if they succeeded there, they were afterward to be delivered in Fraserburgh and other towns. Edward proceeded to prepare his illustrations. About two hundred were put in readiness. He was also negotiating for the purchase of a powerful magnifying glass, so that his patrons might better see the minute wonders of Nature as exhibited in her works.

As there was then an institution at Banff, which had been formed, among other purposes, " For the Discovery and Encouragement of Native Genius and Talent," Mr. Boyd believed that the members would at once give their hearty co-operation to his proposed scheme.   He proposed the formation of a local committee, in order that the rudimentary lectures might be brought out under their patronage.   Edward was requested to name some gentlemen in Banff with whom Mr. Boyd might communicate on the subject.   This was a poser; for Edward knew only a few hard-working men like himself.   Nevertheless, he did give the name of a gentleman who, he thought, might give his assistance.   When the gentleman was applied to, he politely declined.   Edward was asked to name another.   He named another, and he also declined.   Thus the proposal, from which Mr. Boyd had expected so much, fell to the ground, and it was no more heard of.

Shortly after this event, Mr. Boyd died suddenly.   Edward thus refers to the event: "It was but yesterday, at noon,* that my friend the Rev. Mr. Boyd, of Crimond—while full of life and strength, and with every prospect of enjoying many, many long years to come—left his young and courteous partner and two blooming little ones, to enjoy a short walk with a neighboring gentleman.   Alas! short was the walk indeed, and, woe is me! never to return.   A few paces, and he dropped down and almost instantly expired.   Alas! another of my best friends gone.   Cruel death! if thy hand continues to strip me thus, thou wilt soon, very soon, leave me desolate; and then who will take notice of the poor naturalist?   Well may the parish of Crimond say, 'We have lost that which we may never again find.'   Well might Mercy weep, and Religion mourn his premature departure, for in him they have lost a friend on earth; and I, alas! a friend too, and a benefactor."

Edward completed his article on "The Birds of Strathbeg" only two days after Mr. Boyd's death.   It had been written out at his instance, and was afterward published in the *Naturalist*.   It was one of the first papers to which Edward subscribed his own name.

---

* August 22d, 1851.

So soon as Edward's name and address appeared in the *Naturalist* and *Zoologist*, he was assailed by letters from all parts of the country. English dealers asked him to exchange birds with them. Private gentlemen offered exchanges of moths and butterflies. Professors, who were making experiments on eggs, requested contributions of eggs of all kinds. A naturalist in Norfolk desired to have a collection of sternums, or breast-bones, of birds. "I have no doubt," says Edward, "that many of my correspondents thought me uncceevil, but really it would have taken a fortune in postage-stamps to have answered their letters."

But although Edward received many applications from naturalists in different parts of the country, he himself applied to others to furnish names for the specimens which he had collected. We find a letter from Mr. Macdonald, secretary to the Elgin Museum, referring to eighty-five zoophytes which Edward had sent him to be named. Edward had no other method of obtaining the scientific names for his objects. "The naming of them," said Mr. Macdonald, "has cost me some time and trouble..... Some of the zoophytes are fine specimens; others are both fine and rare. One or two have not as yet been met with on our shores. They seem to be quite new." We also find Edward communicating with Mr. H. F. Staunton, a well-known London naturalist, relative to moths, butterflies, beetles, and other insects.

But Edward could not live on zoophytes and butterflies. His increasing family demanded his attention; and shortly after his article on "The Birds of Strathbeg" had appeared in the *Naturalist*, we find him applying in different directions for some permanent situation. He was willing to be a police-officer, a tide-waiter, or any thing that would bring in a proper maintenance for his family. With this object, one of his friends at Fraserburgh made an application to Mr. Charles W. Peach, then an officer of customs at Wick.

Mr. Peach was a well-known naturalist, and he has since become distinguished in connection with recent discoveries in geology. Mr. Peach had once visited Edward, in company with Mr. Greive, the customs officer at Banff. In answer to the application made to him from Fraserburgh, he said:

"*I do* know our friend Mr. Edward, of Banff, and I have thought a great deal about him of late. I have wondered how he was getting on in bread-and-porridge affairs. Oh, these animal wants! How often do they ride rough-shod over the intellectual man, not so much on his own account, as for those dependent on him. I have been thinking of Edward's excellent wife and her flock of seven girls, which I saw when at Banff. They were all neat and clean, and well cared for, in a wee bit roomie—the walls covered with cases of birds. When we called, there was a sweet-cake and a glass of wine for myself and Mr. Greive. I was unhappy at refusing his wine—for you know I am an out-and-out teetotaller — but I took his cake with thankfulness. And now, what can I do for that good man and his wife and family?...."

Mr. Peach went on to say that a great many Glut-men were employed at Wick harbor, to patrol the shore night and day, and prevent the landing of brandy, tobacco, and other excisable articles; that he could give Edward employment for a time at that work, but that it could not be permanent. His age was beyond that which would allow of his being appointed a tide-waiter. Mr. Peach added, " I will not lose sight of the appointment of subcuratorship. This would be the very thing. If forty or fifty pounds a year could be obtained, that would be glorious!"

These suggestions ended in disappointment. Edward could not remove to Wick to accept a temporary appointment; and the subcuratorship could not be obtained. He therefore went on with his old work—natural history and shoe-making. But he must have been pressed by the growing wants of his family, as we find his collection of birds advertised for sale at the beginning of 1855. Again he had recourse to his savings-bank; and again it relieved him, though he parted with the results of his work during many laborious years.

He still went on writing for the periodicals. At the end of 1855 we find an article of his in the *Zoologist*, entitled "Moth-hunting; or, An Evening in a Wood;" and in the following year he commenced in the same periodical "A List of the Birds of Banffshire, accompanied with Anecdotes." The list was completed in eight articles, which appeared in 1856 and the two following years. Although his publications were received with much approval, they did not serve to increase his income, for he never received a farthing for any of his literary contributions.

Before parting with Edward's descriptions of birds, a few extracts may be given from his articles in the *Zoologist*. And first, about song-birds:

"The song thrush or mavis (*Turdus musicus*). Who is there that has ever trod the weedy dale or whinny brake in early spring, and, having heard the mellow voice of this musician of the grove, was not struck with delight, and enchanted at the peculiar richness and softness of his tones? For my own part, I must say that of all the birds which adorn and enliven our woods, I love this one the most. There is to me a sweetness in his song which few, if any, of the other song-birds possess. Besides, he is one of the first to hail with his hymn of praise the young and opening year.

"Next to the mavis, the lark or the laverock is the bird for me, and has been since I first learned to love the little warblers of the woods and fields. How oft, oh! how oft, has the lark's dewy couch been my bed, and its canopy, the high azure vault, been my only covering, while overtaken by night during my wanderings after nature! And, oh! how sweet such nights are, and how short they seem—soothed as I have been to repose by the evening hymn of the lark, and aroused by their early lays at the first blink of morn!

"The goldfinch is also a good singing-bird. If any one wishes to have a cage-bird to cheer him with its song, let him get a male hybrid between this species and the canary, and I am sure he will not be disappointed..... The goldfinch's nest is one of nature's masterpieces. What a beautiful piece of workmanship! how exquisitely woven together! how light, compact, soft, and warm in its internal lining! and how complete! What hand could imitate the woolly, feathery, mossy, cup-formed, half-ball-like structure? How vain the attempt!

"The bullfinch, though much admired as a cage-bird, can not be said to be much of a songster. It is kept more for its beauty than its music, though it is sometimes able to 'pipe' a very pretty tune. Now, with respect to its food. Great numbers of bull-finches are annually destroyed by our gardeners and nursery-men because they are supposed to be destructive. Now, it is a fact well known to ornithologists that although the sparrow, greenfinch, chaffinch, wren, bull-finch, and other birds, do not themselves actually live on insects, yet these form the chief food for their young. Such being the case, what an enormous and countless number of noxious and destructive creatures must they destroy! But we poor short-sighted mortals do not know this. We are all in the dark as regards the good they do us. Let them meddle with any of our seeds or fruits, and the hue and cry is, 'Get guns and shoot every one of them.' I hope a better day will soon arise for these lovely little birds, when they will be cherished and encouraged rather than hated and destroyed."

The story is told of an ancient philosopher having been killed by an eagle that dropped a tortoise upon his head for the purpose of breaking its shell. The story seems to be confirmed by the practice of the carrion and hooded crows, thus described by Edward: "They are to be found on certain parts of our coast all the year round. · Our keepers destroy them whenever the opportunity occurs. I wonder that our fishermen do not destroy them also, as they feed upon a certain crustacean (*Carcinus mœnas*) which is often used for bait. One would think that the crab's shell would be proof against the crow; but no. He goes aloft with the crab, and lets it fall upon a stone or a rock chosen for the purpose. If it does not break, he seizes it again, goes up higher, lets its fall, and repeats his operation again and again until his object is accomplished. When a convenient stone is once met with, the birds resort to it for a long time. I myself know a pretty high rock that has been used by successive generations of crows for about twenty years.

"Besides being fond of crabs, these carrion crows are fond of fish, and though they are good fishers themselves, they seldom lose an opportunity of assailing the heron when he has made a successful dive. They rush at him immediately, and endeavor to seize his food from him. Early in the summer of 1845, while loitering about the hills of Boyndie, I observed a heron flying heavily along, as if from the sea—that rich and inexhaustible magazine of nature— and pursued by a carrion crow, followed at some distance by two magpies. They had not proceeded far when two hooded crows made their appearance, and quickly joined their black associate. The heron had by this time got into an open space between two woods, and it would appear that his enemies intended to keep him there until he had satisfied their demands. During the whole time that the affray lasted, or nearly half an hour, they did not suffer him to proceed above a few yards in any way, either backward or forward, his principal movements being in ascending or descending alternately, in order to avoid the assaults of his pursuers. Having chosen their battle-ground, I crept behind a whin-bush, from whence I had an uninterrupted view of the whole affair.

" The manœuvring of the crows with the heron was most

admirable.   Indeed, their whole mode of procedure had something in it very remarkable.   So well did each seem to understand his position, that the one never interfered with the other's point of attack.   One, rising higher than the heron, descended upon him like a dart, aiming the blow in general at his head; another at the same time pecked at him sideways and from before; while the third assailed him from beneath and behind.   The third crow, which pecked at him from behind, seized hold of the heron's feet, which, being extended at full length backward, formed a very tempting and prominent object for the crow to fix on.   This movement had the effect, each time, of turning the heron over, which was the signal for a general outburst of exultation among the three black rogues, manifested by their louder cawings and whimsical gesticulations—no doubt laughing (if crows can laugh) at seeing their opponent turning topsy-turvy in the air, which, from his unwieldy proportions, was rather a comical sight.

"During one of his somersaults, the heron disgorged something, but, unfortunately for him, it was not observed by any of the crows.   When it fell to the ground, the magpies, which were still chattering about, fell upon it and devoured it.   Finding no relief from what he had dropped, and being still hard pressed, he again disgorged what appeared to be a small fish.   This was noticed by one of the hooded crows, who speedily descended, picked it up, and made off with it, leaving his two companions to fight the battle out.   The heron, having now got rid of one of his pursuers, determined to fly away in spite of all opposition. But his remaining assailants, either disappointed at the retreat of their comrade, or irritated at the length of the struggle, recommenced their attack with renewed vigor.   So artfully did they manage, that they kept the heron completely at bay, and baffled all his endeavors to get away. Wearied at last of the contest, he once more dropped something, which, from its length, seemed to be an eel.   On its being observed by his opponents, they quickly followed it. In their descent, they fell a fighting with each other. The consequence was that the eel, falling to the ground, was set upon by the magpies. The crows gave up fighting, descended to the ground, and assailed the magpies. The latter were soon repulsed. Then the crows seized hold of the eel with their bills, and kept pulling at it until eventually it broke in two. Each kept hold of its portion, when they shortly rose up and flew away among the trees. In the mean time, the heron was observed winging his way in the distance; sick at heart, because he had been plundered by thieves, and robbed of the food which he had intended for his family."

The carrion and hooded crows also attack hares and rabbits. "While walking one morning along the Deveron with a friend, our attention was attracted by what seemed to us to be the faint cries of a child in distress. On looking in the direction from which the sounds proceeded, we beheld two crows pursuing and tormenting a hare, by every now and then pouncing down upon it. Each blow seemed to be aimed at the head; and each time that one was given the hare screamed piteously. The blows soon had the effect of stupefying the creature. Sometimes they felled it to the ground. We eventually lost sight of the crows, but doubtless they would at last kill and devour the hare. I remember, while out on the hills at Boyndie, witnessing another though a less daring attack. Concealed among some trees and bushes, waiting for a cuckoo which I expected to pass, I observed a half-grown rabbit emerge from some whins, and begin to frolic about close by. Presently down pops a hoodie, and approaches the rabbit, whisking, prancing, and jumping. He seemed to be most friendly, courteous, and humorsome to the little rabbit. All of a sudden, however, as if he meant to finish the joke with a ride, he mounts the back of the rabbit. Up springs the latter, and away he runs. But short was his race. A few sturdy

blows about the head from the bill of the crow laid him
dead in a few seconds."

By the year 1858 Edward had accumulated another
splendid collection.   It was his third, and probably his best.
The preserved birds were in splendid order.   Most of them
were in their natural condition—flying or fluttering, pecking or feeding—with their nests, their eggs, and sometimes
their young.   He had also a large collection of insects, including many rare beetles—together with numerous fishes,
crustaceans, zoophytes, mollusks, fossils, and plants.

WHITEHILLS AND BAY OF BOYNDIE, FROM BANFF LINKS.

Although Edward still continued his midnight explorations, he felt that he must soon give them up.   Lying out
at night can not be long endured in this country.   It is not
the cold, so much as the damp, that rheumatizes the muscles
and chills the bones.   When going out at night, Edward
was often advised to take whisky with him.   He was told
that, if he would drink it when he got wet or cold, it would
refresh and sustain him, and otherwise do him a great deal
of good.   Those who knew of his night-wanderings wondered how he could ever have endured the night air and
been kept alive without the liberal use of whisky.   But Edward always refused.   He never took a drop of whisky

with him; indeed, he never drank it, either at home or abroad. "I believe," he says, "that if I had indulged in drink, or even had I used it at all on these occasions, I could never have stood the cold, the wet, and the other privations to which I was exposed. As for my food, it mainly consisted of good oatmeal cakes. It tasted very sweet, and was washed down with water from the nearest spring. Sometimes, when I could afford it, my wife boiled an egg or two, and these were my only luxuries. But, as I have already said, water was my only drink."

In 1858 Edward had reached his forty-fourth year. At this age, men who have been kindly reared and fairly fed are usually in their prime, both of mind and body. But Edward had used himself very hardly; he had spent so many of his nights out-of-doors, in the cold and the wet; he had been so tumbled about among the rocks; he had so often, with all his labors, to endure privation, even to the extent of want of oatmeal—that it is scarcely to be wondered at if at that time his constitution should have begun to show marks of decay. He had been frequently laid up by colds and rheumatism. Yet, when able to go out again, he usually returned to his old courses.

At last his health gave way altogether. He was compelled to indulge in the luxury of a doctor. The doctor was called in, and found Edward in a rheumatic fever, with an ulcerated sore throat. There he lay, poor man, his mind wandering about his birds. He lay for a month. He got over his fever, but he recovered his health slowly. The doctor had a serious talk with him. Edward was warned against returning to his old habits. He was told that, although his constitution had originally been sound and healthy, it had, by constant exertion and exposure to cold and wet, become impaired to a much greater degree than had at first been supposed. Edward was also distinctly informed that if he did not at once desist from his nightly wanderings, his life would not be worth a farthing. Here, it appeared, was to be the end of his labors in natural history.

Next came the question of family expenditure and doctor's bills. Edward had been ill for a month, and the debts incurred during that time must necessarily be paid. There was his only savings-bank — his collection of birds — to meet the difficulty. He was forced to draw upon it again. Accordingly, part of it was sold. Upward of forty cases of birds went, together with three hundred specimens of mosses and marine plants, with other objects not contained in cases. When these were sold, Edward lost all hopes of ever being able again to replenish his shattered collection.

Although Edward's strength had for the most part been exhausted, his perseverance was not. We shall next find him resorting to another branch of natural history, in which he gathered his most distinguished laurels.

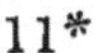

11*

CHAPTER XIV.

BY THE SEA-SHORE.

EDWARD had for some time been extending his investigations to the tenants of the deep. His wanderings had for the most part been along-shore in search of sea-birds. But as early as 1856 we find him corresponding with Mr. Macdonald, of Elgin, as to zoophytes; with Mr. Blackwood, of Aberdeen, as to algæ; and with Mr. C. Spence Bate, of Plymouth, as to crustacea. Now that he had to abandon his night wanderings, and to give up his gun, he resolved to devote himself more particularly to the natural history of the sea-shore.

Here was a great field open for him. The Moray Firth had never been properly searched for marine productions. It was full of fish, and also of the various marine objects that fish feed upon.

When Professor Macgillivray called upon Edward, at Banff, he expressed his surprise at the meagreness of the list of crustacea and testacea found along the Moray coast. In fact, the catalogue of fishes (excepting herring, cod, haddock, and the other edible fishes) was almost barren. There was no want of marine objects; the principal want was in careful observers. To this extensive field of observation Edward now proposed to devote his special attention.

He had considerable difficulty to encounter in proceeding with this branch of scientific work. He had no dredge of any sort. He had no boat, nor could he obtain the loan

of one.   How, then, did he proceed?   He gathered together
all the old pots, pans, pails, and kettles which he could procure in his neighborhood.   He filled these with straw, grass,
bits of old clothes, or bits of blankets.   A coat and trousers cut down were found very useful.   These were Edward's sea-traps.   Having put a heavyish stone at the bottom of the trap to weigh it down, and attached a rope to
the upper part, he lowered his traps into the deeper rock-
pools along the coast.   Some of them he threw into the
sea from the point of a rock, attaching the rope to a stone,
or to some strong algæ.

When the traps were drawn up, Edward obtained from
them small fishes, crustaceans, mollusks (with or without
shells), star-fish, worms, and the smaller kinds of sea-mice.
He took them to a shallow pool and shook out the contents; and when he had picked out what he thought might
be useful, he packed the traps again and set them in their
old places.   He usually visited his sea-traps once a month;
but in winter he visited them less frequently, as he rarely
took any thing at that time of the year.

Edward visited the rocky shore for many miles east and
west of Banff.   He turned over the loose stones, turned up
the algæ, peeped in beneath the corners and shelves of the
projecting rocks.   He went to the pools, and often had the
pleasure of seeing the inhabitants working in their native
element.   If he observed something that he wanted, he
would make a dive at it, though the water might get up to
his head and shoulders.   Sometimes he fell in bodily; but
that did not matter much if he secured his object.

Here is the manner in which he once caught Bloch's
gurnard (*Trigla Blochii*).   Edward observed one of them
swimming in a rock pool.   It had, by some means or other,
come pretty close inshore during high water, and had got
entangled among the rocks, so that it had been unable to
make its way out again with the receding tide.   The pool,
though not deep, was pretty large, so that it gave Edward

a great deal of trouble and occupied a considerable time to capture the fish. "If it had not," says he, "been a rarity, I should most certainly have given in and acknowledged myself beaten long before my object was accomplished; for, between water and perspiration, I was in a pitiable plight before I gained the victory. As it was, however, I was well repaid in the end, besides the fun; that is, if there is any other person than myself so foolish as to call splashing up to the shoulders and eyes among brine, sea-weed, and slippery rocks, 'fun.' Although the fish is not large, mine is a splendidly marked specimen. In the water, and while shooting across and athwart the pool, its bright colors had a most beautiful appearance. The spot on the first dorsal is rather of a dark-purplish color than black, and very conspicuous when the animal is swimming. I am not aware of this species ever before having been detected on this part of the coast."

Knowing from observation that many marine objects are cast on shore at the rising of each tide, especially when the weather is stormy, Edward walked along the margin of the incoming wave, ready to pick up any thing that might be driven ashore. Sometimes he would observe some object in the water—a fish or a shrimp of some unusual kind—which he desired to capture. He followed it into the sea with a piece of gauze tied on a small hoop; and fished for it until he had caught it. He discovered many new objects in this way.

It is almost incredible what may be got along the sea-margin by carefully searching the incoming wave. This, however, required unwearied assiduity. Edward discovered many of his rarest insects among those driven ashore by the wind. It was thus that he obtained most of his rare crustaceans. He himself had no doubt that, had his health been prolonged, he would have discovered many more.

Besides these methods for collecting marine objects, he found that tangle roots were a special hiding-place for many species that were beyond the power of the dredge, and that never entered the traps set by him along shore. They were not, however, beyond the power of the elements. But for the tempest, that tears them from the rocks and dashes them on shore, such objects would never have been found. Whenever a storm occurred in the Moray Firth, Edward immediately went out, collected the tangle which had been driven in, cut off as many roots as he could carry with him, and carefully examined them at home.

He was also greatly helped by the fishes themselves, as well as by the fishermen. It is true that he had no dredge and no boat. But big fish were themselves the best of all dredgers. They fed far out at sea, at a depth where the dredge could scarcely reach. The fishermen caught them, and brought them into port, full of what they had swallowed. Edward therefore endeavored to obtain the contents of their stomachs. For this purpose he sent some of his daughters to the neighboring fishing villages. They went to Macduff and Whitehills twice a week, and to the Banff fishermen daily. The object of their visits was to search the fishermen's lines, to bring away the sea-weed and all the stuff that was attached to them, and to secure as many of the fish stomachs as they could find. One of his daughters was sent to Gardenstown, where she lived with a friend. From thence she sent home her collection of fish stomachs twice a week by the carrier. All this rubbish (as most people called it) was carefully examined by Edward. From these searchings he obtained most of his rarest crustaceans. "It is quite wonderful," he says, "what is to be got in this way. Indeed, no one would believe it who has not made the experiment."

Take, for instance, the cod's bill of fare. "It is to the stomach of this species," says Edward, "that I am most indebted for many of the rarest of the testaceous and crustaceous specimens that I possess. I will only mention what I have myself seen: crabs and lobsters of almost every description (except *Homarus vulgaris*, which I have never yet found), from the prickly stone crab (*Lithodes maia*) up to the hard parten (*Cancer pagurus*), and the larger the better. Shells of every sort, particularly *Fusus antiquus* and *Buccinium undulatum;* no matter whether inhabited by their original possessor, or by a hermit in the form of a pagurus, it is no obstacle to the voracious cod. Shrimps, fish-lice, sea-mice (*Aphrodita aculeata*), sea-urchins, with now and then a star-fish ; 'dead men's paps,' as they are called here (*Alcyonium*), and actinias—no matter what they may be attached to, whether a shell or a stone,* provided these are not themselves fixtures—all are gulped by this most unceremonious fish.   The eggs, capsules, or purses of the dogfish (*Scyllium*) and the skate, with the roe and the ova of other species, particularly when deposited on sea-weed; the algæ and the zoophytes also walk down the cod's gullet, so that nothing may be lost.   As for the *Holothuridæ*, or sea-cucumbers, few, if any, of them escape.   Now and then fragments of the medusæ are swallowed; feathers, with the remains of sea-fowl; and, on one occasion, the skeleton of a *partridge*, with the wings, feet, legs, and head adhering. Pieces of pewter and of cloth occasionally ; and once a cluster of beech-nuts, with part of a domestic fowl.   As for fish !—why, the fish does not swim that the cod, when hungry, will not attack, and, if successful, swallow.   In short, nothing seems to come amiss.   But this outline of the cod's bill of fare does not include all that the animal preys upon and devours.   It is enough, however, to show its epicurean propensities.   The cod is extensively fished for along this part of the coast, and may be termed *the poor man's salmon.*   Great numbers are salted and dried, and in that state are sent to the Southern markets.   The haddock,

---

* "It is only about nine months since I took from the stomach of a cod a stone which weighed above three pounds, to which the remains of an actinia were still attached."

like the cod, is extensively taken, and largely cured and forwarded South. Like the cod, the stomach of this species is also a rich mine for the naturalist, as the reader may already have anticipated from the foregoing list."*

In order to obtain all these products of the sea, Edward went round among the fishermen from Crovie to Portsoy, and pressed them to help him in his researches. He told them that many an object of great interest to naturalists was daily thrown away. Though it might be of no use to them, it might prove of great use to science. "Oh!" said the fishermen, "we canna tell what the fellow wants: we get so muckle trash upon our lines. Are we to keep it all?"

"Yes," replied Edward, "keep it all. Lay it carefully aside, and I or my daughters will call for it." A few of the fishermen did what Edward told them to do; but the others "couldna be fashed."

Edward published his advice to the fishermen in the *Banffshire Journal.* "How little trouble," he said, "would it be for any fisherman who might find a rare fish, crab, shell, or zoophyte, or such-like object attached to his lines, to get it examined and named, so that its occurrence might be recorded! This could be done, and then he could, if so minded, dispose of it to the best advantage. Or what great 'fash' could it be for them to keep the cleanings of their lines for a like scientific purpose?

"It is quite astonishing what amazing numbers of minute creatures are at times to be found among the refuse of only one boat's lines. No one would believe it, except those who are in the habit of carefully examining such things. The ocean is, as it were, one vast and boundless expanse of life, and the inhabitants thereof about as numberless as the sands by the sea-shore. I have myself, and that, too, under the most disadvantageous circumstances, picked off from a

---

* *Naturalist,* 1855.

dead valve of *Cyprina Islandica* nine distinct species of shells, three different kinds of star-fish, and five separate sorts of zoophytes, besides worms and a number of other parasitical animals. Yet this is nothing to what is at times to be met with; and yet such things are, I may say, all but universally thrown away for no other or better purpose than that of being trod upon and destroyed. I will now, in order to show the truthfulness of my statement, enumerate a few of the objects which have thus been cast aside by those who had brought them on shore, but which were again picked up by my *gleaners*, and thereby redeemed, as it were, for a time from destruction, by being deposited in my collection—*Anomia patelliformis, Circe minuta, Venus casina, Venus fasciata, Tellina proxima, Tellina crassa, Mangelia linearis, Pentunculus glycimeris, Psammobia tellinella, Astarte compressa, Corbula nucleus, Emarginula reticulata, Thracia villosinsinla, Chiton lovis, etc., etc.*

"Now, I don't say that these are all new species, but I say that they are among the rarest of our shells. The two first named are, if I mistake not, new, not only to us, but new to this northern part of the island. In works on conchology, no mention is made of either having been previously found on the shores of the Moray Firth, although they are not unfrequent on other parts of the British coast."

The fishermen of Macduff helped him greatly. Among the rare fishes caught by them were the sandsucker (*Platessa limandaides*); the small spotted dogfish (*Scyllium canicula*); the blue-striped wrasse (*Labrus variegatus*), a very rare fish; a specimen of the cuttle-fish (*Loligo vulgaris*), the length of which was four feet, with a splendid gladius of above fifteen inches long. In enumerating these fishes brought to him by the fishermen of Macduff, Edward asked, "What are our own Banff fishermen and those of Whitehills about, that they never bring in any rare objects of this sort? Do they never get any thing attached to their lines worthy of notice—worthy of a place in a naturalist's cabinet, or in a corner of the Museum? Why won't they help us? Just because of their want of will. They, like many more, go about in what might be termed a state of daylight somnambulism—that is, with eyes and ears both open, and yet they neither see nor hear of any of these things.

Edward's appeal was at length responded to. The fishermen began to collect things for him, and they allowed his girls to strip their nets of the "rubbish" they contained. One evening some unknown fishermen sent him a present of a saury pike (*Scomberesox saurius*). Edward's family were surprised at hearing some person, very heavily shod, ascending the stairs. One said it was a horse and cart; another said it was the Rooshians. The door was suddenly opened and flung bang against the wall, when in rushed —neither the horse and cart nor the Rooshians—but a little urchin, out of breath, with his mouth wide open. There he stood, staring bewildered round the room, but with a fish of a silvery hue dangling from his hand. After he had regained his breath, he roared out, "Is Tam in?" "No." "'Cause I ha'e a beast till him." "Fa gi'ed ye't?" "A man." "Fatna man?" "Dinna ken!" "Fat like was he?" "Canna tell." "Fat had he on?" "Dinna mind; only that he had a coat ower his airm." "Fat said he t'ye when he gi'ed ye the beast?" "Oh, he bade me take it till Tam Edward, and get a penny for't till mysel."

The fish was accepted, the penny was given, and the boy tramped down-stairs again. On returning home, Edward found a splendid specimen of the above rare fish. The next number of the *Journal* acknowledged the receipt of the fish. In the article describing it, Edward said: "By whom the fish was sent, or where it was found (though doubtless in the neighborhood, from its freshness), remains as yet a mystery. However, thanks to 'the man with the coat ower his airm' in the mean time, and to many others whose kindness and attention, though their gifts are not

particularized here, are nevertheless duly appreciated.   Likewise, and in an especial manner, thanks to the fishermen
generally of the district, particularly to our own and those
of Whitehills, not only for their now unremitting attention
in securing whatever they deem worthy of notice themselves; but also, and above all, for their very valuable assistance given, and their warm-hearted kindness shown to
my young folks when they go a-gleaning among them."

Indeed, Edward's young folks were of great help to him
at this time.   Several of his eldest girls went about from
place to place in search of rare fish, and they were sometimes very successful.   For instance, one of them, while
living with Mr. Gordon, at Gardenstown, went on a zoolo-
gizing excursion toward the village of Crovie.   As the two
were rounding the Snook, they observed a small fish being
washed ashore.   Mr. Gordon kicked it with his foot, thinking it was of no use, and remarking that it was a young
sea-cat.   "Na," said Maggie, "it's nae sea-cat; it's ower
thin for that.   I dinna ken fat it is; but I'll take it, and
send it hame to my father, for he bade me never to miss
naething o' this kine."   So the fish was sent home, and it
proved to be a very fine specimen of Yarrell's blenny.

On another occasion she sent home a specimen of the
black goby, or rock-fish (*Gobius niger*), which had been
taken from the stomach of a friendly cod.   This was the
first fish of the kind found in the Moray Firth; and of the
six species of gobies found along the coasts of Great Britain, it is the one most seldom met with.   Maggie also made
a good "find" at Fraserburgh, while on a zoological tour
with her father.   She was rummaging about among the
sands, near Broadsea, accompanied by some of her acquaintances, when she observed something sticking up out of the
sand.   At first she thought it was a piece of tangle.   She
was about to leave it, when, prompted by curiosity, she
gave it a pull, and, lo and behold! instead of a sea-weed,
she brought out a long spindle-like fish.   She at once took

it to her father, who found it to be a splendid specimen of
the equoreal needle-fish (*Syngnathus æquoreus*), a fish that
had never before been found in the Moray Firth.

A thought may here strike the reader. How was it
that Edward knew that there were six gobies found along
the coasts of Great Britain? How did he know that the
equoreal needle-fish had never been found in the Moray
Firth before? And, last of all, how was it that he knew
the scientific names of the fishes, the zoophytes, and the

BROADSEA, NEAR FRASERBURGH.

crustacea, which he collected? The names were, for the
most part, Latin. Yet he had never learned Latin. He
must, then, have learned them from books. No: he had
no books. He often ardently desired books, but he was
too poor to buy them. His earnings were scarcely sufficient to enable him to feed and clothe his children. Under
such circumstances, a man can not buy books. Sometimes
his children fared very badly, especially when he was laid
up by illness. At such times they had almost to starve.

How was it, then, that under these difficult circumstances,
and amidst his almost constant poverty, Edward was enabled to carry on the study of science without the aid of
books? He did so by the help of correspondents at a dis-

tance. When he had collected a batch of objects, he sent them off by post to naturalists in different parts of the country, for the purpose of obtaining from them the proper names. They referred to their scientific works, and furnished him with the necessary information.

Edward sent his specimens of crustacea to Mr. Spence Bate, of Plymouth, Devonshire; his fishes to Mr. Couch, of Polperro, Cornwall; and many other objects to correspondents in Norwich, York, Newcastle, Birmingham, and London. The Rev. George Gordon, of the manse of Birnie, Elginshire, was one of his first correspondents respecting the crustacea. Mr. Spence Bate was then engaged (in conjunction with Professor Westwood) in writing the "History of the British Sessile-eyed Crustacea." Mr. Gordon first forwarded to him some of Edward's specimens, and Edward afterward corresponded directly with Mr. Bate. Thus he obtained his scientific knowledge, not from the books in his own neighborhood, but from the books of gentlemen sometimes living at the opposite ends of the island.

There was, indeed, some talk of supplying Edward with books, to enable him to pursue his scientific researches. At a public dinner in Banff, the principal speaker, after paying a high compliment to Edward for his wonderful perseverance, and his devotion to natural science, proceeded to describe the great influence which books exercised in developing the powers of the human mind. After informing his audience that they did not know the value of the man they had got among them, he said: "Assist and encourage him by all the means in your power, but "—here he paused, and all eyes were turned upon him—"but," he continued, "give him no money [loud cheers]. I know him, as you all do, to be no drunkard, no idler, but a sober, hard-working man. But still, I again say, give him no money. Give him BOOKS; provide him with the means of reading, and he is just the man to make money for himself." The auditors thought that they had done sufficient justice to Edward by cheering the proposal of the orator; but it was words—mere words; for Edward got neither a book, nor even the leaf of a book, from any of his local admirers.

How different from this cold counsel was the enthusiasm of Edward when speaking of his favorite science! In an article which appeared in the *Naturalist* on the rayed echinodermata of Banffshire, after regretting the small amount of observation and research which had been made along the shores of the Moray Firth, he said: "It is a great pity that the Moray Firth was never dredged by naturalists, as I am led to believe it never was, on a scale worthy of its waters. If such were done, and done as it should be, I am quite sure, from what I know, that many a valuable rarity, and, I have no doubt, many new species, would be procured, and better got than those already known. If I were but possessed of half the means that some are, it should not long be so. Wind and weather permitting, I should have it dredged from the one end to the other, over and over again. Alas that Nature, that fair and comely damsel, whom I supremely admire and love so well, should have called me into existence at the very moment when *want* and *starvation* stood hand-in-hand, ready to stamp the unconscious heir of immortality with their accursed brands! Money, it is said, is the root of all evil; but tell me, ye who know, what the want of it is!"

We have already said that Edward, because of his want of books on natural history, obtained the principal knowledge of the objects which he discovered from gentlemen at a distance. But even this was not accomplished without difficulty. It was not always a pleasant task, and sometimes it was rather expensive—expensive at least for a poor man. He occasionally encountered disagreeable rebuffs. Some complained that they could not read his writing, and that what he said was unintelligible. Another hinderance was, that when he sent a number of new specimens to naturalists at a distance, they were often kept, and thanks only were returned. But he was scarcely in a position to resent this conduct. At last he sent none but those of which he had duplicates, preferring to keep them without a name rather than run the risk of losing them altogether.

Mr. Edward Newman, of London, editor of the *Zoologist*, was one of those who helped Edward with books. He also named many of Edward's beetles and other insects, which were sent to him for identification. The correspondence* between them originated in Edward's articles on the birds of Banffshire, which began to appear in the *Zoologist* in August, 1856. Mr. Newman sent Edward several books on natural history, together with his own "List of British Birds." In February, 1858, we find Mr. Newman sending Edward a copy of the "Insect Hunters," his most successful book. Mr. Newman said to Edward, "I think it really wonderful that you should have acquired the great knowledge you have obtained under the circumstances in which you have been placed." Mr. Newman asked for some information about fishes, which Edward promised to supply. The result was, that many new fishes were found in the Moray Firth, simply from Edward's determination to search, collect, and preserve them.

---

* Most of Edward's correspondence has been lost, destroyed, or used for "kindling." He never had the least idea that old letters could be useful. When the author made inquiry about them, Edward said, "I fear there will be a great blank there. I am not aware when I began to correspond; and as for keeping letters, I had no reason for that; still, I may have some, and I will try and find them." After about a week, he said, "I have found no old letters yet; but my wife tells me that she saw a box, about two years ago, in an old lumber garret, which she thinks may contain some useless old papers of mine. I will try and get it out, and make a search. I might have had many hundreds, if not thousands, if I had kept them. The postman, as well as my master and shop-mates, were all surprised at the great number of letters I received for many years." At last the box in the garret was discovered, and a small collection of letters was found in it, which the author has made use of in writing the latter part of this memoir.

Edward had also much correspondence with Mr. Alexander G. More, with respect to the distribution of birds in Great Britain during the nesting season. Edward was appointed the observer for Banffshire and the northern part of Aberdeen. He communicated a great deal of information about birds and birdnesting, which was afterward published in the periodical called *The Ibis.*

But his most important communications were with Mr. Couch as to fishes; and with Mr. Spence Bate, and the Rev. A. Merle Norman, as to crustacea; which will form the subjects of the following chapters.

CHAPTER XV.

DISCOVERIES AMONG THE CRUSTACEA.

THE reader will find this chapter, as well as the next, rather uninteresting. But it is necessary that the chapters should be written, in order to show the contributions which Edward made to the scientific discoveries of his day.

Mr. C. Spence Bate, of Plymouth, the well-known zoologist, entered into correspondence with Edward in 1856, while the latter was engaged in collecting marine objects along the sea-coast of Banff. It appears that Mr. Bate had sent to Edward some publications on natural history, and that Edward requested Mr. Bate to name the various crustaceans which he sent him. To this Mr. Bate willingly assented, and a correspondence began between them, which continued for many years. Most of the letters have been lost, and those which have been preserved "in the box in the lumber garret" are not of very great interest.

Edward seems to have been particularly busy between the years 1861 and 1865. Multitudes of bottles were sent, during that interval, from Banff to Plymouth. The bottles were often smashed in passing through the post. Sometimes there was only a mass of débris to examine. In one batch there was a new species of Leucothoii; in another, part of an Eusirus—"the *first* British specimen."

In one of his letters Mr. Bate says: "There are two minute specimens of a prawn which I do not recognize. They are too much damaged for examination; but if you can find any perfect ones like these, I should like you to send them to me. I will send you shortly a paper that I have recently published in the "Annals of Natural History" on the "Nest-building Crustacea." If you know or meet with any anecdotes relative to these animals, I should be glad if you would communicate them to me, as I am endeavoring to collect all of that kind that I can. I assure you that your letters are always welcome, and much valued."

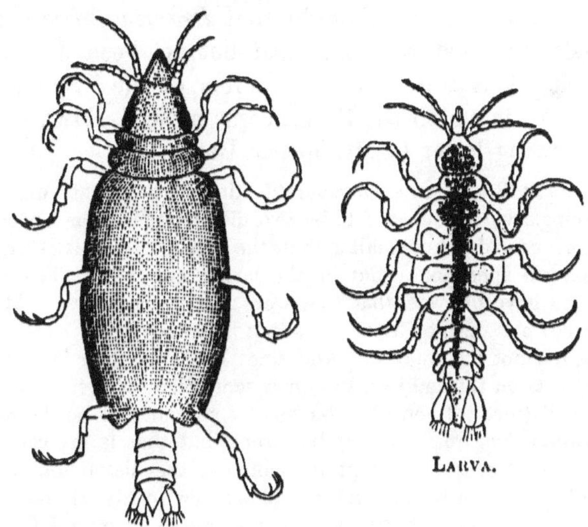

PRANIZA EDWARDII.

In the midst of Edward's explorations, he discovered a new Isopod, which he forwarded to Mr. Bate. It was specifically named, in honor of the discoverer, *Praniza Edwardii.** On subsequent examination, and after comparing it with the Anceus, Messrs. Bate and Westwood changed the name into *Anceus Edwardii.*†

The Anceus is only about a sixth of an inch in length. But, in natural history, size goes for nothing. The mi-

---

* "Annals of Natural History," vol. ii.
† "History of the British Sessile-eyed Crustacea," vol. ii., p. 201.

nutest animal is equal to the largest, in point of value and interest. The Anceus creeps on the bottom of the sea, but it swims with great rapidity—propelling itself forward by the quick motions of a series of ciliated fins placed beneath the tail. The Anceus, in its young state, is parasitical, and is furnished with a sharp process at the apex of the anterior lip, to form a strong lanceolate organ, with which the animal cuts its way through the skin of the fish on which it preys. It was at first thought that *Praniza Edwardii* was a female, and that the male had not yet been discovered. On seeing this stated in the number of the "Sessile-eyed Crustacea" in which the Praniza was noticed, Edward wrote the following letter to Mr. Spence Bate :

"My DEAR SIR,—Some considerable time ago, I sent you, among other things, what I believed to be two distinct species of Anceus, the one being considerably smaller than the other. Of the lesser, there were several specimens; but of the larger, only two. The answer which you gave me was, that they were *Anceus maxillaris*. At this I was somewhat disappointed. I admit that the larger were of that species, but not the smaller. And since I received your last number, which treats on this subject, I am now more than ever convinced that they are distinct. I consider the smaller specimen to be the male of the *Praniza Edwardii*. I may be wrong, but that is my conviction. I need not, of course, attempt to point out the distinctions to you ; but perhaps you will allow me to state a few words on the subject, and what makes me think that he is the male of *Praniza Edwardii*.

" In the first place, I would say that this little fellow is decidedly a deep-sea species—that is, so far as my experience goes. I have never found him but on the old shells and stones brought up by the fishermen's lines. There he seems to prowl about seeking what he may devour—prying into every crevice and corner in search of food, and also into the tenantless worm-cases with which these old shells and stones are generally incrusted. Now these are exactly the habitats and manners of the *Praniza Edwardii* when adult. Where I find the one, I am almost sure to find the other. I have found them together, and taken them out of the same worm-tube. But though this does not amount to an entire proof, still it helps to strengthen my conjecture that they are male and female.

" In the second place, besides the striking disparity in size, the mandibles in this species appear to me to differ considerably from

the same organs in the *Anceus maxillaris*. Here I have never seen
them to overlap each other as they do in the one just named. And,
having frequently kept them alive, I have seen their mandibles open
and shut times without number; and, so far as I could make out,
they never crossed each other in the least. Indeed, I do not think
they could have done so, from their construction. They seem to me,
when they do shut, to go together in the fashion of a rat-trap when
closed. And, besides several other distinctions which I have been able
to discern, there are two or three small bunches of stiff hairs or spines
projecting from the front of the head which I do not see in *Anceus
maxillaris* and the others which you describe. I would also point out
that there is a most remarkable similarity in the tail or hind-part of
this species and the same portion of the *Praniza Edwardii.*"

In support of his views, Edward forwarded some further
specimens of the supposed male to Mr. Bate for his inspection. We have not been able to find Mr. Bate's answer. It has doubtless been lost, like many of the missing
letters. But we gather from a future letter of Edward that
Mr. Bate considered the specimens to be *Anceus rapax.*
"Never having seen a description or plate of that species,"
said Edward, "I can say nothing as to that matter.....
But, call him what you like, I am more than ever persuaded
that he is the tight little husband of *Praniza Edwardii;*
and, as such, I now intend to place them together, and to
name them accordingly."

Many of the crustacea which Edward collected did not
belong to the sessile-eyed order, which Mr. Bate was studying and classifying. These crustaceans he sent to other
observers. For instance, when Mr. Bate was about to set
out for Paris to examine Milne-Edward's typical crustacea,
he received from Edward a letter containing some ento-
mostracea which had been collected from the stomach of
a mackerel. "I do not," replied Mr. Bate, "study the
entomostracous crustacea myself; so I gave some of those
you sent me to Mr. Lubbock, and some to Dr. Baird, of the
British Museum, from both of whom I hope you will hear."

In a future letter, Edward sent Mr. Bate some worm-like

parasites found on a short sun-fish taken near Banff. " The genus," said Edward, " is very little known in this country. It has hitherto been found only on the flying-fish. It seems, however, to frequent the sun-fish. This was not previously known. When once these creatures take a firm hold, it is impossible to shake them off or get rid of them, they sink so deep into the animal's body. There are from two to three longish barbs which protrude from the neck, close to the head, and which appear to serve exactly the same purpose as the barb does on the hook. One which I cut out —and no easy matter it was—had its head sunk at least an inch and a half into the fatty ridge of the fish. In the *Illustrated London News* of July 10th, 1858, there is an illustration given of a flying-fish with a parasite attached to its back, and having a lot of barnacles adhering to it. The fish here figured is said to have leaped from the sea into the mizzen chains of the East-Indiaman *Monarch*, while on her homeward voyage from Calcutta. The parasite in that case was quite different from the one I obtained from the sun-fish. It was there called *Pennella Blanvillii.*"

In one of his communications, Edward sent Mr. Bate some parasites which he had taken from the gills of a crab. Many of the crustaceans found by him were so minute that they could scarcely be examined in detail with the naked eye. Mr. Bate accordingly, with great kindness, made Edward a present of a microscope to enable him to carry on his minute investigations. "It is," said Mr. Bate, in his letter announcing the departure of the parcel, " what we call a simple microscope, and I think you will find it adapted for examining things out of or in doors. It is made portable, and can be used upon the rocks as well as in a parlor. It is similar to one which I use myself for every thing, excepting when I examine into structural anatomy. I was not able," added Mr. Bate, " to have it prepaid farther than Bristol ; so I beg to inclose a few stamps, which I hope will cover it for the remainder of the way."

Edward at first found a difficulty in managing the microscope, on which Mr. Bate sent him a long letter illustrated by diagrams, informing him how he was to use it. "I am sure," he said, "you are too sharp a fellow not to understand it thoroughly after these few hints have been given you..... I will also send you a pocket lens, which you will find very useful..... You will find it convenient during this cold weather (November 24th) to bring home any thing, and then look at it at your leisure, rather than study it upon the sea-shore."

Mr. Bate must have been a thoroughly kind and good-hearted man. He may possibly have heard something of the circumstances of Edward, and he was now on the look-out for some higher vocation for the naturalist than that of "ladies' shoe-maker." The Rev. George Gordon, also a zoologist, who was in constant communication with Mr. Bate, may have probably informed him of Edward's ambition, which was to be appointed curator or subcurator of some important museum. Hence Mr. Bate's letter to Edward. After informing him that Mr. Lubbock would shortly ask him to make a collection of crustacea, and advising him to send certain fishes in proof-spirit to the British Museum, he proceeded:

"I have one thing more to say; but I write in ignorance of your circumstances, and therefore, if I tread upon a *corn*, pray forgive me. I have been asked if I can recommend a person to the College of Surgeons, whose duty will be to attend upon the curators and professors, and make preparations, and do other work in natural history. The salary is one pound ten shillings a week. If such a thing will suit you, let me know, and I will write to propose you. If the place is not filled up, I think it might be got."

This letter raised a glimmer of hope in Edward's breast. Was he really to be rewarded at last for his efforts in natural history, by an appointment which would bring him into communication with scientific men? It may be mentioned

that Edward had already been appointed keeper of the
Scientific Society's Museum at Banff, at a salary of two
pounds two shillings per annum. This was, of course,
merely a nominal remuneration, and the occupation did not
tend to feed Edward's thirst for further knowledge in natural history. He was therefore most willing to accede
to Mr. Bate's proposition; and he sent in his application,
accompanied by testimonials, to Professor Quekett, of the
Royal College of Surgeons.

Unfortunately, Mr. Bate had been misinformed as to the
nature of the proposed appointment. "I am fearful," said
Professor Quekett, in his letter to Edward, "that some of
your kind friends have misinformed you as to the nature of
the appointment which is vacant. It is only that of fourth
museum porter. The duties are: to keep the room clean,
dust bottles, etc., at the wage of a guinea a week. Now,
from what I learn of you through your testimonials, and
from what I have heard of your reputation and high standing as a naturalist, I think such an appointment is far beneath your notice."

Edward's hopes were once more blighted. Science could
do nothing for him, and he returned again to his cobbler's
stool. He had become accustomed to disappointment;
nevertheless, he continued to pursue his work as a naturalist. In fact, he went on working harder than before.
As Mr. Bate was only engaged with one branch of the
crustacea—the sessile-eyed—and as other naturalists were
engaged in investigating other branches of marine zoology,
Edward was referred to these gentlemen, more particularly to the Rev. A. Merle Norman, of Sedgefield, Ferry hill,
County of Durham; Mr. J. Gwyn Jeffreys, of London; and
Mr. Joshua Alder, of Newcastle-on-Tyne, all of whom were
great sea-dredgers.

Zoologists usually take up some special subject and work
it up. They freely correspond with their fellow-zoologists
in different parts of the country with the object of obtain-

ing their help, which is rarely or never withheld. There is a sort of freemasonry among naturalists in this respect. Thus, when Mr. J. Gwyn Jeffreys opened his correspondence with Edward, he said, "No introduction can be necessary from one naturalist to another." While artists and literary men form themselves into cliques, and cut each other up in social circles and in newspapers, naturalists, on the contrary, seem to be above such considerations of envy and uncharitableness.

There is also a fellow-feeling among them, and they are ready to help each other in various other ways. Thus, when Edward was informed by Mr. Spence Bate that the Rev. Mr. Norman was working up the British entomostracous crustacea, including the fish parasites, Edward immediately began to scour the coast, and wade along the waves as the tide came in, plunging into the rock-pools, in order to procure the animals of which Mr. Norman was in search. He did this regardless of his health, and also regardless of his pocket.

A long correspondence had already taken place between Edward and Mr. Norman; but in the midst of it Edward was again laid up by illness, which lasted for about six weeks. The correspondence dropped for a time, but it was afterward renewed. Mr. Norman, in his letter of May 12th, 1862, observed: "I have been absent from home ever since I received your last note, or I should have answered it before. I am extremely sorry to hear of the cause, your serious illness, which prevented your answering my two last letters, and seemed to end a correspondence from which I had derived so much pleasure, finding in yourself such a kindred, nature-loving spirit. I am rejoiced, however, that God has mercifully raised you up again after so much suffering, and that you are recovering the blessings of health and strength.

"Many thanks for the promise of your kind offices for me in procuring fish parasites. Our knowledge of them is at present but limited, and a large number of species new to our Fauna may, I am satisfied, be found, if properly looked after. I trust, therefore, that you may extend your knowledge of the crustacea of the Moray Firth to this branch of the subject."

It would occupy too much space to detail the contents of the letters which Edward received from Mr. Norman and Mr. Spence Bate while their respective works were in process of publication. But there are several facts in them worthy of being noticed. There was one crustacean about which some difficulty had arisen. It was the *Mysis Spinifera*, which Edward had first found in the Moray Firth in the year 1858. He had sent it to one of his correspondents, in order that he might give it its name. But it remained unnoticed and unknown for a period of about four years, when it was rediscovered in Sweden by M. Goes, who at once published the fact. "Thus," says Edward, "the first finder, as well as the country in which this crustacean was first found, have both been ignored in the records of science."

Edward discovered many new species, some of which had never been met with before, and others which had not been met with in Britain. Some were recognized and named, but others were not. "The number of specimens I collected," says Edward, "was immense. It must have been so from the various methods I adopted to procure them, and from the fact that I never lost a single opportunity of obtaining even but one object when it could be got. Labor, time, cold, wet, privation, were nothing, so that I could but secure the specimen that I sought for. . . . . There are still several new species which I discovered and sent to gentlemen years ago. All I knew about them, from letters I received in return, is that they were *new;* but whether they have ever received names, or whether the discoveries have been made public, I do not know."

Mr. Spence Bate did every justice to Edward in the discoveries which he made of *new species*, in connection with his branch of the sessile-eyed crustacea. In one case, Edward caught only the anterior moiety of a small crustacean (*Protomedeia hirsutimana*), and yet Mr. Bate includes it in his list, and gives a drawing of it. Mr. Bate also did every justice to the accurate description of the habits of the species which Edward forwarded to him. For instance, Edward discovered the *Vibilia borealis*, a new species, in the Moray Firth, on which Mr. Spence Bate observes:

"Hitherto the species of this genus have been taken only as pelagic, in tropical or subtropical latitudes. It is an interesting fact that this species should have been taken off the coast of Banff, from whence it was sent us by that very successful observer, Mr. Edward, who, in writing, says: 'I can say little as to its habits. I took eleven, and kept a few alive for a short time, but observed nothing in their manners beyond that which may be seen in the majority of species. I supplied them with plenty of sand, and also with a few marine plants, but they seemed to be neither burrowers nor climbers, as they never went into the one, nor appeared to care for the other. They, however, swam a little. This they do somewhat after the manner of *Callisoma crenata;* in other words, they rise gradually from the bottom until they reach the top ; then, putting on more power, they swim round and round the vessel. With close observation, I observed that the superior antennæ were kept pretty well up and very widely apart, whereas the inferior were always directed downward. All the legs were kept doubled up. I never saw them stretched out. They would then sink once more to the sand at the bottom. There they would rest, sometimes for a few minutes, sometimes longer, when they would again repeat their voluntary evolutions. They did not, however, always rise to the surface: the journey was sometimes performed to about mid-water. They are, when alive, a most beautiful colored species, variegated not unlike *Urothroë elegans*, and rivaling that animal in brightness of tints. I took one, however, that was all over a most brilliant red. I have been told that this species has never been found outside the medusa. However this may be, all mine were. And what appears to be most extraordinary is, that we have had no medusæ here this season. During the months of July, August, and September, I have seen them, generally, by hundreds and thousands.'" Mr. Bate proceeds to say, "Mr. Edward informs us that he has seen specimens of these crustaceans thrown on the shore in extraordinarily large quantities. After a storm one night, he saw them forming a band an inch and a half deep for thirty yards along the beach."*

Mr. Bate so much admired Edward's enthusiasm in the cause of natural history, that he more than once urged him to publish his observations: "I received from you," he says, "a few days since, a parcel of *Eurydice pulchra*, in sand, one of which only was alive. I have been much interested in watching its active habits, and the manner in which it buries itself in the sand..... I wish that you would write some papers on the habits of these creatures. Keep a few at home under as favorable conditions as possible. I am sure much is yet to be learned about them. I know no one better fitted to work out the subject than yourself. For instance, get some of the *Podocerus capillatus*, and find out how it spins the web that makes the nest; and closely watch all their ways."

Edward might no doubt have written and published many papers in the scientific journals. He might have gained praise, fame, and honor. But what mattered these to him? The principal thing that he wanted was time— time not only for his investigations, but to earn money for the maintenance of his family. He had now a wife and eleven children to support. He earned nothing by science: he earned every thing by his shoe-maker's awl. What

---

* "History of the British Sessile-eyed Crustacea," by C. Spence Bate and J. O. Westwood, vol. ii., pp. 525, 526.

could the *Podocerus capillatus* do for his family?   Nothing whatever! His entire labors were gratuitous.   Properly speaking, naturalists should be gentlemen of independent fortune.   At all events, they should have some profession to live by; while Edward had nothing but his wretch-
edly paid trade of shoe-making.   The wonder is, that, with
all his illnesses, arising for the most part from the results
of exposure, he should have done so much, and continued
his self-sacrificing investigations so long.   But he seems to
have been borne up throughout by his scientific enthusiasm,
and by his invincible determination.

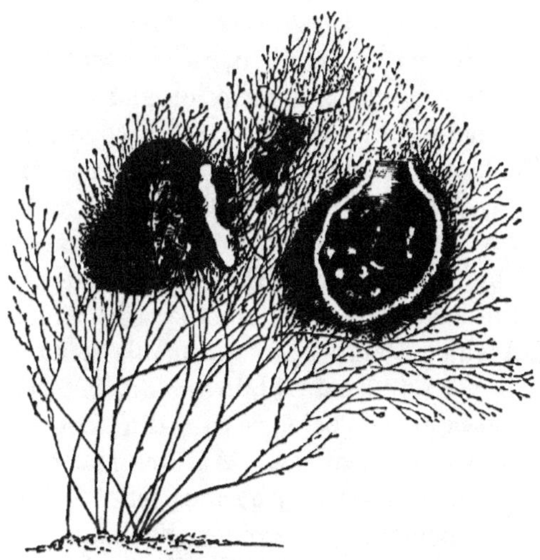

NESTS OF NEST-BUILDING CRUSTACEA.

The *Podocerus capillatus*, to which Mr. Bate repeatedly
directed Edward's attention, is a very interesting crustacean.
It is about a quarter of an inch long.   It is beautifully variegated, and builds its nests in a very bird-like manner in
submarine forests.   Edward found it in the rock-pools off
Banff, where it built its nests on *Corallina officinalis*.   The
nest consists chiefly of a fine thread-like material woven
and interlaced.   The form of the nest is somewhat oval,

the entrance being invariably at the top. "These nests,"
says Mr. Bate, "are evidently used as a place of refuge and
security, in which the parent protects and keeps her brood
of young until they are old enough to be independent of
the mother's care." The preceding illustration is taken
from Messrs. Bate and Westwood's book. In this case, the
nests were built in Plumaria, off Polperro, Cornwall.

A few extracts from Mr. Norman's and Mr. Bate's letters
will serve to show the numerous new species which Edward continued to forward to these eminent zoologists.

Mr. Norman (September 24th, 1862) writes: "The Mysis
I referred to in my last letter is undescribed; and I propose to call it *Mysis longicornis.* Might I be allowed to
keep the specimen? I retain it, at any rate, for the present, in order to draw up a description and figure.

"I have made a most important discovery since I last
wrote. On looking again at the specimens [of the Parasites taken by Edward from the sun-fish], I find that I had
confused two species together as *Læmargus muricatus,* and
had passed by as the male of that species (looking at them
only with the naked eye) a distinct species, which is *new* to
Britain, and which I am at present unable to name."

Mr. Norman wrote again (January 3d, 1863): "Thanks
for the Hyperia, which belongs to a different species from
those you previously sent me. At present I can not name
them. The Annelid—a very curious fellow—I know nothing of. I will name the sea-spider *Nympham.* The treasure of the bottle was, however, the little white shrimp. It
is *new* to Britain, and possibly to science. We will call it,
at any rate for the present, *Thysanopoda ensifera,* new species. The genus is a very interesting one; and only one
species, *Thysanopoda Couchii,* was previously known in our
seas."

A few days later, Mr. Norman wrote to Edward: "I
gladly accept your suggestion that the Thysanopoda should
be called *T. Batei* (instead of *ensifera*), and I am as glad as

you are to pay the compliment to Mr. Bate..... Your observations on the habits of the Thysanopoda are very interesting."

Edward evidently supplied his correspondent with abundant examples, for on the 27th of January, 1863, Mr. Norman writes: "The parasite on the fin is *Anchorella rugosa*
—not a common species. I hope you will procure more.
The *Pagurus cuanensis* bore on its back an example of a
highly interesting genus of parasitic crustacea, *Peltogaster*.
The specimens do not belong to the species hitherto recognized in our seas; perhaps they are still undescribed."

Mr. Bate also wrote to Edward during the same month
of January: "I think that your last long-legged shrimp
may be a new genus. If so, I propose calling it *Polledac-
tylos*..... There are other things of much interest also.
Do try what you can do in the way of collecting specimens
of the young of crabs, etc. Your species of *Stenothoë cly-
peatus* is *new* to Britain."

During the next few months Edward was in constant
communication with Mr. Bate and Mr. Norman, who named
for him an immense number of crustacea. Many of them
were new to Britain; some of them were new to science.
On March 6th Mr. Bate writes: "The little fellow was a
Pettidium purpureum. The long-legged Mysis are hand-
some chaps. The second is, I think, *Œdiceros sasignatus:*
if so, it is *the first* taken in Britain." Again, shortly after,
Mr. Bate asks: "Do you recollect a little fellow just like
this? [giving a diagram]. I never saw the like of it before.
Where did you get it? Do get me more! Is it a wood-
borer? I am afraid that you will scold me when I tell you
that I have not yet examined the green bottle which you
sent me previously. I am just in the midst of describing
a number of crustacea put into my hands, belonging to the
Boundary Commission between America and British Co-
lumbia. When I finish this work, I will write to you again."

A few days later Mr. Bate examines the green bottle, and

writes a letter to Edward, in which he gives him the names of seventeen crustacea which it contained. Mr. Bate was as voracious for further discoveries as Edward himself was. In a letter of December 10th, 1863, after giving an account of the various works on which he was engaged, he says: "Now, because I am working hard in the path that you love so well and labor so industriously in, and so adding to your own fame, do not say that I don't deserve the results of your researches."

Fame! that "imagined life in the breath of others!" What could fame do for poor Edward? What about his bread-and-cheese?

Curiously enough, the letter last mentioned did not at first reach Edward. It was reposted by Mr. Bate, with the observation, "This has just come back to me as a returned letter, because Banff was unknown at the post-office."

Mr. Norman also continued to furnish Edward with the names of his various crustacea, though he could not name some of them. For instance, on the 13th of May, 1863, he wrote to Edward: "The shrimps you have sent completely puzzle me. I must wait for a time until I can solve the mystery. I believe that they all belong to one species, yet there are three, if not four, distinct forms. The general characters are so much the same, that I can not think there are two species..... But the curious thing is, that I have not yet seen a single specimen of the species carrying eggs. I hope that you will yet find some, as it will be most interesting to clear up not only the question of sex, but also to find out the manner in which the eggs are carried. These forms are among the most interesting things I have seen for a long time, because it would almost seem as though we had a crustacean with three phases, just as the bee has —male, female, and worker." After giving a number of names, Mr. Norman proceeds: "And, lastly, the parasite from the common gurnard is a species *new* to Britain."

In his next letter Mr. Norman informs Edward that he

is again going to Shetland on a dredging expedition with
his friend, Mr. Jeffreys. They are to go in a steamer, and
"ought to do good work." How Edward envied them—
going dry-footed, well fed, well clad, and in a steamer, while
he was working along-shore, with no tools but his hands
and his bag-net!

Mr. Norman returned from Shetland in July, and immediately recommenced his correspondence with Edward.
"One of your shrimps," he said, "is *Caligus isonyx, new* to
our fauna, and a very interesting one it is. The male is
as yet unknown. I hope you may succeed in meeting with
it." Toward the end of the year Edward forwarded a number of species new to Britain—among others, *Eurycercus
hamellatus* (obtained from the stomach of the perch), *Chon-
dracantha solex, Mysis mixta*, and others. In one bottle of
crustaceans *three new species* were found. The zoologists
were evidently in ecstasies. Mr. Norman exhibited the results of his researches at the next meeting of the British
Association. In a letter, dated the 15th of September, 1863,
he observed: "I inclose a list of *fifteen* Moray Firth Am-
phipoda, which you have found, and which are unknown to
me. If you now, or at any future time, should be able to
favor me with specimens of any of them, I shall be extremely obliged." The specimens were afterward sent to Mr.
Norman.

On the 6th of February, 1864, Mr. Bate wrote to Edward:
"You will be glad to learn that your little specimen is *Opis
Essichtii*, and that it has not been found previously in Britain. I have reconsidered the little Hyperia, and think that
you are right; your remarks convince me that my first opinion was the more correct. You will therefore call it *Hyperia
medusarum*."

Mr. Bate was then publishing in parts his work on "The
Sessile-eyed Crustacea." He sent Edward the several parts
as they appeared. About the beginning of 1855, Mr. Bate
says: "You will soon get a new part of 'Crustacea,' and

then you will find that all my time and attention have been occupied with the isopods. So *do* try and look out for some of these, and leave the Amphipods alone for a little while."

And again: "Please never apologize for writing to me about natural history. We have now been such long correspondents, that unless I hear from you now and then, I begin to fancy myself forgotten. Your letters always give me pleasure. The crustacea that you speak of is a *Vibilia*, the *first* taken in the British Islands. Please let me know its habitat, and as much of its habits as you can."

In the mean time Mr. Norman was appealing to him for specimens of the Echinoderms, as he was about to prepare a paper on the subject. "I want your aid," he said; "I know you will kindly give it me. The *Urothoës* are extremely difficult, and I want specimens from as many parts of the coast as possible, of all varieties and sizes, and from all depths of water. Will you collect for me some from your neighborhood, from young to the largest size of all you can meet with, keeping distinct those from the shore and those from the deep water? It is important that they should be well preserved..... Please get the specimens as soon as possible, and send them to me by rail."

Edward obeyed the behests of his several correspondents. He searched the rock-pools, fished with his bag-net along the shore, and found various new specimens, which he sent to his friends. But he could not find the Echinodermata in deep water, for he had no means of reaching them. He had no boat, no dredging apparatus. Perhaps his correspondents forgot—perhaps they never knew—that he was a poor hard-working man, laboring at his trade during the day, with only a few hours in the early morning and a few hours at night which he was able to employ in their service.

Not only did he work for his correspondents so industriously, but he also worked for others to whom they referred him. Thus Mr. Norman desired him to send his Sponges to Mr. Bowerbank, and his Ascidians to Mr. Alder, of Newcastle, who were engaged in working up these subjects. The investigators did not know—for none of them had ever seen him—that Edward had the greatest difficulty in earning money enough to maintain his large family. Sometimes, in fact, he was on the brink of starvation. And yet he worked for his naturalist friends as willingly and as hardly, perhaps more hardly, than if he had been a gentleman of independent fortune.

When the "History of the Sessile-eyed Crustacea" came out, the assistance which had been rendered by Edward to Mr. Bate was fully and generously acknowledged. Let any one look over the book, and he will find of how much service Edward was to Mr. Bate while he was preparing the work for publication. Mr. Bate frequently speaks of Edward as "our valued, able, and close observer." In addition to the references to Edward already mentioned, we may subjoin the following: In speaking of the *Lysianassa longicornus*, Mr. Bate says that it "has been forwarded to him by that obliging and indefatigable naturalist, Mr. Edward, of Banff;" that his only specimen of *Anonyx obesus* has been sent to him by Mr. Edward; that the *Phoxus Holbelli* has been sent to him from Banff "by that indefatigable lover of nature, Mr. Edward;" that the species of *Darwinia compressa* was first taken, by Mr. Edward, at the entrance to the Moray Firth; that the first species of the *Calliope Ossiani* had been received from Mr. Edward, "from which specimen the original description in the catalogue in the British Museum has been drawn up." Mr. Bate also stated that he only knew of the genus Eurisus through an imperfect specimen which had been taken by Mr. Edward in the Moray Firth, "the first and only British representative of the genus that we have seen." So, too, with the genus Protomedia, of which "only two specimens were collected at Banff by Mr. Edward." A moiety was obtained of the first species, which was called *Protomedeia hirsuti-mana.* In the second case, the entire crustacean was obtained, of which Mr. Bate made a drawing and description, and he named it *Protomedeia Whitei,* " in compliment to Mr. Adam White, author of a popular history of the British crustacea." Only a single specimen of the *Cratippus tenuipes* was sent him by Mr. Edward, who knew nothing of its habits. Mr. Bate also stated that he " had only seen three specimens of the *Phoxus fusticaudatus,* which were discovered by his valued correspondent, Mr. Edward, of Banff, attached to the brachiæ of the common soldier-crab."

Besides these discoveries, Edward found an immense variety of crustaceans of other orders in the Moray Firth, which had never been found before. Some of these were new to Britain, some of them new to science. But we will not bewilder the reader by introducing the jaw-breaking names of the newly discovered crustaceans. We have thought it right, however, to mention a few of those introduced in Messrs. Bate and Westwood's " History of the Sessile-eyed Crustacea," for the purpose of confirming the statements which we have made as to the indefatigable enthusiasm of Edward in the pursuit of natural history. It must also be mentioned that the sessile-eyed crustacea constitute only a single order, and that on the one side of them there are the Stalk-eyed crustacea, and on the other the Entomostracous crustacea.

There is one point, however, that must be referred to before we conclude this heavy chapter. The impression prevailed at one time that the Hyperioidæ were parasites of the Medusa, or Jelly-fish. In 1862 Mr. Bate acknowledged the receipt of a crustacean, which he denominated *Hyperia medusarum.* He said, " If I am correct, this is the first time that I have known it as British." In a subsequent letter (December 23d, 1863), Mr. Bate said: " It is an interesting circumstance that you should have found the Hyperia and Lestrigonus free on the shore; inasmuch as they have previously only been known as inhabitants of the floating Medusa.   I wish you would direct your attention further to the subject.....   Hunt and be successful."

The Rev. Mr. Norman also communicated with Edward about the same time, and informed him "that the atylus is not a parasitical species, though there *are* some crustacea (Hyperia) which are parasitical upon Medusa."

Upon further investigation, Edward came to the conclusion that the Hyperia is no more the parasite of the Medusa because it is sometimes found upon it, than a crow is the parasite of a tree because it sometimes lights upon it.   As Edward's name was now frequently quoted in matters of zoology, he thought that it might be of some use to give the results of his observations to the world on the subject. Hence the appearance of his "Stray Notes on Some of the Smaller Crustaceans," which shortly after appeared in the Journal of the Linnæan Society.*

It is probable that the facts in that paper, as stated by Edward, had some influence on the minds of Professor Westwood and Mr. Spence Bate; as *Hyperia medusarum* does not appear in their list of sessile-eyed crustacea, the last part of which was published at the end of 1868.

To give an idea of the indefatigable industry of Edward in his researches among the crustaceans, it may be mentioned, that of 294 found in the Moray Firth, not fewer than *twenty-six new species* were added by Edward himself!

---

* Linnæan Society's Journal (*Zoology*), vol. ix., p. 143–147.

CHAPTER XVI.

DISCOVERIES AMONG ZOOPHYTES, MOLLUSKS, AND FISHES.

At the same time that Edward was occupied in searching out new species of crustaceans for Mr. Spence Bate and Mr. Norman, he was also collecting marine objects for other naturalists. He found numerous star-fish, zoophytes, mollusks, and sponges, which he sent to his naturalist correspondents to be named.

Edward always endeavored to bring home the fishes, crustaceans, and other sea objects that he captured, alive; for the purpose of watching their manners and habits. He had always plenty of dishes in readiness, filled with sea-water—some having sand on the bottom, some mud, some bits of gravel, and others bits of rock—the latter being covered with Algæ or Zoophytes. Into one of these vessels he would put his living specimens, in order that he might watch and learn something of their various characteristics. Some of his observations were published in the *Zoologist*, and were regarded as highly interesting, many of them being new to science.

This could hardly have been otherwise, for it was his habit, first to *observe*, and then to kill. He never had any mercenary object in view in wandering about with his gun and his traps; he only desired to obtain knowledge; and what he observed he told as plainly and clearly as he could, without knowing whether his observations had been printed before or not. He only regretted that he had so little time to publish his descriptions of the habits of animals, fishes, and crustaceans.

One of Edward's most delightful studies was that of the star-fish. He published an article on the subject in the *Zoologist*. His object in doing so, he said, was to induce others to employ their spare time in discovering the star-fishes found along the Banffshire coast, and to make them publicly known. "If this," said he, "were done generally throughout the country, we might, ere long, be able to form something like an adequate notion of what we really do possess; but until that be done, we can not expect to arrive at any thing like a perfect idea of what our British fauna consists of, or where the objects are to be found. Let naturalists, then, and observers of nature everywhere, look to and note this, that all who can may reap the benefit."

Edward was as enthusiastic about the star-fish as he was about any other form of animated being. He would allow none of them to be called "common." They were all worthy of the most minute investigation, and also worthy of the deepest admiration. Of the daisy brittle stars (*Ophiocoma bellis*) he says: "They are the most beautiful of this beautiful tribe which I have ever seen. Their disks differ considerably from the star-fishes ordinarily met with, being of a pyramidal or conical form, sometimes resembling the well-known shell *Trochus tumidus*. In color they are like the finest variegated polished mahogany; their disks exhibiting the most beautiful carved work. The rays are short in proportion to the size of the disk—strong, and closely beset with short, thick, hard spines. I may add that the specimens I allude to were procured from that heterogeneous repository of marine objects, the stomach of a cod, which was taken about thirteen miles out at sea."

Edward's children also helped him to procure star-fishes. "I remember," he says, "my young friend Maggie, and three of her sisters, once bringing me a large cargo of the granulated brittle star (*Ophiocoma granulata*)—nearly two hundred of them, which they had gathered up where the fishermen clean their lines. I remember being particularly struck with the numerous and brilliant colors displayed by the cargo, exhibiting, as they did, all those tints—perhaps more than it is possible to name—from the brightest scarlet down to the deepest black, scarcely two being alike. Their disks, too, were remarkably varied; some were of a perfect oval, while others were pentangular; some were flat, while others were, in a measure, pyramidal, and what, in truth, may be termed triangular in form."

Of all his daughters, Maggie seems to have been the most helpful. She went down to Gardenstown to obtain the refuse from the fishermen's lines, to collect fish, crustacea, and such-like, and send them home to her father by the carrier. She sometimes accompanied him along the coast as far as Fraserburgh and Peterhead. One evening, while Edward was partaking of his evening meal, Maggie entered, and accosted him joyfully, "Father, I've got a new star-fish t' ye, wi' sax legs!" "I hope so, Maggie," he answered, "but I doubt it." After he had finished his supper, he said, "Now, Maggie, let's see this prodigy of yours." After looking at it, "Just as I thought, Maggie," said he; "it's *not* a new species—it's only an *Ophiocoma Ballii*, but rather a peculiar one in its way, having, as you said, 'sax legs' instead of five."

Of the rosy-feather star (*Camatula roseacea*)—which Edward had long been searching for, and at last found—he says: "What a pretty creature! but how brittle! and oh, how beautiful! Does any one wonder, as I used to do, when he hears of a stone-lily or of a lily-star, as applied to this genus? Then let him get a sight of a crenard-star, and sure I am that his surprise will give place to admiration. And how curious! It was once supposed to have been the 'most numerous of the ocean's inhabitants,' whereas now there are only about a dozen kinds to be found alive—one only in the British seas, and that but rarely met with.

Well, I am proud to be able to record its occurrence on the Banffshire coast. The specimen I allude to was taken from the stomach of a cod."

But still more wonderful is that rare species, the great sea-cucumber (*Cucumaria frondosa*), the king of the Holothuridæ family, found on the Banffshire coast. Edward's specimen was brought up on the fishermen's lines. "When at rest," he says, "it is fully sixteen inches long. It is of a very deep purple on all except the under side, which is grayish. It is a most wonderful, and at the same time a most interesting, animal. What strange forms and curious shapes it assumes at will! Now it seems like a pear, and again like a large purse or long pudding. Sometimes it has the appearance of two monster potatoes joined end-ways, from which it diverges into a single bulb, with no suckers visible; and again it looks as long as my arm, rough and warty-looking. Its tentacula too, how curious they are! Simple to appearance, yet how complete and how beautiful withal. What strange forms and what beauteous creatures and inconceivable things there are in the ocean's depths! What a pity it is that we can not traverse its hidden fields and explore its untrodden caverns!"

Edward found numerous zoophytes along the coast, which excited his admiration almost as much as the star-fish. Of one species, called "dead-men's paps," "sea-fingers," etc. (*Alcyonium digitatum*), he says, "It is frequently brought ashore by the fishermen, attached to shells and stones. It is curious to observe the strange and fantastic forms which these creatures at times assume. They are loathed by the generality of people when found on the sands. But were they to be seen in their proper element, with the beautiful leaf-like tentacula of the little polyps, thousands of which compose the living mass, these feelings of loathing would give place to wonder and delight. Touch one of those polyps, and it instantly contracts and withdraws its tentacles, while the others continue their movements. But touch them again and again, and they will shrink and hide themselves in their fleshy home, which becomes greatly reduced in bulk. Wait a little, and you will observe the pap assume its natural size, and the surface will appear roughish and covered with small protuberances. From these asperities the numerous polyps may now be noticed, slowly, and almost imperceptibly, emerging one by one; and having gained a sufficient height, their slender and fragile arms, or tentacula, will also be observed cautiously expanding, which, when nearly fully developed, gives to the whole mass the enchanting appearance of a bouquet of flowers of the richest dye, or of a gaudy-colored wreath of beautiful and delicate blossoms, combined in one cluster, enough to excite wonder and admiration even in the dullest mind."

Without following Edward farther in his description of the zoophytes, we may proceed to state that he was for some time engaged in collecting mollusks for Mr. Alder, of Newcastle, who was engaged in writing a paper on the subject. Having observed the great number of tunicata, or acephalous mollusks, found upon the fishermen's lines, Edward proceeded to collect and examine these lower productions of marine life. As usual, he wished to have them named, and he sent a large number of specimens to Mr. Alder for the purpose. Some of Mr. Alder's letters have been preserved, from which a few extracts are subjoined:

"I have received yours of the 16th inst. (October, 1864), and also two parcels of Ascidians. I shall be most happy to receive and name for you any Tunicata you may send. Our communications may be mutually advantageous, as I should like to have information concerning the Tunicata of your coast, being engaged upon a work on the British species. In the first parcel that came I could only find one specimen, though you mentioned parts of two or three. It was, I think, a Botryllida incrusting the stem of a sea-weed, but of what species I can not say. In the second parcel, received this morning, there is a piece of *Leptoclinum punctatum*, and also part of an ascidian which appears to be *A. parallelograma*. The Botryllida are very difficult to distinguish unless they are quite fresh. I have never heard of *Aplidium lobatum* being found in this country. It is a Red Sea and Mediterranean species..... I am much obliged to my friend Mr. Norman for recommending you to send specimens to me, and I shall be glad to hear from you again."

The specimen of *Aplidium lobatum* which Edward sent to Mr. Alder was cast ashore at Banff; though its usual habitat is the Indian Ocean, the Red Sea, and the Mediterranean.

In a future letter Mr. Alder says: "I received your box containing a specimen of *Ascidia sordida* (young), and also a Zoophyte, the *Alcyonidium gelatinosum*, for which accept my thanks. I see that you have been very successful in discovering small fish. Your account of them is very interesting. I wish any one on our coast would pay attention to these things, but we have no one living permanently on the coast that cares any thing about natural history."

Edward afterward discovered a fine specimen of the *Onychoteuthis Bartlingii* or *Banksii*. It was the first met with in Britain—the range of the species being said to be from Norway to the Cape and Indian Ocean. This specimen was found on the beach betwixt the mouth of the river Deveron and the town of Macduff. Doubtless many other specimens of this and other marine animals had been cast upon the beach before, but no one had taken the trouble to look for or observe them. Many, also, of the fishes and marine objects which Edward was the first to discover had probably been haunting the Moray Firth for hundreds or thousands of years; but science had not yet been born in the district, and there were none who had the seeing eye and the observant faculties of our Banffshire naturalist.

Edward also discovered a specimen of the *Leptoclinum punctatum*, which had been thrown on shore during a severe storm.   It was of a most beautiful greenish color, variegated with steel-blue.   This specimen he sent to Mr. Alder, who answered him in the following letter: "The Ascidian which you have sent me is a Leptoclinum, and may probably be a new species.   There are few of that genus with star-shaped calcareous crystals imbedded in them. The species that you have sent has the star-shaped crystals, and differs in color from any I have seen, being of a greenish-blue color.   I put it into water to moisten it after it came, and it stained the water of a blue color.   I presume, therefore, that it would be of that color when fresh.   It seems, from the sea-weed to which it is attached, to be a littoral species.   I shall be glad of any other information which you can give me about it."

This was the last letter Edward received from Mr. Alder. As he was about to send off another large cargo of Tunicata to Newcastle, containing three new species, he received notice of Mr. Alder's sudden death; and knowing of no other person who could name his Ascidians, he ceased collecting them, although there is still a rich field for students of Mollusca along the Banffshire coast.   "It is young, ardent, and devoted workers," said Edward, "that are wanted to bring such things to light."

We next proceed to mention Edward's researches as to new fishes.   Having discovered a specimen of Drummond's Echiodon—the first that had ever been found in the Firth —Edward published an account of it in the *Zoologist* for April, 1863, and offered to afford naturalists the opportunity of examining it.   The article came under the notice of Mr. Jonathan Couch, of Polperro, in Cornwall, who was then engaged in writing his celebrated work on British fishes; and he entered into a correspondence with Edward on the subject.   The first letter that Mr. Couch wrote to Edward did not reach him.   It was returned to Polperro. Banff seems not to have been known at the General Post-office.   Another letter, with " N. B." added, reached its address. Mr. Couch requested an inspection of the curious fish, together with an account of its exact color when fresh from the sea, and also the particular circumstances, of weather or otherwise, under which so large a number of the fishes had been taken. The information asked for was at once furnished by Edward. Dr. Gray also requested a specimen for the British Museum, which was forwarded to London.

Now that Edward had found another opening for his discoveries, he proceeded to send numerous new specimens of fish for Mr. Couch's identification. Mr. Couch having informed him that he was then employed upon the wrasses, Edward immediately began to search for wrasses, and shortly after he dispatched numbers of them to Polperro. Among the specimens of *Wrasse latrus* which Edward sent to Mr. Couch, there was one which Cuvier described as being found only in New Guinea, on the farther side of the world. "And yet," said Mr. Couch, after examining the fish, "I can not suppose that fishes from New Guinea can have visited you." The finding of this fish at New Guinea and at the Moray Firth furnished only another illustration of the scarcity of observers in natural history ; for it must certainly, like most other species, have existed in numerous other parts of the world besides these.

In describing his little fish, Edward says : "Although I can not say much of importance concerning the traits of our little friend, still there is one which can not be passed over in silence. It is this : on coming out of the water after I took the prize, I had occasion to lay it down upon the sand until a bottle was prepared for its reception and exclusive use, as I was anxious to take it home alive, so that I might see and learn as much of its habits as possible. While thus employed, I was rather surprised at seeing it frequently leap several inches at a time. Thinking that the damp sand might have in some way or other aided the operation, when I got home I placed it on a dry board

to see how it would perform there.   It did just the same.
Away it jumped, jump after jump, until I was fully satisfied that there was no difference as to place ; after which I
put him again into his little aquarium.   I now observed,
however, that the tail, which is pretty large, was the chief
and most important object used.   The head and shoulders
were first raised a little, and then, by a doubling of the tail,
which acted as a kind of spring, the animal was, by a slight
jerk, enabled to raise and propel itself forward, or to either
side, and not unfrequently right over.   In the water, too,
when touched with any thing, instead of swimming away,
as fish generally do, it merely leaped or jerked to one side
in order to avoid the annoyance.   I am not exactly aware
whether this gymnastic performance is a common propen-
sity with this family of fishes or not, but it was so with
this specimen."

After further observations, Edward came to the conclusion that these little fishes were inhabitants of our own
seas, but that they differed from those which Cuvier had
described.   He was of opinion that, from the differences
which he had observed between the true wrasses and the
fish in question, it might yet be necessary, after further investigation, to place it in a *new* or *sub-genus*.   In that case
a portion of the name would require to be changed, and
until then Edward held that its name should be the "microscopical wrasse of the Moray Firth."

Another batch of little fishes which Edward sent to Mr.
Couch led to an interesting correspondence.   Edward no
sooner found an opening for further work on the sea-shore,
than he went into it with enthusiasm.   As Mr. Couch was
approaching the conclusion of his work, Edward seemed
to become more energetic than before.   Thus Mr. Couch
had written out and sent off his history and description of
the Echiodon to be printed, before he knew of Edward's
discovery.   And now there arrived from Banff another batch
of specimens, containing a little fish, which Mr. Couch de-

clared to be a *new species*, and even a *new genus*. At first he supposed it to be the mackerel midge, but, after a careful examination, he declared it to be entirely new. Mr. Couch concluded his letter containing his views as to the new fish with these words: "You will perceive that I set a great value on your communications, and I shall take care to acknowledge them when I speak of these different species."

Edward, in his reply to Couch, observed: "I was aware that the new fish was not the mackerel midge, for I have examined it. But this is a far more splendid species; in fact, its colors and resplendence equal, if they do not excel, those of the pretty argentine. The one I sent you first, I kept alive for two days. It was one of the most restless and watchful fishes I had ever seen. I took it with a small hand-net, which I used for taking the smaller crustaceans. I only took one at first; but a few days after, I took several together. I also found some cast ashore on the sands. Those that I send now are old and young. There is a little thing just out of the egg; it has the ovary sac still attached. Be kind enough, when you write me, to let me know the name of the fish."

In replying to Edward, Couch said : "Your last box has reached me, with its contents in good order, for which I heartily thank you. I have already written an account of the fish. My intention is to give it the name of *Couchia Thompsoni;* and as I shall particularly refer to you, I think it may prove to your advantage to obtain as many specimens as possible, to answer any demands that may be made upon you..... The reason why I have not answered you sooner is, that I have been much distressed by the loss of my eldest son—an eminent surgeon living at Penzance, in attendance on whom I was at that town for a fortnight. He was eminent in many departments of science, and was only forty-six years of age when he died. You may judge from this that I have had but little disposition to active ex-

ertion for some time past. I submit, as he was able to do,
to the will of God, but there is difficulty in saying from the
heart, 'His will be done.'"

Edward discovered the above new fish in May, 1863.
After a few weeks it disappeared from the coast, and nothing further was seen of it until the following May, when
Edward took a few specimens. It disappeared again, and
re-appeared toward the end of August. "As this," he says,
"was a lucky chance, and one not to be lost, I took a considerable number, not with the intention of destroying the
beautiful little creatures—as beautiful they truly are—but
for the purpose of ascertaining how they now stood as to
size. Being satisfied as to this, I committed the most of
them again to their native element, and right glad they were
to be set once more at liberty. I found that, although late
in the season, they had not in any way increased in bulk,
as compared with those which were taken in spring. From
this important and opportune circumstance, too, it is now
my firm and decided belief that their average length does
not exceed an inch. It would seem that they are a deep-
water fish, and, herring-like, only visit the shore occasionally. Like that fish, too, they are gregarious—that is, they
go in small shoals. They seem to be about the fleetest,
most active, and most vigilant of the finny tribes. Besides
what I observed in the sea itself, I kept a number of them
alive, placed in the window before me when at work, so
that I had both the pleasure as well as the satisfaction of
observing their habits at my leisure; and I was well repaid
for my time and patience."

So soon as this discovery became known to the scientific
world, numerous inquiries were made to Edward for specimens of the "new fish;" and, among others, Dr. Gray sent
for some specimens for the Home Department of the British Museum.

Edward continued to ply Mr. Couch with new species of
fish. On the 5th of September, 1864, he said: "I herewith

send you another small fish, which I hope you will give me your opinion upon at your leisure. I freely confess that I am at a loss about it. Although small, it is so well proportioned in every respect, so firm, and so compact, that I can not believe it to be a young specimen. I took it about a fortnight since, in a small shoal of Thompson's Midge; and though I have been netting each day since then, I have not yet met with another."

Mr. Couch was equally at a loss with Edward. At first he said, " It appears to be a *Wrasse labrus,* but it is not exactly like any of the known kinds." In his next letter he said, " I think your little fish is the young of the rock goby." This did not satisfy Edward. He answered that " the fish, though little, was a full-grown fish ; and that it might possibly be one of Thompson's Irish fish." " No," replied Couch ; " it will be plain to you that it is not Irish, from Mr. Thompson's own description," which he then gave. At last he thought it to be " the true mackerel midge." He examined the little fish again, and finally came to the conclusion that it was a long-lost fish—Montagu's Midge, or the silvery gade.

Colonel George Montagu was an old soldier and sportsman, who had flourished in Devonshire some seventy years before. Living in the country and by the sea-shore, his attention was directed to the pursuit of natural history. At first it was his hobby, and then it became his study. He observed birds carefully : this was natural to him as a sportsman. He published an " Ornithological Dictionary of British Birds." But his range of study broadened. The sea-shore always presents a great attraction for naturalists. The sea is a wonderful nursery of nature : the creatures that live in and upon it are so utterly different from those which we meet with by land. Then, every thing connected with the ocean is full of wonder.

Colonel Montagu was an extraordinary observer. He was a man who possessed the *seeing* eye. He forgot nothing that he once clearly saw.   He was one of the best naturalists, so far as logical acumen and earnest research were concerned, that England has ever seen.   The late Professor Forbes said of him that, "had he been educated a physiologist, and made the study of nature his aim and not his amusement, his would have been one of the greatest names in the whole range of British science.   There is no question about the identity of any animal that Montagu described. . . . .   He was a forward-looking philosopher; he spoke of every creature as if one exceedingly like it, and yet different from it, would be washed up by the waves next tide.   Consequently his descriptions are permanent."   We might also say of Edward, that, although comparatively uneducated, he possessed precisely the same qualities of observing and seeing.   Nothing that once came under his eyes was forgotten.   He remembered, and could describe fluently and vividly, the form, habits, and habitats of the immense variety of animals that came under his observation.

Now, this Colonel Montagu had, in 1808, discovered on the shore of South Devonshire the same midge that Edward rediscovered in 1864 on the shore of the Moray Firth. Colonel Montagu had clearly and distinctly described the fish in the second volume of the "Memoirs of the Wernerian Natural History Society;" but he had not given any figure of it.   He named it the silvery gade (*Gadus argenteolus*).   The colonel passed away, and with him all further notice of his fish.   It was never again observed until, fifty-six years later, it was rediscovered by Edward.   Future writers on British fishes ignored it.   They believed that Colonel Montagu had been mistaken, and had merely described the young of some species already known.   Even Mr. Couch, the most accomplished ichthyologist of his time, had swept it out of his list of British fishes.   But Montagu was too close an observer to be mistaken.   As Professor Forbes had said of him, "There is no question about the

identity of any animal that he described....consequently
his descriptions are permanent."

Hence the surprise of Mr. Couch on receiving from Edward the identical fish that had so long been lost. "There
is one of your little fishes," he said in his reply to Edward's
letter, "that I am satisfied about, and the history of which
is a matter of much interest. You are well acquainted
with the little mackerel midge, first made known by myself, and which has been denominated *Couchia glauca* by
Thompson. But, previously to this, Colonel Montagu had
published an account of a species much like it, but differing
in having only two barbels on the snout. It does not appear that any figure was given, but he speaks of them as
occurring in Devonshire, where he lived. No one has seen
a fish which answers to his description since that time—I
suppose more than fifty years ago ; and it has been judged
that some mistake was made, especially as he never gave a
notice of the midge with four barbels. Yet Montagu was
a good naturalist, and a correct observer. He calls his fish
silvery gade ; for he wrote before Cuvier made these fishes
into a new genus, termed Motella. But your fish answers
closely to Montagu's lost fish. When I inform you that
Montagu gives the number of rays in the fins, you may
judge how closely he examined this fish. When my 'History of British Fishes' is ended, I intend to give a few as
a supplement, and as ascertained too late to fall into the
regular order. This little fish will find a place there, when
I shall take care to mention your name as its rediscoverer."

In a notice which Edward afterward gave of the fish he
observed : "I may mention that this genus of little fishes,
designated with the appellation of *midges* from their small
size, and containing three species, are now authentically
known to be inhabitants of the Moray Firth, all three, both
young and old of each, having been procured here—a circumstance which perhaps can be said of no other single
district but our own. This, not so much for the lack of the

fish themselves, as from the want of *searchers* for these things ; for we can not allow ourselves to think for a single moment that they could be found in so widely distant localities as Cornwall, Belfast, Devon, and here, and not be met with at intermediate places. Such a thing appears to me to be one of those affairs called *impossibilities.* Let those, then, who live on the coast, and have time and a mind for these things, or whether they have time or not, if they have the will—let such, I say, look better about them, and I doubt not but they will find many of these little gems, as well as other rarities of a similar and kindred nature."

Edward had not yet finished his discovery of midges in the Moray Firth. In November, 1865, he sent to Mr. Couch a specimen of a little fish which he had caught, and which seemed quite new to him. Mr. Couch replied that it was not only new to him, but new to science. Mr. Couch expressed his regret that the midge " had come too late to find a place by the side of its near relation, Montagu's Midge, in his work, the last number of which had just been published." He also added : " As your little fish is certainly new, I have thought of sending an account of it to the Linnæan Society, in which case I should think it only a piece of justice to affix your name to it."

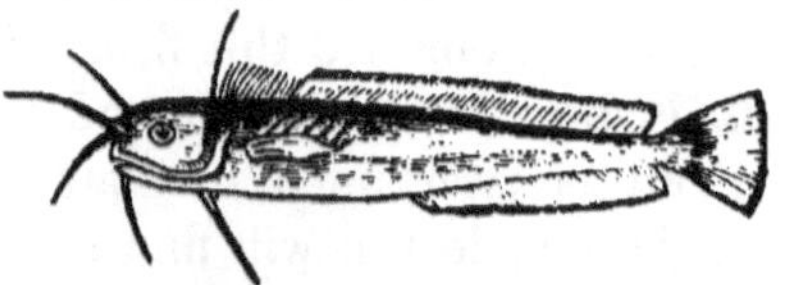

EDWARD'S MIDGE—*Couchia Edwardii.*

Mr. Couch accordingly prepared a paper for the Linnæan Society,* in which he embodied Edward's description of the fish, and of its habits and habitat. He also attached to it the name of Edward's Midge, *Couchia Edwardii.* In the course of Mr. Couch's paper he says:

---

* *Linnæan Society's Journal;* " Zoology," vol. ix., p. 38.

"Long before the discovery of the mackerel midge as a separate species, an account had been given by Colonel Montagu of a kindred fish, which he supposed to be common to the coast of Devonshire, and which he described as being distinguished by the possession of a pair only of the frontal barbs ; and yet for more than half a century this species of midge had remained in obscurity, until it was again brought to light by the diligent and acute observation of Mr. Thomas Edward, of Banff, who found it in some abundance in the Moray Firth, and kindly supplied the writer with examples, which enabled him to give an account of it, with a figure, in the concluding portion of the fourth volume of his 'History of the Fishes of the British Islands.' The five-bearded species had been already represented in a colored figure in the third volume of the same book, as also in Mr. Yarrell's well-known volumes. But a vacancy still existed in the analogy between the species of the nearly allied genera *Motella* and *Couchia ;* and it is this, again, we are able to supply through the persevering diligence of Mr. Edward, whose intelligence enabled him to detect the existence of another species, and whose kindness has, with an example, communicated materials which enable the writer to produce, with a satisfactory likeness, a somewhat extended notice of its actions, the latter of which will be described, as far as can be, in this attentive observer's own words. The length of the example from which my notes were taken is an inch and five-eighths ; and as half a dozen others were about the same size, it may be judged to be their usual magnitude, as it does not differ much also from that of *C. glauca* and *C. Montagui.* Compared with the latter, its shape is more slender, the pectoral fin rather more lengthened and pointed, the ventral fins longer and slender, the cilia on the back, along the edge of the membrane, more extended, apparently more numerous, and very fine ; barb on the lower jaw long; but what especially marks this little fish as distinct from the other species is, that, besides the pair of barbs in front of the head, there is a single one of much larger size in front of the upper lip, and which points directly forward with a slight inclination downward, thus analogically answering to the middle barb that projects from the snout of the four-bearded rockling (*Motella cimbria*). It is probable that there are teeth in the jaws, but they can scarcely be seen, and there is a row of pores along each border of the superior maxillary bone. Some further particulars of this fish I prefer to give in the words of its discoverer, who describes its color as a beautiful deep green along the back when caught, the sides brilliantly white ; but when it reached me, preserved in spirit, it was blue, with a tinge of the same along the lateral line. In some examples in Mr. Edward's possession the color on the back was a faint yellow, with a narrow stripe of bluish purple on the side, and in all of them the silvery hue of the lower portions of the body is found to rise nearer the back than in the other species of this genus. The back also and head were thickly covered with very small, dark, star-like spots, which, together with two narrow yellow streaks extending from the top of the head, above the mouth, and diverging to the eyes, had disappeared when subjected to my examination. Iris of the eye silvery, the pupil bluish green; the fins dull gray, as also the pair of barbs; but the single one on the lip at its root is almost of as deep a color as the top of the head and back.....

"I regard it as no other than an act of justice to the discoverer of this fish to assign to it the name of Edward's Midge (*Couchia Edwardii*), of which the specific character is sufficiently obvious."

Mr. Edward followed up this paper by a fuller description of the midge, after he had had an opportunity of observing a much larger number of specimens.*

It is scarcely necessary to describe at length the large number of new fishes belonging to the Moray Firth which Edward for the first time recognized and described. For instance, the bonito, the tunny—fishes for the most part found in the Mediterranean—the pilot-fish, the bear-fish, the short sun-fish, the bald-fish, the scald-fish, and several species of sharks. Strange fishes such as these had occasionally been found before; but Edward never missed the opportunity of carefully observing them and describing their habits, sometimes in the *Zoologist* and the *Naturalist*, and at other times in the *Banffshire Journal*. He also endeavored to secure as many specimens as possible for the Banff Museum, of which he was curator.

When Edward informed Mr. Couch of the struggles and difficulties he had to encounter in the formation of a museum, the latter replied: "I can sympathize with you, with a smile, at your annoyances and disappointments as regards your attempts at a museum; but a real love of nature, and

---

* "A few Additional Particulars regarding *Couchia Edwardii*. By Thomas Edward, A.L.S." *Linnæan Society's Journal;* "Zoology," vol. x.

even a wish for any thing beyond a very slight acquaintance with it, is rare, and can scarcely be infused into any
one not naturally endued with so great a blessing. With
your museum there ought to be a collection of books on
natural history. . . . .   What you say about the new midge
reminds me of what occurred when I first announced the
discovery of the mackerel midge. A paper on it was read
before the Linnæan Society, but they hesitated to publish it
—thinking, I believe, as in the present case, that the fish
was a young condition of some other known species. . . . .
There is much in the internal structure of fishes that is not
known generally, but which can only be ascertained by dis-
section.   In fact, the riches of nature are inexhaustible; but
if we can not discover all, there is no reason why we should
not continue our search after more of them. The most
unsatisfactory part of the subject is, to find how greatly in
some instances our best authorities are mistaken."

The works of Mr. Couch and Mr. Spence Bate being now
published, and both of these gentlemen having been so much
indebted to the investigations of Edward, it occurred to
both of them to endeavor to get him elected an Associate
of the Linnæan Society, as a reward for his labors. Mr.
Couch, in his letter to Edward of the 1st of November,
1865, says: "There is another thing which I think worthy
of your notice; for, as the world goes, honor is of some
value; and the honor I refer to is of intrinsic value, at the
same time that it will cost you nothing.   In the Linnæan
Society there is a company of associates (A.L.S.), limited
to thirty; but at this time I think there are no more than
twenty-eight.   These associates are entitled to several priv-
ileges in the society; and in order to be elected, it is necessary to obtain the recommendation of at least three of the
Fellows, which I suppose you can procure.   I shall feel a
pleasure in signing the necessary application, and, if applied
to, I have no doubt Dr. Gray will do the same."

Mr. Bate warmly concurred in the proposal. The application was drawn up, signed, and sent to the Linnæan Society. Dr. Gray was of opinion that a similar application should have been made to the Zoological Society for Edward's admission as an associate. But this does not seem to have been done. At length the day of the election arrived, and on the 5th of April, 1866, Edward was unanimously elected an associate.* Mr. Couch wrote to congratulate him. He said, "The number of associates is now limited to a few, so that it is very difficult to get elected; but, then, it is a greater honor."

It never rains but it pours. A few months later, Edward was unanimously admitted a member of the Aberdeen Natural History Society, at its monthly meeting, held in Marischal College; and in March, 1867, he was furnished with the diploma of the Glasgow Natural History Society.

"But a prophet is not without honor, save in his own country." Although Banff possessed an "Institution for Science, Literature, and the Arts, and for the Encouragement of Native Genius and Talent," the members did not even elect Edward an honorary member. The Linnæan Society —perhaps the most distinguished association of naturalists in the world—had discovered Edward's genius and talent, and elected him an associate. But the scientific men of Banff fought shy of the native shoe-maker. It may, however, be added that the Banff Institution, finding no native nor any other genius and talent to encourage, became defunct in 1875, and handed over their collection to the corporation, whose property it now is.

---

* On looking over the records of the Linnæan Society, we find that on the 1st of February, 1866, Thomas Edward was proposed as an associate by C. Spence Bate, Jonathan Couch, A. Hancock, W. N. Brady, J. E. Gray, and M. W. Baird. He was elected by ballot on the 5th of April, 1866.

CHAPTER XVII.

ANTIQUITIES—KITCHEN-MIDDENS.

EDWARD had now been working for about ten years along the sea-shore—collecting crustacea, mollusks, fish, and marine objects. He had won his honors, and lost his health. His medical attendant had often warned him to give up night-work, and avoid exposure of all kinds. But though Edward had given up night-work, and partly recovered his health, he would not give up the study of nature.

He was now, however, compelled to abandon it altogether.* The doctor was called in again, and found him utterly prostrate. It was the old story—fever and sore throat, the results of exposure, and perhaps of insufficient sustenance. His illness was more serious now than it had been before. In course of time, however, he recovered. The doctor again had a serious talk with him. He even threatened him with a lunatic asylum if he did not altogether abandon his out-door researches.

When Edward was able to move about, he learned, to his unutterable grief, the truth, which he would fain have concealed from himself, that his career was at an end as regarded his further researches into the mysteries of nature. Though his mind remained as vigorous as ever, his bodily

---

* This must have been about the beginning of 1868. The last letter which Edward received from Mr. Spence Bate was dated the 3d of March, 1868. In that letter Mr. Bate referred to some specimens of the Eisclados and Themisto which Edward had sent him about three months before. The correspondence then ceased.

constitution had been seriously injured. He had lost the elasticity of manhood, and never recovered it again.

Edward was so completely broken down, that he was in a great measure disabled from working at his trade. What, then, was he to do? His doctor thought that it would be better for him to give up the trade of shoe-making, and try something else. He advised him to study electricity, with the view of setting up a galvanic battery. He gave Edward books for the purpose of studying the subject. But, on considering the matter, Edward came to the conclusion that he did not know enough of the mechanism and economy of the human system to apply the power medicinally. Still the doctor urged him. Numerous patients came to him to be galvanized, and he had not time to attend to them himself; he would send all his customers to Edward. But Edward had no desire to be a quack, and to pour galvanism, of which he knew little, into a body of which he knew less. At length he came to the determination not to take up the system of treating disease by electrical methods.*

He was next advised to obtain some situation in connection with natural history—such, for instance, as the curator of a museum. He was already the curator of the Banff Museum, but the remuneration was almost nominal. In 1852 he had been appointed curator, at a salary of two guineas a year. After about twelve years' service, his salary was increased to four guineas a year.† Even that was but a nominal consideration. Edward naturally desired to obtain some position with a salary sufficient to maintain him. But he possessed no influence; he was too shy to

---

* Of the mischievous results of treating disease by electricity without medical knowledge, a remarkable instance is to be found in the "Life of the Rev. F. W. Robertson, Brighton."

† We are glad to find that, since the Museum has been handed over to the corporation, the Provost and Council of Banff have been a little more liberal to their distinguished townsman.

push himself forward; he had no one to help him to obtain any situation; and he eventually gave it up as a hopeless project.

His attention was next turned to photography. He obtained a treatise on the subject; he read and studied it; and then he purchased chemicals and a camera. To obtain these, he again drew upon his savings-bank by selling another portion of his natural-history collection. He found the practice of photography very agreeable, and he was at length enabled to take a very fair portrait. But he found that really good portraits could not be taken except in a glass-windowed apartment provided for the purpose. He had no such apartment, and he had not money enough to build one. His portraits were taken in the open air. Perhaps, too, he wanted that deftness of hand and delicacy of treatment which, had he been younger, he would more readily have mastered. For by this time Edward was growing old and stiff-handed. Besides, there were other photographers in the town, better provided with capital and machinery, and it is scarcely to be wondered at if his trade in photographic pictures should have been but small. Yet some of his portraits, more particularly of himself and his family, are exceedingly well done.

In the mean time, however, the activity of his mind and the closeness of his observation would not allow him to remain at rest. He had done what he could for science. But there were other things to be thought over and written about. One of the subjects that attracted him was antiquities; and he began with the antiquities of Banff. Several articles on the subject appeared in the *Banffshire Journal*, which were thus introduced by the editor: "We recently mentioned that our townsman, Mr. Thomas Edward, was engaged in preparing notes on the antiquities of the town and neighborhood. We have pleasure in giving the following extract from his MSS. The extract, it will be seen, embodies two important practical suggestions—one

as to the obtaining and re-erecting in the town the Old
Cross of the burgh; and the other as to the erection of a
drinking-fountain."

What Edward said about the ancient cross of Banff and
the proposed drinking-fountain may best be given in his
own words:

"Banff, like every other town, had its 'cross.' Where
this ancient relic of ours had stood during the various revo-
lutions of the burgh, we are not aware. We are told, however, that its last stance was on the Low Street, nearly opposite the foot of the Strait Path. From this we believe
it was suffered to be removed (to our praise as a communi-
ty be it spoken) to adorn the top of a dove-cote about a
mile from the town, and on ground with which the public
have nothing to do. On inquiry, we learn that it is still
the property of the town. If this is correct, then we say,
Get it back. Yes, we say, Get back our venerable and
time-honored cross. No one can fail to observe the almost
universal restoration of the old works of antiquity which
is going on throughout the country. Although nothing of
this kind has yet taken place here, our ancient cross must
be redeemed, and the sooner it is done the greater will be
the credit due to those who accomplish it.

"Our charitable bequests, as is well known, are many
and valuable. Still, we lack at least one—one which would
cost but little, and at the same time be a universal good.
There are many very wealthy individuals in and belonging
to the burgh, some of whom may yet be persuaded to give
us this desideratum. We allude to a drinking-fountain.
These things, too, be it remembered, are becoming universal, although we have none of them. We maintain that it
would be a great and an inestimable boon to the place.

"But some may ask, What has this to do with antiquities? Well, perhaps not much yet, but we trust it will
soon have. We have said that a drinking-fountain would
cost but little. Once erected, the interest of a small sum

annually would pay for the water, and keep the place in repair; and besides tending to be a blessing to thousands, it would be an interesting and conspicuous ornament to the town, and one of the most refreshing which modern ingenuity and gratitude could devise or rear. Supposing that some of our philanthropic friends, who may wish to have their names carried down to future generations as being benefactors and lovers of their species, might yet think well of our suggestion, and give us a fountain, could not our cross be placed upon it as a crowning stone? We think so. And sure we are that no better emblem, nor one more expressive, could be given to a place of the kind. But although nothing of this kind may take place, still we would urge the restoration of our old and venerable cross."

The article produced no results. The suggestion about the cross trod upon the toes of some person of local influence, and the idea of its restoration was soon stamped out. The drinking-fountain also remains to be erected.

Edward was more successful in his investigations of the Kjökken-mödding at Boyndie — a much more interesting piece of antiquity. Kitchen-middens, or refuse heaps, have been discovered in large numbers along the shores of the Danish islands. Not less than a hundred and fifty have already been found in Denmark. They consist chiefly of castaway shells, of the oyster, mussel, cockle, and periwinkle, intermixed with the bones of quadrupeds, birds, and fish. Some of them also contain fragments of pottery and burned clay, and rude implements of stone and bone, which were evidently dropped by those who took their meals in the vicinity of the heaps, or who threw them away as useless.

These shell-mounds vary in height, in breadth, and in length. They are from three to ten feet high, and sometimes extend to a thousand feet in length, while they vary from a hundred to two hundred feet in width. It is evident, from these remains, that some prehistoric people were accustomed to live along the sea-shore, or to frequent it when food failed them in the interior, and live upon mollusks and fish. That they ventured out to sea in canoes hollowed out of the trunk of a single tree (such as are occasionally found in Danish peat-bogs) is obvious, from the fact that the bony relics of deep-sea fish, such as the cod, the herring, and the skate, are occasionally found in the shell-heaps. No remains of any agricultural produce, nor of domesticated animals (excepting the dog), have been found in them; so that it is probable that the people who then occupied the land were exclusively hunters and fishers, and that they knew nothing of pastoral or agricultural pursuits.

Who these ancient people were has been the subject of much conjecture. It is not improbable that they were Lapps or Esquimaux. The most ancient skulls which have been found in Denmark, near the shell-mounds, are small and round, indicating the small stature of the people. Sir Charles Lyell says that they bear a considerable resemblance to those of the modern Laplanders. It is probable that a great part of Europe was originally peopled by Lapps, and that they were driven north by the incoming of a more civilized race from the east. There are still remnants of the Lapps in the island of Malmön, off the coast of Sweden; in North Connaught, and the island of Arran in Ireland; in the island of Lewis, off the western coast of Scotland; and in several of the Shetland Islands.*

When the discoveries in Denmark came to light, and were republished in this country, investigations began to be made as to the existence of similar shell-mounds on the

---

* Dr. Beddoes, in his "Stature and Bulk of Man in the British Isles," says, "The black-haired Shetlanders are of low stature, with features approaching the Finnish type, and of a melancholic temperament" (p. 13). The island of Lewis also, in the Hebrides, indicates an aboriginal substratum of population of Finnish type and short stature.

British coast. We do not know whether the first investigations were made along the shores of the Moray Firth, but they are the first of which we have any account. Numerous shell-heaps had long been observed along the coast. They were raised above the level of the highest tides; and the impression which prevailed was, that they had been collected there at some early period by an eddy of the ocean. The shelly deposits were also adduced in proof of a raised sea-margin.

The kitchen-midden at Boyndie, near Banff, had long been known as a famous place for shell. Hence, probably, its name of Shelly-bush. About forty years since, Edward's attention was drawn to it by a man who had picked up shells from it when a boy. Edward set it down in his mind as an old sea-margin, and although often passing it in his journeys by the sea-side, he never thought of it as any thing else. When Professor Macgillivray, of Aberdeen, was walking with Edward along the links, about the year 1850, the latter pointed out to him the shell-bank. The professor remarked that it did not look like any other raised beach that he had ever seen.

Years passed; but what with cart-wheels going over it, and rude hands picking at it, the shells and bones which it contained at length became more clearly exposed. Still it was held to be but an ancient sea-beach. Then came the news from Denmark about the kitchen-middens. A paper by Mr. (now Sir John) Lubbock appeared in the *Natural History Review* for October, 1861, which had the effect of directing the attention of archæologists to the subject. "Macgillivray's remark," says Edward, "instantly flashed upon me. I looked at the Shelly-bush shells in our collection, and compared them with the raised beaches of King Edward and Gamrie. I saw the difference in a moment, and smiled at my own stupidity. Away I went to the Bush, and the happy result was, that before I returned I had the inexpressible delight of ascertaining that the old

sea-beach was neither more nor less than a veritable kitchen-midden."

The Rev. Dr. Gordon, of Birnie, near Elgin, had already
found a similar accumulation of shells on the old margin
of the Loch of Spynie, formerly an arm of the sea. The
mound is situated in a small wood on the farm of Brigzes.

SPYNIE CASTLE AND LOCH.

It had been much diminished by its contents having been
carted off from the centre of the heap, as manure or top-
dressing for the adjoining fields. The mound—or rather
couple of mounds, for it has been cut into two parts—must
have been of considerable extent. It measured about a
hundred yards in length by about thirty in breadth. The
most abundant shell found was the periwinkle, or the edible "buckie," as it is usually called. Next in order was
the oyster; and magnificent natives they must have been.
The Bay of Spynie was then a productive dredging-ground.
On the extensive flat around it, wherever a canal or ditch is
dug up, the shells of oysters are yet to be met with, seem-

ingly on the spots where they lived. Yet the oyster, as well as the primitive people who fared on it, have long since passed away.

The third shell in order, in this bank of shells, is the mussel, and then the cockle — all edible. "There is evidence enough in these mounds," says Dr. Gordon, " to show that they have been the work of man, and not the effect of any tidal current, or any other natural cause. The shell-fish which the remains represent are, with scarcely an exception, edible, and continue to be eaten to this day. In all deposits by the sea, there is abundance of species that have ever been rejected as food. The shells are full-grown, or adult shells. In collections made by the sea, the young animals are abundant, and often predominate. Now, no movements of wind and water could have thus selected the edible and the adult, and left behind the noxious and the young. They must have been gathered by man, and for the purpose of supplying his wants. Many other arguments have been brought forward to prove this, so that no doubt is now entertained about the matter. One strong proof is, that the oyster and the periwinkle are never found living and mingled together in the same part of the sea. The former exists between tide-marks, the other in deep water. The cockle delights in sand; the mussel must be moored to a rock or hard bottom. In different parts of the masses of shells at Brigzes, there are to be seen many stones that have been subjected to considerable heat. They probably have been used in this state for cooking, as is known to be the case among people of primitive habits to this day."

The shells found by Edward in the kitchen-midden at Boyndie corresponded in a great measure with those found by the Rev. Dr. Gordon at Brigzes. Thus, he found the periwinkle, the highly esteemed buckie, the limpet, the horse buckie (in some places called the dog periwinkle), the mussel; bones of various kinds of wild animals, such as the deer, the hare, and the rabbit; the remains of several species of fish, such as bones of the skate; a few of the crab family; fragments of pottery, and small bits of charred wood and ashes. The ashes are just like those left from a wood or peat fire. Small stones, also, were got, partially blackened, as if they had been used for cooking purposes. One very common ingredient among the fish was that part of the head known as the "lug been"—a bone usually given to the children of the family to pick.

"A remarkable fact," says Edward, in his account of the Boyndie kitchen-midden, "and one not mentioned in any account of a similar place is, that while some of the shells crumble to dust almost with the least touch, others are still so hard that they would require the fingers of a giant to pound them. The enameling of some of the limpet and mussel shells is still as beautiful as almost to persuade one that the animal had been but newly taken out. On the other hand, some are so far gone and so soft as to feel like a piece of wet blot-sheet. But what appears to be the most remarkable peculiarity in these two very opposite extremes is, that the shells thus spoken of may be found in the same handful and from the same spot. Another very striking feature is, that in handling the old 'muck,' one's fingers soon get nearly as black as ink. Here, also, as in all the other shell-accumulations, the larger bones are broken—not cut, but broken up longitudinally, or what might rather be called splintered. This has been done, it is thought, to get at the fat or marrow, of which these early people seem to have been very fond. They broke the bone, just as we break up with some heavy instrument the large toes of a lobster or parten, in order to reach the food."

M. Engelhardt, in describing the kjökken-möddings of Denmark, says that no human bones have been found among the shell-heaps. Sir John Lubbock has also said that "the absence of human remains satisfactorily proves that the primitive population of the North were free from the practice of cannibalism." Recent investigations have, however, cast some doubts upon this statement. For instance, Mr. Laing, M.P., read a paper before the Ethnological Society on the 14th of December, 1864, in which he described the results of his investigations of the kitchen-middens at Keiss, in Caithness, about eight miles north of Wick. Large masses of periwinkle and limpet shells, mixed with bones, flint splinters, and bone instruments of the rudest sort, were found. Among the bones, part of the jaw of a child was discovered, which had been broken as if to get at the marrow ; and affording ground for presumption that cannibalism was prevalent, or, at least, was occasionally resorted to among the race to which the remains refer.

No human bones were found in the shell-heaps of either Boyndie or Brigzes ; so that Mr. Laing's remarks may, after all, prove to be a mere conjecture. "One thing," says Edward, "must be observed—that no implements have as yet been found mixed up with our shells ; but whether this would indicate an earlier or a later date, it would be premature even to hint. Flint flakes, a portion of a flint knife, and a stone axe or hatchet, have been found near some of the Morayshire mounds, but not in them. They are, however, considered to belong to the same period. In the same way, the flint flakes, arrow-heads, elfshots, found in the lower part of Banffshire, as also the two curious rough-looking bits of stones formed like knives, lately dug up near Banff, and now placed in the Banff Museum, doubtless belong to the same by-gone days. Of this, however, we have a proof beyond doubt, that those who had for a time sojourned at Boyndie had, like the men of Denmark, gone out to sea-fishing. This we learn from the fact that spines of large rays or skate, bones of other big fish, such as the cod, ling, and haddocks, bits of old sponge-eaten shells, as the scallop (*Pecten maximus* and *opercularis*), the cow shell (*Cyprina Islandica*), and the roaring buckie (*Fusus antiquus*), are found in our shell-mound. Now these can not be got except in pretty deep water; and although no traces of any of their vessels have as yet been met with near the mound, still one, a *canoe*—very similar to the ancient Danish canoe —was dug up some years ago from a piece of marshy ground betwixt Portsoy and Cullen.

"During a recent excavation of the mound in the presence of a clerical friend, we came upon the two following species of shells not previously noticed — the flat-topped periwinkle (*Littorina littoralis*), and the gray pyramid shell (*Trochus cinerarius*).   These shells are both very common among the rocks at the present day.   As the list indicates, the periwinkle was the most frequent shell in the mound; but we went deeper down, and the farther we went into the bank, the limpet was most predominant, and, in fact, was almost the exclusive shell.

"Taking all these circumstances into account, and weighing the matter carefully over, we can not come to any other conclusion than that the kitchen-middens must be of a very remote age.   We know nothing of the people who formed these mounds of shells and bones.   Tradition and history are altogether silent.   Archæology seems powerless to help us, and ethnology's vision fails to penetrate the depths of obscurity.   It would appear to be one of those mysteries of the past which baffle even the wisest."

Edward collected further samples of articles taken from kitchen-middens for the museum, including a series of shells —the oyster, the cockle, the periwinkle, and the brown buckie, or whelk—gathered from the shell-heaps on the farm of Brigzes, near Elgin.   He had also several other fragments of antiquity collected in the museum, one of the most interesting of which was the joint-bone of some extinct animal.   The story connected with this bone is rather curious.

Before Edward had any official connection with the museum, he visited it one day in company with his master, and there he first saw this particular bone.   He was struck by its size, thickness, and peculiar shape. The idea flashed across his mind that he had seen something like it in a picture, but he could not remember where. Seeing his intent glance, the curator asked him if he knew any thing about it? "Nothing," said he, "except that it appears to me to be a semi-fossilized bone of some of the pre-Adamite monsters that are dug up now and then; but what it is I can not tell." "It looks to me," said the curator, "to be nothing more than the root of a tree : in fact, I am sure it is. If it were a bone, as you say, surely some of the gentlemen composing the Scientific Society would know." "Give it time," replied Edward, "and some one will yet be able to tell us all about it." "Time, indeed!" said the curator; "we have had it lying here far too long. I have often thought of throwing it into the fire, and I will do so when I have next the opportunity. It would never have been here but for that old fool [naming a previous curator], whose only aim seems to have been to get the place filled up with useless trash."

In the mean time the previous history of the bone may be given. Some sixty years before, when a mill-dam was being enlarged at Inverichny, in the parish of Alvah, near Banff, one of the workmen came upon a dark-looking object imbedded in the bank among clay and shingle, about six feet from the surface. After being disengaged, it was found that the object was very like a large hour-glass, though not tapering so much toward the middle. There were differences of opinion among the workmen about the nature of the thing. One said it was a "been," another said it was "an auld fir knot." One man tried to break it into pieces with a spade, but he failed. The hard bone turned up the edge of the spade. It was handed about, to ascertain if any body could make any thing of it. At last it got into the hands of Captain Reid, of Inverichny. He showed it to the three most important persons in his neighborhood —the minister, the doctor, and the dominie.

The minister, though he could say nothing about the bone, knew that there were great leviathans in the waters, for he had read about them in the Scriptures; but he had never seen any notice of such things being found in clay-banks. The doctor, after looking at it, and turning it round and round, said that if it was a bone, at least it did not belong to the human structure. The dominie, like his other learned friends, could throw no greater light upon the subject. He did not think it was a bone at all, but only a monstrous piece of petrified bamboo! Then the men of science of the Banff Institution were applied to, but they could make no more of the object than the minister, the doctor, and the dominie. Finally Captain Reid presented it to the museum of the Banff Scientific Society, and there it remained until Edward first saw it.

It would appear, however, that the curator had become tired of the bone, or whatever else it was, and wished to get rid of it. He removed it from the case in which it was deposited, and threw it among the rubbish of the museum. When Edward was appointed sub-curator of the museum, about nine years afterward, his first natural impulse was to go to the table where the bone had been deposited, but, lo! it had been removed. He searched the whole place, but no bone was to be found. He feared lest the curator had carried out his intention, and burned it.

Next morning Edward received orders to destroy a lot of useless stuff which lay on the floor, consisting of broken-down astronomical and philosophical instruments, moth-eaten beasts, birds, and fishes, together with other wrecked specimens of the long-neglected museum. Edward went to work, and while grouping among the rubbish at the bottom of the heap, he came upon a round dark object. He brought it up, and, lo! it was the "auld been"—in other words, the old bone! It had not been burned! He cleaned it and put it in the old place.

When the curator next made his appearance to ascertain

how far the burning had gone, he gave a glance at the case where the bone had been replaced. He stood aghast. " You have put this thing on the table again !" he shouted. " Yes," replied Edward. " Do you know," rejoined the curator, "that by so doing you are insulting myself, and the gentlemen of the society, who requested all objectionable matter to be removed from the collection ?" " I am very sorry for that," said Edward. "Then remove it at once, and burn it with the rest." Edward removed it accordingly, but he did not burn it. He took it home, and kept it there until he was able to replace it in the museum.

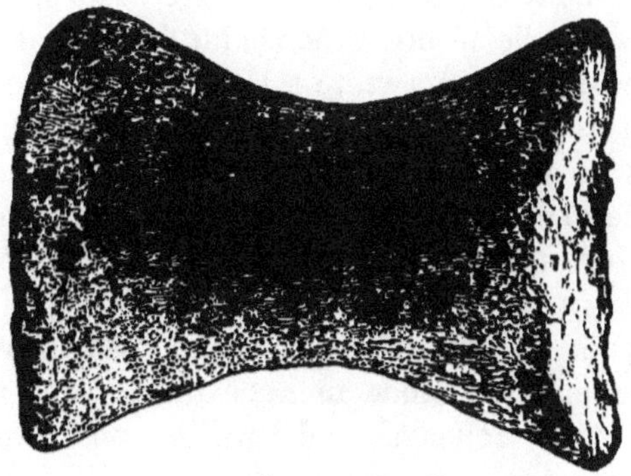

THE " AULD BEEN."

When the curator next entered the apartment, he glanced at the place where the bone had been, and seeing that it had been removed, he said nothing further about it. Shortly after, Edward was himself appointed curator, and, having the control of the collection in his own hands, he restored the bone to its former place. He was still most anxious to know of what animal the bone had constituted a part. He never failed to direct the attention of visitors to the bone, and to inquire of them whether they could give him any information about it. Thus time rolled on, and, despite of all his endeavors, the bone still remained unknown and un-named.

At last Sir Roderick Murchison and Professor Ramsay

honored the museum with a visit, in September, 1859. Edward was sure that Sir Roderick would be able to tell him all that he wanted to know respecting the bone. It was the first thing that he put into Sir Roderick's hands. "Can you tell me what that is, sir?" He took it up, turned it round and round, and over and over, and remarked, "That is a most extraordinary bone;" and then he asked when and where it had been found. Edward told him all the facts he knew respecting it, and added, "But can you tell me to what animal it belonged?" "No, I can not tell," replied Sir Roderick. Neither did Professor Ramsay know any thing about the bone. "You see," said Sir Roderick, "this does not lie in my way. This is not exactly a geological specimen. I am more a *stone* man than a *bone* man. Besides, it is often a difficult matter to distinguish small fragments or single bones of a skeleton, especially such a remarkable one as this, and to determine with certainty to what creature it belonged. But," he added, "if you have any stones in your collection unnamed, or any particular rock in your neighborhood that you can show us, and which you and the stone men of the district are in any doubt about, my colleague and I will be most happy to sort them out for you. As regards the bone, I'll tell you what to do. Send the bone to London, to Professor Owen. He's your man. He's made up of bones. He'll soon tell you all about it. And more, you can give him my compliments, say you saw me, and that I told you to send it."

Edward did not, however, send the bone to London. He knew, from experience, that such things, when sent so far away, rarely came back. That had been the case with many of his crustacea. He therefore kept the bone at home, and continued his inquiries of the *savans* who from time to time visited the museum; but he never succeeded in obtaining any favorable answer to his questionings.

Years sped on, and still the bone remained unknown. At last, when Edward was rummaging over some old books,

he came upon the second volume of the *Penny Magazine.*
While turning over the pages by chance, he saw a picture
of old bones which had much puzzled his brains some thirty years before.   And now he remembered that it was the
picture of the bones here drawn that had first given him
the idea that this bone in the museum was the remnant of
some extinct animal.   And here was the creature itself
from which the bone had been taken.   It was the *Plesiosaurus dolichodeiras;* the bone in the museum being one of
the femurs of the fore-paddle of that long-extinct monster.

To make assurance doubly sure, Edward took a photo-
graph of the bone, and sent it to a scientific correspondent
in London; when he had the pleasure of being informed
there was no doubt whatever that the bone was one of the
femurs of the fore-paddle of the Plesiosaurus.   Here, then,
was a discovery well worth all the care, the trouble, and the
anxiety which the bone had occasioned.   It may also be
mentioned that, so far as is known, no other fragment of
the Plesiosaurus has yet been found in Scotland.   They
have been met with in England in the secondary strata, and
on the Continent, principally in the Oolite and Lias.   The
bone in question is now one of the most cherished relics of
the Banff Museum.

BANFF MUSEUM.

CHAPTER XVIII.

CONCLUSION.

Edward's labors were now drawing to a close. He had fought the fight of science inch by inch, until he could fight no more. He had also fought the fight of honest poverty—a great triumph and a great glory.

> "The honest man, though e'er sae poor,
> Is king o' men, for a' that."

It is said that the man who can pay his way is not poor. Edward could always do that. He was in no man's debt. He had lived within his means, small though they were. Toward the end of his life he could only earn about eight shillings a week. But his children were now growing up; and as he had helped them in their youth, they now helped him in his age.

He had become prematurely old. His constitution had been seriously injured by his continuous exposure to the night air. He had repeated illnesses—inflammations of the throat and lungs, inflammations of the stomach and bowels—each attack rendering him weaker than before, until at last he altogether gave up his researches, and confined himself to shoe-making—occasionally attending as curator at the museum.

Yet he never could get rid of his love of nature. He continued to admire the works of the Creator as much as ever. On recovering from one of his illnesses, he went to Huntly for a change of air. His wife accompanied him.

When she proposed doing so, he asked the reason. "Oh!" she replied, "just to keep ye company, and to help ye." Accordingly she went with him. While at Huntly, he felt his old craving for nature returning upon him. He wished to go out and search the woods, the mosses, and the burns, as before; but his wife never left him.

Whenever he indicated an intention of penetrating a hedge or leaping a wall, she immediately interfered. The hedge would tear his clothes, and she could not accompany him in jumping dikes. He demurred, and said that if he went across he would "come back again." But that did not suit her purpose, and she would not let him go. As evening approached, she said, "We'll awa back noo." He protested that he would rather stay out. "No, no," said she, "I'm no gaun intill a hole like a wild beast; and, besides, the nicht air would kill me." In fact, as he afterward observed, "he had fallen into the hands of the Philistines."

Edward still took pleasure in wandering along the coast, and surveying the scenes of his former exploits. One day he took a friend round to Tarlair, to look at the rock from which he had fallen. Standing on the high ground above the shore, and looking down upon the rock-pools beneath the promontory, he observed: "I set many of my traps down there. I filled them with sea-weed, and sometimes with a piece of dead fish. The sea came in and filled my traps, and sometimes brought in many rare crustacea. I set my traps along the coast for about ten miles, from Portsoy to Melrose Head. Many a time have I scrambled among these rocks. But when I took ill, and the inflammation went to my brain, I had to leave all my traps, and there they are still."

"What a fine chance that will be for some future ichthyologist," said his friend; "he will find the traps ready-made, and perhaps full of new species of crustaceans!" "Weel," said Edward, "it may be sae; but I dinna think there'll be sic a feel as me for mony a lang year to come!"

14*

Although he had long given up searching along-shore for new specimens of fish, crustaceans, or mollusks, yet he had still another discovery to announce. There was a new fish remaining in his possession which had been entirely lost sight of. He had taken it in 1868, while searching among the rock-pools at the links. He kept it alive for two days, and when it died he put it into a bottle, intending to send it to Mr. Couch; but, somehow or other, the bottle got lost, and, though he turned the house almost upside down, he could never find it.

Only about a year ago, while turning over his papers to find the letters referred to in the preceding pages, he found the bottle containing the new fish at the bottom of the box. How great was his delight! But what was he to do with it? Mr. Couch was dead, all his fish friends were dead, and he did not know to whom to apply to name the new fish. But as he was about to proceed to Aberdeen to see Mr. Reid, who was so kind as to offer to paint his portrait, he took the fish with him. Mr. Reid procured an introduction for him, through Dean of Guild Walker, to Professor Nicol, of Marischal College. The professor did not at first recognize the fish, but, on referring to his works on ichthyology, he found that it was a specimen of Nilsson's goby, a species not before known to have been taken in British seas.

Notwithstanding the thousands of specimens and the hundreds of cases that Edward had been obliged to part with during his successive illnesses,* he has still sixty cases filled with about two thousand specimens of natural objects.

---

* After parting with the greater part of his third collection in 1867, Dr. Gray of the British Museum wrote to him: "I wish I had known that you had one or more collections to dispose of, as I should have been very glad to have purchased specimens of the Mollusca, Annelids, star-fish, Holothurea, Echina, and small fishes of the coast of Banff-shire, as I like to get specimens from the different parts of the coast. Should you have any more, please let me know." But the request came too late.

During his life-time he has made about five hundred cases with no other tools than his shoe-maker's knife and hammer, and a saw; and he papered, painted, and glazed them all himself.

As to the number of different species that he has accumulated during thirty years of incessant toil, it is, of course, impossible to form an estimate, as he never kept a log-book; but some idea of his persevering labors may be formed from the list of Banffshire fauna annexed to this volume.

Many of his discoveries have already become facts in history; but a large proportion of them can never be known. His specimens were sent to others to be named, but many of them were never afterward heard of. This was particularly the case with his shrimps, insects, zoophytes, corals, sponges, sea-slugs, worms, Tunicata, or leathern-bag mollusks, fossils, and plants. "Had any one," he says, "taken pity on me in time (as has sometimes been done with others), and raised me from the dirt, I might have been able to name my own specimens, and thereby made my own discoveries known myself."

Many of Edward's friends told him that he should have extended his inquiries into Aberdeenshire and the Northern counties; and that he should have explored the coasts of the Moray Firth in all directions. Others told him that he should have written and published much more than he did, or was ever able to do; and that he should have given many more facts to the public. The only reply that he gave to such advisers was, that he had neither the opportunity nor the means of doing so, having to work for his daily bread all the time that he was carrying on his researches.

He had another difficulty to contend with, besides his want of time and means. When he did publish what he had observed with his own eyes, and not in books through the eyes of others, his facts were often disputed by the higher class of naturalists. He was under the impression that this arose from the circumstance that they had never been heard of before, and that they had now been brought to light by a poor shoe-maker—a person of no standing whatever. This deterred him, in a great measure, from publishing his observations, as he did not like his veracity to be called in question; and it was not until years after, when others higher up the ladder of respectability had published the same facts, that his observations were accredited—simply because they could no longer be denied.

Toward the close of his labors, Edward, on looking back, was himself surprised that in the midst of his difficulties—his want of learning, his want of time, his want of books—he should have been able to accomplish the little that he did. He had had so many obstructions to encounter. His bringing-up as a child, and his want of school education, had been very much against him. Then he had begun to work for daily bread at six years old, and he had continued to labor incessantly for the rest of his life. Of course, there was something much more than the mere manual laborer in him. His mind had risen above his daily occupation; for he had the soul of a true man. Above all, he loved nature and nature's works.

We need not speak of his stern self-reliance and his indomitable perseverance. These were among the prominent features of his character. Of his courage it is scarcely necessary to speak. When we think of his nightly wanderings, his trackings of birds for days together, his encounters with badgers and polecats, his climbing of rocks, and his rolling down cliffs in search of sea-birds, we can not but think that he taxed his courage a great deal too much.

A great point with him was his sobriety. For thirty-six years he never entered a public-house nor a dram-shop. He was not a teetotaler. Sobriety was merely his habit. Some of his friends advised him to take "a wee drap whisky" with him on cold nights; but he never did. He himself believes that had he drunk whisky he never could have stood the wet, the cold, and the privations to which he was

exposed during so many years of his life. When he went
out at night, his food consisted for the most part of plain
oatmeal cakes; and his drink was the water from the nearest brook.

He never lost a moment of time. When his work for
the day was over, he went out to the links or the fields
with his supper of oatmeal cakes in his hand; and after
the night had passed, he returned home in time for his
next day's work. He stuffed his birds, or prepared the
cases for his collection, by the light of the fire. He was
never a moment idle.

Another thing must be mentioned to his credit — and
here his wife must share the honor. He brought up his
large family of eleven children respectably and virtuously.
He educated them much better than he himself had been
educated. They were all well clad and well shod, notwithstanding the Scottish proverb to the contrary.* Both parents must have felt hope and joy in the future lives of their
children. This is one of the greatest comforts of the poor
—to see their family growing up in knowledge, virtue, industry, well-being, and well-doing. We might say much of
Edward's eldest daughter, who has not only helped to keep
her parents, but to maintain her brother at school and college. It is families such as these that maintain the character and constitute the glory of their country.

But to return to Edward and his culture. In one of the
earliest letters which the author addressed to him, he made
inquiry as to the manner in which he had become acquainted with the scientific works which are so necessary for the
study of natural history. "You seem to wonder," he said
in his reply, "why I did not mention *books* in my memoir.
You may just as well wonder how I can string a few sen-
tences together, or, indeed, how I can write at all. My

---

* "The smith's meer and the shae-makers' bairns are aye the worst
shod."

books, I can tell you, were about as few as my education was brief and homespun.

"I thought you knew—yes, I am sure you knew—that any one having the mind and the will need not stick fast even in this world. True, he may not shine so greatly as if he were better polished and better educated; but he need not sink in the mire altogether.

"You may very likely wonder at what I have been able to do—being only a poor souter,* with no one to help me, and but few to encourage me in my labors. Many others have wondered, like yourself. The only answer I can give to such wonderers is, that I had the WILL to do the little that I have accomplished.

"If what I have done by myself, unaided and alone, and without the help of books, surpasses the credulity of some, what might I not have accomplished had I obtained the help from others which was so often promised me! But that time is past, and there is no use in saying any thing more about it. If I suffered privations, I had only myself and my love of nature to blame."

He was sometimes told that it was his "pride" which prevented him from being assisted as he should have been. His answer was, that he did not know any thing about pride. But if it consisted in not soliciting aid when in want, and in endeavoring to conceal his poverty even when in need of help, in order that the world might not know of the misery which himself, his wife, and his family suffered, then he did not hesitate to say that he and his wife were proud. They never refused a kindly gift, but they always refused public charity.

"Although," he says in a recent letter, "I have not known the pangs of want for some time, thanks to my children, I could scarcely have failed to do so in the years that are past: it would have been beyond the common run

---

* "*Souter*, a shoe-maker. *Ne sutor*, etc.

of things if I had not.   What working-man, especially
what journeyman shoe-maker, could have brought up and
educated a large family without at times feeling privation
and the pressure of poverty ? There are other trades which
have their dull seasons; but, unlike most other tradesmen,
shoe-makers are not, from their low pay, able to lay any
thing by, even when they have plenty of work. And, as a
matter of course, this made the struggle, when it did come,
all the worse to bear.

"From these facts and others which I have told you before, I say, and am ready to maintain against every opposition, that no one who steps this earth, or even crawls upon
it, need ever despair, after what I have done, of achieving
whatever of good they have once set their minds on. Firm-
ness of purpose and the will to do and dare will accomplish, I may say, almost any thing. The will is the key
that opens the door to every path, whether it be of science
or of nature, and every one has it in his power to choose
the road for himself."

Notwithstanding Edward's power of will and indomitable perseverance, and the amount of useful scientific work
which he has accomplished, it was easy to see that he was
rather disappointed at the results of his labors. It is true
that his zoological labors did not enable him to earn money: indeed, he had not worked for money considerations.
Natural science is always unremunerative, especially to those
who have to work for their daily bread.* Nor had his self-
imposed labors lifted him above his position in any way.
He began life as a shoe-maker, and he continued a shoe-
maker to the end. Many called him a fool because he
gave himself up to "beasts." He himself says, "I have
been a fool to nature all my life."

---

* We are sorry to observe that the late Mr. Jonathan Couch, for
whom Edward made so many of his researches at Banff, died in reduced circumstances, rendering it necessary for his daughters to go
out in search of employment.

"If it had not been for the industry of my children," he says, "my wife and myself would have been in starvation these many years back, as all that I have been making could scarcely have kept myself in bread. So that is something. But if ever I complained about my life, I never meant it to be in that way. Had the object of my life been money instead of nature—had I pursued the one with half the ardor and perseverance that I did the other—I have no hesitation in saying that by this time I would have been a rich man.

"But it is not the things I have done that vex me so much as the things that I have *not* done. I feel that I *could* have accomplished so much more. I did not want the will, but I wanted the means. It is that consideration that hurts me when I think about it, as I sometimes do. I know what I have done, and from that I can conceive how much more I might have done had I got but a little help. Think yourself—only think for a few moments—of a poor, illiterate working-man struggling against every sort of privation for so many years, with no other object in view but simply to gain a little knowledge of the works of creation —think of that, and say if I can be blamed because I occasionally grieve that I had no help, when it would have enabled me to do so much more than I have already done. For these reasons I sometimes consider my life to have been a blasted one—like a diamond taken from the mine, and, instead of being polished, crushed to the earth in a thousand fragments."

Still, Edward must, to a great extent, have enjoyed a happy life. He was hopeful and cheerful. He had always some object to pursue, with a purpose. That constitutes one of the secrets of happiness. He had an interesting hobby: that is another secret. Natural history is one of the most delightful of hobbies. He had the adventure, the chase, the capture, and often the triumph of discovery. He must have found great delight in finding a new bird, a new

star-fish, a new crustacean, a new ascidian. It must also
have been a pleasure to him to be in correspondence with
some of the most enlightened men of the time; to have
received their congratulations upon his discoveries; and to
have been rewarded with the titular honors which they had
to bestow.

But what did they think of him at home? A man may
be a well-disposed man out-of-doors, yet altogether different in his domestic circle. Follow him home, and see what
he is there. We have seen that Edward was a happy father and a happy husband. His children, as we have said,
were brought up well and virtuously. There was no better-
conducted family in Banff. When young, they assisted him
in his labors among his fishes and crustaceans; and, when
old, they were proud to help him in all ways. Is not this
a great feature in a man's character?

What did his wife say of him? When reminded of his
wanderings about at night, and asked what she thought of
them, she replied, " Weel, he took such an interest in beasts,
that I didna compleen. Shoe - makers were then a very
drucken set, but his beasts keepit him frae them. My
man's been a sober man all his life; and he never negleckit
his wark. Sae I let him be." Wise woman!

Scotch people are very reticent. They rarely speak of
love or affection. It is all " understood." It is said that
a Scotchman will never tell his wife that he loves her, until
he is dying. But you can always tell, from the inside of
a house, what the woman is, and how her husband regards
her. In these respects, it may be said that Edward, though
poor and scrimp of means, has always enjoyed a happy
home; and that is saying a great deal.

It is not, however, the amount of love and respect with
which a man is regarded at home that satisfies him, so
much as the esteem with which he is regarded by his fel-
low-men. When a man works gratuitously for science, and
labors for the advancement of knowledge, he seems entitled

to admiration and respect. But Edward did not think that his labors had been properly recognized. This seems to have vexed him very much. He had often been promised aid in the shape of books, but no such aid ever came. "All my honors," said he, "have come from a distance. I have kept the museum of the Banff Institution for about twenty-one years, for, I may say, almost nothing; and though the Linnæan Society thought me worthy of being elected an associate, the people here did not think me worthy of being an honorary member of their society. Still, I am not complaining. The people of Banff had no right to make me a gentleman."

The truth is, that it was a misfortune for Edward to have lived so far from the centre of scientific pursuits. Banff was a place comparatively unknown. In the pursuit of science a man requires fellowship: he especially requires the fellowship of books. Banff could do little for him in this respect. Had he lived in a larger town, with a library at his command, he could have acquired the friendship of scientific men, who are rarely disposed to be narrow in their "encouragement of native genius and talent," however poor the student may be.

But it was difficult for Edward to remove to any other place. He had his family to provide for, and he had not the means of removing them elsewhere. He was tied like a limpet to its rock. Still, he did all that he could to improve his position where he was. He tried to secure an appointment in connection with the police; but having no influence, he failed. He applied to the London College of Surgeons for a curatorship; but Mr. Quekett having informed him that it was only a fourth portership that was vacant, he failed there too. Then he studied electricity, for the purpose of assisting a doctor in electrifying his patients; but, thinking that he might kill more than he could cure, he gave up the idea of proceeding further. He next tried photography, but, not being provided with sufficient capital,

"AND HERE I AM STILL."

he gave up that too. The last application he made was for an appointment as subcurator of the City Industrial Museum of Glasgow, but he received no encouragement.

After abandoning photography as a means of subsistence, he returned to his old trade. "As a last and only remaining resource," he said, in June, 1875, "I betook myself to my old and time-honored friend — a friend of fifty years' standing, who has never yet forsaken me, nor refused help to my body when weary, nor rest to my limbs when tired —my well-worn cobbler's stool. AND HERE I AM STILL on the old boards, doing what little I can, with the aid of my well-worn kit, to maintain myself and my family; with the certainty that instead of my getting the better of the lapstone and leather, they will very soon get the better of me. And although I am now like a beast tethered to his pasturage, with a portion of my faculties somewhat impaired, I can still appreciate and admire as much as ever the beauties and wonders of nature, as exhibited in the incomparable works of our adorable Creator."

THE FAUNA OF BANFFSHIRE.

[Only a selection of the Fauna is given in the following pages. Had the insects, reptiles, star-fishes, zoophytes, mollusks, plants, etc., which Edward found in Banffshire been given, it would have more than filled the present volume.]

THE FAUNA OF BANFFSHIRE,

By THOMAS EDWARD, A.L.S.

MAMMALS.

MELES TAXUS [*Badger* or *Brock*]. See p. 107.
Sparingly met with in our wooded districts.

MUSTELA MARTES [*Pine Martin*].
Found chiefly in the higher parts of the county. One was observed,
in 1848, to descend from a tree in the hills of Boyndie, and go
into a rabbit's hole. The hole was stopped up, and a spade was
brought to dig the animal out. It had, however, escaped by another outlet from the burrow.

MUSTELA PUTORIUS [*Polecat* or *Fumart*].
See p. 118.

MUSTELA VULGARIS [*Weasel* or *Whitret*].
More frequent than the polecat. While the latter would seem to
delight more in plantations and whins, the other would appear to
think more of old dikes, grassy hillocks, and small cairns of
stones. Both are very destructive, killing much more than they
devour. See p. 112.

MUSTELA ERMINEA [*Ermine* or *Stoat*].
This species is often mistaken for the weasel. They are very similar during summer, their colors being then the same. In winter,
however, the ermine changes to a pure white, excepting in a portion of the tail, which is always black. In this state they are all
but universally called "*White*," or rather "*Fite Futrates*." The
true weasel never changes.

LUTRA VULGARIS [*Otter*].
Often met with in suitable localities along the sea-shore, as well as
by many of our streams and streamlets. See p. 117.

CANIS VULPES [*Fox, Tod Lowrie*, or *Reynard*].

  A well-known animal, especially in the country districts. See pp.
  112, 205.

FELIS CATIS [*Common Wild Cat*].

  The wild cat is now, perhaps, extinct with us, though at one time it
  was frequently found in the woods and rocky glens of the more
  alpine portions of the interior. One which I had the pleasure of
  seeing, and which was killed in Glen Avon, measured over four
  feet in length, and was well proportioned in every other respect.
  It was altogether a very formidable-looking animal.

TALPA EUROPÆ [*Mole* or *Mowdiewort*].

  This harmless creature is often met with. It is very useful to agri-
  culturists by turning up the fertile soil, yet they constantly wage
  war against it. Pure white varieties are sometimes met with.

ERINACEUS EUROPÆUS [*Hedgehog*].

  Ever since I remember, "hedgey" was altogether unknown, or, at
  least, very seldom seen, in Banffshire. Now he is plentiful, and
  seems to be still on the increase. See p. 112.

VESPERTILIO PIPISTRELLUS
VESPERTILIO DAUBENTIONII } [*Bat* or *Backie*].

  These are both to be found here. The first is the most common.
  It appears that we have another species of bat here. It is larger
  than either of the other two. I have met with it in our woods.

SCIURUS VULGARIS [*Squirrel*].

  It is only of late that this agile and tricky little quadruped has become domiciled in this county.

MYOXUS AVELLANARIUS [*Dormouse*].

  I am not quite sure whether we have this animal or not. I think I
  have taken it, but am not able to ascertain the fact with certainty.

MUS MUSCULUS [*Common Mouse*].

  There is no doubt about this sly little domestic. Specimens of various colors—such as white, gray striped with white, reddish, and
  yellow—sometimes occur. Musical individuals of the genus are
  not infrequent. See p. 113.

MUS SYLVATICUS [*Long-tailed* or *Wood-mouse*].

  Is to be found in almost every conceivable situation, except in
  towns.

MUS MESSORIUS [*Harvest Mouse*].

  This sleek little thing, the smallest of British quadrupeds, is now
  well ascertained to be a native of Banffshire. I have myself taken
  it several times.

Mus rattus [*Black Rat*].

This, the native British rat, though at one time very abundant, is so no longer. It has been expelled or driven back, as the Celts have been by the Scandinavians, by the Norway rat. The black rat is seldom seen now. Pure white varieties have been found.

Mus decumanus [*Norwegian Rat* or *Rottin*].

Very plentiful, and bids fair, ere long, to extirpate his weaker relative, the black rat. See p. 115.

Arvicola amphibius [*Water-rat*].

To be found on the banks of all our streams. It is sometimes turned up with the plow, at a considerable distance from the water. It is a curious circumstance that the water-rats of England are mostly of a light-brown color, while those of Scotland are usually jet-black.

Arvicola agrestis [*Short-tailed Field Mouse*].

Plentiful, and very destructive to young trees.

Arvicola partensis [*Meadow Mouse*].

Like the last in appearance and habits. It is recognizable by its much longer tail.

Sorex araneus [*Common Shrew*].

Plentiful.

Sorex fodiens [*Water Shrew*].

Found along burnsides, and occasionally in ditches.

Sorex remifer [*Black Water Shrew*].

Not so frequently found as the last. The water shrew is very difficult to be taken. I never could manage to trap any of them: they baffled all my ingenuity. My only resource was the gun, and even with it I have often had enough to do. I have sat for from six to seven hours without moving, watching for an opportunity of shooting the water shrew, and been doomed to disappointment at last.

Lepus timidus [*Common Hare* or *Maukins*].

Very plentiful in the low grounds. See pp. 110, 246.

Lepus variabilis [*Blue* or *Alpine Hare*].

This species is only to be met with in the hills and mountains, except when driven down by stress of weather. In very severe winters they occasionally descend in great numbers to the lower part of the county, at which time they are of a pure white.

Lepus caniculus [*Rabbits*].

Very plentiful, in every conceivable spot, from the rocky shore, the sand-bank, the quarry hole, the stony cairn, the old dike, the garden, the orchard, and the open field, to the thickest woods. White, black, cream-colored, striped, and pied varieties occur. See pp. 111, 246.

CERVUS ELAPHUS [*Stag, Red* or *Highland Deer*].

This, perhaps the fleetest, as he is the noblest, of our wild animals, still holds his place in the county, though not now so numerous as he used to be.

CERVUS CAPREOLUS [*Roe Deer*].

The roe seems to be more widely distributed than the red deer; and while the latter usually inhabits the more sequestered heath, grassy dells, and wooded glens of the higher lands, the other is mostly found in the plantations and copses of the lower levels. See p. 110.

PHOCA VITULINA [*Seal* or *Selch*].

Stray individuals of this aquatic tribe pay us a visit now and then. They are common in Cromarty Firth.

DELPHINUS PHOCÆNA [*Porpoise* or *Sea-hog*].

This is another watery visitant, much more frequently seen than the seal.

DELPHINUS DELPHIS [*Striped Porpoise* or *Dolphin*].

A specimen of this beautiful porpoise was taken here in 1853.

DELPHINUS TURSIO [*Bottle-nosed Porpoise*].

This species is said to have been taken here, though there are some doubts as to the fact.

DELPHINUS DEDUCTOR [*Pilot Whale*].

Several of these have from time to time been met with. There are other species of whales which have been captured here. One, reported to have been a monster for size, is said to have been found among the rocks, so far back as about the beginning of last century, betwixt the Boyne and the point known as the King's Head, but of what species is not accurately known. It is stated in the "Statistical Account of the Parish of Rathven," which extends about ten miles along the coast west of Cullen, that the porpoise, the grampus, and the spermaceti-whale are frequently seen along the shore.

BIRDS.

AQUILA CHRYSAETOS [*The Golden Eagle*].

The eagle breeds in the highest parts of the county, in the rocky heights near Ben Avon (see p. 123). They have also been seen hovering about the sea-braes between Banff and Portsoy.

AQUILA ALBICILLA [*The Erne* or *Sea-eagle*] has also been found.

AQUILA HALIAETUS [*The Osprey*, *Fish-hawk*, or *Fishing Eagle*] has also been found. A very fine male specimen was shot among the high cliffs of Gamrie Head. Another was seen at Melrose, a few miles from where the other was obtained.

FALCO PEREGRINUS [*The Peregrine Falcon, Blue* or *Hunting Hawk*].

The peregrine is one of our native hawks, and breeds annually, though very sparingly, and usually in inaccessible places in some of our highest headlands. Peregrine falcons have been taken from their nests in Troup Head. As to the manner in which they devour their prey, see p. 207.

FALCO ÆSALON [*The Merlin*].

A daring little fellow that breeds on several of our hills, more particularly on the Knock, the Bin (Huntly), Auchindoon, and Ben-vennis. When strolling along our sea-braes early one morning, I heard a tremendous noise of rooks and jackdaws ahead of me, and on coming to the spot I found them attacking a little merlin. One would have thought that such a host would have smothered the little creature in a twinkling. But such was not the case. The crows did not assail him all at once, nor yet singly; but three, four, and as many as seven, would be on him at a time, the main body keeping at a short distance, encouraging their companions, as it were, with their cawings. After a while one of these storming parties would retire, and then another would sally forth to the charge. The merlin, however, being of lighter mettle and swifter of wing, managed, with wonderful dexterity, generally to avoid their attacks; now rising, now descending, and now turning in a zigzag direction, first to one side, then to the other; and succeeding, while doing so, in giving one or other of his adversaries a pretty severe peck, which had the effect of sending him screaming away. At last, however, a crow, which seemed more courageous than the rest, rushed at the merlin with such fury that I actually thought he would have swallowed him up at once, or sent him headlong into the sea. But no! the merlin withstood the shock, and contrived to deal his assailant a thrust as he approached and passed him. The merlin now rose considerably higher, and was followed only by this single opponent, who returned with redoubled fury to the combat. Up, up they soar, fighting as they go. They close, they scream, they grapple, and their feathers fly like dust. Down they come, locked in deadly embrace. I run to catch them both. But no! See! they part, mount again and again, scream, close, and, as before, fall, but not this time to the earth; they part and mount again. But 'tis now their last time; for the hawk, rising several yards above his bold and venturous antagonist, rushes down upon him with a yell, such as hawks alone, when irritated, know how to utter, and with such force that both fell right down into the sea, above which they were then fighting. I looked to see them rise again, but they did not. After a little splashing, all was over with the crow, but not with the hawk: he was still alive, although in a very precarious situation, from which he made several unsuccessful attempts to rise, but could not. It would seem that in dealing the death-blow to his tormentor he somehow or other got himself entangled, perhaps by his talons entering some of the bones of the crow, from whence he could not extract them. Both met with a watery grave, for on my leaving the place they were both fast drifting seaward, a breeze blowing off the land at the time, with the crows hovering over them and still cawing.

FALCO NISUS [*The Sparrow-hawk*].

This is another daring individual. When standing on our links not long since, and speaking to one of our keepers, something struck me on the breast and fell to the ground. Instantly, and like a flash of lightning, down rushed a sparrow-hawk, and picked up a thrush from betwixt us; it rose with its booty, and was out of sight before we could raise our guns to fire at it. The keeper grumbled a great deal at our seeming stupidity.

FALCO TINNUNCULUS [*The Kestrel*].

This mouse, insect, and caterpillar eating bird — or hawk, if you will — is very common with us. When a boy, I kept, among a host of others, several of this species. I remember that when a mouse, a young rabbit, a leveret, and a middle-sized rat were presented at the same time, either of the former was sure to be pounced upon, while the latter usually lay unheeded. Since then, during my thirty years of taxidermal practice, I have often dissected this bird, and found in its stomach the remains principally of the smaller quadrupeds, insects (chiefly beetles), and caterpillars. Yet this poor bird is persecuted with as much severity as birds of the most destructive kind.

Falco palumbarius [*The Goshawk*].
One was shot at Tomintoul a short time ago, and two others—one at Hillton, the other at Macduff. It is rather a rare bird.

Falco milvus [*The Kite*].
This bird was once plentiful here, but it is now rarely seen. A splendid specimen was recently shot at Eden, about four miles from Banff.

Falco buteo [*The Buzzard*].
Occasionally met with.

Falco lagopus [*The Rough-legged Buzzard*].
More frequent than the last. One in my collection was killed on the hill of Dunn, and another in the museum was shot at Forglen. The nests of this species have also been found in the neighborhood, though rarely.

Falco apirorus [*The Honey Buzzard*].
A still rarer species. A splendid specimen was shot at Gamrie a few years ago. They are usually termed " Gleds " with us.

Falco æruginosus [*The Marsh Harrier*].
Specimens of these birds are occasionally shot in this neighborhood.

Falco cyaneus [*The Hen Harrier*].
Occasionally met with. The male is known here by the names of gray, blue, and lead hawk ; the female by the name of ring-tail.

Falco cinerascens [*Ash-colored Harrier*].
I have only met with one of this species here. It was a first-rate specimen—a male, and a very pretty bird.

Strix otus [*The Long-eared Horned Owl*].
Plentiful. I once found a nest of this bird with eggs about the middle of March. See p. 124.

Strix brachyotus [*The Short-eared Owl, Woodcock, or Grass Owl*].
A migrating species with us. Specimens are frequently met with by sportsmen when out shooting snipes, woodcocks, etc.

Strix flammea [*The Barn Owl*].
This bird, though common in England, is very rare with us. I know of only four being procured within twenty-four years. One is in my own collection.

Strix aluco [*The Tawny or Brown Owl*].
Almost equal in numbers to the long-eared owl, which is plentiful.

Strix nyctea [*The Snowy Owl*].
One of the most magnificent of the owl tribe. What a splendid and showy bird! I think the term "glistening" or "spangled" might,

with all truth and justice, be applied to this shining species. What a noble-looking bird! What beautiful eyes! the pupil dark, and the iris like two rings of the finest burnished gold, set, as it were, in a casket of polished silver. I am glad, nay, proud, of being able to give this king of British owls a place in my list, and of being able, perhaps for the first time, to say that at least one pair have been known to breed within the district. A few miles west of Portsoy, and not far from Cullen, stands the bold and towering form of Loggie Head. In connection with this rocky promontory, and about midway up its rugged height, there is a narrow cave or chasm called " Dickie Hare." In this cave a pair of these owls bred in 1845. Unluckily, however, for them, a party of fishermen belonging to Cullen, returning one morning from their vocation, discovered their retreat by observing one of the birds go in. This was too good to lose sight of, so up the dangerous and jagged precipice scrambled one of the crew, and managed to reach the aperture where the bird disappeared; but instead of only one, as he expected, he was not a little surprised to find that he had four to deal with—two old and two young ones well fledged; and the apartment was so narrow that only one person could enter at a time, so that help was out of the question ; and his ambition grasped the whole. What was he to do, or what could he do? Turn? —then the birds would have flown. No! but, just as I would have done had I been in his place, he set upon them all; and, after a prolonged and pretty severe battle, in which he got himself a good deal lacerated and his clothes torn by the claws of the birds, he succeeded in capturing them all alive, except one of the young ones, which fell a sacrifice to the struggle. The state of excitement which the little town was in as the man landed with his prizes, and the news of his morning's achievement spread, may in some measure be imagined, but can hardly be described.

STRIX PASSERINA [*The Little Owl*].

I gave this bird a place on the authority of a Mr. Wilson, who informs me he saw one in a wood near this place.

MUSCICAPA GRISOLA [*The Spotted Fly-catcher*].

It is somewhat strange, but not less strange than true, that this sylvan and garden-loving species should also be found nestling and inhabiting our wild and rocky ravines; yet such is the case. I have met with them twice.

MUSCICAPA ATRICAPILLA [*The Pied Fly-catcher*].

I have a specimen of this bird, a male, in my possession, which was shot about thirteen miles from this place.

Cinclus aquaticus [*The Dipper* or *Water Cockie*].
  Every means has been put in requisition to destroy this little bird.
  It was abundant thirty years ago; but it is now rarely to be seen.
  It was supposed to destroy the young salmon, hence it has been
  shot down wherever found. But I have never, as yet, found any
  thing appertaining to fish in its stomach, and I have dissected
  about forty; water insects and their larvæ being what I have
  most frequently observed.

Turdus viscivorus [*The Missel Thrush*].
  About twenty years ago such a bird was scarcely known among us,
  but now it bids fair to outnumber the common species; for, as the
  one gains ground, the other seems to lose it.

Turdus pilaris [*The Fieldfare*].
  A winter visitor. We call them " Hel-in-piets;" that is, " Highland
  piets." They arrive in October, and depart in April. Some seasons they occur in thousands, but in others only sparingly.

Turdus musicus [*The Song Thrush* or *Mavis*].
  Usually very common in this neighborhood, but becoming super-
  seded by the missel thrush. (For its singing propensities, see p.
  242). There is one fact in connection with the rearing of these
  birds which I must not omit to mention—namely, that if any of
  the young refuse to open their mouths to receive food when offered, the old one knocks them soundly on the head with his bill
  until they do so. I have observed this frequently, and was not a
  little amused at it.

Turdus iliacus [*The Redwing*].
  A winter visitor, like the fieldfare, but not nearly so numerous.

Turdus merula [*The Blackbird, Blackie*].
  Generally distributed, but not in great plenty in any place. White
  varieties have occasionally been met with, as well as pied. When
  the winter storms send the thrushes to the sea-shore to seek for
  food, this bird betakes himself to farm-steadings and stable-yards,
  so that he never suffers so much as the thrushes do.

Turdus torquatus [*The Ring-ouzel*].
  Rare. A few breed now and then among the higher districts of the
  county.

Accentor modularis [*The Hedge-sparrow*].
  Generally distributed, but nowhere in abundance.

Sylvia rubecula [*Robin-redbreast*].
  This rather bold, red-breasted gentleman, or cock-robin, as we call
  him here, is somewhat more numerous than the last.

15*

Sylvia phœnicurus [*The Redstart*].

Frequents our gardens, and breeds there.

Sylvia tithys [*The Black Redstart*].

I am only aware of two of these birds having been seen in our county.

Sylvia rubicola [*The Stone-chat*].

Sylvia rubetra [*The Whinchat*].

Neither of these birds is very numerous with us; but they may occasionally be seen in suitable localities. The first is with us all the year, and the other, though migratory, is occasionally seen in winter.

Sylvia œnanthe [*The Wheat-ear*].

A summer visitor. Wheat-ears generally appear on the sea-coast first, from whence they disperse inland. They are called with us the "Stone chatterer."

Sylvia phragmitis [*The Sedge-warbler*].

Comparatively rare. It is only of late years that this bird has visited us. How pleasant and enchanting it is to wander by the margin of the running stream either at latest even or at earliest morn, or even during summer's midnight hours, and hear the sedge-warbler pouring forth his long, harmonious song—himself all the while hid in some neighboring bush. See pp. 66, 126.

Sylvia atricapilla [*The Blackcap*].

Rarer even than the last. A most noble songster, though I prefer the thrush.

Sylvia cinerea [*The Whitethroat*].

More numerous than either of the two last. It arrives about the same time.

Sylvia sibilatrix [*The Wood Wren*].

Very rare. It is only seen at intervals, though it is supposed to breed here.

Sylvia trochilus [*The Willow Wren*].

Common throughout the whole county. It is found in plantations, whins, brooms, and in gardens and orchards. It generally nests on the ground. It is a very lively songster.

Sylvia rufa [*The Chiffchaff*].

The only bird of this kind that I have seen is one that I took myself in the Duff House policies.

Regulus crestatus [*The Golden-crested Regulus* or *Wren*].

Wherever there are suitable woods, this bird is to be found among us in pretty fair numbers.

Parus major [*The Great Titmouse*],

Parus cæruleus [*The Blue Titmouse*],

Parus ater [*The Cole Titmouse*], and

Parus caudutus [*The Long-tailed Titmouse*].

These birds all exist in the county in about equal numbers.   It is rather an interesting and pleasant sight, and one which I have often witnessed, to see small bands of these lively, active little birds, together with the gold-crests and creepers, all in company, foraging about among the leafy trees in winter; the tits on the branches, the creepers on the trunk, and, if there is no snow on the ground, the gold-crests generally lower down, near about the roots.   All is life, bustle, and animation, each cheering the other with its tiny note.   See p. 80.

Parus palustris [*The Marsh Titmouse*].

This bird is very seldom seen among us.

Parus crestatus [*The Crested Titmouse*].

This rare British tit is an inhabitant of the higher and middle districts of the county, where it breeds occasionally.

Bombycilla garrula [*The Wax-wing*].

This bird is an occasional winter visitor.   Some seasons large flocks appear, then only a few; then, again, perhaps none; and this may be the case for many succeeding seasons.

Motacilla Tarrelli [*Pied Wagtail*].

Wherever there is a stream or a quarry, you will meet, in summer, with a pair or two of these active little insect-eaters.   During winter they are invariably to be seen on lawns, or about mills and farm-steadings.   They remain with us all the year round.

Motacilla boarula [*The Gray Wagtail*].

This is our yellow wagtail, being known by no other name.   Though generally distributed throughout the country, it is not nearly so abundant.   It sometimes breeds in company with the sand martin.

Motacilla campestris [*Ray's Wagtail*].

Only an occasional visitor with us.   They breed plentifully among the hillocks which stretch along the line of coast between the Don (Aberdeenshire) and Newborough; then again from Peter-head to Fraserburgh.

Anthus arboreus [*The Tree Pipit*].

This bird is frequently seen; it breeds near Inverkeithnay, Rothie-may, and Inveraven.

ANTHUS PRATENSIS [*The Meadow Pipit*].
 Plentiful throughout the whole county.

ANTHUS OBSCURUS [*The Rock Pipit*].
 Known all along our coast.

ANTHUS RICARDI [*Richard's Pipit*].
 I have only seen this bird once, at the foot of the Knock Hill.

ALAUDA ARVENSIS [*The Sky-lark* or *Laverock*].
 Universally distributed along the whole length and breadth of the
 county. It is, I think, the most numerous bird we have. Toward the months of October and November a great diminution
 of its numbers takes place; but a little after New-year's-day
 they again begin to make their appearance. Where they have
 been in the mean time, I have never been able to ascertain; one
 thing is certain, however, that I have seen them returning from
 the east and from the north, in immense numbers. See pp. 128,
 242.

ALAUDA ARBOREA [*The Wood-lark*].
 I have seen but one of these birds—in the avenue of Duff House.
 It was alone and in song at the time—May 27th, 1850.

EMBERIZA NIVALIS [*The Snow Bunting*].
 Seen in large flocks during winter, and exhibiting a motley mixture
 of pure white, jet-black, dull tawny, and deep chestnut—a beautiful band across the wings being conspicuous only in flight.
 They arrive about the beginning of November, and depart about
 the first of April. They sing beautifully, in a sweet, low lilt.

EMBERIZA MILIARIA [*The Corn Bunting*].
 This bird is not very numerous with us.

EMBERIZA SCHŒNICLUS [*The Black-headed Bunting* or *Ring Fowl*].
 It frequents the mosses. I have found their nests in bushes, among
 reeds, or on the ground. It is called the "Moss Sparrow" by the
 country people. I once saw a black variety of this bird, and another almost yellow.

EMBERIZA CITRINELLA [*The Yellow-hammer*].
 More numerous than either of the two last. The common name
 here is "Skite." It is not particular as to the place where it
 builds its nest. I have seen one built in a rut on a cart-track,
 close by the way-side. On passing afterward, I found the nest
 had been destroyed by a cart-wheel passing over it.

EMBERIZA COILUS [*The Coil Bunting*].
 Very rarely found in this quarter.

FRINGILLA CŒLEBS [*The Chaffinch*].
Abundant.

FRINGILLA MONTIFRINGILLA [*The Brambling*].
A winter visitor. A few may be met with every season.

FRINGILLA MONTANA [*The Tree Sparrow*].
To be found in several localities throughout the county.

FRINGILLA DOMESTICA [*The House Sparrow*].
Numerous.

FRINGILLA CHLORIS [*The Greenfinch*].
Pretty generally distributed .throughout the country, and especially
in woody places. The bird is easily tamed.

FRINGILLA COCCOTHRAUSTES [*The Hawfinch*].
A rare bird with us.

FRINGILLA CIRIS [*The Painted Finch*].
A migratory species. Only one specimen has been seen.

FRINGILLA CARDUELIS [*The Goldfinch*].
These birds have in a great measure been captured by the bird-
catchers. See p. 243.

FRINGILLA SPINUS [*The Siskin*].
Fewer than before. They have been thinned by the bird-catchers.
A tamable bird.

FRINGILLA CANABINA [*The Linnet*].
There is no house bird that possesses so many names as this one.
It is the rose lintie so long as it retains its red breast ; but when
that is gone or wanting, it is then the gray lintie, the whin lintie,
the brown lintie, and so on. Cultivation is driving the linties
away, by tearing down every whin, knoll, and brae, where it is
possible for the plow and spade to work their way.

FRINGILLA LINARIA [*The Lesser Redpole*].
This is found most plentifully in the higher districts of the county ;
but in severe winters large flocks of them descend to the lower
grounds.

FRINGILLA BOREALIS [*The Mealy Redpole*].
A rare species.

FRINGILLA MONTIUM [*The Twite*].
Another mountain as well as sea-shore rocky species. It is the
most elegant of all our linnets.

LOXIA PYRRHULA [*The Bullfinch*].
This is another prize for the trapper. But great numbers are an-

nually destroyed by gardeners and nursery-men, who believe that they are destructive. Yet their principal food consists of insects; and insects are also the chief food for their young. I hope a better day will arrive for these lovely little birds, when they will be cherished and encouraged rather than hated and destroyed. The bullfinch is easily taught to whistle or to " pipe " familiar tunes.

LOXIA CURVIROSTRA [*The Cross-bill*].

This bird is on the increase. They nest with us, and have done so for some years. There is a great diversity of color and size among them.

LOXIA PITYOPSITTACUS [*Parrot Cross-bill*].

While walking one morning round the Whinhill, and just as I reached the south side, I was rather surprised at hearing the voice of what I knew to be a stranger. On looking to a low, bare wall, about three or four yards in front of me, I beheld, in all his pride and beauty, a male parrot cross-bill. This is the only instance, to my knowledge, of its existence among us.

LOXIA LEUCOPTERA [*White-winged Cross-bill*].

About fifty years ago, a large flock of these birds suddenly made their appearance on the "Castle trees," in this neighborhood. Their strange appearance and gaudy plumage soon attracted notice, nearly the whole town flocking to see the "foreigners." They appeared quite exhausted, many of them dropping from the trees.

STURNUS VULGARIS [*The Starling*].

The starling has been rapidly increasing of late years. At one time single starlings were rarely to be seen, whereas flocks of this bird now appear toward the close of every season.   •

STURNUS PREDATORIUS [*The Red-winged Starling*].

A pretty bird, which occasionally visits this county.

PASTOR ROSEUS [*Rose-colored Pastor*].

This is another rare beauty, occasionally seen in this county.

CORVUS CORAX [*The Raven*].

A few of these birds inhabit the precipitous parts of the coast, where they breed in company with the falcon, kestrel, gull, guillemot, etc. The raven will tame pretty well; it will talk hoarsely, and do mischievous tricks.

CORVUS CORONE [*Carrion-crow*], and

CORVUS CORNIX [*Hooded Crow*].

Both occur in about equal numbers. See p. 243.

CORVUS FRUGILEGUS [*The Rook*].
Many large rookeries exist in the county. See p. 127.

CORVUS MONEDULA [*The Jackdaw*].
Very plentiful. See p. 45.

CORVUS PICA [*Magpie*].
One of the most bashful of birds. It is very sparingly distributed,
and in some places is scarcely known. Our keepers both shoot
and trap them wherever found.

PICUS MAJOR [*Greater Spotted Woodpecker*].
Several pairs of this showy bird have been procured within our district. It is also found in the higher parts of the county. A
specimen was shot near Banff, and when dissected its stomach
was found crammed with two species of grub, of a creamy or
grayish color. It contained also several beetles and a small
spider.

PICUS MINOR [*Lesser Spotted Woodpecker*].
More rare than the last. One sent to me, fourteen years since,
from Mayen, where it was shot, and another seen on the Lodge
hills, are all that I am aware of. Very probably others have occurred.

YUNX TORQUILLA [*Wryneck*].
The late Professor Macgillivray, of Marischal College, Aberdeen, informed me that one was taken at or near Portsoy, by a pupil of
his. One, now in the Banff Museum, was taken six years ago,
about fourteen miles from the town.

CERTHIA FAMILIARIS [*Creeper*].
Wherever there are suitable woods, these birds are sure to be
found. We sometimes read and hear, as extraordinary occurrences, that nests have been found in the hearts of trees that
have been sawed up. Now, to those acquainted with the facts,
these occurrences are easily accounted for. I know a tree myself which contains *two* nests, both with eggs. About seventeen
years ago there was in the side of this tree a small aperture,
about six feet from the ground, which led downward to a cavity
in the centre of the trunk. The opening was so narrow out-
wardly that it only admitted two of my fingers, but widened as it
proceeded to the bottom, a distance of about eighteen inches.
In this hole, at the time referred to, a pair of creepers built their
nest and laid eggs, after which they disappeared. Next season a
pair of blue titmice acted in a similar manner; and they also disappeared, doubtless in consequence of being tormented by boys,

and of the narrowness of the entrance. The growth of the tree
caused the hole to get less and less every year, and it has been
for several years so completely closed that the point of the finest
needle can not be inserted. The tree, a sturdy beech, has the
two nests and eggs in its very core. It is thus evident how easily
these "extraordinary occurrences" may be accounted for.

TROGLODYTES EUROPÆUS [*Wren*].

The dear little wren, the lion of small birds, with his short, jerking
little tail, I have known and admired from childhood. Who that
has trod the woods in spring or summer has not heard a very
loud though by no means inharmonious song, proceeding from
some bush or bank, and not admired it. And who is there, if he
did not know the bird, that would not be surprised beyond measure at so small a creature being able to make such a loud noise?
Of all the deserted nests I have ever met with, those of the wren
would, I am sure, count twenty per cent. over any other species.
I am unable to account for this, but perhaps it arises from their
building several before they get one to please them. I once
found one of their nests in an old tin kettle, which had become
fixed among the branches of a holly. The wren, like other birds,
does not sing so well in confinement. When in their native
haunts, there is a pathos in their voice, and a music in their melody, which makes the heart thrill with pleasure.

UPUPA EPOPS [*Hoopoe*].

Three or four of these pretty birds have occurred here : one was
taken at Duff House, in 1832, by a Mr. Mackay, in such a state
of exhaustion as to allow itself to be captured by hand ; another
was seen by myself, a few years back, in the same place ; and
two others are said to have been since obtained in other parts of
the county.

CUCULUS CANORUS [*Cuckoo*].

This is another sweet and darling gem. Well do I remember, when
only a little fellow, rummaging about the Den of Rubislaw, near
Aberdeen, how surprised I was on hearing the sound of "Cuckoo,
cuckoo," from a small plantation close by, and how overjoyed I
was when I obtained a sight of the bird ; and now that I am old,
the sweet voice of the harbinger of sunny days still cheers me.
They are not very numerous with us along the sea-coast, but are
very frequent in the higher districts. They generally appear
about the end of April. It is said that they can retain their eggs
for a number of days after they are ready for extrusion. I will
relate, without comment, a circumstance of this sort which came

under my own observation. A female specimen, shot in a garden here, was brought to me to be preserved. On dissecting it, I was agreeably surprised at finding in the oviduct an egg as perfect as if it had been obtained from a nest.

CORACIAS GARRULA [*Roller*].

I am only aware of one specimen of this pretty and rare bird being obtained in our county: it was a splendid specimen, killed on the hills of Boyndie.

MEROPS APIASTER [*Bee-eater*].

I give this species a place here from having heard that a greenish bird, somewhat less than a thrush, with a longish bent bill, and with two feathers of the tail longer than the rest, was killed in a garden between Huntly and Dufftown, about seven years ago. It has since been found at the hills of Boyndie, about two miles from Banff.

ALCEDO ISPIDA [*Kingfisher*].

Several of these sparkling gems have been taken here at different times. See p. 66.

HIRUNDO RUSTICA [*Swallow*], and

HIRUNDO RIPARIA [*Martin*].

These birds are in about equal numbers. The latter generally nestle in the corners of windows, the former in barns, etc.; they also breed along the sea-shore wherever there is a cave or projecting rock suitable. White and cream-colored varieties are sometimes met with.

HIRUNDO URBICA [*Sand-martin*].

Wherever there is a bank of any height, and not too hard, whether along the sea-shore or river-side, or a quarry or sand-hole, a colony of these active little creatures is almost sure to be met with during summer. It is surprising to see how they perforate these places, and the depth to which they will sometimes go, especially when we consider the remarkably feeble instruments with which they do it—namely, a very small and slender bill, and feet equally small and tender.

CYPSELUS APUS [*Swift*].

Of all our migratory species this is generally the last to arrive, and the first to depart. Next to the sky-lark, the swift appears to ascend highest in his aërial flights; and a very beautiful sight it is to see it, on a clear, still evening, gamboling about so far above the earth, and, it may be, screaming its farewell requiem to the departing sun. The swift is the first to depart, toward the end of August or beginning of September, and it returns about the middle of May; the sand-martin next, or about the second or third week in September, and it usually returns about the third week in April; and the swallow and house-martin commonly about the first week or middle of October, and they re-appear about the 1st of May. Before I part with this interesting tribe I must become a little arithmetical. We are frequently told, and justly, of the great benefit swallows and other insect-feeders do, by the countless herds of noxious creatures which they destroy. I will relate an instance of my own experience in this respect. Picking up a swallow which had been shot by a friend, I found that its mouth was crammed with gnats and flies. Some of them were alive. They all seemed attached to the mouth by a glutinous fluid. The bird had apparently been catêring for its young. Being desirous of making a further examination, I wrapped it in paper and put it in my pocket. On reaching home I opened the paper, when a number of the gnats buzzed out into my face, much to my regret; but I succeeded in counting upward of 70, and I am quite sure there were more than 100 in all. Now, it is a well-known fact that both birds assist in rearing their young. Well, say that they visit the nest every ten minutes (which is under the mark), and that every time of doing so each bird conveys 70 insects; this in an hour amounts to 840; in a day of twelve hours, which is but a short day for a swallow at that season of the year, to 10,080; in a week of seven days, to 70,560; and in a fortnight, to 141,120. But if we carry the calculation a little farther, by supposing that the birds rear two broods in a season, although the number is often three, we have, at the ratio at which we have been counting, a total of 282,240 insects destroyed in one year by *two birds alone*, while rearing their two broods!

Caprimulgus Europæus [*Night-jar*].

  Of late years this species would appear to have become more numerous, but it is still very far from plentiful.

Columba palumbus [*Ring-dove*].

  Or, as we have it, *Cushie Doo*. This bids fair to become one of the greatest pests of the farmers. The wild pigeons have increased amazingly within the last few years, and the damage they do is incalculable. This increase is caused by the almost total destruction of the hawk tribe, which tended greatly to thin their numbers.

Columba livia [*Rock Dove*].

  A few pairs breed in the caverns along our coast. It is a rare case,

however, to get a pure specimen ; as domestic pigeons from the
farms near sometimes breed with them.   I have seen white specimens, as well as those of a sand color.

COLUMBA TURTUR [*Turtle-dove*].
   Three or four specimens of this species are said to have been seen,
   and some of them obtained, within the county; but whether wild
   ones, or individuals that had escaped, has not been ascertained.

PHASIANUS COLCHICUS [*Pheasant*].
   Introduced, but seems to thrive very well ; it is a beautiful ornament
   to parks and woods.   Partially pied varieties sometimes occur,
   and another, called the " silver pheasant."

TETRAO TETRIX [*Black Grouse*].
   Exists chiefly in the higher districts.

TETRAO EXOTICUS [*Red Grouse*].
   Exists on all our moors and hills, but not in great numbers.

TETRAO LAGOPUS [*Ptarmigan*].
   Less frequent than either of the two last.   Ptarmigans inhabit the
   summits of our highest mountains; they are seldomer seen than
   those which frequent the lower ground.   Like all others of the
   grouse tribe, they are yearly decreasing in number.

PERDRIX CINEREA [*Partridge*].
   Pretty common.   A very cunning and faithful mother is the female;
   for when she has eggs she never goes out, if time permits, without
   hiding them so carefully that it is almost impossible to detect
   their whereabouts ; and if you take her by surprise, away she
   hobbles on one leg, and a wing trailing on the ground, as if wounded.   See p. 231.

PERDRIX RUFA [*The Red-legged Partridge*].
   Commonly called the French partridge : it has been recently found
   in Banff.

PERDRIX COTURNIX [*Quail*].
   That this species is a regular visitor I am not prepared to say ; but
   that it is an occasional visitor and breeds here is beyond all doubt.
   Nests and eggs of this species are sometimes met with in cutting
   grass ; they are generally passed over as those of the land-rail.

CHARADRIUS PLUVIALIS [*Golden Plover*].
   Where moor-fowl occur, the golden plover is generally to be met
   with.   When the hills, heaths, and fields are covered with snow,
   the plover comes down from his alpine abode, and stays at the
   sea-side, where great numbers fall an easy prey to the gun of the
   sea-side fowler.

CHARADRIUS MORINELLUS [*Dotterel*].

Occasionally met with. On once asking an old keeper from the higher grounds as to where this species breeds, he replied, " On the gray slopes of the highest mountains, far above all the other birds, except the ptarmigan." I am doubtful whether it breeds with us at all.

CHARADRIUS HIATICULA [*Ringed Plover*].

These breed with us, and remain all the year round. I have found their eggs on the sand by the beach, and forty miles inland. They likewise nestle on the shingly banks and islands along our river-courses. They are known here by the names of " sea-lark " and " sunny liverock."

VANELLUS MELANOGASTER [*Gray Plover*].

Rather rare, and I believe only a winter visitor.

VANELLUS CRISTATUS [*Lapwing*].

Found on heaths and moors, and in fields, where they breed. Many of them leave us toward winter. This is another species which endeavors to mislead you when searching for its eggs. Of all our field and heath birds, the lapwing is one of the most useful in destroying destructive insects, such as *Zabrus gibbus*, etc.

STREPSILAS INTERPRES [*Turn-stone*].

An occasional visitor, generally in winter. See p. 220.

CALIDRIS ARENARIA [*Sanderling*].

A regular visitor, generally arriving in August, a few of them remaining through the winter. I have met with them, too, in summer, when their predominant color, instead of being whitish, is a most beautiful reddish fawn. On their first arrival here they are very tame, allowing you to approach within a yard or two. See p. 164.

HÆMATOPUS OSTRALEGUS [*Oyster-catcher*].

Why this bird is called oyster-catcher, I can not understand. Had it been named " limpet-catcher," I could have understood it. I have crawled among the rocks in order to see them feed; when I have seen the limpet driven from its hold, and scooped out of its shell with as much apparent ease as I could have picked up a *Gammaris locusta ;* but I have never seen it attempt to catch an oyster. On this part of the coast its food generally consists of the limpet, and very rarely of *Acmæa testitudinalis*. I have counted as many as forty-one of the former in the stomach of a single bird, while of the latter I have not met with more than three or four examples. The oyster-catcher is a summer visitor with us, arriving here to breed. Now and then it may be seen during winter. Large flocks visit us some seasons, generally in September, and, after remaining for a day, proceed farther south. "Seapiet" is the name the bird is known by here.

Ardea cinerea [*Heron*].

We have some small spots where these birds breed, but which hardly deserve the name of heronries. At one time, however, they were in greater numbers. I remember taking from the stomach of one a large water-rat, three middle-sized trout, and fifteen minnows. Some time ago, a person belonging to this town, while passing through one of the streets, was startled at being hit on the head by something which had fallen from above, and which proved to be a small fish—the five-bearded rockling—apparently quite fresh. On looking up, he saw nothing but a "craigie" passing over the houses, pursued by a number of crows. Of course the fish had dropped from the heron; but the man could not be persuaded that it had not dropped from the clouds.

Ardea purpurea [*Purple Heron*].

One of these birds is said to have been shot about thirteen miles from hence. My late friend, the Rev. Mr. Smith, saw fragments of the bird some time afterward, and believed it to be of this species.

Ardea egretta [*Great White Heron*].

Two of these birds were observed to frequent various parts of our coast about twenty-six years ago; but a specimen has not since been procured.

Ardea stellaris [*Bittern*].

Three or four of these birds are known to have paid us a visit. One in the Banff Museum, a very pretty one, was killed near Banff about twenty-four years since; another in the moss of Park, and one or two at Balveny.

Platalea leucorodia [*Spoonbill*].

One of these rarities was found in a ditch in a wood near here, by a young naturalist; he says it could easily have been shot, for he approached quite close to it, and it did not appear at all shy. It has since been found in this neighborhood.

Ibis falcinellus [*Glossy Ibis*].

On one occasion I perceived three of these birds hovering about the coast for a whole day, but I could not get a shot at them; it was in winter, and during a very severe storm.

Numenius arquata [*Curlew*].

Plentiful in certain localities along the shore in winter; they retire in spring to the alpine and sub-alpine districts. Their note in winter is simply "Whaup," with sometimes a loud scream when come upon suddenly. In summer, however, and while among the moors and hills, it is more varied, being then "Poo-l-ie, poo-l-ie," then "Coor-lie, coor-lie," with a long "Wha-a-up" at the end. They are not then so shy as when seen by the sea-shore.

NUMENIUS PHÆOPUS [*Whimbrel*].

Seldom a summer passes but a whimbrel or two may be met with along the shore, and sometimes in some of our mosses. I think they breed with us. They are generally very shy, and not easily approached. Their call-note at once distinguishes them from the curlew.

TOTANUS CALIDRIS [*Redshank*].

We have this red and long-legged gentleman rather sparingly with us, but we have him all the year. There are certain spots coast-wise not much frequented, where, for seven or eight months in the year, you will seldom, if ever, fail to meet with a few; and when disturbed, their wild scream accords well with the solitary places which they frequent, especially where there is a low hol-low murmuring from the ocean. This is another species, which, lapwing-like, will flap about you when in the way of their nests, and for noise they exceed them completely. They generally breed in marshy and boggy places, and about the grassy margins of lochs, but I have also found them among bents and dry sandy places by the sea-shore.

TOTANUS HYPOLEUCOS [*Common Sandpiper*].

The common sandpiper (or, as we have it, "kittie-needic," from its cry) is one of our summer birds; there is scarcely one of our streams but has its "kittie-needies" in the season. They breed on the banks.

TOTANUS GLOTTIS [*Greenshank*].

This is a rarity with us. I have one in my possession, out of two which were shot in the moss of Banff.

RECURVIROSTRA AVOCETTA [*Avocet*].

More rare than the preceding.

LIMOSA MELANURA [*Black-tailed Godwit*].

Only two specimens have been taken here.

LIMOSA RUFA [*Bar-tailed Godwit*].

A few of these may generally be observed every autumn, either by the sea-side or in our mosses. They do not stop long with us, a few days at most sufficing. Perhaps we have not suitable localities for them.

MACHETES PUGNAX [*Ruff*].
Rare. Three, I think, have been obtained, all birds of the year, and all in autumn.

SCOLOPAX RUSTICOLA [*Woodcock*].
Though a pair or two have been known to breed, the woodcock can hardly rank with us but as a winter visitor. In some seasons they are more numerous than in others. Does the snow affect the coloring of this species? My reason for asking this question is because, in very severe and snowy weather, I have seen many of them of a remarkably light color; but in milder seasons, and when there were little or no storms or frost, I have never seen any of them with the same gray-like coating.

SCOLOPAX GALLINAGO [*Common Snipe*].
Though many of these breed and remain with us all the year, still we receive great additions annually from elsewhere, and generally toward the end of autumn; but neither during summer nor winter are they so plentiful as they were. Drainage is said to be the cause of their comparative scarcity.

SCOLOPAX GRISEA [*The Brown Snipe*].
Some specimens of this bird have been met with near Banff, but it is rarely seen.

SCOLOPAX GALLINULA [*Jacksnipe*].
A winter visitor only, so far as I am aware, and by no means so numerous as the preceding. The jacksnipe would appear to be a solitary animal; at least, I have never seen more than two of them together (of course in winter), but more commonly only one; in fact, they are nearly always seen single. Unlike the others, however, I have seen them return to the same spot three times, after being as often fired at.

TRINGA SUBARQUATA [*Curlew Sandpiper*].
I have only met with one specimen of which I can speak with certainty.

TRINGA CANUTUS [*Knot*].
A few generally visit us every autumn on their southward passage. They are remarkably easy of approach.

TRINGA MINUTA [*Little Stint*].
A very fine little fellow. I once had a desperate hunt after one. See p. 139.

TRINGA TEMMINCKII [*Temminck's Stint*].

Mr. Taylor, gamekeeper to the Earl of Fife, once shot a specimen on the Deveron bank.

TRINGA VARIABILIS [*Dunlin*].

This bird breeds in a few of our marshy places, and may now and then be met with along the coast. Toward autumn large flocks appear, but they do not remain long. Specimens may be picked up occasionally, during winter, almost pure white, except the bill, legs, and feet, which retain their usual color. This species appears to differ considerably in size, the legs and bills included, the larger birds often having the shortest bills.

TRINGA MARITIMA [*Purple Sandpiper*].

A rock-loving species while with us, never leaving the rocks unless from necessity. They are gregarious, and huddle so closely together that I have known as many as twenty-three killed at one shot. I have killed them occasionally during summer, their color being then of a rufous or rusty character, or more like that of the dunlin, the purple gloss and dark-gray plumage of winter having all but disappeared.

GALLINULA CREX [*Land-rail*].

"Corn craig" or "crake." Very sparingly distributed here. It arrives generally at the beginning of May, and departs usually in September; but I have seen it as late as December. These birds often feign themselves dead when hard pressed, rather than fly— a fact that may seem incredible to those who have paid no attention to such things. Is it possible that these birds remove their eggs on its coming to their knowledge that their nests have been discovered? I knew of a nest which contained seven eggs. I took one, and, wishing to get all that the hen would lay, left the remainder untouched; I also carefully obliterated all my footmarks, to prevent others from suspecting any thing if the nest were found. I went back three days afterward, when, although there were no signs of human foot-prints, all the eggs were gone.

GALLINULA PUSILLA [*Little Crake*].

Only one of this British rarity has been procured here, so far as I know. It occurred at a place called Thornton, on the banks of the Isla.

GALLINULA CHLOROPUS [*Moor-hen*].

The "water-hen." In consequence of our having but few lochs, and those very small, we have not many of this species. As skulkers, they almost rival the land-rail.

Rallus aquaticus [*Water-rail*].

Far more scarce than the last; in fact, it is almost a rarity. Perhaps their skulking habits prevent their being oftener seen.

Fulica atra [*Coot*].

An occasional visitor. On the loch of Strathbeg (Aberdeenshire), where they are pretty numerous, they breed, and remain all the year round. In very wet summers the water of this loch rises at times considerably above the usual level: on such occasions I have seen the coot sailing nobly along with her nest beneath her.

Phalaropus platyrhynchus [*Gray Phalarope*].

Three specimens were procured on the sands of Sandend.

Phalaropus hyperboreus [*Red-necked Phalarope*].

One specimen, a male, was shot on the beach here, in the spring of 1855.

Anser.

Of the genus Anser we are remarkably scanty. Several kinds of geese have from time to time been procured, and not an autumn or spring passes without many large flocks being seen passing and repassing, but to what species they belong it is difficult to say. That the *Graylag* (Anser ferus), the *Brent* (A. bernicla), the *Egyptian* (A. Ægyptiacus), and the *Spur-winged* (A. gambensis), have been met with, is beyond doubt; but that these are all that have visited us, it is hard to say. The *Brent* is very numerous in certain seasons along the coast.

Cygnus.

The genus Cygnus is still more scantily represented. Some of them visit us in passing to and from their breeding-grounds.

Anas tadorna [*Common Sheldrake*].

This pretty bird is only a winter visitor with us, and then not in large numbers.

Anas clypeata [*Shoveler*].

This pretty bird is quite a rarity here. In the latter part of the winter of 1837–'38, which was of great severity, a mutilated specimen of the shoveler was found dead among the rocks at Blackpots.

Anas strepera [*Gadwall*].

Another great rarity, so far as I am aware; one, a female, procured in the Deveron by Dr. Leslie, about the time the shoveler above alluded to was picked up, is the only one I know of.

Anas acuta [*Pintail Duck*].

I remember being roused rather early one morning, many years ago, by a loud knocking at the street-door, and a person calling at the top of his voice, "Rise, man, Tam! I've brought a rare bird t' ye —a duke." Being awake, I immediately jumped up. On seeing the bird, I was delighted to observe a beautiful male pintail. It had been shot that night on the Deveron.

ANAS BOSCHAS [*Wild Duck*].

Plentiful, especially in winter. Among the sandy bents almost close to the ocean's verge, and on the tops of our heath-clad hills and moors, I have found this species breeding; as well as on a tree about thirteen feet from the ground, and on a rock in the craigs of Alvah. This latter nest was placed on a ledge fully thirty feet above the water, and had eight or nine feet of perpendicular rock above it. There is a hill near here, which I believe they used frequently to nestle on, but which they have now quite deserted—viz., Fern or Whin hill, better known as Gallow hill. It was on this hill—or rather piece of ground, for it hardly deserves the name of hill—that the celebrated freebooter M'Pherson finished his earthly career. It is a rough and stony place where he lies, covered with heath and whin. The pheasant and wild duck used not unfrequently to breed on his very grave. On a small island on the Deveron stood a tall old poplar. About five feet from the ground it divided into two arms, one stretching upward, while the other bent over the river, and it is with this one that I am now concerned. In 1839 the Deveron, like the other rivers in Scotland, rose far above its usual height, so far, indeed, that it reached the arm of the tree alluded to, on which it deposited a good deal of rubbish. A female wild duck built her nest, a few years afterward, among the débris thus left, and succeeded in rearing a brood of thirteen young ones. Neither nest nor bird, though known of by some salmon-fishers who had a station close by, was disturbed. One morning the female was observed by these men to leave her nest and fly up and down the water in an unusual manner. Presently she was joined by the male, and both disappeared beneath a bank a little above where the nest was. The fishermen, who had watched them, observed the female reappear alone, and, after flying up and down once or twice, again settled down on the water, just below the tree which contained the nest. After sailing about for a few minutes, she was heard to give "a quack," when down went something into the water, and presently a young one was seen by her side. Away she swam with it to the bank referred to, consigning it to the charge of the male; after which she returned, and, having again sailed about for a short time, gave another "quack," when down came another youngster, which she also led away to the bank. In this way she continued until all were safely removed. The female never gave more than one "quack," and she never carried more than one young one at a time, nor did she return after taking away the thirteenth.

Anas querquedula [*Garganey*].
Two specimens of this species were shot in December, 1840; and one is said to have been obtained at Cullen, in the spring of 1841.

Anas crecca [*Teal*].
Occasionally met with in winter.

Anas Penelope [*Widgeon*].
One of our rarest duck visitors. A splendid male specimen was killed at Boyndie in September, 1853.

Anas Americana [*American Widgeon*].
A mutilated male specimen of this rare duck, shot on the Burn of Boyndie, in January, 1841, was for many years in my possession.

Anas marila [*Scaup duck*].
Pretty frequent during winter.

Anas fuligula [*Tufted Duck*].
Very rare.

Anas clangula [*Golden-eye*].
A regular winter visitor, generally coastwise; but they are also met with on mill-dams some miles inland.

Anas glacialis [*Long-tailed Duck*].
Abundant, but always keeping near the coast. I have shot them when in their full breeding dress, which gives them quite a different appearance. In spring they are very clamorous, pursuing each other through the water, and diving and skipping about like Merry-andrews. The noise they make on such occasions is so loud that I have heard it, on a still morning, nearly three miles off. They are generally among the first birds to arrive and the last to leave.

Mergus cucullatus [*Hooded Merganser*].
I was told by an old gunner and bird-stuffer that he had shot a specimen of this species, but I can not vouch for his accuracy.

Mergus serrator [*Red-breasted Merganser*].
Not very plentiful. All along the coast, in suitable localities, they are met with, singly, and two or three together, rarely more.

Mergus merganser [*Goosander*].
A winter visitor. The male is a very showy gentleman. As many

as seven or eight specimens were procured at one shot, on the Deveron. I have seen as many as five or six together.

PODICEPS CRISTATUS [*Great Crested Grebe*].
An occasional visitor.

PODICEPS RUBRICOLLIS [*Red-necked Grebe*].
Of more frequent occurrence, but generally in immature plumage.

PODICEPS AURITUS [*Eared Grebe*].
Less frequent than the last.

PODICEPS MINOR [*Little Grebe*].
A winter seldom passes without an opportunity occurring to obtain this species. It is one of the most expert divers we have.

COLYMBUS GLACIALIS [*Great Northern Diver*].
Some seasons pretty plentiful. Splendid specimens are at times procured, but they are generally immature.

COLYMBUS ARCTICUS [*Black-throated Diver*], and

COLYMBUS SEPTENTRIONALIS [*Red-throated Diver*].
Winter visitors, in about equal numbers. A few of them gradually fall victims every spring to getting entangled in the bag-nets set for salmon. They not unfrequently visit our larger streams, where they make great havoc among the smaller of the finny tribe.

URIA BRUNNICHII [*Brunnich's Guillemot*].
Has been once met with.

URIA TROILE [*Common Guillemot*],

URIA LACHRYMANS [*Ringed Guillemot*],

URIA GRYLLE [*Black Guillemot*],

MORMON FRATERCULA [*Puffin*], and

ALCA TORDA [*Razor-bill*].
All these species breed with us, but the black guillemot only rarely. I have procured several ringed guillemots both in winter and summer; I have also been shown places in the cliffs where the fishermen say they breed.

ALCA ALLE [*Little Auk*].
A winter visitor. In December, 1846, a terrific sea-storm raged here for the greater part of the month. At its termination I counted between the Burn of Boyne and Greenside of Gamrie, a distance of about nine miles, nearly sixty of these little birds lying dead, besides a number of guillemots and razor-bills. Great numbers were also found dead in the fields throughout the county.

Carbo cormoranus [*Cormorant*].

Frequent, except for a short time during summer. A pair or two may breed with us, but that is all. Like the divers, they destroy great numbers of fish.

Carbo cristatus [*Shag*].

Only, I believe, an occasional visitor.

Sula bassana [*Gannet*].

A spring and autumn visitor, and occasionally during summer and winter. When overtaken, as they sometimes are, by strong north winds, I have known them driven to great distances inland, where they are frequently seen lying dead. Immature specimens are now and then procured during their autumnal passage. From their different plumage, they are looked upon as distinct from the "solan goose," as the gannet is here called.

Sterna cantiaca [*Sandwich Tern*].

An occasional visitor, generally in summer.

Sterna Dougallii [*Roseate Tern*].

Two specimens have been obtained between Banff and Cullen.

Sterna Hirundo [*Common Tern*].

Sterna arctica [*Arctic Tern*].

Annual visitors, generally in autumn. During some seasons they come in immense numbers. Although they do not breed with us, they do so on part of the sandy shores of the adjoining counties of Aberdeen and Moray.

Sterna minuta [*Lesser Tern*].

This pretty little lady-like bird does not breed with us, but does so in the places mentioned for the two preceding. It is only an occasional visitor.

Sterna nigra [*Black Tern*].

I know of only one instance of its having been found here.

Larus Sabini [*Sabine's Gull*].

I had an exciting chase after a specimen, but failed in capturing it. It was the only one I have seen or heard of here.

Larus minutus [*Little Gull*].

I believe only two specimens have been met with.

Larus capistratus [*Masked Gull*].

I am informed that two of these birds were killed about thirty years ago.

Larus ridibundus [*Black-headed Gull*].

Like the common and arctic terns, this species, although it has no breeding-grounds with us, breeds on either side in great numbers, and is a frequent visitor here, chiefly in spring and autumn.

LARUS TRIDACTYLUS [*Kittiwake*].
Breeds with us, but not in such numbers as formerly.

LARUS EBURNEUS [*Ivory Gull*].
Several specimens have been shot near Gamrie. It is a polar bird, almost pure white.

LARUS CANUS [*Common Gull*].
Abundant during winter and spring. The gull may be met with all the year round, though I believe it does not breed with us.

LARUS LEUCOPTERUS [*Iceland Gull*].
Sometimes, during winter, a specimen of this Northern bird may be obtained, but mostly in an immature state of plumage.

LARUS FUSCUS [*Lesser Black-backed Gull*].
Met with now and then, but not in great plenty. It does not nestle here.

LARUS ARGENTATUS [*Herring Gull*].
Breeds at Gamrie Head and at Troup. Numbers are taken when young by the fishermen and their children, and brought up quite tame, walking about the villages like poultry.

LARUS MARINUS [*Great Black-backed Gull*].
Like his lesser brethren, this gentleman is but a visitor here, and generally goes before he gets his black coat.

LARUS GLAUCUS [*Glaucous Gull*].
A female, in an immature state of plumage, was killed in Gamrie.

LESTRIS CATARRACTES [*Common Skua*], and

LARUS RICHARDSONI [*Richardson's Skua*].
Both are to be met with as visitors, the latter the rarer of the two.

PROCELLARIA GLACIALIS [*Fulmar Petrel*].
An occasional winter visitor. I had a specimen sent me from Gamrie, which approached a boat so closely that one of the fishermen knocked it down with an oar: this was several miles out at sea.

PUFFINUS MAJOR [*Great Shearwater*], and

PUFFINUS OBSCURUS [*Dusky Shearwater*].
Only winter visitors.

THALASSIDROMA PELAGICA [*Stormy-petrel*].
A visitor, like the rest of its kindred, but more frequent, and may

be met with at intervals all the year round. The superstitious dread of this little bird by sailors and fishermen is well known.

With the stormy-petrel ends my List of the Birds of Banffshire. Many species given as "rare" may turn out to be of frequent occurrence, and many given as "occasional visitors" may prove to be natives. Species, too, not mentioned in this list may have to be included in the birds of the county; and no one will be more pleased to hear of such additions than myself.

FISHES.

LABRAX LUPUS [*The Bass* or *Sea-perch*].
  This is a rare species with us, only three having come under my notice. One of these, a beautiful specimen, was found dead in our river, the Deveron, not far from its mouth, in 1839.

ACERINA VULGARIS [*The Ruff* or *Pope*].
  One is said to have been obtained off Troup Head about forty-two years ago.

TRACHINUS DRACO [*The Great Weever*].
  Occasionally found. The fish is said to be possessed of very poisonous qualities, insomuch that a prick or even a mere scratch from either of the rays (which are hard and spinous) of the first dorsal or back fin causes the severest pain imaginable. On the Continent, where they are more numerous than they are here, and where they are used as an article of food, there is a very stringent law which forbids them being brought to market, or even exposed for sale in any shape whatever, unless these spines are all cut off; and in order to enforce obedience, parties found transgressing the law are severely punished.

TRACHINUS VIPERA [*The Little Weever*].
  Specimens of the little weever are not unfrequently met with; which would seem to indicate that they are more numerous in the Firth than the preceding.

MULLUS BARBATUS [*The Red Surmullet*].
  This and the striped red mullet (M. SURMULETUS) have both been obtained, the latter being the most frequent.

TRIGLA CUCULUS [*The Red Gurnard*].
  Is pretty frequent; as is also

TRIGLA HIRUNDO [*The Sapphirine Gurnard*].
  Some splendid specimens of this latter fish are annually brought on shore by our fishermen toward the end of autumn.

TRIGLA GURNARDUS [*The Gray Gurnard*].

This is our commonest gurnard; and, judging from the numbers taken, must be very numerous. They are known here by the term of " crunack." They are not much esteemed as an article of food, even among the peasants; and they are, in consequence, seldom brought to market.

TRIGLA PÆCILOPTERA [*The Little Gurnard*].

Somewhat rare. I remember once taking one from the stomach of a great Northern diver, which was shot between Findochtie and Speymouth, in the spring of 1840, and which was sent me for the purpose of being preserved.

COTTUS SCORPIUS [*The Short-spined Cottus*].

Pretty frequent.

COTTUS BUBALIS [*The Long-spined Cottus*].

Rather plentiful. I find them in abundance in pools left by the tide, or beneath stones at low water. Many of them exhibit some most beautiful markings.

COTTUS QUADRICORNIS [*The Four-horned Cottus*].

I have never found this species but in the stomachs of other fish; which leads me to conclude that they generally inhabit deep water, or, at least, that they do not come so near the shore as the preceding species.

ASPIDOPHORUS EUROPÆUS [*The Armed Bull-head*].

This is another stomach species. But I have found these, also, though very sparingly, among the rocks at low tide.

GASTEROSTEUS TRACHURUS [*The Rough-tailed, Three-spined Stickleback*] and

GASTEROSTEUS LEIURUS [*The Smooth-tailed Stickleback*] are both plentiful, the former along the coast, and the latter in our streams and rivulets.

SPINACHIA VULGARIS [*The Fifteen-spined Stickleback*].

Common among the pools along the shore. I have seen this species with sixteen and seventeen spines. They are known among our fishermen by the very peculiar denomination of " Willie-wan-beard."

CHRYSOPHRYS AURATA [*The Gilt-head*].

I have only seen two specimens of this fish which have been procured with us. The one was taken off Buckie in 1841; and the other was brought on shore at Portsoy in 1839. They appear to be scarce, from the fact that the fishermen do not know them.

Pagellus centrodontus [*The Sea-bream*].
  This is a more common species — numbers appearing annually.
  In some seasons they appear in greater abundance than in others.
  They are sold here under the name of "perch."

Brama Raii [*Ray's Bream*].
  Rare.

Cantharus griseus [*The Black Bream*].
  A few of these are generally procured every autumn, or about the
  beginning of winter. They are known and sold here under the
  term of "old wife."

Dentex vulgaris [*The Four-toothed Sparus*].
  Although this species, like many more, bears the name "*vulgaris,*"
  or *common*, it is not so with us. I am only aware of one specimen, which was taken off Troup Head.

Scomber scombrus [*The Mackerel*].
  This beautiful and highly prized fish generally appears on our
  part of the coast about autumn; in some seasons, in great
  plenty; in others, not so numerous.

Scomber colias? [*The Spanish Mackerel?*]
  As will be seen, I have placed this species here as doubtful. A
  mackerel differing in many respects from the one noted above,
  and which agrees very well with *Scomber colias*, was taken off
  Portknockie, but by the time I had the pleasure of seeing it, it
  was a good deal disfigured. Still, as I have already said, it exhibited many of the markings and other characteristics of the
  Spanish mackerel.

Thynnus vulgaris [*The Tunny*].
  Several specimens of this fish have, from time to time, been taken
  with us. A very large one was captured in a salmon-net at Portsoy. It measured over nine feet in length, and six feet in girth.

Xiphias gladius [*The Sword-fish*].
  A small specimen of this fish—rare on this part of the coast—was
  caught in our harbor by a shrimper.

Naucrates ductor [*The Pilot-fish*].
  A very fine specimen of this rare and rather peculiar fish was
  taken in our bay some years ago, and was exhibited as a curiosity. It was unknown in the place, and also to the person who
  took it; but an old tar chancing to see it, who had seen some
  service abroad, having hitched up his trousers, and rid his mouth
  of a yard or two of tobacco-juice, exclaimed, with something of a

16*

knowing air, "Well, I'll be blowed if that aint a pilot! and a
pretty one it is, too. We used to see them often when sailing
in the Mediterranean."

CARANX TRACHURUS [*The Scad* or *Horse-mackerel*], or, as it is termed
here, the "buck-mackerel," is not very numerous, and is very
seldom used as an article of food. Its appearance here is usually about the time of herring-fishing. I once found a rather
strange variety of this species. It was about the usual size, but
it was all over of a most beautiful golden yellow, finely striped
and variegated with numerous lines of the brightest blue, except
the fins, which were of the finest carmine.

LAMPRIS GUTTATUS [*The Opah* or *King-fish*] has occurred on several
occasions; as off Troup Head, at Black Pots, on the shore near
Portsoy, and at Buckie.

MUGIL CAPITA [*The Gray Mullet*].
I am only aware of two specimens of this mullet which have been
procured within our limits; the one at Gardenstown, the other at
Cullen.

BLENNIUS MONTAGUI [*Montagu's Blenny*].
One specimen taken from the stomach of a haddock.

BLENNIUS GATTORUGINE [*The Gattoruginous Blenny*].
I have met with this species only on two occasions.

BLENNIUS YARRELLII [*Yarrell's Blenny*].
Rarely met with. I have a splendid specimen in my collection,
which was found cast on shore between Gardenstown and Crovie.

BLENNIUS PHOLIS [*The Shanny* or *Smooth Blenny*],

GUNNELLUS VULGARIS [*The Spotted Gunnel*], and

ZOARCES VIVIPARUS [*The Viviparous* or *Green Blenny*],
Are all to be met with among the low-lying rocks along our line of
shore.

ANARRHICHAS LUPUS [*The Wolf-fish*].
Frequent, but seldom used as food. I find them pretty often cast
on shore dead, after a storm; which would seem to indicate that
their habitat is not always in deep water.

GOBIUS NIGER [*The Black Goby*].
These, inhabiting the rocky parts of the coast, become, at times, the
prey of the haddock, etc. Though they do not seem to be numerous in this arm of the sea, I meet with them occasionally in
the stomachs of fishes.

Gobius minutus [*The Freckled* or *Spotted Goby*].
This is another stomach species; as also the

Gobius Ruthersparri [*The Double-spotted Goby*], which appears to be the rarest of the three.

Callionymus lyra [*The Gemmeous Dragonet*].
This splendidly colored fish is frequently met with; and the so-called

Callionymus dracunculus [*Sordid Dragonet*] is found in about equal number; for it is a general maxim that where the husband is there also should the wife be. Ichthyologists cling to the idea that these fish are distinct species. Out of about one hundred specimens which I have dissected, I have never yet found any thing like *roe* or *ova* in those having the long rays on the first dorsal, and which are known as the gemmeous; and, in like manner, I have never yet met with any thing at all pertaining to a *milt* in those having the short rays, and which are known as the sordid dragonet. My conclusion is that they are only male and female of the same species.

Lophius piscatorius [*The Angler* or *Fishing-frog*, or, as it is called here, the "Sea-devil"] is frequently met with, but is not used as an article of food.

Labrus bergylta [*The Ballan Wrasse*].
Pretty frequent during summer.

Labrus mixtus [*The Blue-striped Wrasse*].
Rare. A very pretty specimen was taken off Macduff.

Crenilabrus melops [*The Gilt-head*].
Rare.

Crenilabrus rupestris [*Jago's Gold-sinny*].
I have only seen one of this species in the neighborhood. A beautiful specimen which I found one winter's day was cast on shore at the links.

Acantholabrus exoletus [*The Small-mouthed Wrasse*].
Like the last, only one specimen of this fish has, as yet, come under my notice, and that one was captured off Troup Head.

Cyprinus auratus [*The Gold* and *Silver Carp*, as it is termed] has been introduced, and has thriven pretty well, as at Macduff, where it has propagated to an amazing degree.

Leuciscus phoxinus [*The Minnow*].
This pretty, active little fish is to be found in most of our streams. It is curious to see it stated in works on ichthyology that this species is not to be met with north of the Dee, Aberdeenshire.

BELONE VULGARIS [*The Gar-fish*, or, as it is called here, the "Green-been"] is by no means scarce at certain seasons.

SCOMBERESOX SAURUS [*The Saury Pike*].

Not so often met with as the last. In fact, it must be termed rare.

SALMO SALAR [*The Salmon*].

This valuable and highly prized fish is found both along our coast and in our fresh waters. At one time, they were very numerous in the Deveron. From a *pot* or *hole* which once existed a little below the bridge which spans the river, at a little distance from the sea, and not far from the town, as many as one hundred, and sometimes more, have been taken at a haul. This was before stake and bag nets were so thickly planted along our sea-shore as they are now.

SALMO ERIOX [*The Bull* or *Gray Trout*].

Some large individuals of this species are often taken.

SALMO TRUTTA [*The Salmon-trout*].

These were at one time believed to be the young of the salmon; and the tacksman gave orders that they should not be taken. Previously, they had been fished for with small-meshed nets, and sold as trout, under the name of "finnock." Time passed and the river beheld another tacksman, who, differing from his predecessor, gave orders that they should be again taken. Accordingly, they are now annually fished for, and are once more sold as "sea-trout," "white trout," and "finnock."

SALMO FARIO [*The Common Trout*].

In all our streams. These also are taken, and sold with the last-mentioned.

OSMERUS EPERLANUS [*The Smelt*].

Rare with us.

CLUPEA HARENGUS [*The Herring*].

This species abounds along this coast toward the middle of summer and the beginning of autumn. The fry of this fish is met with nearly all the year round.

CLUPEA LEACHII [*Leach's Herring*].

A rather smaller-sized herring than the common species. It is generally met with in small shoals in May and June.

CLUPEA SPRATTUS [*The Sprat* or *Garvel Herring*].

This is also met with about the same time, but in smaller numbers.

ALOSA FINTA [*The Twaite Shad*].

Rare. A very fine specimen was taken in our river last summer about a mile from the sea.

ALOSA COMMUNIS [*The Alice Shad*].
  The same may be said of this species—it is rare. They are termed
  "rock herring."

MORRHUA VULGARIS [*The Cod*].
  It is to the stomach of this species that I am most indebted for
  many of the rarer of the testaceous and crustaceous specimens
  which I possess. For the cod's bill of fare, see p. 253. The
  cod is extensively fished for along this part of the coast, and may
  be termed *the poor man's salmon*. Great numbers are salted and
  dried, and in that state sent to the Southern markets. I have
  occasionally met with a cod of a red color, in all save the fins,
  which are generally of a yellowish tinge, and never larger than a
  common-sized haddock. They are known here by the name of
  "rock codlings."

MORRHUA ÆGLEFINUS [*The Haddock*].
  Like the cod, it is extensively taken and largely cured, and forwarded South. Our Buckie haddocks are well known for their excel-
  lence, and are famed for their superior qualities. Like the cod,
  the stomach of this species is also a rich mine for the naturalist.

MORRHUA LUSCA [*The Bib* or *Whiting Pout*].
  Frequent; but not often brought to market, although they are most
  excellent eating. The fishermen generally cut them up and use
  them as bait.

MORRHUA MINUTA [*The Power Cod*].
  Not known as an inhabitant of the Firth until recently. They are
  excellent eating. It is a great pity that they are so small and
  scarce.

MERLANGUS VULGARIS [*The Whiting*].
  Often taken, but not so much admired as the Haddock.

MORRHUA POLLACHIUS [*The Pollack* or *Sythe*].
  Frequent.

MORRHUA CARBONARIUS [*The Coal-fish*].
  Like the last. When young, great numbers of them are occasionally taken in our harbors in small-meshed nets. They are termed
  "gerrocks."

MERLUCIUS VULGARIS [*The Hake*].
  Found occasionally.

LOTA MOLVA [*The Ling*].
  Fished for with the cod, and cured in the same manner. When
  salted and dried, they are called "kealing."

MOTELLA QUINQUECIRRATA [*The Five-bearded Rockling*].
Frequent in the pools left among the rocks by the tide.

MOTELLA CIMBRIA [*The Four-bearded Rockling*].
Rare. I have not met with it often.

BROSMIUS VULGARIS [*The Torsk* or *Tusk*].
Taken with the cod and ling, and cured in the same fashion.

PHYCIS FURCATUS [*The Great Forked Beard*].
This fish is of rare occurrence with us, and that only at long intervals.

PLATESSA VULGARIS [*The Plaice*].
Plentiful, and highly prized by many for its very delicate flesh and agreeable flavor.

PLATESSA FLESUS [*The Flounder*], or, as it is called here, the "common fluke," and the

PLATESSA LIMANDA [*The Salt-water Fluke*], are also pretty frequent. In the stomachs of these fish I occasionally find, among other matters, *Tellina fabula*, *T. tenuis*, *T. punicea* (a most beautiful little shell), *Natica Montagui*, *N. Alderi*, *Philine scabra*, *Cylichna truncata*, *C. cylindracea*, etc.

PLATESSA MICROCEPHALA [*The Smooth Dab*] and

PLATESSA POLA [*The Pole Dab*] are not so often met with.

PLATESSA LIMANDOIDES [*The Yellow* or *Rough Dab*] and the

PLATESSA ELONGATA [*Long Flounder*] are of rare occurrence.

HIPPOGLOSSUS VULGARIS [*The Halibut*] and

RHOMBUS MAXIMUS [*The Turbot*] are both met with, inhabiting deep water. They are seldom taken near the shore. The former is the more plentiful. The latter is known here as the "roan fluke," and always commands a ready sale and a high price. The other is called the turbot; and though it sells well, it is not so valuable as the true turbot, nor yet so eagerly sought after by the higher classes.

RHOMBUS VULGARIS [*The Brill* or *Pearl-turbot*].
This species is occasionally taken along with the two preceding, but must rank as rare with us.

RHOMBUS HIRTUS [*Muller's Top-knot*] occurs at intervals along our whole line of coast.

SOLEA VULGARIS [*The Sole*] is not so common with us as its name would seem to indicate.

Solea pegusa [*The Lemon-sole*].
Rare.

Monochirus linguatulus [*The Solenette*] is of more frequent occurrence.   I have found it in the stomach of the cod and haddock.

Lepidogaster Cornubiensis [*The Cornish Sucker*].
I remember finding a small fish, on one occasion, where our fishermen clean their lines, and which resembled the above in almost
every particular.   It is the only specimen that has come under
my notice.

Lepidogaster bimaculatus [*The Two-spotted Sucker*].
Brought on shore, now and then, among the refuse entangled in
the fishermen's lines, and occasionally in old shells, such as *Fusis
antiquus, Buccinum undatum,* and *Cyprina Islandica,* etc.

Cyclopterus lumpus [*The Lump-sucker*].
Frequent.   Known here by the name of "paddle cock."   Not used
as an article of food.

Liparius vulgaris [*The Unctuous Sucker*].
Of partial occurrence.

Liparius Montagui [*Montagu's Sucker*].
I have only once met with this beautiful little fish here, and that
but lately.   It was brought on shore in an old shell.   I should
think it rare in the Firth.

Anguilla acutirostris [*The Sharp-nosed Eel*] and
Anguilla latirostris [*The Broad-nosed Eel*] are both found.   The
former is the most numerous, and brings the highest price.

Conger vulgaris [*The Conger* or *Great Eel*].
This large species is often met with, but is not used as food.

Ammodytes Tobianus [*The Sand-eel*] and
Ammodytes lancea [*The Sand lance*].
The latter the most numerous.   Both these are used by our fisher-
men for bait.

Syngnathus acus [*The Great Pipe-fish*] and
Syngnathus typhle [*The Lesser Pipe-fish*] are both met with, and are
accounted by the fishermen to be superior to any other bait.

Syngnathus lumbriciformis [*The Worm Pipe-fish*] is met with, and
is not so rare as one might expect.

Hippocampus brevirostris.
This rare and peculiar horse-headed looking creature has been met
with here.   Two were found cast on shore at the sands of
Boyndie, near Banff, after a severe sea storm.

ORTHAGORISCUS MOLA [*The Short Sunfish*] and

ORTHAGORISCUS OBLONGUS [*The Oblong Sunfish*] have been occasionally met with. Several have been brought on shore by the fishermen of Gardenstown, Crovie, and other places.

ACIPENSER STURIO [*The Sturgeon*].
Rare. One has been taken in a salmon-net.

SCYLLIUM CANICULA [*The Small Spotted Dogfish*].
Found occasionally.

GALEUS VULGARIS [*The Tope*].
I am only aware of two instances in which this fish has been found within our limits: the one near Buckie, the other in the bay of Banff.

ACANTHIAS VULGARIS [*The Picked Dogfish*].
Plentiful; often too much so.

SCYMNUS BOREALIS [*The Greenland-shark*].
In May, 1849, a large specimen of the above shark was captured by some fishermen belonging to Pennan, off Troup Head. When brought on shore, it measured thirteen feet nine inches in length, and eleven feet in circumference where thickest.

ECHINORHINUS SPINOSUS [*The Spinous Shark*]. See pp. 210, 211.

SQUATINA VULGARIS [*The Angel-fish*], or, as it is here called (like the angler), the "Sea-devil," is sometimes procured. A large specimen was cast into our harbor during the winter of 1851.

TORPEDO VULGARIS [*The Cramp-fish* or *Electric Ray*].
A specimen of this fish is said to have been taken about six miles off Loggie Head, near Cullen, in 1817. Others are stated as having been caught.

RAIA OXYRHYNCHUS [*The Sharp-nosed Skate*].
Large individuals of this species are sometimes taken, with the more frequent of our rays. One measuring upward of seven feet in length, and over five in breadth, was captured by our fishermen some years ago.

RAIA INTERMEDIA [*The Flapper-skate*].
A small skate, agreeing in many essential points with the flapper, was taken, in a bag-net set for salmon, some years ago, said to be a young one of the above species, and as such I include it here.

RAIA BATIS [*The Blue* or *Gray Skate*] and

RAIA CLAVATA [*The Thornback*].
Taken, occasionally, in great numbers; the former being the most numerous and the most prized.

Raia radiata [*The Starry Ray*].
This small species is picked up now and then.

Petromyzon marinus [*The Lamprey*], or, as it is called here, the
"Lamper-eel," is often met with.

Petromyzon fluviatilis [*The River Lamprey*].
Considered rare. A very fine specimen was taken in the Deveron
some years since.

Petromyzon Planeri [*Planer's Lamprey or Lampern*] has also occurred. These fish are generally termed "Nine-ee'd Eels," and
are by no means held in high estimation.

Gastrobranchus cæcus [*The Myxine or Glutinous Hag*].
This very curious and singular animal, whether you call it a fish or
a worm, is of frequent occurrence.

ADDITIONS.

Perca fluviatilis [*Perch*].
Several of these fishes have been taken in the Deveron.

Trigla Blochii [*Bloch's Gurnard*]. In the Moray Firth, at Banff.
An example of this gurnard (or, as we call it, "crunack") was
captured here in a rock-pool. See p. 251. I am not aware of
the species ever having been detected on this part of the coast
before.

Sebastes Norvegicus [*Norway Haddock*].
One taken off Buckie in 1859 is the only instance of this fish having been taken on our coasts.

Thynnus pelamys [*Striped Tunny*].
A fine specimen of this tunny is in our Museum, taken off Whitehills in 1867.

Auxis vulgaris [*The Plain Bonito*].
Several of these have now come under my notice. One taken in a
herring-net off Cullen measured over twenty inches in length and
twelve in circumference behind the first dorsal. One very peculiar feature connected with it was, that if stroked down when wet
it gave the hand all the appearance of having come across a piece
of metal newly black-leaded. I am not aware of this peculiarity
being mentioned in Yarrell or elsewhere.

Zeus faber [*The Dory*].
I have now ascertained that many of these fish have been taken
here, chiefly in salmon-nets. It would seem that the dory is by
no means an uncommon summer visitor on this part of the coast.

CAPROS APER [*Boar-fish*].

At least one example of this curious-looking fish is now known to have found its way to our shores. It was taken in a bag-net near Crovie in August, 1862, and was sent here to be stuffed and named.

TRICHIURUS LEPTURUS [*Silvery Hair-tail* or *Bald-fish*].

A very fine specimen of this fish, which is rare in the British seas, and especially on the east coast of Scotland, was found in the Firth here in April, 1876. Although the head and tail were a good deal injured, it measured over twelve feet in length.

GOBIUS GRACILIS [*Slender Goby*].

Frequent.

GOBIUS ALBUS [*White Goby*].

Frequent also. Numbers of these little fish are to be met with in our rock and sandy pools, while others are only to be found at extreme low water.

GOBIUS NILSSONII [*Nilsson's Goby*]. See p. 322.

LABRUS DONOVANI [*Donovan's Wrasse*].

A specimen of this wrasse was captured in the Bay of Boyndie in August, 1863. The fishermen said that there were more, but they only managed to hook the one, and looked upon it as a curious species of mackerel. It was mostly of a beautiful pea-green color, but striped with numerous yellowish lines.

LABRUS MICROSCOPICUS [*Microscopical Wrasse*].

It was during the summer of 1861 that I first observed this minute species. It was not, however, until 1864 that I had an opportunity of submitting a specimen for examination to some of our best ichthyologists, among whom was Mr. Couch. See p. 291.

TINCA VULGARIS [*Common Tench*].

One specimen taken in our bay in 1864 is the only example I have seen. It is now in our Museum.

SCOPELUS HUMBOLDTII [*Argentine*].

This beautiful little creature would seem to be a regular winter visitor with us. I took it first in January, 1863; and, since then, I have never missed it during that month. It is of various sizes. I have taken argentines from under one inch to about three inches in length. I have never seen them in summer.

COUCHIA GLAUCA [*The Mackerel-midge*].

Of all the little fish that I have yet found, this one resembles the five-bearded rockling more than any of the midges do the other rocklings.

Couchia Thompsoni [*Thompson's Midge*].

 I first took a few of this species in May, 1863. They were new to me, and as I could not find them in Yarrell, nor in other works of the same kind which I had an opportunity of consulting, I thought they might prove an undescribed form. Since that time, however, I have seen Mr. Thompson's work, and have now no doubt but that my fish are identical with those taken by that gentleman in Strangford Lough, County Down, in July, 1838, and named as above. See p. 293.

Couchia Montagui [*Montagu's Midge*].

 I first obtained this species in October, 1864. See p. 296.

Couchia Edwardii [*Edward's Midge*].

 First taken at Banff, November, 1865. See p. 298.

Raniceps trifurcatus [*Tadpole-fish*].

 Several of these are now known to have been found in this part of the Firth.

Rhombus megastoma [*The Whiff*].

 This species seems to be rather rare with us. I have a very fine specimen which I found at the place where our fishermen clean their lines.

Rhombus arnoglossus [*The Scald-fish or Smooth Sole*].

 This would appear to be another very scarce species with us. I have never met with it but in fish stomachs, and very seldom there. It is about the smallest of British flat-fish.

Monochirus variegatus [*Variegated Sole*].

 This species would appear to be met with occasionally. Two pretty large ones were exposed for sale in our market in September, 1860.

Echiodon Drummondii [*Drummond's Echiodon*].

 In March, 1863, I took the first specimen of this strange-looking fish that I had ever seen. Since then, however, I have met with it several times, and always in winter—save once, when I obtained it in summer. They were unknown in the Firth before. Specimens from here are now in the British Museum, London.

Acestra æquorea [*Equorial Pipe-fish*]. This species and the

Acestra anguinea [*Snake Pipe-fish*] are both occasionally found. The latter, however, are seemingly the most frequent.

Chimæra monstrosa [*Northern Chimera*].

 A specimen of this deep-sea and rather rare species was brought into our harbor in 1859 on board a herring-boat. It was found floating, and quite dead. The first dorsal was somewhat injured, and the cord-like portion of the tail was wanting. It was unknown to the fishermen who found it, and who, for want of a better name, called it the "*devil.*"

SCYLLIUM MELANOSTOMUM [*Black-mouthed Dogfish*].

I am led to believe that this species does occasionally occur with us. It is generally mixed up with the commoner sorts.

ZYGÆNA MALLEUS [*Hammer-headed Shark*].

A specimen of this strange-looking animal was found dead on the shore about two miles beyond Whitehills in 1861. It was a middling-sized specimen, measuring about five feet in length and about eighteen inches across the head. It had lain some time, for the skin was blackish, and had the appearance of charred or burned leather.

LAMNA CORNUBICA [*Porbeagle*].

It is now well known that the porbeagle finds his way here occasionally, and usually about the herring season. There is a very fine specimen in our Museum.

ALOPIAS VULPES [*Fox-shark*].

So far as I have been able to learn, this shark appears to be very rarely met with here. It has, however, been found.

NOTIDANUS GRISEUS [*Brown* or *Mediterranean Shark*].

A large specimen of this shark was taken in the Firth here, and brought on shore at Whitehills in December, 1857. After being exhibited in Banff by the fishermen, its captors, as an unknown monster, it was bought for the Banff Museum, where it now is. This shark is the first known to have been found in the British seas.

RAIA MIRALETUS [*Homelyn Ray*].

Occasionally met with.

RAIA SPINOSA [*Sandy Ray*].

This species is well enough known to the fishermen, but they do not often take it.

RAIA CHAGRINEA [*Shagreen Ray*].

This is also occasionally taken.

AMMOCÆTES BRANCHIALIS [*Pride* or *Mud Lamprey*].

We have, at least, one species of this peculiar genus as an inhabitant of the Deveron.

CRUSTACEA.

STENORHYNCHUS ROSTRATUS.
" TENUIROSTRIS.

INACHUS DORSETENSIS.
" LEPTOCHIRUS.

HYAS ARANEUS.
" COARCTATUS.

EURYNOME ASPERA. From deep water.

CANCER PAGURUS [*Parten*].

PIRIMELA DENTICULATA. In rock-pools, and from deep water.

CARCINUS MÆNAS. See p. 244.

PORTUMNUS LATIPES. Among sand at low tide.

POLYBIUS HENSLOWI.

PORTUNUS PUBER.
" HOLSATUS.
" CORRUGATUS.
" DEPURATOR.
" MARMOREUS.
" LONGIPES.
" PUSILLUS. From stomachs of fish.

PINNOTHERES PISUM. Inside of *Mediola mediolus.*
" VETERUM. Once from Gamrie; inside of *Pinna pectinata.*

EBALIA TUBEROSA.
" CRANCHII.
" TUMEFACTA or BRYERII.

ATELECYCLUS HETERODON.

DROMIA VULGARIS.

LITHODES MAIA.

PAGURUS BERNHARDUS. Common in rock-pools when young.
" PRIDEAUXII.
" CUANENSIS. Both these are brought in from deep water.
" LÆVIS. Frequent in the stomachs of flukes.
" FERRUGINEUS. This little fellow was only added to the list in 1866.

PORCELLANA LONGICORNIS. In rock-pools.

GALATHEA SQUAMIFERA.

GALATHEA STRIGOSA.
" DISPERSA.
" NEXA.
" ANDREWSII.

MUNIDA BAMFFICA. From deep water.

CALLIANASSA SUBTERRANEA.

GEBIA STELLATA.
" DELTURA.

CALOCARIS MACANDREI.

HOMARUS VULGARIS.

NEPHROPS NORVEGICUS.

CRANGON VULGARIS.
" SPINOSUS
" SCULPTUS.
" TRISPINOSUS.
" ALLMANNI.

NIKA EDULIS.

ATHANAS NITESCENS.

HIPPOLYTE SPINOSUS.
" or DORYPHORUS GORDONI.
" VARIANS.
" CRANCHII.
" THOMPSONI.
" PANDALIFORMIS.

PANDALUS ANNULICORNIS.

MYSIS FLEXUOSA.
" LAMORNÆ.
" VULGARIS.
" SPIRITUS.
" MIXTA. First taken as British at Banff, in 1863, by T. E.
" SPINIFERA. Burrows in sand. First taken at Banff by T. E. in 1862, and some years afterward in Sweden, by M. Goes.
" ACULATA.
" HISPIDA. N.S. Taken at Banff by T. E. in December, 1863.

CYNTHILIA FLEMINGII.

THYSANOPODA COUCHII.
" LONGIPES.
" NORVEGICUS.
" ALATA.

Thysanopoda ensifera.   N.S.   Taken at Banff by T. E. in 1863.
      "   Batei.   N.S.   "   "   "   1862.

Diastyyis Rathkii.
      "   echinata.

Cuma scorpioides.
      "   costata.   Burrows in sand.
      "   lucifera.   New to Britain.   Found at Banff by T. E. in July,
          1865.

Halia trispinosa.

Venilia gracilis.

Talitrus locusta.

Orchestia littorea.
      "   Mediterranea.
      "   Deshayesii.
      "   brevidigitata.   N.S.   First taken at Banff by T. E.

Allorchestes Nilssonii.
            "   Imbricatus.

Nicea Lubbockiana.

Opis quadrimana.   N.S.   First taken at Banff by T. E.

Montagua monoculoides.
      "   marina.   With eggs in December.
      "   Aldere.
      "   Pollexiana.   Eyes red.   With eggs, in November and
             December, of a greenish color.   A most beautiful va-
             riegated species.
      "   Norvegica.   First taken at Banff as British by T. E.

Lysianassa Costæ.
      "   Audouiniana.
      "   Atlantica.
      "   longicornis.   With young in December.

Anonyx longicornis.   Of a straw color, spotted with red.   Eyes
          large, oblong; white, with red markings.
      "   Edwardsii.   Eyes red, with black spots.   With eggs in De-
          cember.
      "   obesus.   N.S.   Eyes red, round, and small.   First taken at
          Banff by T. E.
      "   denticulatus.
      "   Holbolli.
      "   minutus.

Anonyx Plautus.　N.S.　First taken at Banff as British by T. E.
"　　longipes.
"　　ampulla.　Eyes red.

Callisoma crenata.　With eggs in November.

Lepidepecreum carinatum.　N.S.　First taken at Banff by T. E.

Ampelisca Gaimardii.　With eggs in December of a green color.
"　　belliana.

Phocus simplex.
"　　Holbolli.　With eggs in December and March.
"　　plumosus.　Two other new species of this genus have been
"　　　taken at Banff by T. E., but are not yet named.

Westwoodilia cæcula.
"　　Hyalina.

Œdiceros parvimanus.　With eggs, which are of a bright orange-
　　color, in September, October, and November.　A sand-burrower.

Œdiceros saginatus.　With eggs, which are reddish, in January.
　　First taken at Banff as British by T. E.

Monoculodes longimanus.　N.S.　First taken at Banff by T. E.
"　　carinatus.　N.S.　First taken at Banff by T. E.
"　　Stimpsoni.

Kroyera arenaria.　With eggs in August and September.
"　　altamarina.

Amphilochus manudens.

Darwinia compressa.　N.S.　First taken at Banff by T. E.

Sulcator arenarius.

Urothoe Bairdii.　Eyes black; with eggs in December.
"　　marinus.　With eggs in December.
"　　elegans.　Burrows in sand.

Liljeborgia Shetlandica.

Phædra antiqua.

Isæa Montagui.

Iphimedia obesa.
"　　Eblanæ.

Otus carinatus.

Pereionotus testudo.

Acanthonotus Owenii.

Dexamine spinosa. With eggs, which are of a greenish color, in April.

Dexamine Bedlomensis. Color a deep and brilliant orange, occasionally mixed with red and brown. The eyes, which are slightly raised, are round and of a bright crimson. The female, which is similar to the male, has eggs, which are of a pea-green, in April and May, and again in October.

Atylus Swammerdamii. With eggs, which are of a brownish color, in September.

Atylus gibbosus.
"   bispinosus.

Phersua bicuspis.
"   fucicola.

Calliope læviuscula.
"   Ossiani. N.S. First taken at Banff by T. E.
"   grandaculis.

Eusirus Helvetiæ. N.S. Taken at Banff by T. E., the first of the genus taken in Britain. A burrower, and very sluggish in its habits.

Leucothoe articulosa.
"   furina. First taken as British at Banff by T. E.

Hora gracilis.

Stimpsonia chelifera.

Microdeutopus gryllotalpa.
"   Websterii.
"   anomalus.
"   versiculatus.

Protomedeia hirsutimana. N.S. First taken at Banff by T. E.
"   Whitei. N.S. First taken at Banff by T. E. With eggs, which are of a very dull green, in November.

Bathyporeia pilosa. Eyes red.
"   Robertsoni.
"   pelagica. Eyes red.

Melita palmata.
"   obtusata.
"   proxima. With eggs, which are of a purplish color, in December. Eyes brownish.

17

MELITA GLADIOSA.

EURYSTHEUS ERYTHROPHTHALMUS.
  " BISPINIMANUS. N.S. First taken at Banff by T. E.

AMATHILLA SABINI.

GAMMARUS MARINUS.
  " GAMPYLOPS.
  " LOCUSTA.
  " TENUIMANUS.
  " EDWARDII.
  " PULEX.

MEGAMDERA SEMISERRATA.
  " LONGIMANA.
  " OTHONIS.
  " ALDERI.
  " BREVICAUDATA.

EISCLADUS LONGICAUDATUS.

AMPHITHOE RUBRICATA.
  " LITTORINA.

SUNAMPHITHOE HAMULUS.

PODOCERUS PULCHELLUS.
  " VARIEGATUS.
  " CAPILLATUS.
  " PELAGICUS. Eyes black.
  " OCIUS.
  " FALCATUS.

CERAPUS ABDITUS.
  " DIFFORMIS.

DERCOTHOE (CERAPUS) PUNCTATUS. With eggs in June.

SIPHONDECETES TYPICUS.
  " CRASSICORNIS.

NÆNIA TUBERCULOSA. With eggs in December. The female has the palms of the two first pairs much narrower than the male.

NÆNIA RIMAPALMATA.

CRATIPPUS TENUIPES. N.S. First taken at Banff by T. E.

COROPHIUM LONGICORNE.
  " BONELLII.

Vibilia borealis. N.S. First taken at Banff by T. E.

Themisto crassicornis. First taken as British at Banff by T. E. Great hordes of this species occasionally visit this part of the coast, and large numbers are sometimes destroyed in consequence of coming too near the land.

Lestrigonus exulans. Occasionally in vast numbers.
    "   Kinahani.

Hyperia Galba.
    "   oblivia. In great shoals at certain seasons.
These are the only species of this family which I have ever found on the Medusæ. I consider *Lestrigonus exulans* to be the male of *Hyperia Galba*, and *L. Kinahani* the male of *H. oblivia.*

Hyperia tauriformis. N.S.
    "   prehensilis. N.S.
    "   cyaneæ. N.S.
All these three new species were first taken at Banff by T. E.; the males and females of all three being procured. The males differ but little from the females, except that they are somewhat larger.

Dulichia vorrecta.
    "   falcata.
I look upon these as being male and female of the same species.

Proto pedata.
    "   Goodsirii.

Protella phasma.

Caprella acanthifera.
    "   lobata.
    " ·   typica.

Tanais vittatus. On tangle roots.

Paratanais forcipatus.
    "   rigidus. On tangle roots.

Anceus maxillaris.
    "   (Praniza) cæruleata.
I consider these two to be male and female of the same species.

Anceus (Praniza) Edwardii. N.S. First taken at Banff by T. E. There is another species of *Anceus* or *Praniza* found here which I take to be the male of *A.* or *P. Edwardii.* I find them associated, and they have precisely the same habits. See p. 265.

PHRYXUS ABDOMINALIS.
   "   FUSTICAUDATUS. N.S. First found at Banff by T. E. on *Pagurus Bernhardus* and *Cuanensis*.

ÆGA TRIDENS.
   "   PSORA.
   "   MONOPHTHALMA.

CIROLANA CRANCHII.
   "   SPINIPES.

EURYDICE PULCHRA.

JÆRA ALBIFRONS.

MUNNA KROYERI.

JANIRA MACULOSA.

ASELLUS AQUATICUS.

LIMNORIA LIGNORUM.

ARCTURUS LONGICORNIS.
   "   GRACILIS.

IDOTEA TRICUSPIDATA.
   "   PELAGICA.
   "   EMARGINATA.
   "   LINEARIS.

SPHÆROMA RUGICAUDA.

DYNAMENE RUBRA.

NÆSA BIDENTATA.

CAMPECOPEA CRANCHII.

LIGIA OCEANICA.

PHILOSCIA MUSCORUM.
   "   COUCHII.

PHILOUGRIA RIPARIA.
   "   ROSEA.

PLATYARTHRUS HOFFMANII.

ONISCUS ASELLUS.
   "   FOSSOR.

PORCELLIO SCABER.
   "   PICTUS.
   "   ARMADILLOIDES.
   "   PRUINOSUS.

ARMADILLO VULGARIS.

ADDENDA.

Cheirocratus mantis.

Helleria coalita.

Nebalia bipes. From deep water. Burrows.

Phoxichilidium coccineum. In rock-pools.

Nymphon gracile. ⎫
   "   hirtum. ⎬ Sea-spiders.
   "   grossipes. ⎭

Pallene brevirostris.

Pycnogonum littorale. In rock-pools.

Anomalocera Patersonii.

Cetochilus septentrionalis.
     Both these are occasionally met with during summer in millions.

Notodelphys ascidicola. Found in the branchial sac of *Ascidia mentula* and *communis*.

Peltidium purpureum. From deep water.

Caligus diaphanus.
   "   rapax.
   "   minuta. A variety of the foregoing.
   "   micropus.
   "   curtus. All these are found on various fishes.
   "   isonyx. On the common gurnard. First taken as British at Banff in 1864 by T. E.

Lepeophtheirus pectoralis. On various flounders.
   "   Nordmannii. On the short sunfish.

Chalimus scombri.

Trebius caudatus. Found on a ling, *Lota molva*.

Monima fimbriata, or fimbricata. On the short sunfish. First taken as British at Banff in 1862, by T. E.

Læmargus merricatus. On the short sunfish.

Cecrops Lattreillii. Attached to the gills of the sunfish, both *short* and *oblong*.

Chondracanthidæ solesa. On the gills of *Platessa vulgaris*. First taken as British at Banff in August, 1863, by T. E.

Lernentoma cornuta. On gills of *Platessa vulgaris*.
   "   asellina. On gills of *Trigla gurnardus*.

LERNEOPODA SALMONEA. Attached to the gills of the salmon.

BASANISTES SALMONEA. On the gills of the common trout.

BRACHIELLA BISPINOSA. On gills of *Trigla.* N.S. First taken at Banff by T. E. in May, 1863.

ANCHORELLA UNCINATA. Attached to various fishes, such as the cod, haddock, whiting, etc.

ANCHORELLA RUGOSA.

LERNEA BRANCHIALIS. Attached to the gills of the cod and haddock.

PENNELLA FIBOSA? Found on the short sunfish.

EDWARD'S HOUSE, LOW SHORE.